TROUBLE IN HOLLYWOOD

A Cassidy Adventure Novel

by

Kelly Rysten

CCB Publishing
British Columbia, Canada

Trouble in Hollywood: A Cassidy Adventure Novel

Copyright ©2016 by Kelly Rysten
ISBN-13   978-1-77143-294-8
First Edition

Library and Archives Canada Cataloguing in Publication
Rysten, Kelly, 1960-, author
Trouble in Hollywood : a Cassidy adventure novel / by Kelly Rysten. -- First edition.
Issued in print and electronic formats.
ISBN 978-1-77143-294-8 (pbk.).--ISBN 978-1-77143-295-5 (pdf)
Additional cataloguing data available from Library and Archives Canada

Cover artwork credits: Background graphic by Kelly Rysten: www.kellyrysten.com
Image of clapper board © Jiripravda, used under license from Shutterstock.com
Image of filmstrip © niroworld, used under license from Shutterstock.com

Publisher: CCB Publishing
              British Columbia, Canada
              www.ccbpublishing.com

To my son, Ryan, and my daughter, Kristen, who gave me the unique life experiences needed to write this book and half their names to use for my pseudonym. I would say pen name, but as Ryan would say, "Why use two words when one cool long one will do?"

Other books by Kelly Rysten

Kelly Rysten is the author of the Cassidy Callahan Adventure Novels. Cassidy Callahan is a young woman who grew up on a quarter horse ranch. Given free run of the local hills she developed an eye for tracking, and with the help of Detective Rusty Michaels, she joined the local search and rescue team to track lost hikers. Unfortunately she is also a terrible trouble magnet, and her job brings her into contact with more trouble than the police can keep her out of. One adventure follows another as Cassidy tracks her way from one mishap to the next.

The books are:

Triple Trouble
Published 2009 – ISBN 978-1-926585-41-3

Car Trouble
Published 2010 – ISBN 978-1-926918-03-7

A Cache of Trouble
Published 2011 – ISBN 978-1-926918-87-7

A Double Dose of Trouble
Published 2012 – ISBN 978-1-77143-025-8

A Shot of Trouble
Published 2013 – ISBN 978-1-77143-107-1

Looking for Trouble
Published 2015 – ISBN 978-1-77143-249-8

Kelly is also the author of an action adventure romance novel that incorporates the hobby of geocaching. College student Gwendolyn Brody agrees to enter a geocaching contest to help her friend Tony win a trip to the Caribbean. Follow their hilarious cross country trip as they accidentally grow ever closer to each other.

Geogirl
Published 2014 – ISBN 978-1-77143-150-7

Chapter 1

My name is Cassidy. I'm a skilled trouble magnet. I've served in the Marines, and volunteered my time to Search and Rescue with the local Police and Fire Departments. I've stared down the barrel of a gun more times than I can count, from both ends. People try to kill me on a regular basis. So far none of them have succeeded but some of them have failed miserably. I am not easy to kill. And I am not easily intimidated. Stick a gun to my head and my brain instantly reverts to survival mode. There is no panic, only a cunning, analytical manipulation of infinitesimal and very subtle clues that result in a most uncanny instinctual response and somehow I get out of any situation alive. Yup, I am a tough little gal and proud of it. At least I was until the unthinkable happened.

Chapter 2

How long had it been? It felt like a long time. When I thought about the results of the test my blood felt like ice in my veins. It couldn't be. Please tell me it wasn't true. I definitely was not ready for this. I felt like I couldn't do this alone, but I couldn't talk to Rusty about it. I had to know first, but I was scared to find out. It would change my whole life.

The phone rang and I jumped. What if it was Rusty? I couldn't talk to Rusty like this. He'd see right through me. The phone continued to ring. I looked at the caller ID. Strict. That was safer, though not by much. Lou Strickland was the search and rescue commander. His calls were never good news.

"Hello?" I said absentmindedly.

"Cassidy? I've got a job for you. When can you be at Elk Meadows?"

"Umm, hold on," I said reading the box. Why did they have to make the print so darned small? Let's see…I could get the results in three to five minutes. Okay, five minutes to take the test, half an hour to either faint with relief or run around in panicked circles. "Two hours," I told Strict.

Oh man, if this came out positive I was going to…to…I didn't know what I was going to do.

"Can't you make it a little quicker?"

Normally this question would start me moving but I was too keyed up for his questions to really sink in.

"I'll try. No promises."

"Are you okay? You don't sound right."

"Yeah, I just need to do something real quick and I'll head out. I'll see you up there."

He hung up but I still had the test to run. I read the directions. Shoot, I had to work up a good pee. I went to the kitchen and tanked up on water and checked my gear as I waited for the water to make its way through my system. The gear check was useless. I was so distracted I was barely registering the contents of my pack. I put my concentration into overdrive. Okay, essentials: food, water, stove, tent, knife, magnesium stick, one change of clothes, necessities. Hmm, I might not need the necessities if this came out positive. Sleeping bag. Nights were getting cooler up in the mountains.

Strict didn't say anything about this being official police business so I felt comfortable going with khaki camping pants and t-shirt. I don't know why he didn't push the uniform on me. Technically I was supposed to wear it on any call but I really did track better if left to my old camping clothes.

Come on, stupid water, do your thing, I thought.

I had to call Rusty, he was going to sense the tension but hopefully he would think it had to do with the call.

"Hey, there," he said when he picked up.

"Hi. Strict called. I'm heading out in just a little bit. Base camp is at Elk Meadows. I don't have any real details. Knowing the terrain it could be anything. As long as they avoid the big shale mountain I should be in good shape."

"Why Elk Meadows?" Rusty asked.

"Because that's where they got lost from."

"That place is jinxed."

"Rusty, it's no more jinxed than any other part of the forest. I like it. There are lots of options for hiking out of Elk Meadows."

"Okay, I'll call Strict tonight like usual."

"I'll be home as soon as I can."

"Take care of my girl out there."

"I will." And I might be taking care of more than your girl, I thought.

Oh, man, what a time to have this come up. A search. Rusty would be mad at me for going out on a search if I knew and yet I couldn't turn it down. And I had to know before I left. I wasn't sure why, it just seemed important to know. And if it turned out positive, then what? Would I tell Landon? He was kind of in charge of things medically. I couldn't tell Landon before Rusty. Okay, first things first. The test. More water. Oh, come on! I thought. I looked at the clock. At least the hands weren't moving. I still had time before I had to take off.

An hour later the clock said five minutes had passed. In fact all the clocks said only five minutes had passed. I paced the house. Gear check, complete. Change of clothes, complete. I took the pack out to the Jeep. I paced the house. I washed my hands and a plastic cup. I paced the house. Another five minute hour went by and I decided to try anyway. I ran the test, put the little stick in the cup, and left it for five seconds like the instructions said. I pulled it out, set it on a paper towel and prayed over it. Please say no, please say no.

It didn't say no. When I checked it three minutes later it said yes and at five minutes it hadn't changed its mind. Oh lord, what was I going to do now? I was pregnant.

I lay on the bed for fifteen minutes hyperventilating. Okay, Cass, get a hold of yourself. You have a search to do. Let's go do it. The plurality of that little statement struck me as funny even in my panic. I gathered up all the test taking paraphernalia, put it in a plastic grocery bag and tied the top. I put it in the bottom of the trash bin and pulled plenty of trash over to cover it, then I got in the Jeep and headed for the compound, still hyperventilating.

Landon Wilson was just pulling out of the lot when I pulled in. He turned around and came back. In the car were Landon, Victor Gomez, Thez Brockman, and one empty seat for me. This was going to be a big search. Why did we have three EMTs? Usually I went out with one, maybe two if they expected injuries, or if there was the possibility of searchers being injured. I parked the Jeep and looked through the window of the SAR vehicle.

"What kind of a search is this?" I asked, looking from one man to the other.

They all exchanged glances. No one was smiling. I got a bad feeling about this search. I looked for weapons and could only see their usual service revolvers. No heavy weapons. That was a good sign. Rusty would be furious if I went out on an apprehension knowing I was pregnant. I didn't even want to think about that. Still, why was Strict in such a hurry on this search? Usually I was the one in a rush to hit the trail. He always had the patience of a saint. I had to calm my thinking. I still didn't have an answer out of the guys as I slid into the empty seat and they pulled out of the parking place. That was when I saw the high powered rifles. The officers usually carried both a rifle and a pistol, but these weapons were the heavy artillery.

"Hold it," I told the guys. "I have to know, right now, before we leave the parking lot, what kind of a search this is."

"We don't know," Landon said.

"What do you mean you don't know? You've got all these rifles for a reason."

"We always carry rifles," Landon said.

"Yes. But not these rifles. There are rifles and there are rifles, and believe me I know my rifles. These are not your typical rifles to scare off a coyote in camp. You've got scopes big enough to spot a fly on tree branch at five hundred feet. What are you expecting?"

"Hopefully nothing, we just don't know what we're getting into yet."

"Okay, stop the car. I have to know. I have a good reason for needing to know and I need to know, so fork over what information you do have. You obviously have more than me."

Landon sighed, irritated at the delay. "There was a car chase. It started on the 2 and took off into the mountains. The vehicle dead ended at Elk Meadows and kept going half way across the meadow where it got stuck in the soft dirt. Three guys jumped out and hightailed it for the hills. We don't know if they are armed. We don't know why they ran. We only know they need to be questioned."

"Never fails," Victor added. "One simple speeding ticket and they take off making more trouble than they ever thought possible."

"A car does not dead end at Elk Meadows unless there is a good reason. Even the Jeep has to take it slow because it is so bumpy. These guys really don't want to get caught. They drove into the meadow to get as close to cover as they could. How many guys are up there already?" I asked.

"Ask Strict."

A pause while my brain numbly went in little circles.

"I can't do this," I stated flatly.

"What?"

"You heard me. Let me out. I need to rant at Strict a while. I'll put him in a nice nasty mood for you, but I can't go."

I opened the door and got out. I pulled out my cell phone and scrolled down to Strict's number. I didn't wait for a hello.

"Strict, what's the idea calling me out on a call like this without some clue as to what's going on? I can't go on this call. I just can't. Landon told me the background and I can't make myself go."

"Cassidy, slow down kid." Like I said, the patience of a saint. "Why can't you go? You said you'd be up here in two hours."

"That was before I saw the guys armed to the teeth! You didn't say anything about this being an apprehension. I should have been told!"

"Okay, so it's sort of an apprehension. We hope not."

"No matter what it is, these guys do not want to be caught. No matter what it is, I'm walking into an unknown situation."

"That never stopped you before."

"Maybe I have more at stake right now. Maybe I have extenuating circumstances."

"What are you saying?"

"I can't tell you. I haven't told Rusty yet. Look, nobody's in danger if I don't go. It's not a lost camper who is going to die of dehydration. It's three guys who are resisting arrest. This is a job for the police. You already have a helicopter on this. You've got guys up there already."

"So you refuse?"

"Unless you give me a direct order? Yes."

"What if I give you a direct order?"

"You know what that means."

The line was silent. He was putting puzzle pieces together. "Go tell Rusty."

Gulp, "Yes sir."

Chapter 3

The station was busy even for a Friday. I went to Rusty's office but nobody was there. I speed dialed his cell phone.

"Hello?" There were car noises in the background.

"What's your twenty?" I asked, still in search mode.

"I'm on the road. Why?"

"Are you busy?"

"Yeah, why?"

"How busy?"

"Work busy."

"Should I wait for you at the station or at home?"

"I thought you had a search."

"I did. I turned it down."

That got his attention. I didn't turn down searches.

"Are you okay?" I heard him pull off the road and cut the engine.

"Yeah. I just need to talk to you, in person, Strict's orders."

"Where are you?"

"At your office."

"Okay, stay put," he said with a this-better-be-good attitude.

I sat with a huff. This is not at all the way I wanted this to happen. This was not a hurried conversation in the hallway type of conversation. This was an old brown couch conversation.

"Rusty, no. It can wait. Please, just do what you need to. I'll go home and we'll talk about this later."

"Something's going on and I want to know what it is. I'll be right there."

Darn. I guess I should have been grateful he put me above whatever he was doing but I didn't see it that way at all. It put me in a jumbled up mess of emotions. Here it was, something he had been waiting for the whole time we'd been married. It was special to him and he was going to march into the station all fired up to be mad at Strict and...and this wasn't how it was supposed to be.

Everyone in the hallway turned when Rusty barged in. He hit the door to the back offices with enough force to knock out anybody coming the other way. I retreated down the hall. He was dressed in SWAT team black, his sidearm in easy reach, his rifle across his back. If I didn't know him better I would have taken off running. I was tempted to anyway. He came to a sudden stop in front of me.

"Rusty, please, calm down. I can't talk to you when you're like this."

"What'd he do this time?"

"Nothing. He let me off. He knew I wouldn't refuse the call without good reason."

"Then why are you here?"

"Strict wanted me to tell you something."

"You brought me all the way back to the station to relay a message from Strict?"

"No, Rusty…" I turned away. I needed a few minutes to collect my emotions, organize my thoughts, and a quiet place out of the flow of traffic in the hallway. He followed me to his office, unlocked the door, checked the safety and tossed the rifle onto his desk. It was not like Rusty to toss a rifle, safety or no. It knocked his mail onto the floor beside his chair and stopped with a clunk when it hit his computer.

He sat on his desk, arms folded. There was not a hint of compassion in his eyes. He was hard. He was tough. This was not supposed to be a hard, tough conversation.

"What happened to the search?" he demanded.

"I refused to go."

"Why?"

"Because, I knew you would rather I didn't."

"That never stopped you before." That hurt. He was right, but it still hurt. Maybe it hurt *because* he was right.

"Rusty, I do keep in mind what you would have me do in this job. Occasionally I get roped into things without knowing what I am getting into. I saw it coming this time. I thought it could get risky. Nobody was going to be hurt if I didn't go track it. They had air support. They had their little army. There was no good reason for me to go, so I didn't. It's as simple as that. I thought you'd be glad. I didn't want to drag you back to the station. I wouldn't tell Strict why I wouldn't go on the search, because I hadn't told *you* yet. So he ordered me to tell you… I don't want it to be like this. I don't want you to be mad when I tell you. We both need to be calm."

"You're digging yourself in deeper. Just tell me."

Damn it, he just wasn't getting it. I decided I better not match his attitude or I'd be even sorrier than I was already.

"When Strict called I was debating whether to try a home pregnancy test. When he called, I thought I should know the results before I went out, so I told Strict I'd be there in a few hours, then I ran the test."

I let that little fact sink in and his macho attitude deflated a little. He unfolded his arms and his expression softened.

"When I arrived at the compound and there were three EMTs with automatic rifles I knew this was no lost camper. So I backed out."

"And the test?"

"It was positive. Rusty, I didn't want to tell you like this. I wanted to tell you at home, just us and the big, brown couch. I'm sorry I dragged you in here like this. I didn't want to. I didn't mean to get you all upset. I wanted this to be so different. Even if I didn't know how *I* felt about it I wanted it to be right for you. I…"

He wrapped me in a SWAT team black hug and kissed the top of my head. "It was positive?"

"Yeah. I still need to get a real test from the doctor but… but yeah. It was very positive. And Strict's apprehension seemed like a bad idea, so I didn't go."

He gave a big, wretched sigh. "I am such a dolt. Would you please just slap me one when I do that? Babe… I'm sorry. I just got through a raid and things didn't go well. I chased a teenager away from an apartment full of stolen goods. I hate those calls. At least something good came out of today."

"Did you catch him?"

"Yeah, we caught two." We both sighed with tension and relief, then he asked, "How long? Do you know?"

"No, I wasn't keeping track. It just seemed like things were off by a few weeks so I bought a test at the grocery store."

"How long until we know for sure?"

"I can go in to urgent care and get a test. Or I can make an appointment with my doctor. Considering my history he'll probably want to know pretty soon."

"How sure are you?"

"I wouldn't tell you unless I was pretty sure. I know how you've waited for this to happen."

"How are you doing with it?"

"I don't know yet. Let me get used to the idea."

A few days later my doctor confirmed my fear. I was indeed pregnant and so far everything checked out fine. I prepared for nine months of protective custody. Well, not really, but I knew Rusty was going to be impossibly overprotective and cautious. He lived up to my expectations to the letter.

As word traveled around the station I heard from Landon and then Strict.

"Yes, I'll take typical tracking calls," I told Strict. "As long as it is straight forward backpacking and tracking I'll do anything. I won't do apprehensions. If it's that kind of a call, call Chase. It's what he's good at."

Although I was trained as a soldier, scout, and police officer the idea of shooting another person was paralyzing to me. I almost refused to do it. I'd regretted every shot I ever fired at a person even though it had saved my life more than once and the lives of friends, too. I didn't think I could do it again.

"It takes Chase five hours to get up here. On an apprehension five hours is too long. Besides, he turns us down half the time."

"Tell, him you'll try calling me. That usually gets his attention. He's going to be almost as overprotective of me as Rusty with another little tracker on the way."

"I don't think he knows yet."

"He'll call the ranch. He'll know." And then it hit me that my family didn't know. So Chase didn't know yet. Chase wasn't part of my family. He was a retired cop and tracker based in San Diego. He had closer ties to Rusty's family than mine, but when he discovered there was another talented tracker in the area he began keeping tabs on me and when he found out my nephew, Patrick, showed promise he began keeping tabs on Patrick, too. We couldn't do anything without Chase knowing but I didn't mind. Chase had a good heart in spite of his quick trigger finger. If there was anybody I wanted on my side it was Rusty, Landon and Chase. With those three behind me I thought I'd survive any bout of trouble that came my way.

"Hello? Mom?" I said when the ringing stopped but there was no answer. "Hello? Anybody there?"

"I'm sorry, Cassidy, I was just checking something in the oven when the phone rang in my pocket," Martha explained. "Is everything okay?"

"Yeah, everything is fine. I just have news."

"Oh! At last! I can't believe it! Your mom is going to be so excited!"

"Martha, slow down. I haven't even told you the news."

"I know, but there's only one thing it can be and you can't tell me first. You have to tell your mom so she can tell me. But isn't this exciting! Oh, and Patrick is going to be unbearable with his questions! The pie needs five more minutes. I'll go find your mother. Do you have any names picked out?"

"Martha, we've only known for a few days."

"So? Do you have any names picked out?"

"No, we haven't even talked about it other than joking that if the baby was born on a search we could name it Cliff or Brook. If it was born in a car we could name him Otto. But it was all just joking. Knowing me it could happen anywhere."

"Here's your mother. I can't wait until she tells me!"

"Tells you what?" Mom asked.

"Cassidy's expecting!" Martha said.

"And you told Martha before you told me?" Mom asked.

"No, I didn't tell her. She just assumed right."

"So, you really are? Is everything okay?"

"Yes, everything is fine. I went to the doctor and got checked out and everything is normal this time."

"Oh Cassidy, Jesse's going to be ecstatic! When is your due date?"

"The end of June."

"You sure picked a good time to get pregnant. Being nine months pregnant in the summer is no fun. You'll have fewer searches in the winter. I can't wait!" And then the inevitable question from my mom, "What do you need?"

"Mom, we've got eight months to plan. We don't need anything."

"Of course you do! You have no idea the number of little things you need for the baby. Cribs and changing tables and diapers and wallpaper."

"A baby does not need wallpaper."

"Of course they do! With bright, colorful designs. It's important to provide a visually stimulating atmosphere for a baby."

"If you did that for me, then I think I better tone things down a bit."

"And we need to plan a shower! I can't wait to plan the shower!"

"Mom, I don't have any friends up there and all my friends down here are guys."

"It's okay, we can tailor it to the profession. That sounds like fun, too."

Oh gee, I didn't know what I was getting into telling my mom.

"Why don't you tell Jesse," I suggested. "Then you can both have a plan of attack ready when it really matters."

Several hours later I got a call from Jesse.

"Is this for real?" she asked.

"Yeah, it's for real."

"I can't wait! Do you have names picked out?"

I was beginning to think I better choose a name just so I would have an answer ready.

"Jesse, it's been less than a week!"

"So? Do you have names picked out?"

"No, and I haven't gone shopping and I don't care if it's a boy or a girl and, yes, I am still doing searches and teaching at Farley's school. Nothing has changed."

"Oh, come on Cassidy. What theme did you choose for your nursery?"

"Theme? Babies don't need themes. They just need love and space to explore."

"You. Need. Help."

"I do not need help. I'm doing just fine! I've got eight months to get ready. There's no decorating or shopping or choosing that needs to be done right now."

Next Chase called. The conversation was brief.
"Is it true?"
"Yeah."
"You still taking calls?"
"Yeah."
"I'll talk to Strict."
"Okay."
"Take care of yourself."
"I will."

After that things settled down except for occasional calls from my mom who couldn't keep her charge card out of the mall.

"Don't buy a mobile, I found the cutest one. It's perfect for your baby. It's got little baby squirrels and raccoons and wolves and deer. I've never seen one like it and I just had to buy it."

A mobile? What was a baby going to do with a mobile? You have to understand that I hadn't babysat as a teen. I hadn't changed a diaper until about six months prior. I was completely ignorant of what went into baby care. But I was assuming I wasn't the first and I wouldn't be the last. Babies had survived for centuries, even back in the dark ages when kids became mothers at fourteen, with no hospitals, no technology, no mobiles.

I thought my mom was going overboard, that is until I read a parenting magazine. Oh, man! I scanned through it and found out I was supposed to teach my baby sign language so he could talk before he could speak. I was supposed to show him flash cards of words so he'd recognize the patterns when he got to be four or five. I was supposed to make sure they got x number of servings of anything you could name or they'd suffer some incurable disease. Not only did I need a theme and a mobile, I needed to make my whole house into a giant learning center. All this would bring out a sense of wonder and awe with the world around them and encourage them to explore and begin learning at an earlier stage, which would translate to easier learning for a lifetime. After what I put my parents through I thought I better raise my baby in the secret room. Dirt walls, old rug on the floor, an old couch, a bare light bulb overhead. Give a kid my curiosity and raise them in the secret room and they might balance out to somewhere near normal.

Of course, I wasn't going to do that, but I was beginning to see my mother's shopping trips as a normal part of grandmotherhood and I tried to greet her announcements with enthusiasm. I looked on the bright side. By the time this baby was born I wouldn't have to buy anything and I'd have a theme. I didn't need to do anything except name the kid.

"Rusty, have you thought about what kind of a name you'd like for the baby?"

"I thought that was your job," he said. "You're the one with a family tradition."

"I don't care about the family tradition. We'll name our baby whatever we want. Maybe I don't want my kid named after a trouble maker."

"Now you're sounding superstitious. A name does not jinx a kid for life. I've never known you to be superstitious before."

"I'm not. But I would like your input about a name. The first question everybody asks me is if I've picked out a name. I'm tired of it. I need an answer even if we end up changing our minds. At least I'll sound like a normal parent if I can say I've been thinking about names."

"How about Mike?" he kidded.

"No, not Mike Michaels."

"Michaela?"

"Rusty…"

He laughed at me.

What I found out is that there is no end to the questions people will ask a pregnant woman. After the name question was, "Do you know if it's a girl or a boy?" I never even thought about finding out. And how would you go about doing that? I didn't really want to know but most people insisted it was better to know because you could buy things with the gender of the baby in mind. Since I wasn't buying anything, I didn't think it mattered. The sex of the baby was out of my hands so there was no point in guessing. We'd find out for ourselves when the time came.

Chapter 4

At first I had a very uneventful time. I wasn't bored at home because I was too busy getting used to the idea of having a baby. My mind would run in little bitty circles and I'd worry about it. Then I'd force myself to focus on a task and I'd wonder at how easy this pregnancy thing was. I felt great. Wasn't I supposed to have swollen ankles? Food cravings? Weren't little kids supposed to walk up to me at the grocery store and ask if I was hiding a basketball? I was almost my normal self, except that I felt better. I felt healthier.

"Don't buy bumper pads," my mom said. "I found the cutest ones on sale."

"What are bumper pads? It sounds like something you'd put on a car to protect it from bumps and scrapes while it's in the shop."

"They go around the edges of the mattress so the baby doesn't bump against the crib rails."

"Oh, why would I buy bumper pads?"

"Because you need them. Oh and I found crib sheets so I bought yellow, green and Winnie the Pooh. I don't know if Winnie the Pooh will go with your theme but they were on sale."

"Mom, how many sets do I need? Surely not three!"

"You never know, it can't hurt to have extras. Babies are really good at making messes. When you find out if it's a girl or a boy we'll get you some in pink or blue."

"No, Mom, three is plenty."

Every few days I got a similar call. I'd never fit all this baby stuff into my house! I was getting scared to answer the phone. What would my mom come up with next?

I had just hung up the phone because Mom found some expensive educational toy when the phone rang again.

"Don't tell me, you found little cowboy print diapers," I said sarcastically.

"Cassidy?" It was Strict. Oops. "How are you feeling?"

That was another of those irritating questions. Everybody needed to know how I was feeling, like I was supposed to have some special answer just because I was pregnant.

"I feel like a normal person today. How about you?"

"What?"

"I'm sorry, Lou. I'm fine."

"I've got a tracking case for you. It's important that you take it."

"Okay, why?"

"It's been two days already."

"Where?"

"A young couple took a short backpacking trip out of Devil's Punchbowl. First night up the trail they set up camp. Tess wanted to get a view of the valley so she took her camera and looked for a photo spot. She wasn't going far so she didn't take much. Rich said she probably did not bring any water. She never came back. Rich hiked around and looked for her but he almost got lost when darkness set in. He didn't know what to do. He didn't want to leave because Tess would be up there alone and he was a day's hike from help. After another quick look in the morning he decided he wasn't going to find Tess on his own. He took minimal provisions and hiked out."

"Where's the camp? Burkhart Trail or Punchbowl Trail?"

"Burkhart."

"Okay, we've been over that area before. I can handle that. I just hope the trail hasn't been busy. Two days of tourists can really mess up a trail. I need to call Rusty and then I'll head out."

"Good luck with Rusty."

"Thanks."

"Oh, and Cassidy? Meet the guys at the helicopter pad. We're going to try and drop you off at the camp. Time's too short to waste a day hiking to it."

"Okay."

Rusty picked up on the first ring. Seemed like ever since I told him I was pregnant he was on constant alert.

"Hello?" He said even though he knew it was me.

"Hi! I got a call from Strict. I'm heading out in a little while. We're taking off from the helipad. You know the one?"

"The one by the fire training station?"

"Yeah."

"Are you sure you're up to this?"

"Yeah, I feel great. Strict is saving us a hike by dropping us off at the camp the girl disappeared from. We're kind of in a hurry because she's been missing two days."

"Are you sure you want to do this?"

"Of course I'm sure. It's what I do best. I'll find her and I'll be fine."

"Who are you going with?"

"Strict didn't say. I assume it'll be Landon. If the boyfriend was really worried and thinks Tess might have been hurt maybe Victor will go, too. I'll just have to see when I get there."

"Cass…"

"I'll be fine. You can check in. You know that. And if I'm on this side of the mountain I might even have cell phone reception."

"Cassidy…" a big sigh. He knew I was going. This was a first for him. He still remembered what happened not too long ago. I'd gone out not knowing I was pregnant, not knowing it was a dangerous situation and I'd had complications. He hadn't known anything was wrong until I was being whisked over the mountain to LA. "If anything happens. Anything at all. Any little twinge. I want you to tell Wilson."

"Don't worry. Landon's almost as bad as you are."

"I mean it, babe. I have to know you'll play it safe."

"I'll be fine and I'll report any twinges. Now quit worrying. I've never felt better."

"I can't help it."

"Go over to Kelly's. He always understands your worry. You can go shoot pool or something."

"Okay, take care of my girl out there."

"I will."

Wow, it hadn't been that hard to get away since my very first search and that was because I wasn't going with a team. Rusty couldn't imagine a girl trekking out on a trail alone on a week long search for a missing ranger. But I'd found that ranger. He was Rusty's best friend, Kelly Green, and hopefully they would find something to do tonight so Rusty wouldn't stew.

I loaded the pack into my Jeep and took off for the fire training station. I was eager to be on the trail. I even beat Strict and Landon there. Landon was ready to go but he assessed the situation carefully before he allowed himself to relax.

"You're sure. Everything checks out."

"It's too early for an ultrasound, but the doctor says I'm doing fine. I feel great. Rusty didn't call you did he?"

"No, why?"

"I half expected him to."

"Why?"

"To threaten you to within an inch of your life if I do something stupid."

He smiled at that but he also knew it was halfway true.

"Don't worry, I feel fine and I'm ready to roll and I won't do anything stupid. I've promised Rusty if I even get a twinge in my pinky finger I'll tell you about it. This is ridiculous."

"It wouldn't be if you'd listen to your body and not be so hard headed."

"So what's the hold up?"

"Victor and Jayce. Strict has a feeling this lost camper might have gotten lost for a reason. It might take two of us to handle the repercussions."

"A reason? Like an accident or..."

"Drugs."

"Oh."

"Rich smelled, well, rather rich, when he talked to Strict and it would explain why a simple walk to take pictures turned into a two day stint on a mountainside."

"What do I do? I don't have any experience with people on drugs."

"Just find her and get out of the way. It might be easy if she's had access to more. If she's been two days without she might be a real wildcat. We'll get a lift out. We want to get her checked out as soon as possible in case charges need to be filed. First though, we gotta find her. I'm glad you're up to going. Did you bring cookies?"

"Yeah, I brought cookies. Since Rusty's kept me under house arrest, I've had lots of time to make cookies."

Victor showed up in a hurry. He knew he was late. He grinned broadly as he walked up. We hadn't worked together for a while. He was looking forward to the latest installment of the Cassidy Michaels Adventures.

"Hey Cassidy, so far you're still Skipper meets GI Joe. What are you going to do when you are more like Skipper meets Winnie the Pooh?" Victor asked.

"Ha, ha, very funny."

"Natalia wants to know if you've thought about names for the baby."

Grrr, again? "Yeah, as a matter fact, after hearing that question for the hundredth time we decided we'd do like the Indians and name the baby after the first thing we see after he's born. If it's on a search there's lots of options. For a girl we could name her Brook or Gale, Heather, Ivy, hopefully not poison ivy, Rainy, Savannah, Skye, Star, Summer...how about Windy? It's always windy here. For a boy there's Ash, Bud, Cliff, Dale, Eddy, Ford, Forrest, Rocky, Woody..."

"You're kidding, right?"

"If he's born in a car we can name him Otto and if he's born in Landon's ambulance we can name him Van."

There were three men standing there hands on hips, just waiting for me to wind down.

"Sorry, I just got tired of that being the first thing people say to me."

Another car pulled up and Jayce Thompson emerged. I wasn't too concerned about this apprehension. Lost girl, unarmed. Jayce was along in case legal issues came up.

"All right, let's get a move on," Strict said.

We stowed our gear on board the helicopter, found our seats and gave the pilot the okay. The chopper lifted off and headed over the city and off to the mountains to the south. The pilot had some general coordinates for where the camp was located but he still had to fly around to locate the tent.

As we flew back and forth over the spot that we thought the camp should be, I kept spotting a boulder. Nearby, something fluttered in the wind.

"See that rock?" I called out to the pilot. "See if you can get closer to that."

The helicopter lowered and the details of the camp became clear to me.

"Jayce, I sure hope you brought a big evidence bag!" I said. "Okay drop us here!"

"What?" the three officers exclaimed.

"I don't like the sound of this," Jayce said. "I mean, I know things are always going to get interesting when Cassidy's aboard but why are we being dropped on top of a mountain because you like the looks of a rock?"

"It's not a rock. You're going to have to talk to Strict, maybe even Schroeder about this one! This is cool. I can't wait to tell Patrick about this. He loves animal stories."

The guys all gawked out the little windows. Maybe they should know what they were getting into.

"That rock is not a rock. It's a bear. The only reason a bear would conk out in the open like that is if he had plenty of help. If we are looking for someone who might be on drugs and there's a conked out bear in camp, why do you suppose he's there, sleeping, in the middle of the day?"

"He's...tired?" Jayce said hopefully, although I'm sure he got the gist of it by now.

"How are you going to take a doped up bear back for evidence?" I asked.

"How the hell should I know? This sounds like an animal control call."

"We'll need a vet. We need blood samples to prove the drug charge," Victor said. "We need an officer to collect the evidence at camp while we look for the girl."

"What camp? There is no camp!" Landon said.

"Yes there is," I added. "Do you know what an abandoned camp looks like when a bear has thrashed it and eaten his fill? It looks like a green piece of tent fabric fluttering in the breeze. I bet once we get down there we will see belongings scattered around. But I bet we don't find much in the way of drugs. Do you know how many downers it takes to knock out a three hundred pound bear?"

"And you want to go down there?" Landon asked me.

"Yeah, this is cool. Now I can say I touched a bear in the wild."

"Oh no you don't! You're not touching that bear!"

"Why? He's unconscious. I wish I brought a camera."

"Aw shit," said Jayce. "I've got one. I have to carry one for damage reports and accident scenes. I'll take your picture. It'll prove just how far gone the bear really was."

We all had harnesses on, so two by two we clipped onto the cable and were lowered onto the mountain. Jayce and Landon went first just in case the bear woke up. They were armed the heaviest. Victor and I followed. I always loved the ride down on a cable. The view was great and it appealed to my sense of adventure. To the guys it was just a risky descent. They didn't like being directly under a hovering helicopter.

While I stood on the mountainside and watched the cable being pulled back up into the chopper the guys approached the bear cautiously. Landon bent down staring into the face of the sleeping bear. I got a mental image of Landon shining his little flashlight into the bear's eyes and laughed.

"What's so funny?" he asked.

"I think Jayce better radio for that vet before the bear comes around." I walked up to it and stroked it gently. It reached out lazily with its paw, flexed its claws and dragged his paw back leaving inch deep furrows in the ground. I was glad the bear was peacefully asleep. Jayce snapped a couple of pictures and we got to work.

Chapter 5

The camp was thrashed. The tent was a scrap of fabric and a couple of snapped poles. There were articles of clothing scattered here and there. A few cooking pots had rolled down the hill. Plastic eating utensils were scattered around. No sign of water. Hopefully Tess had some with her.

I looked around for the best vantage point to photograph the valley and headed that direction looking for Tess's tracks. This area was notorious for wind and Tess's tracks were already two days old. They would look like week old tracks on the valley floor, rounded, with very little of the tread left.

I located Tess's and Rich's tracks. The two were not together. Tess's tracks were much smaller and below Rich's tracks because he had been searching for her after she left camp. The tracks didn't look as random as I expected. As far as I knew I had never tracked someone high on drugs before. This might prove interesting from a tracker's point of view. The wind had scoured the tracks and the tread was less plain but they were still recognizable as tracks and still provided most of the information I hoped for while reading a trail. My mission was straightforward. All I had to do was follow Tess's tracks. When I had a start to my search I went back and found the guys still fascinated with the bear.

"Did you get the bear situation figured out?" I asked.

"Yeah, we've got a vet, an army of animal control officers, and two cops enroute. Why do you do these things to me?" Jayce asked.

"Me? I didn't do anything! You act like just because I got called in the bear thought he needed to get involved too. Just because I've had a tiger call and a mountain lion call doesn't mean I do these things on purpose. It's not my fault we have a dopey bear to deal with!"

Victor was snickering.

"What?" I asked, irritated.

"Lions and tigers and bears. Leave to you to have all your bases covered."

Sigh, "I need someone to hit the trail with. I've got a line on the tracks."

"I'll go," Victor volunteered.

At last, I could settle into my tracking. It was fun bantering back and forth with the guys but I had a missing person to find. I went back to my starting place and bent to the task of reading Tess's trail. My pack felt heavy but I knew it would settle into place and feel like part of me soon. I wondered how it would fit in a few months.

Tess's track's followed the hill that faced the valley. Every twenty feet or so she would turn and take in the view. I did, too. It was a big, wide valley below but I couldn't imagine why anybody would want a picture of it. It looked like a dust bowl to me. Joshua Hills at the bottom of the mountains, wide-open desert, then the white expanse of the dry lakebed at the Air Force base. Not exactly picturesque. I followed the tracks across the ridge and then down the far side. Trees closed in and Tess couldn't stay close to the ridge without falling so she followed a game trail east. She had left camp in the evening. She didn't have time to go far and eventually she turned around to go back. Only problem was she turned and went uphill, no particular direction, just uphill, and the uphill she chose didn't lead back to camp. She angled as she went and when she reached the top again the camp was nowhere in sight. I knew where it was. I could point to it, but when she chose a direction to look it was about thirty degrees off from where camp really was. I wonder sometimes about the people I track. Usually I can see why they came to the conclusions they did, but Tess was not even following any form of logic that I could see. Was she thinking clearly? There was really no telling at this point. Some people just get turned around easily.

A helicopter flew overhead. Our vet and animal control backup. I hoped the bear was still around and not giving the guys a hard time. It was hard to believe the bear could ingest enough downers to knock it out for over an hour. I waved at the pilot just in case any of the guys on board were supposed to be with me.

They'd get their handy dandy little GPS gadgets out, compare locations and find us. Guys always appreciated technological backup. The more gadgets they could make use of during a search the more successful it was. I laughed that GPS could also stand for the number of Gadgets Per Search. So far this search had a pretty good GPS rating. Helicopters, rappelling gear, cameras, GPS. We needed to come up with a numbering system. Things like high-powered rifles and all-terrain vehicles had a high GPS rating while rappelling gear had a pretty low one.

Tess had figured out that she was turned around but every time she changed direction she chose wrong. It didn't take darkness long to force her to stop. She sheltered under a dense old oak tree. She sat beneath it for a while until she grew tired and convinced herself she was stuck for the night. She found the most comfortable position she could and curled up on her side to sleep. I found the imprint of the bottom of a water bottle nearby. That was good news. I examined the print trying to guess how much water was in it but there were too many variables. I had no way to know how hard she had set it down. I tried setting my own water bottle next to where hers had been. Just with that simple test hers appeared to be heavier than mine but the print was eroded, she may have pushed down harder. I couldn't really tell. I was glad, though, that we'd identified the time involved. From here on out we were working on the first full day Tess had been out here. The tracks should be a little fresher and I usually got more clues about the person's mental state the second day. It was time to start profiling.

As we headed out again the radio came alive with orders for the guys at camp. I didn't pay attention. That was all police business. My job was to find Tess. The men I worked with lived in constant radio contact with each other and it amazed me how all the transmissions sounded alike, but they could pick up on the ones that pertained to them. It was their job to screen radio transmissions and act on them. They filtered the jumble automatically. I followed tracks automatically.

The place Tess had spent the night wasn't in view of the valley. I don't know what made her decide to head south. Everything I knew about the place said to head north to get to the view of the valley where she started out, then west a little to get back to the camp. All I could do was accept her faulty thinking and follow along.

We entered a large bed of pine needles. It doesn't take pine needles long to hide a trail. First the blanket of needles springs back up. Tracks can be seen with careful observation even after they have sprung back up, but then more needles fall from above covering the, already faint, trail. Often all I could do was circle the bed and find an exit point. In this case Tess's condition was beginning to tell on her. I didn't know if it was drugs or exhaustion but when she reached the bed of pine needles she slipped repeatedly. The needles underneath were darker and rotting slightly. I was able to quickly follow the trail of darker pine needles until the ground was firm again.

I was feeling pretty good about the search thus far. Although tracking is never a speedy endeavor there are good searches and then there are rotten searches. I'd had my share of rotten searches and I was sure I'd see more of them but this one was coming along pleasantly easy. A speedy search progressed at a lazy walk. If the tracks were unmistakable it could progress at a fast walk. I'd tracked at a jog when time was critical, but I worried about missing something and I missed the profiling aspect of the search. I'd also tracked from horseback but that had been tracking another horse and horses leave big, sharp, unmistakable tracks. As long as I walked along from print to print I was doing pretty well.

Tess's trail topped out and she looked down onto miles and miles of rugged mountains with a faint hint of L.A. in the far distance. She didn't know what to think about that. Her logic and her circumstances disagreed with each other and when people are faced with conundrums they follow their emotions. Tess did what I hate to see lost people do. She knew L.A. was before her so she turned right around and made a mad dash back the way she'd come. Now she was headed in the right direction but she'd lost it. She was no longer thinking. She was getting desperate.

"Hold it!" Victor called out.

I stopped and turned around.

"What is it?" I asked.

He walked over to the side of the tracks and plucked an empty water bottle out of the brush. He swirled it around, opened it up, smelled the contents, frowned.

"Looks like she's out of water. She should have held onto the bottle in case she finds more," he said.

"At least we know she had water up to this point."

The radio crackled and Victor answered it. I didn't know how he could understand the voice behind the crackling, but he answered.

"Ten four, everything's fine…okay, stand by."

He got out his GPS receiver and pushed a few buttons. He studied the screen and fired back some coordinates. There was a pause and he was asked about his surroundings. It was dry open forest. He looked at the sky.

"You'll have to be right on top of us to see us but it should be okay for a quick descent." The radio quieted and he said, "We're going to have company."

After a while we heard the helicopter coming over the hill and as it hovered close by Landon and Jayce rappelled down. I was glad for the short rest. Although I felt fine, I did tire faster. My pack felt heavier. The day felt hotter than it should.

"Strict wanted us to catch up before it got dark," Landon explained.

"How's it going with the bear? It isn't still in camp, is it?"

"Naw, but you should have seen the vet's face when we told him we wanted a blood sample. He'd never treated a bear before. He had to shave a spot on the bear's leg and then find a vein. All the time we expected the bear to come to. Every time the bear snored the vet jumped away. They'll send the blood sample to a lab, what kind of lab I don't know. I'm sure somebody somewhere has studied the effects of drugs on black bears but nobody here is quite sure what to do with it. When the bear started coming around we all cleared out. There was no telling what kind of mood it was going to be in."

"So they just let it go?"

"As long as it wasn't hurting anything. One of the guys is keeping an eye on it but it just seemed tired last time I saw it."

"Any signs of drug use in the camp?" Victor asked.

"Just some shreds of what could have been bags to store the drugs in. Those will be analyzed, too. This is going to be a fun court case. I wish I could see it. It'll be like one of those wacky reality TV shows."

"First we need to find our suspect," I reminded them.

Tess's state of mind varied from one moment to the next. I don't know what drove her. Lost people tend to be unpredictable in the best of circumstances but Tess's actions spoke volumes about her drug use. It seemed as if she would get a grasp of her circumstances and think rationally for a while, but after about a half hour her attention faded and she began reacting more emotionally and less rationally. She walked circles around a tree. She thrashed her way through brambles. She led me through places no sane person would think to go.

"Cassidy, are you sure you're on track. This is not making much sense," Jayce said from a clear area beside the brush.

"I know it doesn't, but I see tracks. No thinking person would go this way so it must be Tess, right?"

The tracks led straight through the brush and almost went right off a ledge. Tess lurched to a halt then paced agitatedly back and forth. I looked out over the scene below. Even if she had spotted the camp she wouldn't have recognized it from this far away. She started to follow the top of the ridge and then doubled back. This canyon before her had her puzzled.

The light was fading fast and we were forced to admit we couldn't tackle a climb down into the canyon until morning. I hoped Tess stuck to the high country where her tracks would be clear. A climb down into the canyon meant rocks, cursed rock, the bane of trackers everywhere. We stopped and made camp quickly. We cooked and ate our dinner before any nocturnal animals could get a whiff. I ate my lasagna wishing I had more cheese, a piece of garlic bread, anything to make it more of a proper meal instead of noodles and tomato sauce. "Dangerous Tracker Woman sure has been quiet this time," Victor observed. "We haven't heard one of your tall tales yet."

"Yeah, and I haven't gotten a cookie yet," complained Landon.

I passed the cookie bag around, thankful it came back considerably lighter. I took one, too.

"What story do you want to hear?" I asked.

"I want to hear what happened with Sherri Champlain," Victor said.

"Then ask Landon and Jayce. They were both there. By the way, whoever won the Bubble Wrap War? Rusty said you two were still at it when you got back to the station," I said.

"We both claim to. But I really won because we never did prove he popped them all."

The evening was passed with the guys asking questions and me answering them, gradually moving from one story to another, then it morphed into baby questions, which surprised me. I didn't think guys would be interested in such things. They were asking the wrong person, though. I didn't know the first thing about babies or being pregnant.

"My mom has gone nutso over this," I told them. "If you get a baby shower invitation feel free to ignore it. I told her I didn't have any girl friends to invite to a shower and she insisted we could have one anyway. I don't know what she is going to do. She and my sister might come up with anything. I'll make them keep the cute games to a minimum."

"Cute games?" Landon asked.

"You wouldn't believe the crazy things they do at baby showers," Victor told the single guys. "Diaper changing relays seem to be pretty common. My wife described this game where they had a ketchup bottle suspended from a chandelier and they had to spoon baby food into the bottle as it moved around, simulating trying to feed a squirmy baby."

"You've got to be kidding," I said.

"No. She said there was baby food everywhere by the time the game was over."

"I need to talk to my mom," I said. "Even I won't play something like that."

"Are you going to teach the kid to track?" Jayce asked.

"Sure, even if they never become a tracker it makes a person more aware of their surroundings. They pay more attention to the small life that most people don't notice. I want my kid to be aware of the things around them. I bet you didn't know we were camped right in the middle of a game trail. It goes right under your tent."

"You're kidding," Jayce said.

"No… look, it comes out from under that grassy area, goes right under your tent and disappears in that brush over there. If you get down on hands and knees you can make out rabbit tracks, even mice and voles if you know what to look for."

"Should I move it?" he asked.

"Not unless it bugs you to have animals outside your tent. They won't hurt anything."

"How far are we from that bear?" Jayce asked. "Do you think we need to tie up our packs?"

"You know, the bear might have left Rich and Tess's camp alone, but they left a jar of peanut butter in their tent. There was almost nothing left of the jar or the tent. The few shreds that were left of it had peanut butter smeared on them," Landon said.

"It can't hurt to string up the packs. We don't need anything from them except maybe a flashlight," I said. "Do drugs cause the munchies like pot does? The bear might be pretty hungry."

I was out like a light. Usually I spent some time thinking about where Rusty was and what he might be doing, but I must have been tired from the day's activity.

The rising sun woke me up like usual. I moved to get up and my stomach gave a lurch. Oh man, not now, calm down, calm down. After a little experimentation I figured out that I was in a pickle. If I got up my stomach was going to heave but I had to unzip my tent before I could get to the bushes. It was cold enough that I'd slept in most of my clothes. I was grateful for that. I lay back down and settled my rumbling stomach. When things felt semi normal again I tried to unzip my tent without moving my body. It was no use. I had to barf in the tent or admit I needed help. This was embarrassing. I didn't know which was worse, cleaning up the tent or asking for help. It was a simple thing for them but they'd tease me for the rest of the day. Their teasing was nothing new to me.

"Um, Landon? Are you awake? First light, time to wake up. Time to hit the trail."

Grumbling from the next tent. No intelligible words yet.

"Landon? Can you do me a favor?"

More grumbling. Tent rattling noises. Then nothing. Then just outside my door, "What do you need Cassidy?" It was Victor. That was probably better.

"Can you unzip my door and stand clear?"

"Yeah, you sure?"

"Positive."

"You ready?"

"Ready."

I heard the door unzipping and he stepped aside.

"Okay?" I asked.

"Yeah."

I leaped to my feet, ran into the door, got tangled in the fabric and lurched off into the trees. Oh man! That was close! And it wasn't over for a while either. Every time I moved, my stomach gave another heave but there was nothing in it.

"Anybody got crackers?" Victor asked. "Natalia says saltines help."

"Closest I can think of is granola bars or Cassidy's cookies," Landon said.

"What are you guys talking about?" I called back from the bushes.

"Morning sickness," Victor explained.

"Is that what this is? Oh hell, this is the first time it's happened. Are you sure?"

"What did you eat for dinner last night?" Landon said.

"Backpacker lasagna, same kind I've had every search for the past two years."

"Then it's bound to be morning sickness. Some women have it for the whole pregnancy," Victor said.

"You're just full of good news," I said back.

"Here," said Landon holding out the bag of cookies. I took one but one bite set off another round of almost dry heaves.

"Don't you guys have something better to do?" I asked. "I'll be fine."

"I thought you said you never felt better," Victor reminded me.

"That was yesterday. I'm fine. I'm just sick. But I'm not sick. Just get ready to hit the trail. I'll be there as soon as I…oh yuck."

I was in the bushes for an hour. An hour of daylight wasted. And even after I was able to join the guys I still couldn't eat anything. Everything I tried to eat made me feel worse so I hit the trail with an empty stomach.

Chapter 6

Tess continued to follow the ridge. Sometimes she came precariously close to the edge. I followed her tracks seeing the things she saw, deciding, too, that this was a bad place to go down. She did this for over an hour as the canyon below got shallower and shallower. At last the tops of the trees below reached the top of the ridge. That's when she made her move. I tracked along and suddenly the tracks stopped. Well, they didn't stop. They backed off from the ridge, took about ten running steps and went off the edge. I stopped, shocked by what she had attempted. She wouldn't, I thought. She couldn't.

"I can't look," I said.

There was a tall pine tree with ladder-like branches standing about five feet from the top of the ridge. The drop was about thirty feet to the rocks below. I looked at the tree. Bark had been knocked loose about the same spot a person might hit if they leaped at it. Oh hell. I went to the edge and looked down. Landon put his hands on my shoulders and pulled me gently back.

"What is it, Cass?"

"She jumped. I think she was aiming for the tree, hoping to climb down it, but you know how hard that is to do. It looks easier than it is. We need ropes."

Jayce produced a climbing rope and a brake bar.

"Wilson, you first. You've got the most experience and the best gear."

Landon rappelled down first but he quickly called back up.

"Cassidy! Get down here!"

I left my pack with Victor and Jayce and rappelled down. I found Tess backing away from Landon. She was afraid of the uniform. Landon held back even though it was obvious Tess needed help. She was broken, scraped up and bruised.

"Tess, stop, you're only hurting yourself worse," I told her. "Landon's only here to help. We've been searching the mountains for you. Hold still. You're going to complicate things."

"No! They're not taking me in!" she shrieked. "I'm not going with them." She looked at me, wild eyed.

"They're here to help you. You're hurt. They'll take you to a hospital," I told her, then to Landon, "Toss me a water bottle."

"Water? You've got water?" Tess asked.

"Yeah, don't leave camp without it," I advised her.

"I didn't. Get away from me!" she yelled at Landon. She backed over the rough rocks. It was obvious she had a broken leg and a broken arm. Both arms were scraped and bruised. I presumed that was from trying to grab hold of the tree. I was guessing her ribs were giving her fits, too.

"Tess, settle down. These guys are EMTs. They're here to treat your injuries. They aren't going to hurt you. I've seen their work first hand because they even rescue *me*. Come on, we can do this the easy way or we can do it the hard way. The hard way is going to hurt. You've been hurt long enough. You need help. You know you can't get out of this alone. You tried that already. It didn't work. Let me see your arm. You tried to jump to the tree, didn't you? Hurts to hit a tree like that, doesn't it? Let me see your arm."

It took talking, cajoling, but finally she just seemed to tire of it all. Even after she let the guys get close enough to help her she fought their every move. Victor would sit behind her and position her arm and Landon would struggle with the splint. All the while Jayce was on the radio calling in a report, asking for a helicopter. We had a long, tiring wait for one. When it hovered overhead and the guys strapped Tess into the basket she fought more violently. One of them had to ride up with her to make sure she didn't get loose on the way up. She struggled all the way into town. I had trouble watching it all. I knew she wasn't thinking very clearly but I ached with every lurch of her broken body.

Rusty found me in the hospital lobby pacing, my emotions a jumble.

"Good job, babe," he said, setting my pack aside and wrapping me in a hug.

"Thanks, I guess," I responded.

"What's wrong?"

"Nothing, I've just never seen anybody so strung out before. She fought our every move. I know it's not unusual in your line of work. But we were only trying to help and even though we found her and she'll get treatment, it doesn't feel like a happy ending. I guess I just like happy endings."

"How did the tracking go?"

"It was a fairly normal search, except for the bear and the morning sickness and the struggle to get Tess into the helicopter."

"Okay, tell me about it. I need to know what to expect at work tomorrow."

"It was cool! Well, kind of sad, kind of funny, but cool. I got to pet the bear and everything!" I said as we walked to the Explorer. When I finished telling him about it, he just shook his head.

"Leave it to you. Something has to come up with everything you do."

"That's what Jayce said, like it was my fault the bear showed up. Believe it or not the bear didn't have any inkling what I was doing when it ate a handful of downers."

"So how long does morning sickness last?"

"I don't know. That's the first time I've experienced it. Victor wasn't very encouraging. He says some women have it for all nine months. I'll ask Jesse. It lasted a few hours this morning. At least I don't have a tent zipper to wrestle with tomorrow."

The next morning, the same thing happened. As soon as I moved to get up I either had to lie down and stay down or make a run straight to the bathroom.

"What can I do?" Rusty asked.

"I don't know. On the trail I just had to wait it out. I couldn't eat anything. Victor said saltines help but I'm not going to count on it."

"I can make my own breakfast."

"You sure?"

"Breakfast, I can handle. When it comes to dinner…"

"I can handle dinner. This should pass in a few hours."

He headed to the kitchen and I heard him rattling around in the pots and pans cupboard. He looked in the fridge and decided on eggs. I heard the *crack, crack* and the sizzle as the eggs hit the pan and then the most awful smell wafted down the hall. Ugh! My stomach turned over. I ran to the bathroom. Oh man! What happened? Were the eggs rotten? They couldn't have been rotten. I just bought them three days ago. Plus, if they were rotten Rusty would be as bad off as me. What was going on out there?

"Rusty? What are you doing?" I exclaimed.

He walked down the hall, frying pan in hand and the smell hit me again.

"Arg! Get it away from me! It's attacking!"

"What do you mean, it's attacking? It's just a couple of eggs."

"I know but it smells horrible! And it makes my stomach feel terrible! Take it away. Oh, it's awful!"

Rusty took the pan back to the kitchen and came back without it.

"Are you okay?"

"There's nothing wrong with me, I'm just miserable."

He brought me a glass of ice water and went to eat his eggs. Even the lingering smell of the eggs after they were gone sent me running. I turned on the fan over the stove, opened some windows and hoped the smell went away.

Usually I wasn't one to complain but I called my sister and let loose.

"What's going on?" I asked. "How long does this last?"

"Eight more months," she answered.

"No, the morning sickness. How long does it last?" I could feel her smiling all the way through the phone line.

"It's different for everybody. For me it lasted about three weeks."

"Why does my nose work different?"

"Get used to it. It'll settle down with the morning sickness. While you're waiting for the morning sickness to pass spend the time planning. Mom says you haven't done anything yet and June will be here before you know it."

"Is Mom leaving me anything at all to plan?"

"Of course she is! She just likes to spend money on her kids. She isn't taking over. The planning is all up to you."

And so we talked longer that day than we ever had before, sister to sister. It felt a little off since I was the older sister but she knew all the ins and outs of being pregnant. If she ever needed to track down a kid or a horse thief she knew who to call, too.

I threw all the eggs away. What would set me off next?

Fish, curry, anything with a very distinctive smell sent me running in the mornings. Fortunately we didn't have much use for fish or curry first thing in the morning.

"Are you sure there's nothing that will make it better? You have to eat something."

"All I can keep down is potato chips."

"Babies do not live on potato chips alone."

"I eat lunch as soon as the morning sickness eases. I'm not starving."

"Oh yeah? What does the scale say?"

"I've heard I'll make up for it later."

Rusty really didn't ease up until he'd seen the ultrasound. It proved to him that everything was progressing normally. Having had one ectopic pregnancy he needed to know we were in the clear with smooth sailing ahead. The doctor was very understanding. He let Rusty listen to the baby's heartbeat and Rusty was there when they ran the ultrasound.

"Do you want to know the sex of the baby?" the technician asked.

"No!" we replied simultaneously.

The technician explained the picture on the little TV screen so Rusty would understand it.

"Here's the baby's head. We measure that to tell us how far along you are…"

I lay there with a gallon of water in me while they patiently analyzed the size of the baby and where it was located in my uterus.

"Then we measure the length of the baby…"

Let me out of here! I wanted to scream, I'm about to explode!

"We note the position, though it could change many times between now and your due date…"

When, at last, Rusty was convinced I was going to survive and his baby was growing and thriving, they helped me roll off the table and stand up. I made a mad dash for the restroom, paper sheets blowing in my wake.

"Where did you go so fast?" Rusty asked afterwards.

"You try drinking a gallon of water, then have the appointments backed up, then have a slippery device rolled over your bladder and lay on a table while you are being talked about for half an hour and we'll see what *you do*."

Later Rusty asked, "You really don't care if it's a boy or a girl?"

"I hope it's a boy for you and I hope it's a girl for Mom."

"What about twins?"

"No! I'm not even going to know what to do with one. Besides, the ultrasound would have told us if it was twins."

One thing the morning sickness did was cut my chances of getting in trouble in half. When you spend the morning between the bed and the bathroom, not much can go wrong. But eventually the morning sickness went away and once again I was feeling healthy and fit. Since, apparently, I had a lot to do before the baby was born I went to town a couple of days a week. I went shopping for baby supplies and then I went to the gym. I wandered from machine to machine doing easy exercises and I put in a couple of miles on the treadmill, ready for the next search.

Gradually the guest room filled up with stuff. I didn't like the clutter but there was no place else for it to go and so far I did just think of it as stuff. Things. Things I was supposed to need but had little meaning to me at the moment. Pretty soon the baby stuff and the guest room started fighting for dominance. I finally had to admit the baby stuff needed a place of its own so I rearranged the furniture. Moving the bed and the dresser were awkward but I wasn't about to ask for help. When Rusty came home the bed and dresser were in one corner of the room and the crib and changing table were in another. He came to me with an evil looking glare.

"What do you think you're doing moving all that heavy furniture? If you want something moved just tell me."

"I didn't know I wanted it moved and then all of a sudden it just seemed like the thing to do. You were at work. I don't mind rearranging furniture. It's fun to have a change every once in a while. Now the baby stuff has a place of its own and there's still space for Mom to visit after the baby is born."

"The baby's going to sleep in your mom's room?"

Hmm, I didn't want that. From what I heard, new parents got very little sleep. So we went shopping again, this time for a little bed to go in our bedroom. We chose a little wooden cradle that rocked and placed it in our bedroom beside the bed.

"Babies are really this small?" Rusty asked.

"I hope so, considering where they come from."

Rusty could be so cute for a big, tough detective. One evening we were watching the news for a work related story and he put his ear to my belly.

"What are you doing?" I asked

"Trying to hear the baby's heartbeat."

"I think you need a stethoscope for that," I told him.

"I can hear yours."

"Even over the TV?"

"Maybe I can just feel it."

"Can you feel the baby?"

"No, can you?"

"I don't know. Sometimes it feels like there's butterflies in my stomach."

"When you can feel it will you tell me? I want to feel it, too."

He worried about everything. Was I eating enough? Did it hurt to make love? Could he bring home anything from town? And the inevitable question of how I was feeling that day. He watched me at dinner. He eased up in bed. He frequently brought things from town but not because of sudden cravings for pickles and ice cream. And I was almost always feeling fine, especially if I could get him to forget easing up in bed.

"Don't buy a bouncy horse," my mom told me on yet another phone call, "I found one that looks just like Shasta!"

"Mom, the baby won't be old enough to ride a bouncy horse until he's two. What am I going to do with a bouncy horse for two years?"

"He! You said he! Do you know it's a boy?"

"No, of course not. I refuse every time they try to guess the sex of the baby. I don't want to know."

"Well, I do! Does your doctor know?"

"I don't know. And I won't ask him because I don't want to know."

"Can I ask him?"

"No, because then you'll tell me and I don't want to know."

"I would not."

"Yes you would even if you didn't mean to. You'd start calling the baby he or she and you'd start thinking of names and you have to admit I'd see a pattern. It's what I do best."

"I want to know if I should be looking for little girl things or little boy things!"

"I know, Mom, but you're not going to know until I know and I won't know until they tell me in the delivery room."

"Can I be in the delivery room?"

"Mom! I don't know. I don't even know if Rusty will be. It would take a major catastrophe to keep him away though. He even went to the ultrasound appointment."

"He did? How sweet. That guy…"

"Drives me nuts sometimes."

The phone rang. It was Rusty.

"Hey!" I said brightly.

"Cassidy? Can you help me?" he said seriously. "I need to know what happened here and I need to know quick."

Chapter 7

"Sure," I said. "Should I wear my uniform?"

"Yeah, it might be better."

"Okay, where are you?"

He fired off an address on Foster. It sounded like a downtown call. There wasn't much dirt downtown. I went to change clothes. Five minutes later I was back on the phone.

"Can we skip the uniform?" I asked.

"Yeah, why?"

"Do they make maternity uniforms?"

I could feel the silent chuckle even if I couldn't hear it.

"You're kidding. Already?"

"Yeah, I couldn't button my pants. The shirt's always been big."

"Just get down here."

There was a whole team of cops at the corner of Foster and Evergreen. Why did they have a street named Evergreen in a city that was ever brown? Wishful thinking?

I found Rusty standing with a group of officers next to a squad car. An area barely twenty feet square had been taped off.

"Don't let the tracks get to you," Rusty admonished. "It's a small area. The action was short. We have a teenager who was approached and surrounded by four other kids. There were no weapons involved. Tell me what you see."

I walked the perimeter of the area, then I backed off and found the place where the four had entered the vacant lot. The police may not have thought it was important to tape that information off but it was critical in my thinking.

The boys arrived in a close-knit group.

"Cassidy, what are you doing?"

"Establishing dominance. It's easier to read over here where the group is at ease. Everybody is in their rightful place in the pecking order here. This kid is in charge," I said pointing to one set of tracks. They were forceful tracks. Sure tracks. The person who made those tracks had a purpose in mind. "This kid is his right hand man." I said pointing to another. Both sets were sure of themselves but the right hand man leaned toward his superior, talking as they walked. "This kid isn't sure about things. And he is talkative. He's asking questions as they go." His tracks wandered closer to the older boy and then faltered a little, backed off, caught up. "And this kid just seems to be along for the ride." He was strictly a follower.

"How can you tell?" he asked.

"Mostly by their attitude. The alpha kid is sure of himself. There's no faltering. He knows what's going on and he's on top of it. If I follow it through alpha kid will approach the lone kid, the others will spread out. Most of the talk will be alpha kid and lone kid. Right hand man will need to prove himself, so most of the physical movement will be from right hand man. Some from alpha kid. I'm guessing the other two had very little to do with it. Next time you tape an area off, tape off the whole lot. I'm not convinced it was just these four either."

"But their tracks…"

"We'll see."

The four advanced on the lone boy. Alpha kid strode straight to the boy who appeared to simply be walking down the street. He stopped when alpha kid approached. Heavy traffic blocked one side so the other boys formed a semicircle. First, right hand man peeled off from the group. The other two seemed to know their positions. They jogged into place, blocking any forward movement. Lone boy stopped. He faced alpha kid. I explained all this to Rusty as I went. He patiently let me follow the altercation from start to finish even though there appeared to be a very short segment of time that he was interested in. Alpha kid seemed to be speaking forcefully to lone kid. His weight was on the front of his feet and he stepped forward to make points. Right hand man stepped forward in a threatening stance. The two underlings spread out to cover more area. They shifted from one foot the other. Their weight was on the front of their feet too but they seemed less certain. It seemed more as if they were debating staying involved or abandoning the pursuit. They hung tight knowing bailing out meant a new kind of trouble. Lone boy turned, looking for a way out. He only had the street or the gang to choose between. Alpha kid advanced a step, his weight went to the outside of his left foot and his right foot came up. Lone boy braced. His footprints were solid even as they slid a couple inches due to a hard kick. Then the weight shifted to his toes as he doubled over. Right hand man stepped in and downed the boy with an uppercut. Lone boy fell back. His hand prints in the dirt were small, and he was mad. He grabbed two fistfuls of dirt before making his way to his feet.

"Do you see any sign of injury?" Rusty asked.

"It's hard to tell until he moves. Anybody would get up uncertainly after being knocked around."

I looked more carefully. Was that blood in the sand?

"Okay, maybe, slightly. Do you have those evidence markers you usually carry?"

He handed me one and I placed it on the dirt with the little indicator line pointing to a small dark spot in the dirt.

"Have someone test that," I said.

Lone boy took a step back considering whether to take his chances in the busy street or face his attackers. He stepped toward the street, but right hand man closed in and held him as alpha kid went in for the kill. They gave him a few more punches before right hand man stripped him of his backpack and the group ran away. The two underlings had watched. Their footprints were animated but they stayed back except for closing in just a bit when alpha kid and right hand man advanced. I followed the group. This was the part I was interested in. The two younger kids ran ahead and joined a fifth person, an older, bigger kid who had been standing to the side during the whole altercation. Their meeting was brief. When the group walked up he spoke to them briefly and the two younger kids went on. Then the fifth kid waited and spoke to alpha and right hand man. They argued briefly and then walked off down the street together. I went back to see what lone boy did after the group left. He had fallen back and sat in the dirt. He got up quickly, scattering dirt, and ran down the street. He favored his left leg. I followed him and found some faint blood spots but once he hit sidewalk again all I could go by were the bloodstains. Rusty told me I could stop.

I looked at him hopefully. Then I glanced around. There was always a group or two of gawkers with any police operation.

"Thanks, babe, I hope I didn't mess up your day too much."

"Oh yeah, and there's so much to mess up, too. I have a feeling about this. I think I'll hang around a bit and watch the crowd. I doubt all these people are just curious. I'll let you know when I'm ready to take off."

I went back to the Jeep and sat for a few minutes, letting the gawkers forget me. I put on a light jacket to cover the shirt they had seen me in before and brushed my hair down a little straighter. I observed the three groups. The one by the stoplight seemed to be normal city folk just watching. One group on the backside of the lot acted a little differently. They seemed to know more. I walked around the back of the lot and came in from a different angle so they wouldn't associate me with the police. I wandered over to the group standing there.

"Hey, what's going on?" I asked a Hispanic teenager.

"Huh! D Dawg an' his stick man pulled a switch up on the buster."

"Oh yeah?"

"'Bout time. He 'as long due. Shoulda been more jacked up 'an he was."

I didn't understand a word of what he said. He figured that out and switched to more normal English.

"Hey, what are you doing for vacation? You got plans? You gonna be 'round?"

"No, I'll be out of town," I said.

"Oh yeah? Where to?"

I didn't really have a vacation coming up but I thought he assumed I went to his school.

"My family is going to visit relatives up north."

"Cool! You gonna blow off the reading assignment? Can't get me to read no novel when I could be out with D Dawg."

Now I was a little worried about how to make my break. I'd verified what I thought. Hanging around too long would give me away. I gawked with the rest of the group and gradually made my way around the back of the group and wandered away. Rusty noticed me and tried not to register the alarm he felt. As I walked the long way back to my Jeep I called him.

"See the guy in the black t-shirt with the skull on it? He knows more. I can't understand his street talk."

"What'd he say?"

"He said, 'D Dawg and his stick man pulled a switch up on the buster.' It sounds like he's describing the altercation but I couldn't keep up so I snuck out. Oh and he said it was about time, that he was long due. You might want to try talking to him. I assume you know more street talk than I do."

"Cassidy, *never* do that again. You don't know how much you were risking entering that group. If there weren't cops everywhere you could have been in real trouble."

"I just had a feeling they knew more. All I wanted to do was confirm that. He acted like I was some ignorant, nerdy kid from school."

He spoke to some officers nearby and I could see them walking away.

"Get out of here and call me from some other place," Rusty said. "Don't talk to any officers. Just get in your Jeep and leave."

"Rusty, you're being silly."

"I wish I were. I'll talk to you soon. If you see a tail, call me back."

"They're just high school kids."

"They're just the most notorious high school kids in the valley. Don't do anything to make them associate you with the police or it'll be San Diego all over again."

Gulp. I'd helped a detective named Slick Whitman with a drug problem in a small private school and been found out. I'd been put before a firing squad. I let them fire on me because I was wearing a bulletproof vest but I could just as easily have taken a bullet to the head. Only the fact that they all aimed for the heart and the police were breathing down their necks saved my life that time.

If I'd known the afternoon was going to end this way I wouldn't have parked so close to the police activity. Squad cars circled the block discouraging further activity around the scene. I think Rusty sent them to distract the gang members and give me a clean break so I walked to the Jeep, got in, and drove away watching my tail, not watching the group on the corner, not driving to the station, just in case...I still thought he was over reacting but it seemed logical that if I wasn't supposed to associate myself with the police it would be a bad idea to go to the station and it also seemed logical to not give out any information about myself so I didn't go home. I went to a clothing store. A store that sold junior sized clothes and I browsed until Rusty called me. Let them think I was a nerdy high school kid. When I looked at the clothes though I wondered about the kids these days.

"Cass, you okay?"

"Yeah, I'm fine."

"Where are you?"

"I'm shopping. I went someplace logical for a high school kid to go. And I'm looking at clothes. I think. I hope not. But I think so. How can they wear this stuff?"

"You were raised in a cave," Rusty reminded me.

"I know, but still..."

"You were talking to Manny Mo. It's his street name for Manuel Morales. Usually street names are a little more original than that but maybe his friends called him that and it stuck. Do you know how much tension you caused talking to those guys? White girl, just wandering onto their turf. You could have caused all hell to break loose. You were just lucky they took you for an ignorant, blond, California girl."

"They're just kids."

"They're just kids with a violent background, a knack for trouble and territorial as all get out. You make them question their boundaries and they'll push them. When these kids push they aren't gentle. They come armed and they come with a bad attitude."

"Well, other than my daily disaster was the information helpful?"

"Yeah, thanks. I learned more from Manny Mo but it didn't come easy. We know who D Dawg is. His stick man is Dred. We know who he is, too. I haven't identified the other two kids."

"What's a stick man?"

"Just what you said he was when you were tracking. Everything was just as you said it was. D Dawg got tired of the buster messing up and pulled a switch up. He basically turned his back on him, did an about face and the altercation was the way he went about telling the buster about it. A buster is basically an embarrassment to the gang. He's not cool, he's easily manipulated, naïve...so D Dawg pulled an about face. Only problem was he left too many witnesses and too many clues. Manny Mo wouldn't have talked except you fingered him. Hopefully he won't make the connection."

"I'm glad you know these things. And I'm glad I don't. I forget that kind of people live around here. I guess that's what I get for spending so much time away from town."

"Do us both a favor and lay low for a few days. Let this blow over. If we catch D Dawg and Dred I'll let you know if there is any talk going on that you should be aware of."

I was still walking around the store wondering how they got so little fabric to stay on the hangers.

"Do I need a red, sequined halter top and a matching mini skirt? They have red sequined high heeled shoes, too."

"Sounds dangerous right about now. Besides you never wear heels. Maybe you should be looking at another kind of clothing store."

Maternity clothes. Even the words sounded, uh, maternal. It sounded so unlike me. I could survive on my own in the woods for weeks by whittling snares and digging up edible roots. I could shoot as well as anybody on the force. I could down a buck with a single shot. I could saddle break a horse. But I wasn't motherly.

Chapter 8

"I'm not going to question if you're up to a search," Lou told me. "But I have to trust you to know your bounds."

"What's up?"

"What do you think of a grasslands search?"

"No problem. How old is the trail?"

"A day."

"Details?"

"Local news columnist wanted to do a piece about the windmills so he went up to photograph them. There are miles of windmills, but it's hard to get lost. You can see all around from up on those hills. So we don't know what happened. He didn't show for work the next day. We doubt he had much water since he expected to be near his car all day."

"So they think he's been injured?"

"Can't think of any way to get hurt up there."

"Did they try an air search yet?"

"No, I know the guy's boss so he called me. Want me to send out a plane first?"

"No, if he was lying down in that tall grass he wouldn't be seen from the air. We're lucky it's fall. The grass probably bent and broke as he walked instead of springing back up."

"This should be a quick search. He wouldn't have gone far from his car. I bet he's within sight of it."

"So," I asked. "Are you ready?"

"Ready."

Since I expected to be home by nightfall I left Rusty a note on the fridge: "Gone tracking with Lou south of Tehachapi ETA evening."

I grabbed my daypack because it had tracking tools, snacks and water in it. I met Landon at the compound and we took an SUV out for a look-see.

Everett Miles was a small man, I decided as I examined the tracks near his car. He was wiry and quick and full of energy. He could have called on a real photographer to come out and do this shoot but he went himself, because he needed to get away from his desk. I didn't blame him one bit.

It was windy and cold in the yellowed hills. The windmills stood like sentinels on the hilltops. I'd never seen them still. Today they were going at a good clip. I looked down into the town below. All seemed peaceful. Only the wind and the windmills seemed agitated today.

Miles had taken his camera gear from the back seat of his Ford Taurus and located a good spot to take pictures. It wasn't hard to do. There were windmills everywhere. He climbed a hill to put the car out of view of his camera.

Landon followed as I tracked Miles from one vantage point to another. Several things made this an easy track. The grasses were bent and broken. Miles was always walking on hillsides so his feet bit deep into the soil. He found the camera gear to be burdensome. He paused frequently to shift his load. He carried a camera bag over one shoulder, a camera hung from his neck, and a tripod rested over the other shoulder. Sometimes I could pick out the three legs of the tripod when he stopped to shoot pictures. Other times he just laid the tripod down and shot pictures without it.

I followed the grasses, pausing to make sure I was really on track by parting the grass and finding the tracks beneath. His trail bent the grasses but so did the cattle from surrounding ranches. I had to check periodically. He had taken many pictures just of the windmills, but then his trail took a turn. He'd stopped and crouched in the grass. I found a person sized flat spot in the grass. He spent a moment watching something.

"He's taken a different tack," I told Landon. "Something caught his eye."

"What is it?"

"I don't know yet."

I was curious. There was nothing out here, just grass and windmills and wind. As I looked closer off in the distance there were cattle grazing but that wasn't enough of a draw to attract a newspaper columnist. Miles remained crouched. His equipment made things increasingly cumbersome. He advanced, but fighting the camera bag and tripod were too much. We found them in the grass, the camera bag open. Miles had stripped down his gear to a single camera with a telephoto lens. We figured this out by looking at the contents of the bag. All the normal lenses for landscapes were hastily placed in cases and placed haphazardly in the bag. He'd unclipped the strap and laid it on top. He left the tripod. Whatever he'd seen, he needed stealth for these shots. I tracked him as he crept forward in a crouched position and descended the hill. When he stopped to take pictures he made sure his body formed a good solid base for the big lens. Sometimes he would sit and use his knees for stability. Once he lay in the grass and shot through it. I was getting curious. What was he trying to capture? I took my bearings based on Everett's body position and went to find out.

"Stay here," I told Landon. "I want to know what he's following."

"Why stay here?"

"It'll be quicker. If you come with me we'll have to track our way back. If you stay here I can see you when I find out what I want to know."

"What if I want to see it too?"

"It's probably just a bunch of tracks now. You wouldn't recognize them if you were right on top of them."

He conceded so I took off in the direction the camera had been pointing. There were no tracks to follow so I jogged out about a hundred yards and began searching around on the ground for tracks. I thought it had to be an animal and it was an animal on the move or Miles wouldn't have been following, staying out of sight as much as he could. I knew he was crouching as he walked because his weight was shifted onto the front of his foot. There was very little heel to his tracks. The most likely animals out there were cows, horses, mule deer, or maybe an elk. I highly doubted it was elk. There were rumors of antelope, but sightings usually proved to be light colored cows that happened to be standing at an angle to make them look skinny. How anybody could mistake a cow for an antelope I couldn't imagine but the paper reported an occasional sighting that proved to be false. Nevertheless, when I got out away from where Miles had been shooting pictures I saw hoof prints. They weren't cows or horses or mule deer or elk. They were smaller and lighter of foot and I'd never seen tracks like these before. Maybe there *were* antelope in these hills. I spent a moment studying the tracks. I didn't have much time. I had a missing person to find, but a new animal to add to the others cataloged in my brain was too tempting. I took some quick notes about the spacing, size, and shape. I quickly sketched a track in my little notebook and jogged back to Landon.

"Well? What was it?" he asked.

"I'm not sure. It's nothing I've ever tracked before. I'm guessing antelope. It's the only thing I can think of that would catch his attention this strongly. Just think, the chance to verify antelope after all the false sightings that usually appear in the paper. And he'd have pictures to prove it."

"But you've never seen antelope tracks before?"

"No."

"So it could be anything. This is California."

"Yeah, for all I know it was a gnu."

"A gnu?"

"Yeah, a gnu animal I've never tracked before. I always like tracking gnu animals."

"Cassidy… let's find Everett."

We followed the tracks down into the valley and I wondered the whole time how Everett planned to find his gear again. It was invisible under the grass. If I'd been thinking I'd have stood up the tripod so it could be spotted from a distance. He continued following the antelope until he came to an old fashioned windmill made to pump water. He approached the tank, and climbed up to the spout. The tank was dry, empty except for one battered photographer. The discovery startled me. I hadn't expected the search to end so abruptly.

"Everett Miles?" I asked.

No answer.

"Landon, I think this is where you come in," I said.

Landon looked over the top of the tank.

"What's he doing in there?"

"Maybe I can figure out by the tracks how he got in there."

"It doesn't matter how he got in there. It's up to us to get him out."

"It might matter."

"Why?"

I was looking around on the ground and it wasn't making sense. After he'd found the tank dry he'd investigated the windmill. Maybe he'd photographed it. Then he... he climbed it.

"Why would he climb the windmill?" I asked.

"Because it's there?" Landon answered.

"Maybe he could see the antelope from up there. At any rate, we need to consider the fact that he could have fallen off the windmill into the tank."

Landon vaulted the tank wall and dropped to the bottom. He radioed his findings to Strict, who sent a lift out. We'd have a wait ahead of us. The two of us were not carrying Miles out.

"Cassidy? Can you climb down here okay?"

I took off my pack and climbed over the lip dropping in quietly next to Landon. I watched and followed instructions as he deftly examined the unconscious man. He asked me to hold things in position as he splinted and bandaged. Miles had a nasty swollen gash on the side of his head that seemed to verify a fall from the windmill onto the wall of the tank.

"I wonder how high he fell from," I said.

"It wouldn't take much of a fall onto the metal rim to knock a guy out. I've seen people out cold just from a fall from a standing position."

"Mind if I go look?"

"No, go ahead," he said.

I climbed out of the tank and made my way up the ladder. I was looking for loose boards or rungs as I climbed. I watched for antelope off in the distance just in case they were still around. I was beginning to think this was another false sighting but I couldn't bring myself to believe the hoof prints were anything besides antelope. I'd have to look up the track in my book at home. I was climbing and looking and thinking and then all of a sudden I felt a *whack* on the side of my head and the whack sent me sprawling. I grabbed for the windmill and came to a halt dangling over the tank, hanging by one hand. After the stinging on my head calmed down, I found my footing again.

"He fell from right about here," I said as Landon stared open eyed up at me.

"Are you okay?" he asked.

"Yeah, when climbing a windmill, remember the blades are closer than they appear. Do you have an extra ice pack?"

I climbed down again and Landon handed me an ice pack. I put the cold pack on my wrist and he took it away and put it on my head.

"Don't do stupid things on my watch," he said. "Do you know how touchy Rusty is right now?"

"Yeah, don't worry," I answered. "I'll take care of Rusty. My head is just scratched. The hit startled me but my hand took the brunt of the fall."

"Keep the ice on it."

"That scared me. I was afraid I was going to fall on Everett."

"It scared me, too. I thought you were going to fall. I wasn't even thinking about Everett."

"Why don't I keep my feet on the ground and go back for Everett's camera gear? I'm sure he didn't mean to leave it a half-mile out in the middle of nowhere, and I doubt he can find it on his own. I can track myself back to it."

"Stay here. I don't want you to be half a mile from here and…."

"I'm fine, Landon."

"Can you carry all that stuff?"

"I'm not an invalid. It's just camera gear. I'll see the helicopter coming and I'll be here when it lands."

I followed my trail back to the camera bag and tripod and after a short time I figured out why he had left it. It weighed a ton and it was cumbersome. Things jostled with every move. I finally hooked the bag on the tripod and carried it over my shoulder like a little kid running away from home. I jogged for the windmill, glad to have a ready landmark.

Landon was watching over Everett, who was sitting there groggily.

"Everett, this is my partner, Cassidy Michaels."

"I brought your gear," I told him as I set it down.

Everett looked at me like he couldn't make sense of me. I was used to it. Nobody expected a woman, especially one that looked fifteen.

"How did you find me?" he asked.

"We tracked you from your car," I said.

"How did you find my cameras?"

"We were tracking you so we ran across the spot where you left them."

"So tell me how this search and rescue stuff works."

"Well, that depends on the search," I began. "You just happened to be a classic tracking case so our commander sent out a tracker."

"And who is your commander?"

"Lou Strickland," I said.

"And what exactly does this Mr. Strickland do?"

And so it went, an interview about the whole search and rescue organization. I'd forgotten how curious reporters are about everything. Usually I spent a good deal of effort avoiding them but Everett Miles was a charming man, just out for the day to write a story about windmills. I didn't think about him doing a whole page-long article about search and rescue. After talking to me for a half hour while we waited for the helicopter and then another half hour on the way to the hospital he called Lou and got a rundown of the inner workings and before I knew it there was this huge article explaining how he went out to photograph windmills and finally sighted the elusive Joshua Hills antelope. He had some amazing photos of them in the article. Then it went on to describe his ordeal. There were pictures of Landon and I, then pictures of Lou and some of the gear at the compound. It explained how the rescue organization was a nonprofit organization that relied heavily on donations. Lou was pleased with the article. Any support we could garner was welcome. Lou had the support of Everett's boss for some time, but now the whole newspaper office seemed to rally to our cause.

When I went to Farley's riding school to teach Bailee the next Tuesday, Bailee brought me a copy of the article and, just as she had when I tracked down a movie star several months prior, she asked me to autograph the article for her.

Bailee was becoming advanced enough at horseback riding now that we pretty much just did what she was interested in and that day she felt like taking Mack over the jumps. We saddled Mack for English riding and arranged the jumps. We only did small jumps at the school but she always got a thrill out of leaving the ground, if only for a second.

"Chas, are you going to teach your baby how to ride?" Bailee asked. She has called me Chas ever since I began teaching her. She had a severe speech impediment when I started teaching at the school but she'd overcome most of it due to firm determination and hard work.

"When she's old enough," I answered. "My dad will always have horses for her to ride."

Bailee was determined I was going to have a girl and that she'd be big enough to baby-sit when the time came. Considering Bailee was only ten, I wasn't counting on that. When I'd told her I was expecting she was disappointed because she remembered her mom having to stay home for long periods of time after her brother was born. She thought our riding days were coming to an end. Then the more she thought about it the more she wanted to play big sister to the baby and she relaxed a bit. I wasn't sure how my teaching at Farley's school would work with a baby to care for. In fact, I wasn't sure how I would do anything with a baby to care for. Rusty assured me it would all work out, but I couldn't see how.

"What does the baby want for Christmas?" my mother asked.

"Mom, the baby won't be born until six months *after* Christmas. He doesn't need anything."

"Of course he does!"

Sigh.

At Christmas at the ranch there were gifts labeled to Rusty and Cassidy and "baby within."

"Did I get presents before I was born?" Patrick asked.

"Of course you did!" my mom answered, not remembering.

"How could that happen?" Pat asked, "Mom didn't even know she was pregnant the Christmas before I was born."

It was true. Patrick was born in the fall. Mom blushed.

"Santa Claus knew you were coming," she said.

When we drove home from the ranch the Explorer was packed with baby gear. What was I going to do with all this stuff?

Chapter 9

"Manny Mo is in the hospital," Rusty announced.

"What happened?" I asked as I stirred some vegetables on the stove.

"Word got around. Someone matched your picture in the article Everett Miles wrote to the girl at the investigation. They figured out Manny Mo had accidentally snitched and they taught him a little lesson in caution."

"Gang members read the newspaper?" I asked.

He rolled his eyes.

"They aren't stupid. Most gang members are very intelligent. Their talents are just misdirected."

Okay, so Manny Mo snitched. I wondered what that meant to me but decided I was laying low up here in the foothills anyway. No worries.

"Will he be okay?"

"Yeah, chalk another one up to D Dawg. His rap sheet is getting longer every day."

I knew the pregnancy was progressing because I added a new question to my list. Now, without provocation, people, even total strangers, would ask, "When is your due date?"

I had fun with that one. "Anywhere from June twentieth to the twenty ninth," I told them.

One woman looked at me funny and said, "Well... don't you know when you, um, DID IT?"

And I said, "Yeah, that's how we narrowed it down to nine days. It had to be one of the nine..."

I looked through all the stuff my mom bought. A changing table. A dozen little yellow and green outfits. Was she trying to send me a hint with that? A mobile. It took me a while to figure out the mobile. I knew what one was. I'd had to make them in school. I just didn't know what a baby would do with one. All the pictures faced in a downward position. It was cute.

"Look," I said as I twirled the mobile around. "What's a baby going to do with this?"

Rusty finished putting it together and clamped it to the crib rail.

Oh, so that's how it goes.

He wound it up and it played a lullaby and the animals turned.

Okay, I got it now, but I still didn't see the use in it. It seemed frivolous.

"All these clothes are size six months," I told him. That was another thing that puzzled me. "Babies aren't born size six months or they wouldn't have size newborn or size one to three months."

"Babe, I don't know, I just assume your mom does. Maybe babies outgrow the little sizes. Besides, how big is newborn? There's a big difference between a five pound baby and a ten pound baby. Newborn wouldn't fit both of them. We'll just have to see what fits and use that."

"Well, I've been buying size newborn because it made sense."

Rusty put a baby sock on his thumb. It fit just right.

"Maybe your mom knew you'd do that and bought things for when the baby suddenly outgrew the ones you bought."

"You know, I can deliver a foal. I can train it until it wins races. That's a lot easier than this is."

He wrapped me in a hug and my little belly bumped up against him first. I felt a little flip flop in my stomach.

"Did you feel that?" I asked.

"No, I didn't know I was supposed to be feeling something."

"Here, come to the kitchen. I figured out how to make the baby move."

He laughed, "How did you do that?"

"Whenever I drink ice water he moves!"

I filled a glass with ice and added water. I swirled it around a little, waiting for the ice to melt a bit and chill the water. I took a drink and waited. Nothing. I took another and felt a fluttering. I took Rusty's hand and laid it against the side of my belly just above my right hip. I took another drink.

"There! Did you feel that?"

"No."

"What do you mean? I can feel it plain as day."

"From the inside."

"Did you feel *that*?"

"No"

Rats. I filled up the glass again we went to the old brown couch and I drank another tumbler full of ice water. I put Rusty's hand here and there, wherever I could feel movement, but Rusty just couldn't feel the baby kick yet. Then I spent half the night in the bathroom.

"At least he's an active baby. I know he's healthy because he does his exercises."

"You said *he*. Do you think it's a boy?"

"I switch back and forth. I don't know what it is."

"I think it's a little Cassidy. I can't see her and I can't feel her, even when I know she's there."

"Oh, I hope not. I think if we had another Cassidy all the guys would suddenly find a way to transfer to another city. Schroeder would be forced to hire a whole bunch of rookies and the crime rate would escalate. We wouldn't want to be responsible for the crime rate in the city."

"You're exaggerating."

"Oh yeah? When Patrick was here the guys were relieved to hear he didn't live around here. Big John said he didn't know what the force would do with another little Cassidy in the area. He said it was spooky how much Patrick was like me."

"You just wait, you put that little baby in Big John's arms and she'll have him wrapped around her finger in minutes."

As winter settled in the guys got inundated in ski rescues. They didn't need a tracker in the snow so I settled in for a couple of peaceful months at home. I finished setting up the nursery, still unsure if the room was a nursery or a guest room. When pregnancy really set in it hit with a vengeance. I thought I had breezed through the first trimester with only a few weeks of morning sickness. Now I got hungry an hour after eating. I needed a nap in the afternoon. I couldn't stand for long periods of time. Going to the grocery store was risky. I'd do my shopping and get in line only to feel faint. If I moved around I was fine so I'd get out of line and pretend to shop some more only to get back in line and have trouble again. Finally I asked Rusty to go with me.

"And why exactly am I following you around the store?" he asked.

"I need help checking out," I answered.

"And why do you need help checking out?"

"Because, I don't know why, I just can't stand still. It's like all my blood is no longer in my head and I have to walk around to get it going again. As long as I'm doing something I'm fine, but if you could just check out for me it would help a lot. One time I came here and I thought I'd never get home. The lines were just too long and I had to bail out before I fainted and so I'd walk until my head cleared and get in another long line. You know I wouldn't make you do this if I didn't need help. Usually you get mad at me for *not* asking."

When we stood in line he watched me. I stood with him as long as I could.

"I need to walk," I told him.

"So I see," he replied. "Are you sure you'll be okay?"

"Yeah, as long as I keep moving I'm fine. I'll be back in a few minutes."

I walked a circuit of the store and came back with a little more color. I stood again.

"Why don't you wait for me in the truck? I'll be out in a few minutes."

"Do I look that bad?"

"Guys know not to answer that question."

That meant yes.

"Okay, I'll go sit."

I found the Explorer and got in. I was glad it was winter and not summer or the truck would have been sweltering. I waited and waited, watching the front of the store. A group of kids came out laughing and punching at each other in mock hostility. Then one of them saw me and the group headed toward the truck. I locked the doors.

"Well, look who it is," Manny Mo sneered. "How was the trip up north?" He tried the door, knowing it was locked. "You're lucky I wasn't lookin' for you. When I hunt for a person it's for a reason," he said as he flicked a knife out and tapped the glass with the point of the blade. "D Dawg's in deep shit. He don't like deep shit. You better watch yourself. He be mean when he's cornered. Tell your cop friends they don't want to corner D Dawg. *Nobody* wants to see D Dawg when he's cornered." He held up his hand, which had stitches all the way across the palm. Manny Mo looked to the store and signaled his group to move out. They turned as one and walked across the parking lot.

When Rusty appeared with the groceries I got out to help him put them away.

"Manny Mo is out of the hospital," I announced. "He seemed to be doing fine. He says you don't want to corner D Dawg."

"I kind of figured that. I don't have much choice. Did they give you trouble?"

"No, but they would have liked to."

"Why didn't you call me when they approached?"

"I didn't see a need to. You were busy."

"Cass, these kids walk around armed. If they have something against you they won't hesitate to tell you about it, forcefully."

"They told me about it. There were enough people around that they weren't going to try anything."

"Don't go shopping by yourself. You should have asked for help a long time ago. How long have you been feeling like this?"

"About a month. It's normal, if irritating. I didn't want to keel over in line and find myself staring up at one of Landon's coworkers. I'd never hear the end of it."

As we were unloading groceries the phone rang and Rusty picked it up. I wanted to get the groceries in so the things needing refrigerating could be put away. Rusty glared at me as he walked out to the Explorer still talking on the phone.

"No," he said. There was a pause and then he added, "I still say no."

He looked at me. My color had come back but I guess I'd given him a little bit of a scare at the store. I thought it must have been Strict. Rusty always said no at first.

"If my wife wanted a job, she'd have a job."

A job?

"I don't care how much it pays. If it's that much it's not worth the price. Every job with a price tag that steep has a risk factor involved... You've got my answer. Good bye."

"Who was that?" I asked.

"A man named Arnold Rodeo."

"Who is Arnold Rodeo?"

"He thought you'd know."

"So what did he want?"

"He wanted to offer you a job. Three weeks, fifty grand."

"What! That doesn't make sense. What could I do that is worth fifty grand to someone?"

"Track."

"You're kidding."

"You aren't going to do it."

"Rusty fifty thousand dollars is a lot of money! He wants me to track for three weeks? Why not? I've got three weeks. Strict isn't going to send me out on a lost skier search. That'll pay for a semester of college."

"College? I didn't know you wanted to go back to school."

"I don't. But somebody else might want to someday. Fifty grand will grow in eighteen years."

"No. If he calls back, just say no. A paycheck like that means risk. I'll not have you walking into some risky situation..."

"Did you ask what the situation was?"

"No," he admitted.

"What if it isn't risky?"

"How could it not? Why would anybody shell out that much money for no reason?"

"Do you have any missing people? Kids of rich people?"

"No."

We both puzzled over it. A three week tracking assignment? I couldn't think of any search that would take three weeks and yield anything for the efforts. Usually one week was pushing it. Two was nearly hopeless.

The next morning after Rusty went to work the phone rang again. I picked it up out of curiosity.

"I'd like to speak to Cassidy Michaels," the man said.

"Speaking," I answered.

"Miss?"

"I am Cassidy Michaels."

"I'm sorry, when Sherri said to call you she said you were a tracker. I wasn't sure what to expect. Until I talked to your husband yesterday I thought you'd be a man."

Sherri?

"Let me introduce myself. I'm Arnold Rodeo. That's pronounced Road`ao, like in Rodeo Drive, Beverly Hills? I'm employed as the agent of Sherri Champlain."

Ah, good old Arnie! The makeup case delivering agent. The greasy head in the helicopter. It was making more sense now! Several months before I had tracked down a missing movie star and somehow she had remembered me. That was amazing in itself, that some famous person knew who I was. What in the world did Sherri Champlain need with a tracker?

"Yes, Mr. Rodeo, what can I do for you?"

"Sherri asked me to call you. She's doing a shoot in your area. An action flick. Problem is we have a mysterious person playing tricks on my star. Sherri's tired of it. She doesn't want to go into her trailer anymore because she never knows what to expect. The trailers are all lined up on a big lot. Tracks are everywhere. Sherri is hoping you will accept her offer of a job to either track down and catch the prankster or guard her trailer to prevent further practical jokes."

"What kind of a person are we dealing with here?"

"We aren't sure. So far the pranks have had a chance to cause harm but not great bodily injury. We don't believe it is a danger. We simply want it stopped."

"Fifty grand is a lot of money to spend for a little security."

"Sherri seems to think that you understand her a little more than some rent a cop from a security company."

Ha, that was a good one. I thought Sherri was a spoiled rotten, overly vain California bimbo.

"So you need a tracker to figure out who is playing the practical jokes and a body guard to prevent them from happening?"

"Precisely."

"And I'm to be armed and in uniform?"

"It would further your cause if people could see that Sherri has someone around her who is obviously there for her protection."

"Um, that's a little hard to do right now. Have you seen me? I do not look much like a bodyguard. I look like a teenager and I'm four months pregnant. The armed part I don't have a problem with, although I won't shoot someone unless I am forced to. It takes a lot to force me to shoot."

"Nevertheless, you are who Sherri trusts and you are who she wants to hire."

"Sherri's nuts."

"Can you follow the tracks and find the perpetrator?"

"I'd have to see that for myself."

"Then allow me to invite you to the set."

Oh, shoot. I'd gotten myself into a spot. I threw in my requirements.

"I have a previous commitment Tuesday and Thursday mornings."

"I'm sure we can work around that."

Double shoot.

"Mr. Rodeo, I don't think this situation merits a body guard or tracker."

"Fifty-five grand."

Triple shoot. It looked like Sherri was just as spoiled as I thought. Still, fifty-five thousand was a lot of money.

"What time do things get underway on the set?"

"They like to make good use of the daylight hours. Can you be there at seven?"

Sigh, "No problem, but no promises. I need directions."

He rattled off directions but then said, "Many of the crew are staying at Joshua Hills Station. You can pick up a map from the front desk."

"Okay."

That meant a trip into town but I thought I needed to come up with an outfit that approximated a security uniform. And I needed to come up with a holster that didn't buckle around the waist. I went to a uniform store where all the officers bought their uniforms. They called it their cop shop but the place had uniforms for other professions as well.

"I need a uniform to go with my new figure," I told Lawanda Phillips. Lawanda knew me and Rusty. I just hoped she didn't see Rusty before I talked to him. Rusty didn't have any reason to come here so I thought I was safe. "Not a police uniform. It just has to look official but I'm not impersonating anything."

"What company are you working for?"

"Michaels Security Service."

"Huh, whatchu up to Cassidy?"

"I'm supposed to be a body guard."

"No way, I'm not getting involved in this. This has the makings of a Cassidy disaster."

"I'll talk to Rusty before I get involved. I can't go looking like a teenage girl, especially not a pregnant teenage girl. I need help."

"You goin' to tuck in the shirt?"

"I doubt it."

"Okay, lookee this."

She held up a slightly baggy straight hemmed navy blue blouse and matching Dickies.

"I can get you a name patch in three weeks."

"The job is only three weeks long."

"Yeah? Who are you body guarding?"

"Can you keep a secret?"

"No."

"Then I'm not telling you. I don't even know if I am yet."

"Will you get me an autograph?"

"No promises."

"All right! I know you, you'll do it! Cause you're nice. These guys are all business but I know, if you see a chance you'll try."

"Thanks Lawanda."

Chapter 10

My alarm went off early and Rusty grumbled and tried to turn his off.

"It's just me," I said. "Go back to sleep."

"What are you getting up so early for?"

"I've got an appointment."

"How can you have an appointment this early?"

"It's not until seven. I need to shower and get ready."

He scratched his head and let me be but I could tell he wasn't sleeping any time soon. I showered and changed into my "uniform." I strapped on my 9mm with a shoulder holster. Rusty turned over and his eyes narrowed.

"No," he said.

"It's just Sherri Champlain. She remembered me from when Landon and I rescued her. She just needs babysitting for three weeks."

"No."

"I couldn't see any reason why not to. She's tired of some prankster and wants the pranks to end so she hired me to babysit her. It's all harmless."

"A person doesn't shell out fifty grand for a babysitter."

"They might if they are used to buying five hundred dollar shoes. Rusty it's only three weeks. If I can figure out who is pulling the pranks on Sherri it might be just one day. It's on location, out in the desert, maybe I can track them and figure out who it is real quick and then I can be done with it."

"You didn't commit to this already, did you?"

"Arnie invited me out to the set to see what the job entailed."

"Arnie?"

"That's what Sherri called him."

"Cassidy, just say no."

"They upped it to fifty-five when I hesitated. Should I hesitate some more?"

"Just say no. This has the makings for a Cassidy disaster and I don't care what they give you, it's not worth it to me."

"You think everything is going to turn on me."

"That's because everything *does*."

"You don't want me to work?"

"This isn't work. This is a shady operation."

"It's not a spoiled movie star who just wants some security?"

He hemmed and hawed, "It... might be. But..."

"Trust me, Sherri is spoiled enough to demand what she wants. She doesn't want some impersonal security company. She knows I can track. She asked for me just because she knows me. She's comfortable with me. Besides I promised Lawanda I'd try and get her autograph."

"Oh, there, that settles it. You need to get Sherri's autograph for Lawanda. Cassidy, oh hell, I'm going too," he said rolling out of bed. "Not Lawanda at the cop shop."

"Yeah, she helped me come up with a security maternity uniform. Do you like it?"

He smirked at it. "You look like a hotel maid except for the gun. And what do you need a gun for if you're just baby-sitting?"

"You know just the sight of a gun will discourage people from doing suspicious things around Sherri's trailer."

"Ah, good visual deterrent. A pregnant woman with a pistol."

"Hey, just because I'm pregnant doesn't mean I can't shoot. I still shoot better than…"

"Babe, I know. I know you can shoot. You can shoot my socks off."

"I don't plan to use it."

He pulled some pants on with a frustrated huff.

"Where are you going?" Rusty asked as I drove out into the middle of nowhere. I handed him the map.

"I told you, it's out in the desert."

We pulled up to a chain link fence and a man sitting on a stool motioned for us to stop.

"We're here to see Arnold Rodeo and Sherri Champlain," I said.

He leafed through a sheaf of papers on a clipboard.

"Names?"

"Cassidy Michaels. This is Rusty. He's my bodyguard."

Rusty smirked. The guard didn't bat an eyelash. He was used to people with bodyguards passing through his gate.

"Cassidy Michaels? Mr. Rodeo can usually be found in 4C. You can park in that lot right over there," he said pointing.

"Thank you."

I pulled forward and to the right and found a parking place next to a silver BMW. Rusty and I got out and walked to the area where the trailers were lined up in rows. I kept an eye to the ground. Lots of tracks. Everywhere. Hundreds of tracks. Tracks on top of tracks. People came and went amongst these trailers all day. People with all kinds of shoes. People who were used to this lifestyle. I saw very few impractical shoes. Most wore tennis shoes, a few loafers, a pair of boots. Lots of young people. Lots of people in a hurry. We found 4C. I looked at Rusty and Rusty looked at me. We didn't know if this was an office, or somebody's home away from home. I was guessing an office. I didn't think agents followed their stars around. Arnie was just here to make sure Sherri got her bodyguard. I knocked on the door and a young person opened it.

"Uh, hello? Was the door locked? You can just, like, come in," he said.

"We're new here. The guard at the gate said we might find Arnold Rodeo here."

"Oh, yeah. Hey Arnie, you got company."

A man looked up from behind a laptop. It was a Mac. Arnie looked like a Mac guy. I'd recognize that head of hair gel anywhere. He clicked the mouse a few times, glanced at the screen, and stood. His shiny tie glistened.

"You must be Cassidy Michaels," he said. "I never forget a voice."

"This is my husband, Rusty," I said by way of introduction.

"Yes," Arnie said. "I believe we've met."

Rusty glared at him.

The trailer looked like a break room. Round folding tables were scattered about and a row of vending machines lined one wall. There was a microwave and a refrigerator. Two large trash cans stood by the door. A tower of cases of bottled water stood next to one vending machine. Arnie grabbed a bottle. He offered one to me and one to Rusty but we declined. Then he said, "Follow me," and headed out the door.

We followed him down the trailer steps and around a couple of bends. All the trailers looked alike and I didn't know how anybody could tell them apart. I tried to watch the ground but I thought I might need to know where I was going so I switched my attention to trailer numbers. Everywhere we went the dirt in between the trailers looked like a high school corridor, like five hundred kids filed out every hour. There were so many tracks I didn't know how I'd pick out the prankster without catching them at it and following them. Rusty watched me, taking mental notes. We came to a trailer where a man was taking the doorknob off the door. He unscrewed the screws holding the knob on and then jiggled. It was stuck.

"Another prank," explained Arnie. "Excuse me, could we get by?"

He knocked on the side of the trailer. Sherri came to the door in a huff.

"Look at this! I can't even leave for a minute before something happens. Oh, hi!"

"Hello Sherri, it's good to see you again. How's the leg?"

She held it out for my inspection.

"I had to go to the tanning salon for three weeks to get it to match the other one. Then I had to go to the gym. It was hell. Sweating on those machines. The broken one lost weight and I had to build back up. It was a pain. I'm never going to break a leg again!"

"Looks good to me. Sherri, this is my husband, Rusty."

"Oh! I thought you were a stunt man telling me it was time to do the car chase."

"Believe me, you don't want to be in my car chases," Rusty said. "What happened with the door?"

"That…that joker! He glued my doorknob so it wouldn't turn! The lock was filled with glue! I am so sick of this! One night he glued the whole door shut! I couldn't get out and I had an appointment at six a.m. to have my hair done. And I couldn't get my coffee! Shooting got put off two hours because of that little skunk. He loosened the bolts on my steps so they folded up when I stepped on them. He filled my shoes with honey. They were good shoes, too! Irreplaceable! They were going to be shot in a scene and we had to find new ones. Katrina had to rush to Beverly Hills and find a similar pair. You'd think finding one pair of shoes in L.A. would be easy but they had to have these certain qualities to fit into the scene. She was gone for hours and hours."

"Why me?" I asked.

"Because, you're sneaky. You're the tracker, right? With Landon? Right?"

"Yeah."

"You can find this guy. You can track him and you can arrest his sorry butt."

"I can't arrest him unless I'm here in a police capacity and if I have a senior officer. The most I can do is collect evidence against him and then turn it over to the real police."

"So? You can do that."

"I'm telling you, no," said Rusty.

"He thinks this is going to get dangerous," I explained to them. "So far you'd be stretching it to prove anything illegal was done."

"Vandalism, damage to public property. There has to be something!" Sherri said.

"A slap on the hand, maybe restitution."

She sighed. "Mostly I just want to put a stop to this. I'm tired of never knowing what they are going to come up with next. I'm almost certain it's one of the extras. They come and go a lot and if it is I can leave them behind when we continue shooting in San Francisco. But that's three weeks away! I can't take these pranks for three weeks! I'll go insane."

"And what would you have me do about it?" I asked. After being hunted, kidnapped, and beaten I thought getting upset over a glued doorknob was silly.

"Just be here. If you hang out here with that gun it'll discourage people from trying anything. If they still manage to pull something track them until you find out who it is."

Rusty watched the proceedings with disapproval.

"You're not doing this," he said. "If anybody knows how easily an apprehension can go bad it's me. Even mild mannered little housewives turn into wildcats when they are cornered."

"I know," I said. Having been a mild mannered little housewife who was cornered, I knew what a pain they could be. "No apprehensions," I told Sherri. "You have security guards around here. What have they done?"

"Nothing, it always happens when things are quiet. Then when I discover what happened I call them but it is no use. The person is long gone by then. Then they just laugh at me. I don't know what's worse finding the prank or dealing with security. It's embarrassing."

"Days or nights?"

"Days. That's what makes me think it's an extra. The extras are local people who go home every night. Sometimes the extras are only here for a few hours. Sometimes all day. When the light fails they get sent home."

"Cassidy, you're not going to do this."

"Why? Give me a couple of days. I want to see how this place works. I'm curious about this prankster. It'll be fun to track in this new setting."

"This is *not* a game," Rusty said sternly and Sherri backed off a step.

"I know, but it's intriguing."

"You knew you were going to do this when we left the house," he accused.

"Not one hundred percent, but I couldn't think of a good reason not to. Take the Jeep. Pick me up after work. Let's see how one day goes. Even if nothing happens I'll get lots of practice tracking."

The whole time we were talking, people walked around outside. This was a busy place. I didn't know how someone could set up a practical joke in a place like this. It was too public. The more I thought about it the more I wanted to see for myself what was going on.

"Let me take you home," Rusty said. "You don't belong here. What are you doing even thinking about going along with this wild goose chase? So some person likes to play jokes on people. So Sherri doesn't like it. She can deal with it. There's a joker in every crowd. It's life. Let's get out of here."

"I can't. I'm too curious. I want to figure this out. Even if I don't catch him. I want to see how he works. Go on to work. I'll be fine here. I have a goal and I'll be careful. You don't have to worry. I'll check in with the security guards and they'll be around to help."

I should have listened to Rusty. He reluctantly took my Jeep to work and I wondered how he would get back in to pick me up but here I was, with one spoiled actress, one greasy agent, and a whole new world of people and tracks.

"Okay, first things first. Security has to know who I am."

"O...kay," said Arnie. He marched off and about ten minutes later three guys in uniforms walked up.

"Don't tell me. He glued your shoes to the floor," one guy said to Sherri.

"No, I've hired a new... what are we going to call you? You have to have a title."

"I'm a tracker. You hired me to track."

"But that doesn't sound right. Why would a movie star hire a tracker?"

"To track a prankster."

"It sounds better to call you a bodyguard. Stars have bodyguards all the time."

"Okay, so call me a bodyguard. I don't care."

She looked at the security guards, "This is Cassidy Michaels. She's my new bodyguard. She's going to be keeping an eye on my trailer. She'll spot this guy. She's good. She's the one who found me when I broke my leg in the mountains last summer. If she doesn't spot the idiot who is pulling these pranks she can track them down."

"HA! Ha, ha, that's a good one, Sherri," the younger guard bellowed.

Sherri got irate, "She will too! You just wait and see!"

"It's good to meet you ma'am," said one of the other guards. "I'm Joe. This is Bill and Mr. Disbelief over there is Davin. You run into any trouble just call us. Put it in your cell phone with an *aa* in front so it's the first number you see." Then he gave me a number and I programmed it into my cell phone, never expecting to use it. It never hurt to have options.

I told them thanks and, introductions out of the way, they went away, Davin laughing all the way. Joe seemed to be more on my side though.

"Don't scoff," Joe told Davin, "You didn't see her on TV. There's more to her than it looks."

"*Well*," said Sherri. "I need to have my hair done. I really did think your husband was going to call me to go do the car chase. I need to go get properly windblown."

"I'll keep an eye on things here," I said.

She walked away fluffing her hair up.

Chapter 11

Okay, first things first. I examined the tracks of the security guards. I'd been watching their feet as we talked, so I could tell them apart after they left. Their feet and their tracks told me a lot about their personalities. Joe was matter of fact. He knew his job. He stuck to it. He didn't stress out over it. Problems were handled quickly and efficiently. Bill was lazier. He strolled, toes out. If he got bored he tended to drag his feet. He'd hang out in the break room, talk to girls. Davin was too young to have this job. He didn't keep his mind on the job. Every friendly person who walked by distracted him. He stopped and talked to many people. I realized with a jolt that I'd tracked Davin until I'd lost Sherri's trailer. It took me a few minutes to find it again. I circled the trailer watching for any footprints that seemed to stop or linger. So far so good. I didn't really expect another prank. The door hadn't even been fixed for ten minutes. It would take the prankster at least several hours to come up with another plan.

People walked by. Most of them had things to do, places they should be. I watched their eyes. I watched their movements.

Usually if a person were up to no good their actions advertised it plain as day. They avoided eye contact. They fiddled with things, nervousness coming out their fingertips. They took note of odd things in the place they were hitting. An armed, pregnant woman hanging around where they wanted to work would cause most pranksters to pause. That pause was what I was looking for. It only lasted a second but it was fairly recognizable.

I felt a bit naïve standing there. Half of Hollywood stardom might pass me by but I wouldn't recognize them. I worried that Sherri would ask me if I'd seen her movies. Hmmm, had I? I didn't know. It was very possible that I had not.

Sherri was gone for over an hour. I thought it was easy enough to get properly windblown just standing outside her trailer. Someone could easily have set something up while she was having her hair done. I circled the trailer again, nearly colliding with Davin as I rounded a corner.

"How's it going?" he asked.

"All's quiet on the western front," I reported.

"Exciting job, huh?"

"Oh yeah, but I've had worse. At least I don't have to carry an M16 and challenge everybody who walks by."

"M16?"

"Yeah."

"You?"

"Yeah."

"So what're you really doing here?"

"Keeping an eye on Sherri's trailer. Watching patterns. Taking mental notes about who comes and goes. Noticing any odd tracks that stand out. Why? What are you doing here?"

"Watching the stars, that's all."

"How can you tell the stars from the ordinary people? I can't."

"You're kidding. Everyone knows what Brock Larone looks like. You can't tell me you wouldn't recognize Brock the Rock! And Lynette Casey. She looks like, well, Lynette Casey!"

"Sorry, I don't get out much. I have no desire to meet the stars. The only reason I know who Sherri Champlain is because she got lost near my city and I'm the local tracker."

"So what Joe said is true?"

"I don't know what Joe said."

"He said you tracked Sherri from her campsite, up a mountain and through the woods."

"That's what I do. Anybody gets lost and they can be tracked, I get called in."

"Damn, I never would have guessed it."

"It's okay. That happens a lot."

A group of people walked by talking and heading for the next trailer down. One woman noticed me, gave me an odd look. I made a mental note to watch her in future trips past the trailer.

"Do you ever look at people when you talk to them?"

"Sorry, it just pays to know what's going on around me, especially if I have a puzzle to solve."

"It isn't any of those people."

"Why not?"

"It's their job to make sure Sherri gets ready for the shots. They aren't going to foul things up for her and make her late. It would make them look like they weren't doing their job. Have you tracked any other famous people?"

"Only one, but you may not have heard of him."

"Guy? Gets lost easily? Hmmm...Billy Sellers?"

"No. Who's Billy Sellers? This guy wasn't a movie star or a TV star. He's a photographer. His name is Mark Mireau."

"Oh yeah? You'd think he would know where he is all the time."

"Well, he wasn't lost. He knew where he was. He was over the side of a cliff on the backside of an island."

"No shit. How'd you figure that out?"

"I tracked him and when his tracks led over the cliff I rappelled down and looked around."

"I just can't get over it. You look like you ought to be teaching first grade Sunday School, but you talk about tracking and M16s."

"Time for another circuit."

I could feel the blood draining out of my head. I had to move. I headed around the trailer and when I needed to keep moving I widened my circle. Then I narrowed it again. Davin followed. He dropped behind a bit when I widened the circle and a person walked by that he wanted to greet. When I narrowed the circle again I noticed a pair of footprints veer off the middle of the walkway and pause at the very edge of the trailer. The tracks indicated motion. A purpose. I glanced under the trailer. It was dark in there. I crawled under and looked around but nothing looked unusual. I examined the underside of the trailer and found a lot of odd bumps and bulges, but I didn't know how trailers were built so I crawled back out.

"What are you doing under there?" Davin asked.

"Following footprints. See these tracks leading off from the norm?"

"Nothing much gets by you does it?"

I just brushed off the dirt and kept going, thinking about what I saw in the dark crawlspace. Were trailers really built with boxes and huge bolts and cables running underneath them?

"What do you guys do for lunch out here?" I asked. "When I talked to Sherri this morning I didn't even know if I was staying. I didn't expect Rusty to let me."

He opened the door on another trailer and the aroma of cooking food wafted out.

"Oh, thank you!" I said, taking in the room. It was a buffet of sorts. There were several different casserole type dishes along with side dishes of vegetables and a small salad bar. I took small portions, unsure of the cost or the availability.

"Go ahead," Davin said. "It's here for the workers. People are out here all day. They can't run to town to eat, too much to do. So we eat when we can. Lunch is covered."

"But they don't know that I'm a worker. Besides, I'm Sherri's employee, not the company's."

"Do you analyze everything to death? Just eat. Anybody says anything I'll send them to Arnie."

"Learn anything useful?" Rusty asked me over dinner.

"Yes, I learned that there are security guards and then there are non-security guards. And I need to check something tomorrow. I'm not sure of what I saw at one point so I'd like to take a look at the undersides of some of the other trailers."

"What do you mean non-security guards?"

"Some of them give out more than they guard. This kid has got to learn to guard his words. He may turn out to be useful to me but he shouldn't be in uniform."

"Sounds like somebody else I know."

"That reminds me. I need to wash my uniform. I only have one and I crawled under the trailer today."

"You're not going back, are you?"

"Tomorrow is when I should learn something useful. Either my presence is discouraging them or they will rig something up tomorrow. I want to be there when it happens."

"You're eating like you haven't had a thing to eat all day. What did you do for lunch?"

"They have a trailer there where employees eat. It took me a while to figure that out but I did get enough to eat."

"So you spent a whole day as a body guard and nothing happened?"

"Yep."

"You're losing your touch."

Chapter 12

The next day everybody was walking around bleary eyed. I knocked on Sherri's door.

"Just reporting in," I said. "What happened? You look like…"

She let out a big, long wail. Oops, I'd attacked her sense of vanity.

"That cat! There was a cat outside meowing all night long! I could have shot it if anybody had given me a gun!"

Just then there was a loud, obnoxious sounding meow that radiated from the trailer and bounced off the surrounding trailer walls.

"Did anybody bother looking for this cat?" I asked.

"Davin walked around trying to scare it. He shined a flashlight around and he couldn't find a cat. But it went on and on. I didn't get a wink of sleep."

"*MEEEOOOOOOW*," went the cat, louder than any cat I'd ever heard.

"*That* is *not* a cat," I said. "Why didn't anybody look around? No cat in its right mind would meow over and over all night long, the same meow every time."

I walked around the trailer.

"*MEEEOOOOOOW*"

"Call Davin. I want to talk to him."

I found the place where the fishy footprints had been the night before.

"*MEEEOOOOOW!*"

I crawled under the trailer and waited.

"*MEEEOOOOOW!*"

I followed the sound to one of the odd boxes I'd passed up the day before. Shoot. I pulled the box off the bottom of the trailer. It was a simple recording device cranked up loud with the speaker against the floor of Sherri's trailer.

Davin jogged up to the group outside Sherri's door as I came out from under the trailer, dusty, dirty and irritated.

"*MEEEOOOOOW!*" went the box.

"Let's take a short walk while I explain something to you," I said. I didn't want to chew him out in front of the group. I handed him the box. "Turn this thing off."

"*MEEEOOOOOW!*" went the box.

"How the hell should I know how to turn it off?"

"I'm not saying you planted it but you should have looked for it. A cat does not sit in one spot for long. It does *not* yeowl the same meow over and over and over in perfect rhythm. A cat is *not that loud*. A cat does not go on nightly strolls through the desert looking for people to irritate. What made you think it was a real cat? It took me exactly two meows to decide it was a joke. Sherri said you looked for a cat, but think! Think when these things come up. Does it sound like any cat you've heard?"

"*MEEEOOOOOW!*" went the box.

"How do you shut the stupid thing off?" he asked.

"I don't know. There's no buttons. You may have to shoot it. When Sherri called security how did *you* get the call?"

"I was the last one here."

"*MEEEOOOOOW!*" went the box.

"They don't have night security?"

"Of course they do. I took the call because I hadn't left yet. Plus it's always funny to take Sherri's calls. She makes such an issue out of everything."

"You have a job to do. When she calls, don't just walk around with a flashlight pretending to figure things out. Think about what's going on. It doesn't take much thinking."

"*MEEEOOOOOW!*" went the box.

"Now, does that sound like a real cat to you?" I asked.

"No," he admitted.

"Good, now go put the thing out of its misery. And then bring it back to me."

"Wha? Why?"

"I want to see how it's put together. I want to get a feel for how this guy's brain works."

"If I shoot it there may be nothing left."

I had my doubts if he could even hit it if he shot at it. "Okay, let's take it to the break room and dissect it."

"*MEEEOOOOOW!*" went the box.

We sat down at a table in the break room and set the crude box in front of us. Davin ran off to get a screwdriver. Several more obnoxious *MEEEOOOOOWs* blasted forth while he was gone. The people in the break room getting coffee stared at me with my box. I wanted to hide.

"Here we go," said Davin, sitting down with a small tool kit.

Inside a cheap black plastic box was a recording device connected to a small, travel alarm clock. When the alarm went off the machine started and played over and over. I cut a couple of wires and the meowing stopped. I made a note to look at the underside of the trailer again. There had been other unidentified boxes under there.

Davin followed as I returned to Sherri's trailer and crawled underneath.

"I wouldn't go down there if I were you. There's likely to be rattlesnakes."

"Rattlesnakes hibernate in winter," I stated.

I shined a flashlight around under the trailer and found a second box. I took it to the break room and opened it up. I carefully changed the alarm on the clock and watched the box come alive. This one was coyotes. At least they had recorded more than one howl. It was a small pack of coyotes but again they had messed up. The coyotes were different ages and at this time of year the pups would be more mature than the ones in the recording.

"This guy needs to do his homework," I said. "And he could learn a lesson in subtlety. Less is more. Well, at least it proved to be an interesting morning. I learned something and I have evidence to turn over to the police, should it come to that."

"Evidence?" Davin asked.

"Yeah, that's part of my job. Collecting evidence. I need to remember to carry rubber gloves. Now I'll have to file a report that says I touched the evidence and I'll get chewed out by Javier Delgado. Actually I should take this in and have it fingerprinted. If the prankster is somebody who has been fingerprinted we might be able to get a name."

"Why would an extra have fingerprints on file?"

"You never know. Lots of jobs require fingerprinting. Plus, who says extras don't have a record? My fingerprints are on file."

"Why are *your* fingerprints on file?"

"Because I'm a reserve deputy."

"You?"

"Yeah. I had to, if I wanted to track for the police."

"You are one strange girl, you know that?"

"Yeah."

"Here's your cat," I told Sherri. "Don't touch it. I'm going to have it dusted for fingerprints. Look, we have coyotes, too."

"That's the coyotes?"

"Yeah, why?"

"I've heard the coyotes before."

"And nobody tracked down the box before this?"

"No."

"Well, you should be sleeping better."

She was mad and she looked like she'd been up all night. I just couldn't imagine everybody falling for a recording this long.

It was irritating to know that another prank had occurred right under my nose. I could pin point exactly when the footprints were left under the trailer but I didn't see anyone in the area at the time. Davin and I had been making the rounds of the trailer, talking. Then Davin had fallen behind. It was hard for me to believe it might be Davin. But, if he was a security guard, his fingerprints should be on file. Come to think of it though I knew he had handled the boxes. We had passed them back and forth trying to get the cat to be quiet. Had he touched the coyote box, too? As far as I could remember the coyote box only had the prankster's and my fingerprints on it. And there were far fewer prints on the coyote box. I had known how to open it up the second time around. I shouldn't have touched the buttons, though. Sigh, I needed to think before trying these things, and I needed to bring rubber gloves with me. I put the boxes in plastic bags and set them aside. Time to get to work.

I walked around amongst the trailers. For hours I walked. The makeup crew went by. The hair crew hurried down the walkway between the trailers. A costume person with an armload of clothes rushed by in a hurry. I wondered where Arnie was. I hadn't seen him since the first day. A group of people in ratty jeans strolled by. Extras? It sure would help if I knew a little about the movie making business. It was going to take me a long time to categorize these people on my own.

"Hey there, beautiful!" I heard behind me. I turned around. Oh hell, it was Brock the Rock. What was his last name again? The only reason I knew who he was is because he was Mr. Hollywood himself, and I mean makeup, toothpaste smile, a costume that showed off every muscle he had and might even add a few he didn't have. I looked up and down the little corridor. We were alone. I don't know why I automatically felt for my gun. "Yes, I'm talking to you," he continued. "You're Sherri's new bodyguard?"

"Yeah, sort of. Bodyguard, private eye, tracker. Seems like this little job has been less body guarding and more private eyeing."

"Be careful. I have a feeling this could turn nasty."

"Nasty I can deal with. When this person starts getting nasty is when he starts slipping up and revealing himself. That's when the job gets easier."

"No, when this person gets nasty, is when you get out," he said looking me up and down. "This is no place for you."

"Is that a threat? Because if it is, I've had plenty of experience with people who get downright nasty. I doubt they can beat what I've already been through."

"And you're willing to go through that again? Now?"

That gave me reason to pause, "No, not now. But it doesn't scare me off either."

"It wasn't a threat, just a friendly warning. This started out in fun but I have a feeling this person is going to get tired of fun."

"What makes you say that?"

"Just a change in the tensions around shooting."

"Tension implies a cause. And a cause would point to a motive. What is this person's motive? Where is the tension coming from?"

He shrugged, "Could be a lot of things. Envy, jealousy, a fan who wants to get noticed. Fans do some very odd things to get noticed."

"Do you know more than you're letting on?"

"Hey, a guy always knows more than he's letting on. But if you're asking if I know who is doing these things to Sherri, the answer is no."

"What do you think of Davin?"

"Davin is your best bet. Davin gets around. He talks to everybody. Doesn't do much for security but he does get around. If you really need security call Joe."

"I have a feeling if I call security I'll get Davin anyway."

"Look, I gotta run. If you need security call Joe. If you really need security ask for Spike. I'll tell him he's on call."

"Spike?"

"My body guard. He's not visible, but he's there."

"Then he already knows."

"Huh. Yeah, I suppose he does."

Spike was definitely visible when he came to see me an hour later. He was...he was... well, he was bigger than Rusty. He had influences from an odd mix of people. I imagined his dad as a sumo wrestler and his mom as a fitness trainer. His mom had won the battle over who was going to train up Junior, but he was still huge. He filled a room just by stepping into it.

"Brock said to check in wit' you," he said.

"Okay, thanks," I replied, feeling like a little kid beside him.

"If you need help you call security. Ask for Joe. If you need real help ask for me. Just the fact that you know who I am will tell the guys you're in the know. They'll put you through to me."

"What kind of help?"

"You'll know. If it happens, you'll know."

Gulp. Oh, that kind of help.

"You got kids?" Spike asked.

"No, this will be my first," I replied.

"Brock never assumes folks want these but he thought if you had kids..."

He held out a couple of autographed eight by ten photos. I brightened immediately. Lawanda and Bailee would be thrilled. Lawanda didn't know I was working for Sherri. Now if I didn't get Sherri's autograph I could let Lawanda think I'd worked for Brock the Rock. What was his last name again? Grrr. Spike handed me the photos. Darn! I couldn't read it in the signature either.

"Oh, thank you! I have two friends who will be really excited to get these."

"What about you?"

"Maybe I'd like one to remember you all by, especially if this gets dicey. Hey, you don't have one of you, do you?"

"Me? I ain't no actor. My picture'd crack a camera lens."

I believed it but I'd really rather have a snapshot of Spike and Brock than a high gloss autographed studio photo of Brock the Rock.

"Tell Brock I said thanks."

There was a blood-curdling scream from the trailer. The door banged open and a shaking Sherri Champlain stumbled down the stairs.

Chapter 13

"Aiyeeeee!" she cried, "It's awful! It's horrible and it was this close to me!" She held her hands about a foot apart.

"What is it?" I asked.

"It's a spider! A huge spider!"

Spike blanched. I smiled, glad to have the upper hand. I was really very proud of myself as I led Spike into the trailer. I searched high and low but even a large spider was able to fit into a very small space.

Sherri's trailer consisted of a vanity and sitting area, a small kitchen and a bedroom, with a bathroom separating the two living areas.

I found the spider, an average sized tarantula, walking across the floor under the vanity chair. Spike backed off, clearly not wanting to have anything to do with this eight-legged invader. Hoo boy. I had to catch the thing or Sherri would never believe it was really, truly gone. I looked around quickly, worried the spider would run away. The tarantulas I'd seen in the desert were slow but they didn't have a person trying to catch them either. I wasn't sure how fast they could be if threatened.

There was a large glass canister full of cotton balls on the vanity. I grabbed that and pulled out all the cotton balls. I found a thin magazine and went after the unfortunate spider. As I approached, the tarantula walked toward Spike who gave out a yelp and jumped, shaking the whole trailer.

"It won't hurt you," I admonished him.

"Not if I can help it," he responded.

The tarantula advanced until Spike was backed into a corner. He brought up his boot ready to squash the spider and I flashed him *the look*.

"Don't you dare! It hasn't hurt a thing. I'll catch it and let it go in the desert."

"You'll catch it? Before it gets me? 'Cause if you don't it's the boot."

"You don't want to step on it. Just think of that icky crunch. I can't bear to hear that icky crunch! I'd rather catch it with my hands than hear that awful sound!"

The tarantula took a few more steps.

"Catch it! Catch it!" yelled Spike.

I put the magazine between Spike and the spider and shooed it toward the canister. The tarantula ran off in a different direction and I chased it down again. Spike relaxed a bit when he wasn't cornered anymore.

Davin ran into the trailer. He stood in the doorway hands in pockets, grinning as I followed the huge spider. I was wondering if he was grinning at the odd picture I made, pregnant woman chasing a large spider. Or was he grinning at the obviously distressed, hulking form of Spike, cowering in fear of the same spider? I blocked the spider with the magazine again and it stopped. I cautiously slipped the canister over the top of the tarantula careful not to catch its legs under the rim. I slid the magazine underneath, trapping the hapless critter. As I held it up for all to see, Sherri's face beamed up into the jar from the cover of the magazine, the tarantula sitting squarely on top. Oops. I turned over the canister and the tarantula dropped to the bottom. I replaced the magazine with the lid of the canister.

I brushed off the magazine. "We won't tell Sherri about the magazine. I don't think she'd appreciate knowing it walked around on her face," I said. "Anybody want to take our little friend out to the desert?"

Spike backed off like I was handing him a lit stick of dynamite. I extended the invitation to Davin but he backed off, too.

"Good job, kid," he said grinning.

"We won't tell Brock about this," I admonished both guys.

Davin wasn't so sure. I thought Brock would hear about it as soon as Davin could arrange it. I showed Sherri the captured tarantula, then followed Davin out. He gave me a ride out to the desert in a golf cart that had SECURITY printed front and rear. I chose a sheltered area and let the spider loose hoping he'd find a nice warm place.

"Now to find out how it got in there," I said as I turned around to begin trailer inspection.

"This is the desert. It could have just wandered in."

"It didn't just wander in. Tarantulas are not active in the winter. They like to be nice and warm. They are not going to go hiking out in the open in winter. They'll find a rock that gets warmed by the sun and stay close to that. This tarantula was bought at a pet store and placed in Sherri's trailer just to scare her. But how did they do it? I've been walking around the trailer for two days. I know who came and went. I saw the tracks. They were normal. Everybody came and went just like usual except for the recording box episode."

When we got back to the trailer I crawled underneath with a flashlight again. I shined it in all the nooks and crannies but I didn't see a way for a person to plant a tarantula in the trailer. Then I circled the trailer again. It took three circles with each pass getting more and more detailed before I found it. Sherri's bedroom window was open a crack for ventilation and a slit just along the edge of the screen allowed someone to slide in a slim tarantula-containing receptacle long enough to let the spider loose. Then they simply pulled the empty container out and the tear in the screen was barely visible.

"Sherri isn't going to like this," I said. "That spider started out in her bedroom and it could have been lurking for days. In her bed, in her shoes, anywhere it wanted to go. We won't go into detail about the possibilities. We're just lucky she discovered it in the day time. In the living area."

I knocked on the door of the trailer and Sherri answered it hesitantly.

"Spider hunted down and disposed of," I reported.

She shivered, "I'm going to be feeling creepy crawlies on me for weeks! How did it get in?"

"Umm, it was planted."

"What?"

"Someone put it in your trailer."

"I'm...I'm going to report this. This is awful! It could have bitten me!"

"I doubt it. It was harmless, just ugly. You can still report it but it wouldn't have hurt you. While you are at it call maintenance and have them fix your screen. And keep your window closed."

"Track them down," she said. "Find out who did this."

"Sherri, it could have been planted a week ago. There are no tracks left. They were covered over long ago."

"A week?" she squeaked. "That... that thing has been in my trailer for a week?"

"I don't think so, but it's possible."

"Ooooh, YUCK! YUCK! To think I could have stepped on it in the night. I could have been eating dinner with it! It could have crawled in the shower! I'll have creepy crawlies *forever*!"

"Sherri, it was harmless."

"I don't care, it was gross! It was ugly! It was loose in my bedroom. It could have crawled on me when I was sleeping!"

I sighed and went back to "work." Creepy crawlies were Sherri's department.

"I just hope they don't come up with a scorpion next," I muttered as I walked my circuit.

When I got home Rusty and Kelly were both there. I dived into dinner preparations.

"How many am I cooking for?" I asked the guys, "Can you stay?"

"Yeah, if it's not a problem. Rhonda is visiting her sister in Iowa."

This was going to be fun. Kelly already knew I got into some odd adventures but he had no idea what I'd been up to lately.

"What are you grinning about so much?" Rusty asked.

"You wouldn't believe the day I had. It was very entertaining. And that reminds me. I brought something for you to check out if you have time." I went to the living room and got the recording boxes out of my pack. "Can you check these for fingerprints that aren't mine? On one there should be two sets of fingerprints and on the other there will me three."

"What are they?"

"Recording devices. Get a load of this. They had been kept awake all night by what they thought was a cat meowing. I listened to two meows and decided there was no way this was a real cat so I tracked it down. One box has a cat recording. Only one meow over and over again. I don't know how anybody could mistake it for a real cat. The other one apparently kept them awake another night and it has coyotes on it."

Rusty looked the boxes over. "You want them checked for fingerprints? Cass...I think we have more important things to do than check over some practical joker's work."

"Okay," I said disappointed, "I guess it's not that big a deal. I just thought if we could come up with a name the security guards knew it might put an early end to this job."

"What are you doing?" Kelly asked.

"I'm a bodyguard," I replied.

"You? No you're not. Rusty wouldn't stand for it."

"It's a cushy job. Only three weeks. And the pay is great. There are little side benefits, too. Look what I picked up today."

I found the pictures Brock had given me.

"Bailee and Lawanda will be so excited to get these."

"You're working with *Brock Larone*?"

"So that's his last name! I couldn't remember it for anything."

"He has heavy duty body guards. He doesn't need you."

"I don't work for Brock. I work for Sherri Champlain. And you're right, Brock has a heavy duty bodyguard, named Spike, who is afraid of tarantulas."

Kelly leaned back in his chair. He was ready for the story now, so I dove in. The guys sat back laughing at Spike's expense, imagining me chasing after a tarantula on the loose.

"And it didn't bother you to catch a tarantula?" Kelly asked.

"Well, I didn't *like* it. But Spike made the job a lot more fun."

"And these recording devices were plastered to the underside of the trailer? How did you find them?" Rusty asked.

"I crawled under with a flashlight and looked for them."

"Cassidy, this box could have been anything. It could have exploded when you opened it," Rusty pointed out.

"It was *meowing*. I knew it was a recording. And the other one is exactly like the cat one. They wouldn't make the devices explode. Then they couldn't change them. Leaving them intact they could make any number of irritating noises. I think everything I've seen so far was planted before I came on board. And activity has been normal around the trailer as far as I can tell. There was one set of tracks leading under the trailer the day before the cat box got tripped but I'm not convinced it was the prankster. These boxes just have timers imbedded in them. So really, I don't know much of anything except that there might be fingerprints on the boxes. But if you don't want to check them, that's fine. Maybe if I bring them back out to the set I can use them for bait. Maybe the prankster will try to steal them back."

Rusty shook his head and I knew I had him. Rusty was more interested in getting me off this job than solving the mystery but if that was incentive enough I'd take it.

"I'll take them to the station and see what they can do. But I'm warning you, they have a lot of work to do and a practical joke is not going to be a high priority to them."

"That's okay, just tell them where they came from and they'll want their piece of the Cassidy Michael's adventure."

"No. You never know how people are going to react when they know a famous person is around. You're likely to be followed out to the site and cause all kinds of havoc."

"So you're tracking down recording devices and tarantulas for Sherri Champlain?" Kelly asked.

"So far, yeah. I wonder what they will come up with next."

Chapter 14

Next was a very juvenile stunt, but it led me on my first tracking case for Sherri Champlain. The day started out very boring. No irritating meowing recording devices. No huge spiders prowling the trailer. I walked the circuit, first around Sherri's trailer, then around a larger circle, then the smaller one again. Keeping an eye on people. Many of the people I saw were the same groups as before. The make-up people went by. The hair people. The director followed by an entourage of cameramen. I always thought of movie making as being glamorous but what I saw on site was hardly glamorous. I learned there were as many different positions involved in making a movie as there was in any large corporation. The people dressed according to the environment, mixed with their job description. The hair people dressed casually, in jeans, slacks, blouses, and sturdy shoes suitable for standing at the chair or walking in the desert. They had fantastic hair that barely rustled in the wind. The people out in the field, people like cameramen and directors wore light weight camping type clothes. Workers who were used to the sun wore shorts and t-shirts. The fabric breathed. Everything they chose was very practical. Hardly glamorous.

A group of people I hadn't noticed before came to Sherri's door and knocked. I tried to memorize their faces. Two men and two women. They looked like actors and actresses because they were dressed like they were in an action movie. As with any gathering of faces, Davin showed up, striking up a conversation with the woman dressed in black spandex motorcycle riding gear. I couldn't imagine anybody actually wearing spandex to ride motorcycles and drive sports cars but the effect *looked* good, so who was I to argue?

Sherri answered the door and greeted her visitors then invited them all in. Davin was still talking to the woman in black so he followed and came out again a short time later to let the actors do their job. Things got real boring then. The walkways grew quiet. Sherri and her friends were going over lines or something. I stood at the door until I had to walk. I walked a small circuit and then a big circuit, then a small one, then stood some more. I kept it up until Sherri's friends left and once again all was quiet. I was hoping it was quiet because there was a guard on Sherri's trailer. Even if I was basically harmless to most folks, they also didn't want to get caught. So maybe just my presence was paying off.

It was right about then, when I was convinced a statue of a guard would be just as effective as I was that I heard a long, frustrated wail from Sherri's trailer.

"Waaaaaahhhhhh!" The door banged opened and Sherri just stood there. No harm done, it was just water. But she had steam coming out her ears. "How? How do they do it? You've been outside. I've been inside. Yet they still manage to pull these things on me! How do they do it?"

I perked up. Something had happened, in the time I'd been there. There had to be tracks. There had to be clues. I cursed the fact that I couldn't call on the police to take fingerprints now.

"Show me what happened," I said.

"All I did was go to the sink for a drink of water. That's all! I just turned on the water like I always do and it sprayed all over me. It's never done that before."

She led me into the trailer and showed me the sink. It was a kitchen sink and it had a handy little sprayer for rinsing off dishes. Someone had wrapped a rubber band around the sprayer, pointed it at the front of the sink and left. Simple. So simple a kid could do it, but effective as far as Sherri was concerned. A little water on her costume was as bad as sleeping with a tarantula. She was irate.

"Okay, quick, tell me who was in your trailer?"

"Well, nobody, I lock it when I leave."

"Five people were just here. They couldn't have been nobody."

"But it couldn't have been them. I was talking to them the whole time. Nobody did anything."

"Somebody did something. Who were they?"

"Well…they were Trey Houston, Alonzo Marcos, Whitney Washington and Simone Madison."

"*That* was Simone Madison?"

"Yeah."

"And Davin."

"Davin?"

"He was talking to Simone when they walked in. Then he left so you guys could work. Who else has been in your trailer since you used the sink last? Think."

"No one. You would have seen them if they came in."

"Okay. I'm going to look at the tracks. Maybe someone will stand out."

I went outside and studied the mess of tracks. There were two sets of boots. Not cowboy boots. Not work boots. This was an action movie. What would the two men have been wearing for car chases through the desert? Dingo boots? Hell, I wish I was more fashion conscious. One of the women was wearing high heeled boots and the other was wearing practical shoes with tennis shoe-like tread. The group stayed together until they got to the far end of the trailers and then they split up. After the foursome split up they moved into the busyness of the site and other tracks crisscrossed the tracks I was following. People stared as I concentrated on the trails. Young, pregnant woman walking around a Hollywood movie production, staring at the ground, deep in thought. I didn't care what they thought. I was just doing my job.

"I thought you were odd before," Davin said from across a small clearing.

"You were right before, too," I reminded him.

"I hate to tell you this but you lost the body you were supposed to be guarding."

"It's safely ensconced in her trailer," I told him, still tracking along.

"Do you know that?"

"It doesn't matter. Sherri hired a tracker, so I'm tracking."

His eyes crinkled with amusement. "Oh yeah? Who are you tracking?"

"Simone Madison."

"How do you know?"

"There were five people at Sherri's trailer. The two women were wearing very different footwear. Simone was wearing high-heeled boots. They went with her black spandex costume. I'm tracking the one in high heeled boots."

"So why are you tracking them?"

"Because one of the five pulled a very juvenile trick and I'm supposed to figure out who. Was it you? You were one of the five."

"Could be. That would be just like me. Security guard and all. Yep, it's the uniform. Peg him."

"You're just being sarcastic."

Actually, I hadn't ruled Davin out at all, but he was still a good source of information. If I had to pick a suspect right now, I'd pick Davin, simply because he was overly interested in all the details and he was always there.

"Tell me, while you were in the trailer was anybody standing near the sink?"

"We were all standing in the living room area."

"Nobody wandered over to the sink?"

"No."

Hmm.

I tracked all five trails and they all walked perfectly normally except for Simone who stumbled in a ground squirrel hole and limped a little afterwards. That's what she got for wearing high-heeled boots in the desert. Davin's trail was the most suspicious. He snuck around the building and took off for the perimeter fence, then followed it to the parking lot. What was all that about? He watched, amused as I tried to piece together his own tracks.

"Joe called me. We had to check out a car with no ID on it."

"Could have been mine. The guard at the gate knows me but I don't remember getting a parking pass or anything."

"Tan Jeep?"

"Yeah."

"Sorry."

"Sorry? Why sorry?"

"Not really, one reason I found you was to ask you if it was yours. Looked like what you'd drive. I give you two months after that baby is born and you'll be driving a van or an SUV."

"SUV. We already have an Explorer. My husband drives it."

"About your husband. Why isn't he on the Hollywood scene? He could beat out Brock Larone for this part."

I laughed out loud. "Rusty isn't interested in acting. He can look pretty tough with a buzz cut but he'd never make a good actor. His cop face is pretty good but...no. An actor? Never."

"His cop face?"

"He's a detective. He's used to keeping a calm exterior no matter what is going on around him. Now if you want to find a guy to give Brock some competition look up Rusty's little brother. He'd love a movie part. He's a real ham."

"What's the little brother do?"

"Last I heard he rented kayaks to tourists in San Diego and posed for pictures with girls on the beach. A dollar a shot."

"Is he worth the dollar?"

"He makes more on the pictures than he does on the job. I guess maybe he gets more than a dollar a shot. He looks like he's in a sun tan lotion ad."

I was kicking myself. Another thing that made me suspect Davin was he was so disarming. I thought he could get away with anything just because he had that kind of personality. If it did turn out to be him I'd feel guilty turning him in.

"Well, now that we know the Jeep is yours I'm going to go put a parking pass on it. I didn't want to have it towed away. It's a long walk into town."

And away he went.

I returned to Sherri's trailer.

"We struck out," I told her.

"What do you mean?"

"I followed each person's tracks after they left the trailer but I only learned not to wear high heeled boots around ground squirrel holes."

"What?"

"And you shouldn't either. You could break a leg."

"I don't want to do that again."

"Do what?"

"Break a leg."

"We need to catch this person doing something fishy. Once they leave the area they become one of the crowd again. Think again. When did you use your sink last?"

"When it sprayed me!"

"No, I mean before that." Sherri truly was blonde, I thought.

"I don't use it much. I don't cook. I usually drink bottled water."

I wondered how one simple question could possibly take that much thought.

"I used the sink to soak my nails last night before I went to bed."

"To soak your nails?" Not being a nail person, I had trouble understanding the concept of soaking one's nails other than to wash dishes.

"Yeah, I can soak them all at one time in the sink. It only takes a half inch of liquid."

O...kay.

"And that's the last time you know the sink was working properly?"

"No, I didn't put water in the sink."

Big sigh.

"Okay, when did you last use *water* at the sink?"

"I emptied a half full bottle of water into it yesterday evening."

Patience, Cassidy, patience. I knew I meant business when I called myself by my whole name.

"Okay, when was the last time you turned on the water in the sink and *it worked*?" There, I couldn't get much more specific than that.

Sherri burned off a few thousand brain cells as she considered my question. Finally she said, "I don't know."

How could someone not know when they used their sink last? I used mine. Several times a day. I'd made breakfast and washed the dishes quickly before I left the house that morning. I knew that's when I used my sink last. But to think this was a tough question made me wonder how she had survived this long and maybe I would be doing society a favor by leaving her to the mercy of her prankster. Maybe she'd be forced to think.

"How was your day?" Rusty asked after a big hug. I'd gotten home after him and he was hungry. He was munching on an apple.

"When was the last time you used the kitchen faucet?"

"Two minutes ago. I washed my apple. Why?"

"Oh, nothing. You just proved you're ten times smarter than Sherri Champlain."

"I take it this was a frustrating day."

"I got to do some tracking. That's the good news. Bad news is I learned zilch from it. Oh, I learned a few people's quirks. I categorized a few mannerisms. But I didn't learn who rigged up Sherri's sink to spray water all over her. So…how was your day?"

"Boring. It was my court day. That's why I'm home early."

The courthouse shut down at five o'clock.

"What do you want for dinner?"

"Zeke's."

"Okay, let me change."

Zeke's was a treat. I always liked going to Zeke's. It reminded me of the first day I met Rusty. It was a friendly mom and pop establishment with beat up wooden booths and tacky silk flowers at the ends of the tables. I wondered if the waitresses still had to go by Z names. I hoped it was a passing fad. The girls were tired of them. Nobody wanted to be Zelda and they frequently ran out of girls' name tags, so they had to use boys' names at work. Hopefully Brenda and Jennifer and Lindy had gone back to being themselves again.

I went to change but stopped in frustration. My pants didn't fit anymore. I looked through my dresses. They were all made for skinny people. I flopped down on the bed, discouraged. The baby gave me a kick for good measure.

"What's wrong, babe?" Rusty asked as he lay behind me. He put an arm around me and I moved it down so he could feel the little taps.

"I must have woken him up when I flopped down," I said.

"That's not what's wrong."

"None of my clothes fit and I don't want to go in sweats. I must have grown a few inches in the past several days."

Rusty moved his hand to follow the movements.

"That's my baby?"

"Yep, that's him. He moves around a lot."

"I wish I could feel what you feel. What does it feel like when he does that?"

"It feels like…I don't know how to describe it. I can feel it. But not like you feel things with your hands. It feels like part of me is moving around. But not."

"Does it hurt?"

"No, it doesn't hurt, although I've heard it can get uncomfortable the last month."

He moved to get up, "All right, put on your uniform pants and…" He opened the closet. He pulled out a loose royal blue sweater and held it up for inspection. "What do you think?"

"It's not your color," I said.

The sweater was tight.

Chapter 15

On the way to Zeke's we stopped at a store. A clothing store. It had the M word in the title. Sigh. I walked in and saw all the maternity clothes and almost turned right around. Rusty blocked my way. Okay, okay, I'd look. All the tops looked cheerful and perky and pleased to be the clothing of choice for this most special occasion. When I tried them on I felt very…maternal. And I wasn't comfortable with that feeling. It wasn't that I was displeased with my situation. I just wanted to be one of the guys again and in my condition they would never see me that way. I bought three pairs of pants and three tops because I knew I couldn't leave the store empty handed and I really did need some clothes I could wear. Junior was happy. No more squeezy tight waistbands.

"Hey! Long time no see!" Brenda said when we walked into Zeke's. Oh good, she was Brenda again. "Oh my gosh! You're expecting! Do you know what you're going to name the baby? Do you know if it's a boy or a girl? When is your due date? How have you been feeling?"

I had to give her credit. She knew the drill.

"No. No. The end of June. And I've been fine."

"This is so exciting! I can't wait to see your baby! You will bring him in after he's born, won't you?"

"Of course." I wondered if every business we frequented would ask us to bring the baby back for a visit.

"So, what can I getcha? The usual? Medium Hawaiian and a medium all meat?"

"No, I feel like having Rusty style pizza tonight, so make it a large with all the meats."

"Ooo, cravings," Brenda said.

"No, I just feel like meat pizza. I haven't had any cravings so far."

"You just wait. I've got three sisters and I'm the only one who hasn't been pregnant. Lisa craved peanut butter ice cream. And it couldn't be just any peanut butter ice cream it had to be Ben and Jerry's and it had to be halfway melted in a waffle cone. When Courtney was pregnant it was Ruffles potato chips. It had to be the ones with ridges and it had to be fried, not baked, and she wanted to dip them in bean dip. She hates beans but she had to have bean dip. Then there was Britney she…"

"Brenda, this pizza's getting cold," we heard from the counter.

"Uh oh, gotta run. One large all meat pizza. Got it."

"No cravings yet?" Rusty asked.

"No, but it wouldn't hurt to order cheesecake just to put them off a little while longer."

"We really should start thinking about a name for this kid," Rusty said.

"Okay, toss out some ideas."

"We need to get one of those name books."

"Why? I bet you can rattle off a hundred names just off the top of your head."

"We need to research famous people of the old west."

"Why? I thought we didn't care about Dad's tradition," I pointed out.

"We don't. But if there's a name out there that fits maybe we can find it."

"Well, I'm ruling out Calamity Jane right now," I said. "We see enough calamity without inviting it onto our kid with a name. Doc Holiday is out. Buffalo Bill. Billy the Kid. Wild Bill Hickok. There sure are a lot of Bills in the old west. Jesse James is out. Wyatt Earp has been taken. So has Pat Garrett."

"Garrett hasn't."

"Garrett Michaels? I guess that would work. I'm sure I can find something I like better."

We never did decide on anything and then the pizza came.

"Britney craved chili cheese dogs from Wienerschnitzel," Brenda continued. "They had to have onions on them. Then, later, she switched to sardines, straight out of the can. Ugh! I don't know how she could stand it."

"If we named a boy Bill it would make both sides happy. He'd be named after an old west figure and your dad," I said.

"I think we can come up with something a little more original than Bill Michaels."

"William?" I asked.

"And what about middle names?"

"I don't have a middle name. A kid doesn't have to have a middle name."

"What do you put if someone insists on a middle initial?"

"A."

"A? But that's not right."

"Yes it is, if you read it right. I'm Cassidy, a Michaels."

"Only you would actually do that."

We didn't get very far on naming the baby. I was having a hard time thinking of any girls' names from the old west. My dad was very creative using Jesse and Cassidy for girls' names but there wasn't much left to choose from. I decided an Internet search was in order to track down more names.

Every night Rusty pulled me close trying to feel the baby move but when

I settled down the baby usually did, too. So far the ice water trick was the best thing I'd found to get him moving. I didn't know why Rusty seemed to feel a connection with his baby when the little thumps and bumps hit his hand. He could lie there for an hour just feeling the taps but I could only take so much ice water.

I had a surprise waiting for me the next day. Everything at the trailer was on an even keel but things on the set were not.

"Can you come out there and just observe? Maybe with you there these things won't happen."

"What's going on?"

"I don't know."

I was getting awfully tired of hearing those words. I thought if Sherri would think a bit she might know more.

"I've just never had shooting be this messed up and interrupted before. Every time I turn around something is going wrong. Just little things, but things that never used to before."

I followed her out to where the shooting took place. I found out acting isn't nearly as glamorous as it looks on TV. It wasn't a matter of acting out a whole scene. Sometimes a scene consisted of just one person performing one small action, like walking towards the camera, or a car zooming past. All the pieces were then cut apart and glued back together into what we saw on the screen. It all felt very disjointed to me. Watching Sherri walk toward the camera in six slightly different ways didn't interest me in the least so I began watching the scene as a whole. I placed Sherri in the middle and watched the periphery. It was like watching for wildlife in the woods. I began to put people in their places. The director had a place and a role. The cameramen did too. Most of them had very predictable actions. I watched a person until they fell neatly into the puzzle. Many groups clicked quickly but there were a few pieces outside the puzzle and those were the ones I needed to watch. Once I narrowed down my focus things became more interesting to me. I was looking for the odd man out.

"Cut! Cut! Sherri, what's going on?"

"I don't know, I just can't focus. There's too many distractions."

"Distractions weren't a problem before."

"I know. I just keep seeing something odd."

My ears perked up. I jumped into the scene. Security jumped in, too, and pulled me back out.

"Wait! Sherri, what's odd. Tell me where to focus," I said as the two men gripped both arms. I shook them loose.

"You can't just step into a scene like that," the director admonished me.

"Okay. I just need something to work with here."

"And who are you?"

I looked to Sherri.

She said, "She's trying to help me catch the guy who's been playing all these tricks on me."

The director's head jerked back around. "You?"

I sure was getting tired of hearing that, too. I knew I wasn't who people expected me to be, but why did everybody have to be so obvious about it?

"Yeah, me," I said. "Believe me, I was just as surprised. Sherri, don't point, but tell me who is distracting you. Even if you don't know what he's doing. Tell me who the odd man out is."

"It's not a man, it's a woman. It's the one over there with the long black hair and the squinty eyes."

"Okay, I'll watch her. Even if you're distracted try to keep going. If she thinks one thing isn't working she'll try something else and the more she tries the more obvious it'll be to me."

Only problem with that plan was that a dozen people had overheard me and then anybody who wasn't directly involved in the scene watched the group of people that contained that woman. With five sets of eyes concentrating on her she just faded back. This had one positive affect. Sherri could work again. But it defeated my purpose. I decided to fade, too. I slipped away and found a quiet place to observe from.

The woman was young, even younger than me. She was slim and she'd be shapely with another ten pounds added. She was in costume so I couldn't tell much about her from her dress. She looked like she wasn't afraid of tarantulas. She looked like she could handle a wrench to loosen bolts on a stairway. She looked bitter. She looked like a smile would break her. I wondered what her motive could be, so I kept watching.

My phone vibrated in my pocket, making me jump. Who would call me here? I checked the caller ID. Spencer Freeman? Who was that? Probably a wrong number. I ignored it knowing I was supposed to keep quiet during shooting. The director said cut and was talking to Sherri again. The phone began vibrating again so I answered it. A wrong number wouldn't take long.

"Hello?" I asked.

"Cassidy? Are you okay?"

Spencer knew my name!

"Yeah, I'm fine."

"Where are you? I can't see you."

"Spike?"

"Yeah."

"Your name is Spencer?"

A sheepish silence. "So I was named as a baby. Nobody knew I'd grow up to look like a Spike."

I thought I better keep that in mind when Rusty and I finally chose a name for our baby.

"Brock told me to keep an eye on you," he said.

"I'm standing behind the props watching a woman who was distracting Sherri. She said shooting had not been going well and asked me to come keep an eye on things."

"I know. I was there when she talked to you. I just lost you."

"Thank you," I said.

"What for?"

"For letting me know I could still disappear. That's what I was trying to do. They're shooting again. Gotta go."

We hung up but off in the distance I could see Spike observing quietly. Guess I *could* use some backup. It couldn't hurt.

I turned back to my suspect. Where did the woman go? I looked to Spike but he was watching me. I looked around. This could be fun, I thought as I found a closer hiding place. Where had she gone? I examined each face in the group. Nope, none of them were her. So where was she? I gave Spike a run for his money as I moved lithely from place to place, trying to see around the site. Finally I gave up and figured I'd have to just track the woman so I approached the group, smiled and greeted them. They seemed puzzled about why I was there, but since they already figured I was weird I found the footprints leading away from the group and followed them. This woman was the odd one in her group, too. Of all the footprints in the area of the group she'd been in hers were different from everybody else's. The soles had no tread. At first the trail led me in the direction of the outhouses but before they got there they veered off to the side. I looked ahead in the direction the footprints led. I took cover and inched around the various structures they had built as props. My cell phone buzzed. The text message said, "Get your ass out of there."

I hadn't lost Spike. I caught a movement up ahead and ducked into hiding. The woman darted away and quickly headed back to the group. What had she been doing over here? Now that I could identify her I wasn't too worried about catching her. I was more interested in pinpointing her activities.

When I was certain she was out of the area I headed back to her tracks and followed them to a set of props. Her tracks stopped and stayed in one place as she briefly did something. But what did she do?

Spike slipped in next to me. "If you hired me as your body guard I'd quit!" he said.

I considered it a compliment so I said, "Thanks again."

"What are you doing?"

"Trying to figure out what she was doing over here."

"Well, whatever she did, it ought to have spectacular results."

"Why?"

"This thing launches a car over an eighteen wheeler. It'll be disguised by then but that's what it's for."

"And who's supposed to be driving this car?"

"I think it's time to call Joe," Spike said. "Go keep an eye on Sherri."

"But, I want to see what she did."

"Joe will have to call in the guy that made this thing. They'll go over it with a fine-toothed comb. And I want you to keep your eye on Sherri."

"You're just trying to get rid of me. If I'd have stuck with Sherri we wouldn't know anything about this. This person doesn't work in front of Sherri. She does things when no one is around and then stands back to watch her work."

"You're getting in too deep. You learn too much and you're likely going to be a target."

"I'm not too worried. Tarantulas and water spouts are nothing compared to what I am used to."

"And what is it you are used to?" he asked turning towards me.

"You wouldn't believe me if I told you."

"Try me."

"You see those mountains?" He looked south. The mountains loomed over us. "You drop me anywhere in those mountains with a hunting knife and magnesium stick and I'll make my out and back home within a week. I'll be fed and I'll be fit and I'll have found water."

"That's not this kind of trouble."

"Okay. See those mountains? I've been chased five miles through them by rifle toting drug dealers. Was that closer to the kind of trouble you were thinking of? How about being left for dead in the middle of the desert with no water? How about spending three days in a collapsed mine tunnel? I've been beaten and shot and kidnapped and dragged through the desert tied to the back of a car. Try and name something that hasn't happened to me."

"Ever been attacked by a bear?"

"Yup, it missed me by a foot or two as I climbed a rope into a tree."

"You've been shot?"

"And pepper sprayed and attacked by dogs."

"And you got a job as a body guard? Sounds more like you need one."

"There's no use in it. They'd quit just like you."

"Hey, I haven't quit yet. But you sure don't make the job easy. First rule of body guarding is: don't lose the body. Now, go keep an eye on Sherri while

I show Joe this problem."

"Those guys can be a royal pain!" I complained to Rusty. "As soon as I run into something that might pay off, they shove me off to the side. They make it sound like it's for my own good but it sure doesn't feel that way. If he weren't three times my size, I'd give him what for…"

"Babe, you only need to do one thing to give that guy a hard time and I'm not going to tell you what it is because he's right to get you out of there. I wish I could."

"At least I only work in the afternoon tomorrow. I told Arnie right up front I had prior commitments Tuesday and Thursday mornings. So I'll be at Farley's school in the morning. I can't wait to see what Bailee thinks of the picture I got."

Chapter 16

"I have a surprise for you after class," I told Bailee. "See if you can complete all the jumps nice and cleanly. Take your time setting them up. Make sure you're seated well, you're balanced just right, and Mack is ready, then take the jump. You tend to rush through the course and that's when you get sloppy. When you get sloppy is when you make mistakes and mistakes can be costly when you're jumping."

She rushed through it again.

"Bailee, you've got to slow down. Think before you act."

"But I want to see what you brought."

"Rushing the jumps isn't going to make the time go by faster. Do the whole course, slowly and cleanly and I'll give it to you. Remember, slow, deliberate and clean. It doesn't mean you have to ride at a walk. You know you need some speed to make the jump. But set up the jump so Mack is sure of it, so you're sure of it, and do it once more."

She really was shaping up into a good rider. She really didn't need me to teach her anything. Other kids needed me worse. Bailee just needed a big sister to check in on her every couple of days and the school was something we had in common. She wanted to grow up to be a horse trainer and the school was the only place she had to work with horses.

"How is school going?" I'd ask her each time. School had become a priority to her since she found out her chances of becoming a horse trainer were more likely if she did well in her studies.

"A lot better. I have a friend. Her name is Alicia. She likes horses, too. She wishes she could ride here, too, but I told her what it took for me to get in here."

Farley's school was for handicapped kids. When Bailee had come here it was after an automobile accident had left her with crippled hands and speech problems. She had opened up and gradually learned to speak clearly again and then surgery on her hands had restored them to nearly normal. If she hadn't already been a student here she probably wouldn't qualify to attend but she had earned Farley's respect and she was still making progress. Farley was not one to stand in the way of progress so Bailee kept to her twice-weekly lessons.

She continued, "She didn't want to go to a handicapped kids' school. I love it here. I understand the kids. When I get old enough maybe Farley will let me teach here, too."

She took all the jumps slowly and cleanly, just like I knew she could, given the right incentive. So I gave her the picture.

"Where'd you get this?" she asked excitedly.

"Brock's body guard gave it to me. I'm working on location and Brock is in the movie."

"You work for *Brock the Rock*?"

"No, but I've talked to him. He's a nice guy. If I play my cards right I might get one from Sherri Champlain, too. We'll just have to wait and see."

"I've got to hear all about this!"

"I can't tell you all about it."

"Chas! That's no fair!"

"If I told you about it you'd tell Alicia and Alicia would tell somebody else and pretty soon the whole school would know. I have to respect Sherri's privacy."

"So you're working for Sherri Champlain? Did she get lost again?"

"No, I can't tell you. Maybe after the movie comes out but that could be a year."

"Arg! This is so exciting and you won't talk!"

"It's not exciting. It's irritating. I have to go to work right after lunch and I just hope everything is still in one piece when I get there."

After Bailee's lesson was over we were standing around peacefully waiting for her mom to pick her up. I checked my phone messages praying there were none and, if there were any, they were to tell me to take the rest of the day off. No such luck. The first message was enough to get me going.

"Aaaahhhh! Cassidy, where are you? Oh gee, get it! You know what to do with wild animals loose in the house! Come quick!"

"Who was that?" Bailee asked. "I could hear it all the way over here."

"That was Sherri. I think I better eat lunch quick. Well, not too quick. Hmm, maybe I ought to let her deal with this for a little while. I think I'll take my time."

The next message was from Arnie.

"I know you're busy but we could use some help out here. We've got two animal control officers here tearing the trailer up to find a snake they say is harmless. I think you had better luck last time this happened. Call me back 555-5555."

"Who was that?"

"Arnie."

"You lead an interesting life."

"Thanks, I guess."

The next message was from Rusty.

"Sherri and her agent are trying to get hold of you. Mind if I just shoot them?"

I'll think about it.

Chapter 17

So much for things being all in one piece, I thought as the trailer came into view. All the furniture that could be removed was crowded up in the walkway between trailers and two men thumped and bumped around inside.

"Is Sherri here?" I asked a person standing nearby.

"No, she went to makeup for a facial and a nervous breakdown."

"Good. Who's inside?"

"Two animal control officers."

"Good. Where's their truck?"

"Right over there," he said pointing.

"So far so good." I went over to the truck, grabbed their pole with a loop on the end and took it to the trailer. *Knock, knock.*

The door opened a crack. "Yeah?" a guy asked.

"Mind if I help?" I asked.

"You're crazy. We're chasing a snake."

"What kind?"

"Corn snake, harmless. What are you doing with our pole?"

"I've used one to catch snakes before."

"Ha! You?"

"Ha! Yeah, me." Again. I entered the trailer. "When you took out the furniture you took out all its hiding places. You're just upsetting it chasing it around with your bare hands. Just stop. Sit down and let the snake settle."

"And why should we listen to you?"

"You don't have to. I'll go away and let you work or you can sit there for half an hour or so and watch me work. Which would you rather do?"

They were hot, tired and very frustrated but their honor was on the line. Could they let this little pipsqueak upstage them?

"What have we got to lose?" the big hairy one asked.

"Our dignity," the little guy answered.

"As long as we return with the snake, who cares how we got it?"

"We got to fill out the report."

"I don't care what you put in your report," I told them. "Sherri called me to have a snake caught so I'm here to catch it."

"Sherri... called you... to catch a snake for her."

"Yeah, me."

"Why?"

"I guess because I caught the tarantula."

"You? Caught a tarantula?"

"Yeah me."

The big hairy guy rocked back on his heels and folded his arms over his chest, grinning. "This oughta be good. I say we sit and watch. I want some popcorn. This'll be a blast."

Just then the door opened and Spike walked in. Oh, great.

"Spike, don't tell me you are scared of snakes, too."

Spike looked at the two animal control officers. He couldn't say he was scared of snakes with them there.

"Me? No. Need help?"

"Just have a seat and let the snake settle down."

We all had a seat and silence descended on the trailer.

"It's getting away," the little guy said.

"It's easy to spot. When it settles down it'll be easy to catch," I assured them.

"You haven't spent the past two hours chasing it," the little guy pointed out.

"Once the snake is calm and I find it, I'll catch it in just a few minutes. What are you going to do with it after it's caught?"

"We'll have to take it back to Animal Control."

"You have snake cages at Animal Control?"

"Sure."

"Do people actually come there looking for lost pet snakes?"

"Not often, but sometimes."

After a short wait, I stood and addressed the guys. "Okay, I'm going to go find it. You can watch, but stay out of the way and don't make loud noises. The whole idea is to keep the snake calm. Think like a snake. Snakes are slow when they're calm. Think slow and quiet."

I took the pole, made sure the loop closed enough to hold a snake gently. Then I went through the trailer with my little troop of skeptics behind me. I could tell when I was close because I could feel Spike stiffen. He backed against the wall. The animal control officers laughed at him silently. I spotted the snake nosing the crack next to the closet door. I hoped it didn't try to go under the door. It could do that easily. I lowered the loop toward the snake's head. I followed the snake doing my best to make everything seem nice and calm. No sudden lunges. When it lowered its head and nosed the crack under the door I put the loop on the floor in front of it so if it tried to go under I could pull the loop closed. It took a bit of following and some patience. I could have caught it a few times but I wanted it to be in a place where I wouldn't have to jerk it around, so I patiently followed it until it was a little more out in the open. I let a large loop of rope out from the pole and set it in front of the snake. The snake paused and investigated the rope but found nothing threatening about it. I let the snake slither through the loop, gently pulled the loop smaller. I didn't pull it tight. I didn't want to frighten the snake. When the loop was small and the snake was having a little struggle moving though it I laid the pole down and walked to the end. I picked up the snake gently and treated it like I would a pet and it responded in kind.

"Anybody got a bag?" I asked. "Spike? You want to pet it?" I stepped closer offering the snake to him and he dashed out the door. The big hairy guy produced a bag and I placed the snake inside. He pulled the drawstring top closed and stood back again.

"Hey," I said. "Were either of you on that call up on the mountain where they had a bear full of downers?"

"No, we were chasing down a stray donkey that was walking down the road. How'd you hear about that?" the little guy said.

"I found it. I was tracking the girl who left that camp."

"Somehow that does not surprise me in the least," the big guy said.

"If you see the pictures the officer took they show me petting the sleeping bear."

"What are we going to write in the report?" the little guy asked the big guy.

I offered my opinion, "Just say, the snake was finally caught using a pole and bagged for transport. Usually as long as there's no one to question the report it just gets filed."

The big guy nodded, thinking it over.

"Well, we'll be off. Tell Sherri if she has any more problems with snakes to call *you*."

"Gee, thanks."

They carried the bag gingerly checking the drawstring to make sure it was still secure. I followed them out of the trailer.

"I might catch snakes," I said. "But I am not moving all this furniture back up the stairs."

The guys waiting outside jumped to attention and went to find the proper furniture movers.

"Do you have to be gone all morning?" Sherri asked.

"Why does it matter? This person seems to work whether I am here or not. Did you have your screen fixed? The snake may have come in the same way the tarantula did."

"No, it's just a little hole."

"Just big enough for another snake or tarantula. The snake was harmless. Kids keep those snakes as pets. There was no need to be scared of it. But if you don't want uninvited guests, get the screen fixed and close your window."

"How am I supposed to know if it's harmless? I'm not a snake scientist."

"Neither am I but I've seen corn snakes in pet stores. The officers said it was a corn snake."

"Well, you're a normal person. You're allowed to go to pet stores without a crowd of people following you. I haven't been to a pet store since I was six years old."

Hey, I thought, she called me a normal person! Most people accused me of being decidedly not normal.

"Do you have a dog?" I asked.

"No, I'm not in one place long enough to have a pet. Do you?"

"Yes, I have a sheltie named Shadow."

"That's cool."

"He sits, lies down, stands, jumps, and shakes hands on command. He has an obstacle course in the backyard that he runs every night."

"That's weird." So much for normality. She went on, "I wish I could live in a real house. I wish I could just go to the store. I wish I could go places without hiding. I wish guys liked me for just me. I wish I could have home cooking with no fancy garnishes."

"I've got company coming Thursday evening. You're welcome to join us," I offered.

I wasn't really expecting company but I would be if Sherri said yes.

"Any cute guys?"

"Single?" I asked.

"Of course."

"Landon?" She knew Landon from her little stint up on the mountain. Landon had flown with her to the hospital.

"That might be fun."

"Actually, the person I was expecting is a little girl I teach horseback riding to. But maybe I can get Landon to come, too."

"Your company is a kid?"

"Yeah, she doesn't get much attention at home so she likes coming to my house, and helping me cook. She loves my dog. Her name is Bailee."

"Small group. Home cooking. Why not?"

"What's home cooking to you?" I asked.

"Fried chicken with mashed potatoes and milk gravy, carrots and corn on the cob with butter on it. No dessert."

"Bailee will expect chocolate cake."

She gave me a pleading look but I stood firm. "You don't have to eat it. But Bailee never gets any sweets at home. To her it's a real treat."

"Just the fried chicken is pushing it for me. But I'm *dying* for fried chicken."

"Mrs. Roland? This is Cassidy. I was hoping Bailee could come over to my house for dinner Thursday. I have a guest coming that she would like to meet."

"Who is it? It's not that boy, Randy, is it?"

"No, it isn't Randy. I'd rather she not know who it is until she gets there."

"As long as it's not that boy. He's too old for her and she'll be unbearable if she sees him again."

Bailee had fallen head over heels in love with Randy when she had visited my parent's ranch. I didn't blame Mrs. Roland for discouraging Bailee when it came to Randy.

"No it's not Randy. It'll just be Rusty and I, Landon and a friend from work. But don't tell Bailee that because she'll guess. Just tell her she's welcome to have dinner at Cassidy's house on Thursday."

"Does she need a ride?"

"Rusty can pick her up on his way home."

"All right."

Next was Landon.

"Hello?"

"Landon? This is Cass, I was wondering if you'd do me a favor."

"Um, sure."

"Can you come over for dinner Thursday?"

"How is coming over for dinner doing you a favor?"

"I have a guest who would like to see you."

"Is she single?"

"Yeah."

"I'll be there."

"Actually, you've already met this person. I guess I should be honest with you."

"That sounds like a good idea. Is it your great aunt Matilda?"

"No, it's Sherri Champlain."

"You've got to be kidding."

"No, I've been playing body guard to Sherri and she was saying how she never gets home cooked food, so I invited her over."

"You've got something up your sleeve. I still don't see how doing this is a favor to you."

"You were kind of a package deal."

"Uh huh? And?"

"Okay, I admit the whole purpose of this dinner is so Bailee can get an autographed picture of Sherri and meet her in person. But Sherri wanted to see you."

"Me?"

"And fried chicken, mashed potatoes, carrots, and corn on the cob."

"And cheesecake?"

"No, chocolate layer cake."

"You like cheesecake."

"Bailee likes chocolate layer cake."

"No cheesecake?"

"Oh, all right! I'll pick up a cheesecake, too."

"You know you want cheesecake. How have you been feeling?"

At least it wasn't the first thing he asked me.

"I'm fine. I chased a corn snake today."

"Not a rattlesnake?"

"No."

"I'm disappointed in you. Normally it would be a rattlesnake."

"Sorry."

"I'll be there."

"Dinner at eight? I have to work first. You can come earlier but I think eight is the soonest I can have dinner for five on the table."

"Gotcha."

Chapter 18

Wednesday made me question whether or not there was going to be a Thursday for me. It was the day we jumped the eighteen wheeler. I say "we" even though I had nothing to do with it because when you are on the set and a big stunt takes place everybody is so into it. It's like we're all doing it. As each little step unfolds it gets ticked off in your mind and when the car lands, or doesn't land, in its allotted space on the other side we all react as one. There are high fives. There are sighs of relief. There is a sense of accomplishment. And even though everybody feels their own thing it all jumbles up and we think, we did it!

The prop had been inspected and any problems had been corrected. It no longer appeared to be a giant car launcher. It looked like part of a highway median.

The traffic patterns in a take like this are more like dance choreography. Everybody knew their proper place. Everybody moved in sync. Seventy, eighty, ninety miles per hour. A very fast and furious automotive dance. Everybody followed the plan and everything worked except for one tiny glitch. One little glitch where "Cut!" had no effect.

There's not much a bodyguard can do when the body you are supposed to guard is hurtling down a stretch of road at ninety miles per hour. There's not much I could do when I was focused on my job and suddenly, what I was afraid would befall Sherri, got directed instead to me.

The car Sherri and Brock were in was filmed racing down the highway. The taping was stopped and the stunt doubles were called in. They were ready for the jump. We all watched with bated breath as the plan was set in motion. The cars jockeyed for position. There was the planned screeching of brakes. The planned skidding around, the planned burst of speed, the car swerved, hit the median and went flying over the eighteen wheeler. It landed with another screech and a lurching on the other side. There was the director's, "Cut! Great job everybody!" High fives all around. And the next thing I knew a blue Cadillac Deville was skidding straight toward me on the outskirts of the group, ignoring the cut. It felt like a freight train hit me and next thing I knew medics were standing over me. The woman driving the Deville was standing aside shaking and telling her side of the story. Spike and Brock were standing aside talking in hushed, worried tones. I struggled to get up. Davin squatted beside me so he could look me in the eyes.

"You lucked out," he said.

"I'm good at that," I replied.

"Spike knocked you flat. I'm not sure which is more dangerous, a Cadillac or Spike but he was at least as gentle as he could be. Your husband's on his way."

"Rusty? Why?"

"Standard procedure in an emergency."

"What emergency?"

"Cassidy, you were knocked out. There's an ambulance on the way. We called Rusty. It's just standard procedure. He said you wouldn't go in and that he was on his way."

"Damn."

"Why?"

"He knows me too good."

At least the ambulance crew didn't include Landon this time. If it did I'd have had a bigger fight on my hands. The EMTs descended on me and probably did everything the medics on site had already done. They decided I didn't have any broken bones. They were mostly worried about concussion and the baby. They had pulled the stretcher out of the ambulance and I was standing there arguing that I definitely did NOT need a trip to the hospital, when Rusty strode up. Rats.

He wore that worried look that made me sad and irritated at the same time. He wrapped me in that hug I was so used to now. "Cass, what am I going to do with you? You can't stick with this. You *are* going to get checked out. There's no way you can get out of it. I'm not taking any chances. You can go with them or with me. But you *are* going. I've already called Doctor Ron."

"Okay, Cassidy, what happened this time?" Doctor Ron asked. He was standing there in his white coat, arms folded. Rusty stood beside him wanting to hear my explanation, too.

"A human train wreck tried to save me from a human/Cadillac wreck," I explained as simply as I could.

"What?!" both men said at once.

"We were filming a car stunt and one of the cars was heading straight at me and Spike tackled me right before the car plowed through the place I was standing. I think I hit my head but other than that I'm fine."

"Up on the table."

Doctors and EMTs have learned there's no use being polite with me. Here's what you're doing, now do it, is the attitude they have taken. Doctor Ron shined a light in my eyes, felt for bumps.

"You've got quite a knot back here."

"Does it match the five or six others?"

"Not quite."

"Spike can't help it if I landed wrong. He was just trying to save my hide. Apparently he succeeded, although I did have a plan on how to deal with the Cadillac."

"Which was?" Rusty asked.

"Run like hell," I admitted.

Then there was the other exam, which Doctor Ron wasn't as concerned about.

"Babies are very well protected from bumps and falls. Now if that car had hit you, I'd insist on further tests. But I think, if you will go home and rest and watch for anything suspicious, we'll find out that the baby is fine."

He poked and prodded.

"He's growing nicely. You sure you don't want to know the sex of the baby?"

"No!" Rusty and I said in unison.

"Do you know?" I asked.

"No," he admitted. "But it wouldn't be hard to find out. Just a routine test that I'd have run if you *had* been hit by the car would have told us." He looked at me seriously. "You will take off the rest of the day. Do you hear me?"

"She hears you," Rusty said and I knew I was due for an afternoon's house arrest.

As we were leaving the building I informed Rusty, "We can't take the day off completely. We have dinner guests coming tomorrow and I need to go grocery shopping."

"Does anything slow you down? When were you going to do it if you didn't accidentally get the afternoon off?"

"Very late tonight. And we need to go get my Jeep."

"You're going to go home. You're going to take it easy. If you need something from the store I'll go get it later."

"What about my Jeep?"

"We'll stop by on the way home."

I had to be content with that.

Sending guys out grocery shopping was dangerous but there wasn't much I could do about it. I was stuck. Funny how I was more worried about what Rusty might come home from the store with than I was about having a concussion.

We pulled up to the gate and I explained to the guard that I just needed my Jeep. He allowed me to walk in to it. I hopped in and eased it out the gate and followed Rusty toward home. When we reached the open road he sped up. I pushed on the gas pedal and crept up on him. A mile or so later, he slowed down for a turn and I eased up. Only problem was the Jeep didn't ease up. Rusty turned but I couldn't! I was going too fast to make the turn. I sped through the intersection. I tried to remember what to do if the gas pedal sticks. First I tried pumping it to feel the movement. Big mistake it just sped up, but didn't slow down. Grateful for nice straight roads, I tried prying the pedal up with my toe. It didn't budge. I tried reaching down and pulling on it. It still wouldn't budge. I looked at the speedometer. Sixty. Hell. I could keep this up for a little while but eventually I was going to hit town or hills. I had to do something before I got to town! I couldn't stop and I wouldn't make it through without a serious accident. I felt a rush of adrenaline and that didn't help at all. I fought the panic it brought with it. I focused on the road. I zipped through four way stops, counting my lucky stars there was nobody on these back roads. The road began turning as it made its way into the foothills. I nervously screeched around the turns using both lanes. I rounded a turn and heard a horn blaring, saw a grill coming at me and jerked the wheel aside. The jeep went up an embankment, launched itself into the air and came down with a thump. It sped off through the desert and began slowing. What happened? Why was it slowing? It settled into a crawl and came to a lurching stop in a large mesquite. Pushing branches aside, I stumbled out, shaking.

I was sitting on the ground trying to make sense of the past fifteen minutes when my cell phone rang.

"Where are you going?" Rusty asked.

"Nowhere. Come get me."

"What happened?"

"My gas pedal stuck! I didn't know what to do!"

"Where are you?"

"Go back to where I didn't turn and then look for a mess of cars."

Long pause.

"Are you okay?"

"Yeah, I'm not hurt. But…"

"I'm on my way," he said as I heard the screech of tires in a high speed U-turn.

When my nerves had settled I thought I better check on the other driver. I followed my tracks back toward the road but I was met by a posse of angry people.

"Crazy woman driver!" a fat man in a plumber's uniform grumbled as he waddled up the hill. Behind him was a parade of people. Mr. Plumber saw me and started in on me, red-faced, "How did you manage to get a driver's license? Damn it woman, you're a menace to society. Just wait until the police get here! You're in for a surprise then!"

I was still shaky but mentioning the police calmed me a little. No, I thought, you're in for a surprise.

The woman behind the plumber noticed my condition and stared open mouthed.

"Is everybody okay?" I asked. "Any injuries?"

"No thanks to you!" Mr. Plumber yelled.

"Look, I'm sorry. My gas pedal was stuck down. I couldn't stop! I was just trying to stay on the road. I don't know why it finally slowed down."

This caught the attention of another guy in a mechanic's uniform. He marched past and we all followed him to the Jeep. "You probably knocked it into neutral when you landed," he explained. He opened the driver's door and looked around.

"Don't touch it," I warned him.

"And whatcha goin' to do to stop him, crazy woman driver?" Mr. Plumber said.

The woman cut in, "You leave her alone! Can't you see you're just making things worse?"

"Mommy, I'm going to be late for my soccer game!" wailed a little girl behind the woman.

"Don't worry," she said. "Your coach will understand. There's a few things more important than soccer."

This mom is *not* a soccer mom, I thought.

The mechanic pulled his head out of the Jeep just as Rusty jogged up the hill. "Somebody doesn't like you much," Mr. Mechanic said. "Someone rigged your gas pedal."

Rusty clasped me tight. "Are you sure you're all right?"

"Yes, I was wearing my seatbelt. I just held on and rode it out."

"Why didn't you just stick it in neutral?"

"I didn't think of that. I was thinking too far ahead. I was trying to figure out how to stop before I got to town. I was lucky I got forced off the road."

"Forced off the road!" the plumber said. "Yeah, make it look like it's all my fault, will ya? I tell you, if I'd have been the one to go off the road you'd have a lawsuit on your hands!"

"Mister," Rusty said. "Shut up."

"You just wait! As soon as the police get here we'll see!"

"I *am* the police," Rusty said calmly. "You and you, stay behind. Anybody who wasn't a witness to the accident please go back to your car. You may leave now."

Instead of instilling calm the crowd got all riled up again.

"We can't!" someone yelled. "There's a %@#& plumber's van blocking all the lanes! There's half a mile of cars backed up down there."

About this time we started hearing sirens. I wanted to disappear. This would be all over the station within hours. Rusty slipped into cop mode. He sorted people out according to how much they knew. When that was over we were left with me, Mr. Plumber, the mom, kid, and the mechanic. The mechanic hadn't witnessed the accident but he knew what had been done to my gas pedal.

"That was cool!" the kid said. "You shoulda seen your car! It was like a movie! It went up the hill and into the air like... like. Mom what's that flying car in that old, old movie you saw when you were a little kid?"

"Chitty Chitty Bang Bang," the mom answered.

"Yeah! Like that, except your car didn't keep going. You need wings on that thing."

"I think I'd prefer a working gas pedal," I told her.

Ben Tomlin jogged onto the scene. A big smile appeared when he saw who he was dealing with. Ben was young, energetic and one of the first officers I met after I'd gotten to know Rusty a little bit.

"Ben, take this guy's report," Rusty said indicating the mechanic. "I'll go get traffic flow under control and meet the other responding officers."

Ben looked disappointed. He wanted the full story. But the mechanic sparked his interest by saying, "Get a load of this. You got yourself a case here."

Rusty put an arm around me and guided me down the hill. Oh man! Where did all the cars come from? I was glad they were elsewhere while I was fighting the gas pedal! Cars were honking. Curious drivers were walking up the line of cars. People who had a sunroof were standing with their heads out the top. They all pointed when we appeared at the top of the hill. A black and white cruised up the wrong side of the road and pulled off out of the way. The officer jumped out and looked in the plumber's van.

"Who's the driver of this vehicle?" he barked.

Mr. Plummer reluctantly raised a finger and stepped forward to correct the traffic situation. One by one they found the cars that belonged to witnesses and moved them aside. An officer stood by directing traffic to move in a slow, controlled manner. The mom gave a quick concise report and was allowed to leave. The little girl put in her two cents worth in about just how far my car had flown up in the air and how many times it had bounced coming down. "It was like Tigger! Boing, boing! Mom was scared, but I thought it was cool!" Rusty did not need to hear this.

Mr. Plumber gave his report with much yelling and gesticulating and comments about "that crazy woman".

The officers regrouped and compared reports, then turned to me. Ben placed another form on top of his clipboard and stepped forward.

"How about if I just fill it in myself," I volunteered.

"You'll probably do that, too. We want to hear it firsthand."

"I don't know where to start."

"Start with who rigged your gas pedal and then tell us what happened."

"I don't know who rigged my gas pedal. I have an idea but I can't prove it without tracking her and even then the tracks could be long gone by now if people have been walking over the parking lot."

"Why would someone try and knock you off?"

"Because I'm me?" I asked.

"Not good enough."

"Because they are up to no good and I have been trying to stop them and they don't like it?" I asked.

There was a big frustrated shifting of the ranks.

"Okay, tell us about the gas pedal. We'll get the back story from Rusty."

And so it went, a quick telling of the sticky pedal story.

Dwight Stafford folded his arms, "I like the kid's version better."

"I was too busy hanging on to worry about any similarities to Chitty Chitty Bang Bang," I said.

"Who tampered with your gas pedal?"

"I don't have a name. I don't have proof."

"A description?"

"Okay, if it was the same person I've been watching she's younger than me, a hundred pounds, long black hair, small eyes."

"Height?"

"Five six? A little taller than me."

"Dress?"

"She's an actress. I've only seen her in costume."

"Costume?"

"Evil biker chic, although so far she has driven a car."

"That sounds fitting. Attractive?"

"She would be if she could find a way to be pleasant. Something is eating at her. It's been eating at her for a long time. She's forgotten how to be nice."

"Do you know how many high school kids resemble this description?"

"Yeah. Look guys, I'd love to sit out here and chat but I'm supposed to be resting off a concussion and I need to go grocery shopping for a dinner tomorrow."

"A concussion?"

"This is my second disaster of the day."

"Oh man, you're making up for lost time. How long has it been?" Ben said.

"I'm going home," I announced. "If you need anything else call tomorrow."

A tow truck pulled up. The guys would have my Jeep towed to the station.

Rusty practically dragged me to the old brown couch, ignoring Shadow, who was running around us barking a friendly greeting. When Rusty was like this, he just needed time. Time to make the world feel right again. I wondered what Davin had told him when he called. Something about a car and an unconscious Cassidy. That would have sent Rusty into a panic. Okay, I conceded, he needed this time.

"What a day," he said.

"It definitely wasn't boring."

"You can't imagine my fear when Davin called," he said quietly.

"It always sounds worse than it is," I reminded him.

"So far. It doesn't have to turn out that way though. If there's one thing I've learned at work it's that things can always get worse. And when they get worse they get worse in a hurry. Worse than what I heard was... I didn't even want to think about it. All I knew was I had to be there."

"Let's change the subject. You'll feel better if you put it behind us."

"Who's coming for dinner tomorrow?"

"Sherri, Landon, and Bailee."

"That's an odd mix. How did that happen?"

"Sherri missed home cooked food. I told her I was having company and she was welcome to join us. She wanted to know if my company included any single guys so I roped Landon into coming."

"How'd Bailee get into this mess?"

"Bailee is an autograph hound. Every time I do something that involves Sherri she brings me something to autograph. I thought she'd like to get Sherri's autograph. She doesn't know Sherri's coming. She thinks she is just coming for dinner. Can you pick her up on the way home from work?"

"If you survive tomorrow."

"I'll survive tomorrow. I promise. I only work in the afternoon, but how will I get out there? I have to go to Farley's school and then out to the site."

"The Jeep will be at the station being processed as evidence."

"I know, but I need my Jeep."

"You need this person behind bars. If your Jeep will help put an end to this job, it'll get processed. I need you to put together what you know of the case. Was the woman driving the car the same one that has been pulling pranks on Sherri?"

"I think so. She's an actress. She only has minor parts. I don't understand her motive in all this."

"I don't suppose I can get you to quit."

"All I have to do is catch her at it. I can't prove anything yet but just let me at her. I'll figure it out."

"Not today. Let me hold you. Let me feel that baby move. Let me fall asleep with you in my arms."

He was really rattled. I had to remember I was risking more now. I felt it, but it really came into focus seeing it through Rusty. I carried his hopes and his dreams. He loved this baby. He had a very protective nature and it had expanded since I'd become pregnant. When I got things into perspective it wasn't such an imposition to just snuggle with him on the couch. Part of me was working on the puzzle at work. Part of me was antsy to get dinner planned for tomorrow. But I knew, right now, I needed to just be here, soaking up his warmth, showing him all was well, hoping it really was. He put a hand on my stomach to feel the baby but the baby was sleeping, or at least quiet. I wondered if he had had a busy day, too. I wondered if my baby had felt the same adrenaline rush that I had. I was too busy reacting to the situation to notice if he was more or less active. I hoped he didn't feel alarmed if that rush of adrenaline had hit him the way it hit me. So tiny, I thought, he was so tiny, he didn't need to feel my fears. It's okay little one. No fears. I snuggled closer.

"Can I feel him?" Rusty asked.

"Soon, let him rest. I need to feel him be at peace."

There was a gentle understanding silence. I think it was the first time Rusty had heard me identify with the child within me. It calmed him knowing I felt for him. Her? In a way I wish I knew. But we were at peace. All three of us. I just needed it to stay that way for a few minutes longer.

Junior stayed quiet for a while but when he began moving again the little taps brought a wave of relief. He was okay. He didn't feel distressed. I put Rusty's hand where he could feel it.

When everyone was at ease again it was time to go shopping.

"Let me go," Rusty said, "I'd feel better if you stayed home."

I knew it was dangerous sending a guy grocery shopping alone but to push might make the evening even tougher. So I made a list and sent him on his way. An hour later Rusty began finding out why it was easier for me to just go myself. My cell phone rang.

"What kind of chicken?" Rusty asked.

"Just get a frying chicken cut up. It doesn't even have to be cut up. I can cut it up."

"It would be easier if you didn't have to, though."

"Okay, so get one cut up."

"But we like white meat."

"So?"

"There isn't much white meat on one chicken."

"So get two."

"Okay."

Five minutes later.

"How many potatoes do you need?"

"A bag."

"What size bag?"

"Ten pounds."

"What kind?"

"I don't know. Not the little red ones, get the big brown ones."

"What kind of corn on the cob?"

"Whatever they have."

"Fresh or frozen?"

I should have just gone to the store. I called him back.

"I forgot dessert. Bailee will expect chocolate cake but Landon insisted on cheesecake."

"He only asked for cheesecake for you."

"I know but he still insisted. I told him I'd get one."

"Whole milk or low fat?"

"It doesn't matter. It's for gravy. Sherri wanted milk gravy."

"Low fat."

"Okay."

A minute later.

"How did they come up with so many different kinds of cooking oil? I mean, it's just *oil*."

"Most women would say the same thing about motor oil. Get canola."

"What kind of motor oil should I get?"

"Ten-thirty."

"Good girl."

"Were you able to rest at all?" he asked as he carried in the groceries.

Rest? Yeah right.

Chapter 19

Thursday was Bailee's lesson. Rusty didn't like it but I rode the motorcycle to the riding school. I didn't have any choice. My Jeep was gone. He took the Explorer to work because it had his gear in it. I liked the motorcycle. It was fast, efficient and, I was hoping, tamper proof. Okay, so it had been tampered with before but I didn't think any movie extra was going to know how to wire a gas tank to explode.

"Can I come home with you after riding?" Bailee asked.

"No, I have to work after lunch. Rusty will pick you up on the way home from work."

"Who else is coming? My mom said it was a surprise."

"Your mom talks too much."

"Aw, come on Chas. Just a hint?"

"Nope. You're doing better on the barrels. I wonder if Farley will throw a fit if we try for a winning run."

"I don't know. He's such a control freak."

"I know. But you have to admit for most of these kids that's a good thing."

"How fast is a winning run?"

"Under fifteen seconds."

"Do you think Mack can do that?"

"No. He'll try, but if you pit him against a younger, fitter horse they will beat him every time."

"But I can try, can't I?"

"Sure you can try. You have to maintain control though. The more command you show in the saddle the more Farley will let you try. He has to know that *you know* what you are doing. If you goof around he's going to come down on you. So take this seriously. Take the run like a horse trainer. Watch for little things you need to work on. Then work on those things."

"I don't know how to work on problems. I just know how to ride."

"You'll see something. Run the barrels and then tell me what you find when you get back."

She ran the barrels and, sure enough, she had found something to work on.

"When I come out of a turn I have to already have the next barrel in mind. Finishing the turn and then looking for the next barrel takes too long."

"All right! That was a good observation! It'll shave seconds off your time if you can come out of the turn at just the right moment to head for the next barrel."

I ran home, changed into my uniform, ate lunch and took off for work.

"Can I use my old parking permit for a motorcycle?" I asked the guard.

"Let me update your info. Kawasaki, 250. You want a primo parking spot?"

"No, any old parking place will do."

"See where the other motorcycles are parked? Go over there."

I rode up feeling like my little street legal dirt bike was outclassed. Goldwings and vintage Harleys stood gleaming, freshly dusted after a ride through the desert. Davin stood at the end of the lot, arms folded, grinning.

"What's that?" he asked.

"It's called a Jeep substitute. My Jeep kind of had problems on the way home yesterday. Joe might want to know about it. In fact, I suggest he get a full police report on the incident."

"Oh yeah? What happened?"

"Let's just say it was a sticky situation."

"Honey on your shoes?"

"A sticky gas pedal."

"That can happen. Did you unstick it?"

"No, it's still stuck. I have a little experience if I ever want a job as a stunt double. I did my own version of jumping an eighteen-wheeler, only I was missing a truck to jump over. I landed on the other side, accidentally hit the shift lever into neutral and coasted to a stop. Tied up traffic for an hour. Made a plumber really mad."

"Are you charmed or jinxed?" he asked.

"I think I'm both. How's Sherri?"

"She'll be better when she sees you here. Shooting was canceled after the stunt yesterday because she was in such a state she couldn't do anything."

"The stunt yesterday was a good take though. It was quite an accomplishment to pull it off."

"Do you always give the EMTs such a hard time?"

"You wouldn't believe. There's a standing joke amongst the rescue crews that I'm only allowed one call per station per week. They all know me. They've either worked with me or been called to some disaster I got myself into. I even heard rumors that they were going to create a special radio code for me but that got stopped pretty quick. The higher ups said they couldn't use nonstandard radio codes because it would confuse the outsiders."

We talked as we walked to Sherri's trailer. Davin knocked on the wall outside. There was no answer.

"You want a lift to the set?"

"Sure."

They were between takes when Davin and I arrived. He had to get back to his post so he dropped me off. The director was having a group discussion so I walked around out of the way wondering if Miss Congeniality was present. I didn't see her but she could have been tucked away in any of a half dozen cars. I looked around for Spike but knew he tried to stay in the background. He probably wasn't pleased to see me back so soon.

"Ooooooo Cassidy! You're back!" Sherri said. "Arnie said not to expect you back, money or no. He said almost getting run over by a car was enough to scare off anybody."

"Arnie doesn't know me very well. Every time this person tries something they give me more clues. Has anything happened that I should know about?"

"No. Yesterday afternoon's shooting was canceled and then this morning Brock and I have been working together. We'll start back in sequence tomorrow."

"So the extras aren't here?"

"No, it's been a quiet day."

"Well, whoever our wayward extra is, she was busy yesterday afternoon. She seems to be more focused on me right now."

"Are we still on for dinner tonight?"

"Sure, why wouldn't we be?"

"You were out cold twenty-four hours ago. I wouldn't expect you to have dinner guests after nearly being run over."

"I was still planning on it."

"Good, I'm still dying for good old fashioned fried chicken."

"How'd I end up out cold?"

"Spike doesn't know his own strength."

"He does when it comes to spiders and snakes," I added.

"Well, he was more like, the girl's still alive, job well done. I was debating which was more powerful, Spike or the car. At least Spike isn't quite made out of metal."

"I hope he wasn't hurt. I've been watching for him."

"He's around. If Brock's around, he's around."

"Brock must know something. He sent Spike to watch out for me. He wouldn't do that unless he suspected something was afoot."

"Something *is* afoot, but I don't think it's dangerous."

"It was dangerous yesterday. Two close calls in one day is even pushing it for me."

"Two?"

"While I was at the doctor getting checked out our extra was tampering with my Jeep. It could have been much worse than it was."

"How can we know anything is safe?"

"We can't."

"This used to be funny. It isn't funny anymore. It quit being funny a long time ago."

"Look, I'm not doing you much good. If you fired me Rusty would be glad. I don't care about the money. At first I did. I thought it would make a good college fund for the baby. But, hell, my dad will take care of college. It's not the money. Why don't you hire somebody who can really protect you? I wear this gun, but I wouldn't use it. I've only shot people in a life and death situation and I still have nightmares about it."

"You've shot people?"

"Yeah, a time or two."

"What if we put you under cover? Then you could hang out with the extras and just be one of them."

"I'm not an actress."

"So? All you have to do is be in costume and do what the director says. It can be really boring, because if they don't need extras for a shot you end up spending a lot of time waiting. But you could spend that time talking to the others…"

"Watching the girl who seems to be after us, establishing a motive and getting myself killed."

"But if we can just catch her, maybe we can stop her. I could hire another Spike but we've made progress. Another bodyguard would just be starting from scratch. I'm willing to stick this out, if you are."

"Tell me what the focus is here? I started out watching the trailer. Now we're way out here on the set."

"This person has to be stopped. All we need is proof. Let's put you in the movie. You'll be in on the shooting. You can move amongst the people. You can see things you might otherwise miss. You'll still be on hand if my trailer gets invaded. We need to talk to Nickolai."

"But I don't want to be an actress. What are they going to do with a five months pregnant extra?"

"Shoot from behind. Come on. We can figure out something you can do."

"I say we ask Spike if he has a brother and I go home and be a housewife." I couldn't believe I was saying these things. Usually I wanted to be in the thick of things. I still found this interesting but it felt wrong to subject Junior to the things that could happen in the near future. Reluctantly I followed Sherri as she met with her director and then I saw a real acting job.

"Come on Nick. Cassidy needs to get inside the group of extras." Big hound doggy eyes.

"Don't do that," Nickolai Danti said. He was a middle-aged man already set in his ways. He had a kindness about him that helped when it came to getting what he wanted out of actors. He came alongside them sometimes even getting into the scene himself. In one scene he had actually played a hotdog vendor because he reviewed the take and liked it, director's clothes and all.

"We're only going to be here for two more weeks, but I can't take two more weeks like the last two. Cassidy can put a stop to these pranks. I know she can. Put her in the works."

Nickolai turned to me. "What experience do you have?"

"None, I've never acted in my life."

"Oh, yes you have," Sherri said, "Don't tell me you never asked your dad for a car or a horse. That takes real acting."

"We had horses all over the place. I drove the ranch truck when I was twelve."

"Don't tell him that!" Sherri admonished.

"Sorry."

"What is your normal job?" Nickolai asked.

"I'm a tracker. If given the right set of circumstances I can play a cop."

"A cop? You?"

"Well, I prefer not to but I've got plenty of training. I was in the Marines, I've been through police reserve academy. I can bust down a door, leap a six foot fence, run five miles, and out shoot half the force. I just hope I never have to."

Nickolai stood there for a moment running his fingers through his goatee.

"You can do all that?" Sherri asked.

"Give me a police line or two, actions and everything," Nick said.

Oh hell, I didn't want to do this. The few times I'd actually used my police training it had failed miserably. I looked like a kid playing cops and robbers. Only problem was it was real robbers wielding real guns. I took out my pistol and emptied the bullets. I wasn't taking any chances on accidentally firing the thing. I glanced around, chose a "suspect" turned, drew my empty gun and yelled in the deepest voice I could muster, "Police! Freeze! Put your hands over your head!" The woman stopped and turned, blanched when she saw the gun and put her hands tentatively over her head. I lowered my weapon, "Sorry, Mr. Danti told me to," I explained.

Nick wasn't through with me. It was quite a little audition I put on right there on the set. "This picnic table is a police car. That building holds a dangerous criminal with a hostage. Just show me the posture a cop uses in these situations."

"Well, I assume you mean the crouching behind the car type posture, though unless there is shooting going on they are just as likely to be standing around talking."

I crouched behind the picnic table, gun aimed over the "hood" of the car, head low.

Nick flipped open his cell phone, "Spike, where are you?... Okay, stay there. Cassidy is doing a little audition here. Call me back when she closes in on you." He snapped his phone shut and turned to me, "You get the picture? I want you to find Spike like you were looking for a suspect. Just do what comes naturally."

Double hell. What was I getting myself into? I didn't know where Spike was hiding. Okay, Cass, you may not know where he is but you know where you would be and you know his tracks. They look like rhinoceros tracks. I should have just backed quietly away and said "thank you so much, but I'm going home." But I didn't. I stood there like an idiot and looked over Spike's options.

"Is he watching me or Brock?" I asked.

"Probably both," Nick answered.

I found Brock. That narrowed down my choices considerably. I chose a path that would take me by several nooks and crannies where Spike could be hiding but my final destination was where I expected him to be. Moving in stealth mode I inched from hiding place to hiding place, finding cover where I could, flattening myself against lighting equipment, props, the outhouse. I watched for Spike's tracks. One hiding place after another proved empty until I finally picked up his tracks. He was changing hiding places. When I locked onto the tracks it became a game. It was like hunting Chase in the woods. I forgot all about the hundred or so people milling around waiting to get back to work. I focused on the tracks and on staying hidden and I could tell when I was getting close when the tracks changed in attitude and direction. I closed in on Spike and when I had pinpointed his hiding place I circled around and invisibly came in behind him. I tapped him on the shoulder and stood back, proud of my accomplishment.

"Cut!" called out Nickolai.

"Oh shit," I said, covering my mouth in embarrassment. "He was filming all that?" Then to Spike I said, rather uncomfortably, "Thanks... for watching out for me yesterday. I *have* done the jump-up-on-the-hood-and-scare-the-driver-half-to-death-stunt but this car was moving too fast."

"Jus' doing my job," he replied with a wink. "What made you come back?"

"Jus' doing my job," I replied.

"And what's all this about?"

"Sherri thinks I can do a better job as an extra."

"That weren't no extra audition."

"We'll see."

"You should back quietly out of here. You don't want to get involved in this anymore'n you have."

When I found Sherri again she was grinning ear to ear. Oh, no.

Nickolai and another man were reviewing the shots on a small TV screen.

"Look, right there," he said. "I swear the kid's a natural. How'd she learn to move like that?"

"Sneaking up on cowboys when I was five," I answered. "I just grew up that way."

Nickolai stood up and surveyed the situation again.

"Can you do that with a rifle in hand?" Nickolai asked me.

"Yes, sir, I've carried rifles in my work for years."

"In the morning report to Gloria in 3A. She'll take care of you."

"I think I need to know a little bit more than that," I said.

"Gloria works in Hair!" Sherri said cheerfully, "You did it! You're in!"

"I'll draw up a contract and talk to you about it tomorrow."

"Contract?" I squeaked out.

Oh man. What had I done?

The rest of the afternoon I watched Sherri and Brock as they plotted the next scene on camera. When Nickolai dismissed everybody it was five thirty. Good. I thought I could have dinner on the table by eight if I did it right.

"Do you need directions to my house?" I asked Sherri.

"Why can't I just ride with you? Then I can call for a limo to take me home."

"There's one small problem with that."

"What?"

"I came on a motorcycle."

"You're kidding."

"Yesterday while I was at the doctor's office someone tampered with my Jeep and the gas pedal stuck down. I ended up in the desert and the police took my Jeep back to the station as evidence. I don't know when I'll get it back. So I'm on the bike today."

"I've never ridden on a motorcycle before."

"It's just a little dirt bike, and you can't ride it without a helmet."

"You mean you'll give me a ride?"

"You need a helmet. And a makeup case. You won't like what helmet hair looks like."

"Oh goodie!"

I looked at the bike with doubts but Sherri and I weighed approximately as much as Rusty so we should be okay. She reappeared carrying a helmet that looked like a World War One German Army helmet.

"It has to be a motorcycle helmet," I informed her.

"This is! Look!" She flipped it over and sure enough, the inside was all padded and it had straps and buckles just like any normal motorcycle helmet. I wondered which motorcycle it matched up with.

"You're sure you want to do this?"

"Yeah! It should be cool!"

"You brought your hair stuff, right?"

"Right here."

"Okay."

"This?" Sherri asked standing over the bike, "We're riding to your house on *this*?"

"You definitely don't have to. It's what I've got. It's practical for me."

"Practical or not, *it's barely there!*"

"It's sturdier than it looks. It's made for off road so it'll take a beating."

"O…kay," she said. "But never again!"

"Get on and then scoot back," I instructed her. "Put your feet here." I got on in front of her. "Now scoot close and put your hands around my waist. Lean when I lean."

"Cassidy? Are you sure about this?"

I didn't have time for this. I had dinner to cook.

"Ready?"

"Nooooo!" she wailed as I took off, slowly motoring through the gate. "Cassidy! Wait!"

"It'll feel better once I get up to speed," I yelled back at her.

Her grip tightened. I turned the bike out onto the main road and put on the gas. The motorcycle sped up slowly, not used to this much weight. As we raced down the open road and nothing bad happened she relaxed. A white car appeared on the horizon behind us and I didn't pay much attention to it. It caught up to us just like I expected it to. Cars out on these back roads seldom kept to the fifty mile an hour speed limit. I thought if I wanted Junior to remain unsquished I better keep to the speed limit. The white car came up behind us. Pretty soon it was breathing down our necks.

"Just pass us, you stupid car!" I said.

It inched closer.

"Cassidy, pull over. Just let it by," Sherri said.

I slowed down and scooted over but it followed inching even closer. I looked back at the driver.

"Sherri, you're going to have to hold on tight," I yelled. "It's *her*!"

Chapter 20

"Which her? Oh! No! It's her!" she shrieked into my ear.

I sped up again and the car kept to our tail.

"What the hell is she doing?" I yelled back.

"I don't know, just lose her!" Sherri yelled back.

"Are you sure?" I yelled.

"Yes! Yes! We don't know what she'll do to either of us."

"Okay! Just remember, you asked for it!"

I sped up and gained a little ground. Then I watched for places to get off the road. When one came up I slowed quickly and made a wide turn right into the desert.

"Aiiiiiyyyyeeeee! Casssssidy, what are you doing?" Sherri cried from the back of the bike.

"Losing the car just like you said."

"You're going to kill us! Which way would I rather die? On the pavement or in the middle of the desert? I choose pavement! At least we'll have witnesses on the pavement!"

"You're not dying, just out of your comfort zone. I ride like this a lot. Just hang on."

The car followed us down a dirt road. I put on the speed. Over hills and through dips the car clumsily chased us but when I turned off and rode cross country it had to give up.

"Casssssidy! Stop! Stop!"

"You're getting upset over nothing," I yelled. "Just hang on."

I crossed about ten miles of desert with Sherri wailing all the way about how we were going to die, then I hit pavement and made my way home, Sherri shaking all the way. When we finally pulled up into my driveway Sherri staggered off the bike catching her foot on the seat on her way off.

"Never! Never again! I'll never get on one of those things again!"

I grinned at her.

"Still got your makeup case?"

"Yeah, but I don't know how I kept hold of it through all that."

"I'll show you where you can freshen up."

I took her to my master bathroom because it was more like what she was used to. Even before she'd run a brush through her hair she was gawking at my shower.

"Wow! How'd you get a shower like that? It's like a *dream shower*. It's like from a movie or something!"

"Yeah, it's one of my favorite parts of the house."

"No wonder you're pregnant. That's the sexiest shower I've ever seen!"

"There's towels under the sink."

She looked in the mirror.

"Oh yikes! You weren't kidding!"

"I'm going to go start dinner. I expect the others to get here about seven."

I put Shadow out back and went to start dinner. Peeling potatoes and breading chicken kept me busy. Pretty soon there were potatoes boiling and chicken frying.

"Oh, that smells heavenly!" Sherri said when she emerged from her helmet hair recovery. Not a hair was out of place. "You said Landon was still single? Anyone in the running?"

"No, he, well, he kind of had a thing for me and prefers the search partner role if he can't have the boyfriend role. He's minded his manners since he found out Rusty and I were serious. But he's still very single."

"Who's the kid coming over?"

"Bailee. She's ten. I teach her how to ride horses. That's where I am every Tuesday and Thursday morning. Bailee doesn't need a teacher so much as a big sister. She's had a rough life. She was in a car wreck when she was seven. When I met her she could barely speak and her hands were withered. Since then she's gained confidence. She's had surgery on her hands. And you will find out she definitely talks now. She wants to be a horse trainer when she grows up."

"And Rusty. What did you say Rusty does again?"

"He's a detective. He's the reason I can track for the police department. He encouraged me to go to police academy, so I did."

"What would have happened to me on the mountain if you hadn't found me?"

"You mean if I wasn't the area tracker? It would have taken a lot longer to find you. They would have sent out search parties, but the fact that you were in the brush at the foot of a cliff made you kind of hard to spot. You didn't exactly make it easy by hiding from the searchers. Normally they send out a person with a dog, if they don't have me, but the dog couldn't pick you out over all the other perfumed girls you were camping with. That reminds me..." I said going to the back door. "It's time you met Shadow." I opened the door and Shadow raced in. "Pet him for a minute and he will calm down. Shadow, sit!" Shadow came and sat at my feet. "Stay!" I commanded. He watched me for the release word but I didn't say it. Sherri petted Shadow tentatively. She obviously didn't have much experience with animals.

"Mind if I look around?" she asked.

"No, go ahead."

She walked around gazing at the pictures on the walls and we began a disjointed, long distance conversation.

"Do you think that woman really means to do us harm?" she asked.

"I wasn't going to stop and ask, under the circumstances."

"Yeah, what's this thing?"

I looked around the wall. "It's souvenirs from my honeymoon," I answered.

"It looks like a parachute, a stick and an animal fur."

"That's what it is. I had a rather interesting honeymoon. I have a scrapbook of the calmer parts of it. It's on the coffee table in the living room."

She went into the living room and I heard her leafing through the scrapbook my sister had made.

"There aren't any parachute pictures in here."

"That's because I lost my camera in the plane crash and I didn't get another one until later."

"Who's this?" she asked and I had to go into the living room to see what she was looking at.

"That's me, on a rescue. I rescued a photographer and he gave me those pictures as a thank you gift."

"They're… interesting. I've never seen pictures like them. This one reminds me of your audition today. You should have seen Nikolai. His eyes were all bugged out. At first he's like yeah, okay and then all of a sudden something changed and you…"

"Turned into Dangerous Tracker Woman."

"What?"

"That's what Landon calls it when I slip into a serious tracking mood. He says I turn into Dangerous Tracker Woman."

"I don't know what it is, but Nick sure noticed it. Those two guys were whispering between them saying, 'look at that, did you see that? How'd she do that?'"

"Why did they put me through all that? Spike said that wasn't an audition for an extra. What did I get myself into?"

"I don't know, but the fact that he sent you to Gloria is a good sign!"

"Good to who?"

"Hey! One thing riding your tacky little motorbike did… the photographers didn't know it was me leaving! I'm photographer free!" She wandered over to the shadowbox with my honeymoon souvenirs in it. "Will you tell me about it? It must be an exciting tale. A plane crash? What's the stick?"

"It's an animal snare. I made it to catch food."

"Tell me about it," she insisted, so I told her the very long story about my adventures in the woods of Minnesota until the front door banged open and Bailee ran in.

"Chas! Did you make chocolate cake?"

"No, but Rusty bought one. I hope that's okay."

She started to ask me a question but she turned around and her mouth fell open, "Ooh, oh, oh, it's you!"

"I think I'm still me," Sherri said. "I was last time I checked."

"When Chas brought me an autograph of Brock Larone I couldn't believe it! Now I get to meet Sherri Champlain in person! Oh man, am I supposed to faint or something?"

"Please don't. Who's Chas?"

I interjected, "Bailee's called me Chas ever since we first met."

"When did Brock give you his autograph? You didn't ask for *my* autograph."

"I didn't ask for his either. Spike gave them to me and I gave one to Bailee and I saved the other for another friend who won't get it until this job is over."

"Who's Spike?" Bailee asked.

"He's Brock's bodyguard."

I was turning chicken pieces when Rusty walked in. He gave me a big hug and Sherri gave a big sigh.

"Do you have a bodyguard?" Bailee asked Sherri.

"Yeah, sort of. Right now her title is kind of up in the air because I think she just landed a part in the movie."

"Chas would be a good bodyguard. She knows how to shoot and everything!" Bailee said.

"I know," Sherri said. "That's why I hired her."

"Chas! You're Sherri's bodyguard?"

"I'm afraid so."

"How'd you get a part in the movie? Are you going to be a star, too?"

I glared at Sherri. Rusty glared at me. The doorbell rang. Saved by the bell!

Rusty answered the door and I heard the curt greeting between the two men, "Wilson."

"Michaels."

"Come on in."

Bailee's eyes got big. She had never met Landon before. "Are you in the movie, too? What do you do?"

"I'm an EMT. I work with Cassidy in another life."

"What's an EMT?" Bailee asked.

"Have you ever had an accident and had to go to the hospital in an ambulance?"

"Yeah…" Bailee said. "When I was seven."

"Then you've seen what EMTs do."

"I don't remember it," Bailee said.

"It was a rather serious car accident," I said.

The doorbell rang again. I glared at Landon. "You didn't." I said.

"No! I didn't," he answered.

I glared at Rusty, "Did you?"

"No, I haven't told anybody," he said.

"If this is a photographer, I'm going to be hopping mad," I told them.

It wasn't a photographer. It was Kelly Green.

"Hi, I didn't know I was crashing a party, Rhonda's still at her sister's and I burnt dinner."

"How burnt was it?"

"It was so burnt the fire department sent it in to have it identified by its dental records."

"You can come in if you can keep a secret."

"Okay, I'll go pick up a burger in town."

"Kelly, come in. We have extra."

"But…"

"We don't turn down friends. Even if we didn't have extra, we'd parcel out what we did have. We'd throw another potato in the pot. You know you're welcome here."

Kelly stepped into the room grinning, "Let's see, who have we got here? Landon Wilson, Rusty, Cassidy. Who are you?" he asked Bailee.

"I'm Bailee. I ride horses."

"Good to meet you Bailee. I'm Kelly Green."

"Hey, isn't that a color?" Bailee asked.

"To some people. All the kids in my family have color names. My brother is Hunter and my sister is Ivy. And I grew up in a green house. But my mom had a black thumb. I'm lucky I lived through it." He went on to Sherri. "And you are?"

Sherri brightened immediately. "He doesn't know who I am!"

"Am I supposed to? I don't get around much because I get around too much."

Sherri burned off a few thousand brain cells on that one.

I explained, "Kelly is a forest ranger and he lives in a small town. He's always out and about but he doesn't see much TV or movies."

"Uh oh. This is Cassidy's house," Kelly said. "You could be anybody. Once she rescued Sherri Champlain from a fall in the mountains. Did you know that?"

"Yeah, I kind of figured it out," Sherri said.

"Mr. Green," Bailee said quietly. "This *is* Sherri Champlain."

"You are? Of course you are. It's good to meet you."

"Me too," answered Sherri.

"By the way, Landon did most of the rescuing. I just did the tracking," I added for Landon's sake.

I went to the kitchen and turned the chicken before it decided to become a burnt offering, too. I set the table for six, mashed the potatoes and checked the chicken again.

"Bailee? Can you put this on the table for me?" I asked.

Sherri groaned. It was the chocolate layer cake. It had curls of chocolate all over the top and little drizzles of fudge down the side. When Bailee came back I handed her the cheesecake.

"What's this?" Bailee asked.

"New York cheesecake," I replied. "Landon asked for it."

"How do they make cake out of cheese?" Bailee asked.

"Really, really good," I replied.

"It sounds yucky."

"You can try it if you want. You just have to eat dinner first."

She turned up her nose at the idea.

The dinner conversation left a lot to be desired as far as I was concerned. It started off bad and went to worse. From my point of view. Everybody else seemed to enjoy it. Up to a point.

"How do you eat like this every night with you working? And how do you stay so thin?" Sherri asked.

"We don't eat big complicated meals every night. It's usually much simpler. Sometimes we go out to dinner in town. We don't usually have dessert. Bailee will take home the leftover cake."

"The chocolate one," Bailee interjected, still unsure about the idea of cheesecake. "I want to know if you're going to be in the movie!"

Leave it to the kid to get me in trouble. Rusty's fork paused halfway to his mouth and he and Kelly exchanged glances. He straightened up, ready to listen.

"If I am I won't be very visible. Pregnant women don't make good action movie extras."

"I don't think you're an extra," Sherri said. "If you were an extra Nick would have sent you to Merriam. But he sent you to Gloria. Just wait till tomorrow. You'll see."

"I don't want to be anything!" I said. "I didn't ask to be in the movie. We just suggested I be allowed to mingle with the extras and then the next thing I know this director guy is telling me to give him a police academy demonstration. Somehow in the demonstration I managed to slip into tracking mode and... and I think I better shut up."

"And this magical transformation took place and she turned into, like, an action hero or something. And Nickolai was, like, really jazzed and he sent her to Gloria. Gloria is, like, the *best* in hair. And then there's make up and costuming. You're going to think it is so cool!"

"Yeah, cool," I mumbled. "Sherri, are you sure this is a good thing?"

"Of course! I mean, you'll be, *in there, in the thick of things*. You'll find this berserko Barbie doll. Do you know what she *did today*?"

Rusty really didn't need to hear all this but Sherri had an audience and I couldn't stop her. Nobody was eating, except me. I was nervously shoveling food into my mouth pretending like everything was fine.

"I thought we were going to die!" Sherri exclaimed.

"That's only because you've never ridden a dirt bike before," I said desperate to cover my tracks.

"This woman, who has been playing tricks on us, chased us down in her car and Cassidy and I had to take off into the desert! She followed us down this dirt road. Dust and dirt is flying everywhere! We had to go cross-country to lose her but she only had a regular car. Cassidy takes off across the desert and I thought we were going to wipe out or get skewered on a cactus or something. It was bumpy and rough and I'd never been out in the desert like that before. I thought rattlesnakes or coyotes were going to be out there but we didn't see any animals. I was never so glad to hit pavement again."

"And you didn't want me to take the dirt bike," I reminded Rusty.

"I'm glad we weren't in a car! If we were we couldn't have lost her! We really lucked out!" Sherri went on.

"Yeah, lucky us," I said to myself.

"You have to admit she knows how to drive a car. She did her part of the stunt perfectly, except for the part where she nearly ran you over. Now she tries to run you off the road. She needs a cool car. That old junker of hers just won't keep up. If she had a fast, cool car she could have done some real damage but we out maneuvered her, didn't we?"

"Yeah, we did," I admitted reluctantly, trying to pass food around as a distraction. I didn't have any takers. I sure wish Sherri could see how deep she was digging us in. Pretty soon we'd find ourselves in a six-foot deep, eight-foot long grave and they could just start shoveling the dirt in on top of us. I was sunk.

"That's three times in two days," Rusty said. "Can you identify this person?"

"I think so," I said. "But that's the only link I have to her. I don't know who tampered with my gas pedal, I don't know who has been pulling pranks on Sherri. All I know is this one woman acts differently towards us and I think it is the same woman who tried to run me over. If you could link those fingerprints to her it sure would help. Any proof we can get would help."

"There were fifty witnesses at the set yesterday," Rusty pointed out.

"Yeah, but we're talking about an actress here. Everybody's convinced yesterday was just a freak accident, that she tried to hit the brake but missed and hit the gas," Sherri explained.

"What's this woman's story? Is there something that would make her vindictive toward you?" Rusty asked Sherri.

"There's always a chance. I don't know where she came from. Thousands of people try out for parts and it's impossible to know them all. When you've seen twenty people say the same lines over and over they all start to look alike. They just keep coming and coming. Only a few get chosen. There's bound to be a little jealousy here and there but it never affects shooting like this."

"If there's only a few chosen how'd you get in?" Rusty asked me.

"Beats me."

"Because she's a natural," Sherri said. "Not to the camera but to the feeling Nick is trying to put in this movie. She moves like a ghost. You should have seen her."

"I've seen it," Rusty said.

"What's the movie going to be rated?" Bailee asked.

"I don't know. We never know until it gets all put together. It depends on how Brock and I hit it off in the scene where…" Sherri looked around her and chose, wisely, to stay quiet. "Um, never mind."

"Aw, that's no fair. Is Brock a good kisser?" Bailee asked, breaking the tension at the table.

"It's not like that when you're acting. It's not romantic at all. After ten kisses from ten different angles, it kind of loses its appeal."

"Will I get to see the movie?" Bailee asked.

"That's up to your parents, no matter what it's rated," I reminded her.

"Are there any horses in it?" Bailee asked and I was thankful for her inquisitive mind. It distracted Rusty from things better left unsaid.

"There's lots of them but they are all under the hood," Sherri said.

Bailee's expression rose and then fell in consternation. "What do you mean they're under the hood?"

"She means there's cars with plenty of horse power," Kelly said. "Sounds like my kind of movie."

"Just because you're the one with an old souped up muscle car in the driveway," I said.

"Hey, if I could afford a new souped up muscle car I'd have one."

"If you took the money from the paint, the struts, the custom taillight covers, shiny chrome and the fuzzy dice you might be able to afford a new car."

"My car suits me just fine," he argued and he was right. A bright Kelly green Charger with black racing stripes, it suited Kelly Green perfectly. I thought it could use a hula girl in the back window but maybe Rhonda disagreed with me.

"Did you see Kelly's car?" I asked Sherri.

"No, I got here first, remember?"

"Seems like most of my friends have cars that suit their personalities. Kelly has a Kelly green Charger. Landon has a white Mustang with black stripes. My friend Chase has a Baja Bug. What do you drive?"

"Drive? I haven't driven since I was in high school and my mom made me take driver's ed. Oh, I wanted my license, just like any kid, but then I got into acting and it just wasn't practical to drive everywhere. I am always going places where big crowds are expected and so I want to be dropped off right at the entrance. I call a limo when I need to go somewhere."

"You don't have a car?" Bailee asked.

"No."

"I think you should drive a Zamboni."

All the adults laughed.

"Bailee, do you know what a Zamboni is?" I asked.

"No, but it sounds really cool."

"It is. It's the machine they use to resurface ice rinks."

"Oh. It is? Why would an ice rink machine have a cool name like Zamboni?"

"I have no idea, but I don't think it could keep up on the freeway."

Since Sherri had asked Landon to be here I thought it was about time to give him a chance to talk.

"Has Strict called you out on the usual flurry of snow searches?" I asked him.

"Yeah, I ran into an old friend of yours," he answered.

"Arg, let me guess. Old friend? Not Foe? Meaning I've found him before?"

"Yeah."

"Not Thomas Parker. That's the only person I can think of that would be an old friend and a rescue."

Landon just smiled.

"I thought you said Thomas Parker wouldn't get lost in our neck of the woods for a long time. You said he was attending some out of town college somewhere."

"So he came back for a visit. He asked about you."

"No he didn't. So what's the story?"

"Same o', same o'."

I turned to Sherri. "The first time I rescued Thomas Parker he was missing from a Boy Scout outing. The second time I rescued him he had skied off the back side of the mountain and gotten lost in the snow. I think this is the fourth or fifth time he's been rescued in our district."

"No, that's the fourth or fifth time he's gotten lost. He's been rescued from other things too."

"What's the funniest rescue you've been on?" Bailee asked Landon.

"About three years ago there was this old lady. Her cat had climbed up in a tree and she climbed up to try and get him down. When we got there the cat was calmly licking its paws up in the tree, comfortable as can be. The lady was in a state. She was hanging on for dear life up on branches that were way too small to support her. She'd slipped a couple of times, scaring the neighbors half to death. A neighbor had called an ambulance because they thought she must have broken something, or was about to fall. So there we were staring up at this lady in a little pink, cotton duster with pink curlers in her hair, hanging in a tree. I climbed up as close as I could and talked to the lady, got her into a harness, which was a job in itself. Do you know what an old lady in a duster and a climbing harness looks like?"

"I don't want to think about it," Sherri said.

"Once the harness was on her I could tie her to the tree and then a fire truck arrived and they helped her climb down without worrying about her falling. The cat climbed down on its own because it didn't like all the commotion. It was sitting on the porch when the lady finally found her feet on solid ground again. The lady brushes off her duster and finds her slippers, which fell off in the climb up the tree. She feels her curlers, which were only half in after all the ruckus. She squares her shoulders and huffs into the house going, 'here kitty, kitty, kitty'. Of course the firemen had to chase her down to fill out the report. She ended up putting out tea and cookies. We didn't have time for all that but she wouldn't be hurried. Then there's the calls with Cassidy. There's no telling what those are going to be like. Did you tell them about the drugged bear?"

"What was the scariest?" Bailee asked unknowingly.

Landon's face fell and he looked to me. I looked back.

"Bailee, I don't think that's a good question to ask right now," I said.

"Why?"

"Because... EMTs see some pretty scary things that they don't want to remember."

"Okay," Bailee said matter of factly. "I guess I can understand that. I have things I don't like to remember, too."

I looked around the table. All the guys looked like they were ready to walk out. They were dealing with their own memories of things best forgotten. I thought I could guess what they were thinking. Needing to change the subject, all I could think of was dessert.

"Okay!" I said cheerfully. "Who wants chocolate and who wants cheesecake?"

Eager to get things on a brighter note Rusty said, "Chocolate. Do we have ice cream?"

"Did you buy any?" then, "I'll check." I doubted we had any unless he had bought some. Ice cream was a downfall of mine right at the moment.

"Landon?"

"Can I have both?"

"Sure."

"Kelly?"

"Cheesecake."

"Sherri?"

"Ohhhh, why do you do this to me?"

"I didn't. Bailee and Landon did."

I went on to Bailee.

"How do they make cheese into cake?" Bailee asked.

"Well," Kelly said. "They have these cows that only eat sugar and so the milk is really sweet. Then the cheese is really sweet and it makes good cake."

"Are they hyper all the time? My mom says sugar makes kids hyper."

"You heard about the cow that jumped over the moon?"

"That's just a little kids' story."

"Not so, that was one of those cows that only ate sugar."

"Then why did the little dog laugh?"

"Because it was Kelly's dog," I quickly put in. "He's just telling you stories. You can have a bite of my cheesecake, just to see if you like it. Then, if you do, you can have your own piece."

"Can I still have chocolate?"

"Sure!"

I went to the kitchen and checked on the ice cream situation. We had a little bit. I called over my shoulder, "How many ice creams do I need?" Everybody who wanted chocolate also wanted ice cream. Sigh, I'd have to give up my last scoop.

I divided up the cakes and the last of the ice cream giving Sherri a tiny slice of both.

"You don't have to eat it," I told her.

Bailee took a taste of my cheesecake and gave Kelly a disapproving look.

"They feed the cows sugar," she said in a derogatory way. "Cows are herbivores."

"Sugar comes from sugar cane and that's a plant," Kelly said hopefully.

"It is pretty good," she admitted. "But I like chocolate better. I suppose chocolate milk comes from brown cows and cheesecake comes from blonde cows."

"Well, sure, why not?" Kelly said.

"Chas, you better keep your baby away from that guy," she confided in me. "If he's around much there's no telling what hokey things she will learn."

All the guys laughed but the question piqued Sherri's curiosity.

"Have you thought of a name for the baby yet?" she asked.

"It's a little complicated and I haven't had time to do the research."

This got looks.

"My dad started a tradition of naming babies after old west characters. We don't have to stick to the tradition but, if we did the research and a good name turned up, we might go with that."

"Old west characters? Like John Wayne?"

"Well, that's my dad's name but think older than that. Think pioneer days."

Sherri's expression went blank as she tried to remember her history lessons. She gave up and went to the next question.

"Is it a girl or a boy?"

"We don't know."

"What do you mean you don't know? Everybody knows these days!"

"We don't want to know. We want to be surprised."

"So when's your due date?"

"The end of June."

"I'd be dying of curiosity!"

"I say it's a girl!" Bailee piped up.

"You can only hope, you can't know."

"Maybe if you hope loud enough the baby will hear it."

"It doesn't work that way. Besides, if it did, I'd have a very conflicted baby. I think Rusty would like a boy and my mom definitely wants a girl. She already has two grandsons."

"Why don't you find out? Then it would be settled," Sherri asked.

"Because we don't want to," I insisted.

I thought Sherri was just about ready to give a big yawn and declare that she needed her beauty sleep when Bailee did it again.

"If you become a movie star will you bring me an autographed picture, like Brock's?" she asked me.

"No," I told her. "I have no intention of being in a movie, much less being a movie star."

"You will be if you show up tomorrow morning. You just wait. Gloria will fix you up and before you know it you'll be stuck in a scene. Nick is just dying to see what you can do."

"Hey, hey, heeey," Bailee sang dancing around. "Chas is going to be in mooooovies."

Trying to turn this into something positive I said to Sherri, "I think Bailee is trying very hard to not ask for your autograph. She is a bit of an autograph hound. She even asked for mine after your rescue was written up in a tabloid."

"You want my autograph?" Sherri asked Bailee.

"Yes!"

"What do you want me to autograph?"

"Mostly I'd like a picture, but if you don't have one then I guess my shirt, so I can wear it to school and show it to all the kids."

"Let me see if I brought one." She went to the bathroom and looked through her makeup case. "I only have a little one. The big ones don't fit in my makeup case." Sherri signed the picture and handed it to Bailee. "Will your mom be mad if I sign your shirt?"

"Yeah, but it'll be worth it."

"Then I better not sign it."

I went to my closet and found a t-shirt that was tight.

"Try this on," I told her.

She slipped it on over her clothes and it was about three sizes too big but it wasn't embarrassingly huge either. At least she could wear it for a long time.

"Go ahead and sign that one," I offered.

"Oh cool! Oh cool!" said Bailee. "Sign it real big! Like a concert t-shirt. I can't wait to go to school tomorrow!"

"You will *not* tell all the kids there's an action movie being filmed right outside of town. You know what people do around here when they hear about a movie. Just tell them you got to meet Sherri and she was nice enough to sign your shirt. Now, it's getting late. Your mom is probably wondering what you are up to and you have school tomorrow."

"Awww, do I have to?"

"Isn't Friday show and tell day?"

Her eyes brightened, "Yeah!"

"Just remember, don't tell too much. Are you taking the chocolate cake with you?"

"Can I?"

"Of course."

"I'll have to hide it or my mom will eat it all."

"You shouldn't eat all of it. Share with your family."

"Will you wrap up one slice so I can hide it for my school lunch tomorrow?"

"You are a sneak!" I said, but I wrapped up one slice and covered the rest of the cake with the plastic cover.

When Rusty had driven off with Bailee, Sherri asked, "What do you see in that kid?"

"I see a fighting spirit. A kid who makes the best of a bad situation. She's doing a lot better than she was when I met her."

"Why do you let her tell you what to do?"

"I'm the only one who ever spoils her. Every kid needs to be spoiled by somebody. She can count on me. Even when she can't count on her family. If she doesn't need me for moral support, the least I can do is give her chocolate cake."

"You're an odd one Cassidy."

"It's okay, I like to think I'm a nice kind of odd. You think *I'm* odd. Landon has this fixation with saving my life. So I bring him chocolate chip cookies." I turned to Landon. "I'm sorry about Bailee's questions. I could see it hit."

"Wasn't just me."

Kelly put his arm around me and said to Sherri, "We all have a scary story inside us. Cass...has some terrifying things happen to her. That's why Rusty is reluctant to let her get involved in this movie. He sees trouble brewing. And he's got so much at stake right now. He's going to be unreasonable. Remember, Cassidy, he's only unreasonable because he cares so much. Don't break his heart."

Gulp.

With a "thanks for dinner", a big hug and a loud rumble from his Kelly Green Charger he drove off to his little smoke filled house in the woods.

Sherri got out her cell phone but Landon stepped in, "Need a ride home?"

"Are you sure you want to risk it?" Sherri said.

"No problem."

"You heard what we went through to get here," Sherri said.

"That's because you were with Cassidy. Cassidy is a trouble magnet."

Sherri looked to me. I told her, "Go on, Landon's my bodyguard. You can trust him unless you invite him to spend the night. If you do that, then no promises."

Chapter 21

"Cassidy, what are you thinking?" Rusty said. "You're getting in deeper and deeper."

"I didn't mean to. I didn't know talking to this guy would lead to a part in a movie. It made sense for me to be allowed to mingle with the extras. I was just following Sherri's lead and then all of a sudden they were asking me to do some very odd but doable things. So I did them. It was just simple acting that I learned in academy. And now I have to report to this Gloria person in Hair and it's supposed to be a good thing but I'm not so sure about it, or this contract Nickolai was talking about."

"Now you're on a first name basis with the director?"

"Everybody is. He's not a stuffed shirt. He's personable. He's easy to work with. Everybody calls him Nickolai, if not just Nick."

"What *contract*?"

"I don't know. I won't sign it until I've read it. I'm not committing to anything past the next two weeks."

"You're not committing to anything. Period!"

Was I in a mess, or what?

I opened the door at A3 and peeked in. It looked like a typical beauty shop.

"Go on in!" Sherri said behind me.

"Ooooh there you are!" a woman squealed from behind a beauty shop chair. "I love getting my hands on a new head of hair. Look at you! So pretty! Too bad what we need to do to get you ready for this movie. Are you ready?"

"No." I said.

"Oh, it won't be that bad."

Not that bad! She started out with scissors. I didn't mind a trim. I could actually use one. But what I saw wasn't a trim. It was a hack! My hair looked like she took a weed eater to me. It was short. And not only that, it was spiked. And not only that, she wasn't through yet. Next came a dye job. And another dye job. Then it was gelled and spiked and sprayed and sprayed again. She turned me around and when I saw myself I jumped. Black hair, red tips, spikes. What had I done? I wasn't vain. I didn't put a lot of stock in perfect hair. I was an informal, wash and wear type person. But I also had a husband to go home to. I still had a vision of the me I expected to see and this was *not it*.

"There!" Gloria said cheerfully. "Now go see Theo in A2. Just wait. You've seen only one fourth of the transformation. There is the hair, the makeup, the clothes and then the change as you become your character! Isn't it exciting?"

Shocking was more like it.

Theo didn't bat an eyelash at my new look. She couldn't. Her eyelashes were too heavy to bat. I didn't know how she held her eyes open. She must have had very well developed eye muscles. She looked me over with a critical eye.

"Too cute," she said, puzzling over my face. "We must toughen you up. Have a seat."

She applied foundation and more foundation and more foundation. Eyeliner. She smudged it around a bit. Mascara, more mascara, more eyeliner, more smudging. Smudging in places smudging usually wasn't done. She applied makeup to every exposed piece of skin and then she pulled up my sleeves and put makeup up under my sleeves. I looked at my hands. They were turning color. I was no longer fair skinned. Normally I had a little tan. I was outside so much; I didn't have much choice but tan a little. This was different. This wasn't tan. This was colored. It was…it was, hmmm, what was it? I definitely wasn't one of the good guys. Bailee would never recognize me even if she saw the movie. I doubted I'd even recognize myself! But, I thought, maybe the person who was playing these tricks on Sherri wouldn't recognize me either. This could be perfect, except for the obvious problem of having black and red hair. I was sent to Costumes in A1 or B1 or C1. There were a lot of costumes involved in this movie. I ended up being in the C1 group. I was outfitted in black, dressy grunge. What can I say? It looks different on the screen than it does in real life. I stood in front of the mirror. It looked so unlike me, yet… there was me in there somewhere.

I knocked on Sherri's trailer. She opened the door.

"How come you get to be you and I have to be this?" I asked.

"Cassidy?" She laughed. She came down the steps and walked around me. "Are you sure you're in there?"

"I think so. I'm having a hard time finding myself under all the layers."

"Wow! Wow! It's hard to believe that's really you. Where are you?"

"Try the eyes," I suggested.

"That's amazing! I can't even tell you're pregnant."

"I wonder if Junior is having an identity crisis, too."

"Try not to touch your face. I know that's hard to remember at first. Most people do it a lot without even thinking about it."

"Now what do I do? I can't spend the day like this."

"You may have to. Let's go find out the game plan."

Acting is harder than it looks on the screen, especially if you aren't an actor. Especially if you are five months pregnant and playing an evil hunter. Especially if they've already shot three quarters of the movie and now want you to make up for lost time. First we headed up to the mountains because they had already finished the shooting there but they backed up to try and fit me in. Actually, that was the fun part of the day. At first. I liked being in the woods but as the scene developed I was forced into roles I was not comfortable with. As long as I could forget there were cameras around I was able to be semi-normal. I was instructed to run from point A to point B carrying a black machine gun look alike. It took me a few tries to get started.

"What's wrong? You said the rifle was no problem."

"A real rifle is no problem. This thing is too light. I end up flinging it around because there's no weight to it. And this isn't a rifle. I think if I just keep a firm grip on it I'll be fine. I've just never done this before."

"Okay, try it again."

I went back to point A.

"Action!"

I ran in and out of the trees, machine gun close at hand. Watching my tail, hiding my tracks."

"Cassidy, you're going to die. If they catch you they're going to kill you. You're tired, you've been running a mile."

"Tell you what, let me run a mile again and you can catch me as I come in."

"You want to run a mile?"

"If it will make the scene work. I can run a mile. It'll just take a little time for me to walk it, so I can run it."

"Hold it."

They put their heads together then drove me up the road.

"Can you find your starting point again?"

"No problem."

"You sure you want to do this?"

"Yeah."

He got on the phone and then gave me an okay. I jogged off and broke into a run, trying to conjure up a bad guy. Trent? Stern? Troy? Stern proved effective. Him and his dogs. I thought about a pack of his fighting dogs on my tail. He'd nearly beaten me to death. I remembered the blows, probably more clearly than I had when they fell. When they really happened I was too busy blocking them out. When the police found me I was barely recognizable. Flashbacks of the dogs on me drove me through the woods. Hide your tracks, Cass. The cameras came into view I hesitated, looked for the dogs, took off running pulling the gun up close. I stopped by a tree gasping for breath, checking my back trail. I took off again, hiding behind trees then running flat out again.

"Cut!" Nick yelled.

I sat down in the leaves and cried.

"Are you okay?" a cameraman asked.

I couldn't answer. I hated the fact that I had so many bad memories, so many things from my past that could drive me like this. I hated that I let them get to me.

"Nick?" the cameraman said.

Nickolai squatted down.

"It's okay," I told him. "You couldn't understand."

"Sure I do. You've got ghosts. I wish I could see them."

"It's funny you should call them ghosts. Some of them are dead."

"Is this one?"

"I think so. I heard the gunfire. I don't know the outcome. It was close range. They couldn't have missed." And Rusty…I pushed it aside, stuffed it down. "What's next?" I asked.

"It's been a very physical day for you and we're just getting started. Are you up to it?"

"One thing at a time."

"Are you sure you've never acted?"

"I wasn't acting. I was running for my life. At least it gets to stop before the bad guy catches me."

"You are the bad guy."

"Not *the* bad guy."

"No, but bad enough. You wouldn't want to meet up with yourself."

"Sometimes I don't anyway."

They had me do some things that weren't in the script. How could they be? *I* wasn't in the script. They said they might be able to fit them into the movie at a later date. I vaulted a low wall, climbed a chain link fence. I was put in an alley and had to find my way out. Again, I was being pursued. I pictured the alley in San Diego where I'd been gunned down. I found my break and climbed frantically to the roof.

"What are you doing? There's a ladder right there!" Nick boomed at me.

"Too obvious," I replied from the rooftop.

"Well, try it again and use the ladder. What made you use the meters on the wall?"

"It's how I got up on the barn roof as a kid."

"Why would a barn have meters?"

"Water? Electricity?"

"All right, forget the meters. Use the ladder."

"Have you ever been in a fist fight?" Nickolai asked me.

"I'm a lousy fighter. I'm better at staying out of reach. But, yeah, I have boxed with a detective at the station. I've had training in the Marines in hand-to-hand combat. But I never was much good at it. I have trouble hurting people. I don't like to do that."

"The boxing is a good start. It's more a matter of timing and action. And you don't have to hurt anybody. You just have to look like you mean to."

It wasn't too hard to fight this guy. He looked just like Mario Peccati. When he came at me my guard was up instantly. He swung at me and I ducked but the blow never landed.

"You see how it's done?" he asked. "Now a hook. You jerk back, I follow through."

We worked through the moves. Over and over and over. At times I had to stop, partly from exhaustion, partly because I needed to stop the flashbacks. I was worried about going over the edge and giving the guy a black eye.

"Cassidy, you can't hurt me. I'm a black belt."

"I can't help it."

"You've got to get into it."

"Are you who I'll be fighting in the scene?"

"No, I'm a choreographer."

"Can't I work with the person I'll really be fighting?"

"He's busy. I'm trying to get you up to speed. Okay… again… one, two, three, four, duck, kick, left, trapped."

"No!" I yelled pulling loose. I stood back breathing hard, "Sorry, I can't. I can't be choked."

"It's just a stunt."

"You don't see what I see."

"What do you see, Cassidy?"

"I see Dirk. He really did try to choke me. I…"

"You what?"

"Damn it, Ramon, I had to shoot him. I can't look into your face without flashbacks. When Nickolai says I have ghosts, he isn't kidding. For every fight I go through physically, I go through ten mentally. I don't know if I can do this."

"Okay, let's try this," he said, "one, two, three, four, duck, kick, left, step around, trapped from behind."

"Maybe. Try again."

"One, two, three, four, duck, kick, left, step around, trapped from behind."

To me the actions were dodge, jerk, twist, duck, kick, twist and there was an arm around my neck.

"You know this sequence is going to mean a whole new camera angle."

"Don't remind me of the cameras. I hate cameras."

"Then what are you doing here?"

"Sherri roped me into this job. Nickolai saw something in me and now I'm stuck." Stuck in a job with horrible flashbacks.

When I was able to go home that evening I wanted to rush home and leap into Rusty's arms. One thing stopped me. The hair. It was still black and red. The Explorer was in the driveway when I rode up on the dirt bike. I snuck in silently but he'd heard the bike. He walked out to the living room.

"Promise you won't be mad," I said from behind the kitchen wall.

"Why would I be mad?"

"Promise you won't laugh."

"Babe, what did you get yourself into this time?"

"Just promise. At least try."

He was smiling, that was good news, probably the closest to a promise I was going to get. I stepped around the wall, black and red hair and all.

"Oh Cass, why did you let them do that to you?"

"When you sit in the chair you put your life in their hands. You should have seen me with makeup."

"I'm not sure I want to."

"At least it's short. It won't take long to grow out. I got quite a workout today, running through the woods, climbing walls and fences, learning how to fight without actually hitting anybody. I didn't have time to get into trouble."

"Then the hair is worth it. You can paint yourself purple if you will just stay out of trouble."

"Thanks. I need to sit a bit before dinner. Would you sit with me? Come on, come sit with me." I tugged him to the old brown couch. He sat and I climbed into his lap. "I need some time. Just be here."

"What happened?"

"Nothing has to happen for me to want to spend time with you."

"I know. But I know you, too. What happened?"

"It's flashbacks. Every time they asked me to act out something it brought to mind a fight, a chase. It hurts. Rusty, it really hurts. It's just memories. But it's memories I have tried so hard to forget. And now they aren't forgotten anymore. Why can't I just forget? It was bad enough going through them the first time. Some of them haunted me for months. I finally stuff them away and they all get dragged out in one day. It's just too much. I just need your peace."

"What can I do to make you stop?"

"Two weeks. That's all. It can only hurt for two weeks."

"No… memories can hurt forever. I don't want you fighting memories forever."

"I think today was the worst of it."

"Can I go to the set with you?"

"No, you'd try to stop me. I'll get through this. Just hold me."

"I want to be there for you."

"It's rough and physical and you'd worry. But you'd worry about the wrong thing. I just need you here. Right here. Just be here."

"I'm here."

Next morning Hair was easier, having already gone through the dye process. Makeup was just as tedious as it had been the day before. How could real stars stand it?

"Cassidy, this is Donnal Pierce. He's your opponent."

Donnal Pierce was little bigger than me. I guess they had to match us up size wise so it looked right on film or maybe it simplified camera angles. I didn't know and I didn't question. Ramon stood aside calling out, "One, two, three, four, duck, kick, left, trapped."

Dirk's face flashed before me and a right hook came up and before I knew it Donnal was standing there with a bloody nose. I turned away.

"Ramon, I thought we decided face to face was a bad idea. Donnal… I'm sorry. I'm really sorry. I didn't mean to hurt you. Ramon said we weren't going to do it that way! I got taken by surprise."

People stepped in and helped Donnal control the bleeding.

One thing my little stunt did was make Donnal think I was going to bop him again so he watched me warily. He looked like he was in a real fight. His reflexes were just a bit quicker. Ramon showed him the new sequence. One, two, three, four, duck, kick, left, step around, trapped from behind. Even that reminded me of Trent but I fought the urge to stomp his instep and run away. After an hour of practice I paced the room erasing faces from my mind. Easing feelings. Stuffing away fears.

"Okay, Cassidy, opponent number two. Ready to go again?"

Ramon stepped forward to instruct me again. This one was a longer sequence. He handed me a pole.

He taught me the sequence. Duck, charge, duck, twist, turn, block, block, kick, turn, block, jab, JAB, jab harder, push up with the pole, run forward two steps, turn. Hell, how was I supposed to remember all that? Over and over we practiced it and then he became my opponent. Slowly the fight developed as I knew what to expect during the charge, knew why I was ducking, knew what I was blocking. He sped it up as the sequence got logged in my brain. When the sequence resembled a real fight he brought in my new opponent. This guy was lithe and tall. I had a little trouble adjusting for the height difference but the reason he was chosen was clear when our fight scene developed and he stepped up onto a prop. As I pushed up with the pole he did a flip right over me. I ran forward and turned to finish the sequence.

"Okay? You got it?" Andrew asked.

"I think so," I answered, tired.

Ramon stepped forward. "This time he's not going easy on you. Remember you're fighting for your life here. Put some force behind your blocks."

He came at me again and I slipped into automatic. When he was supposed to be driving me back I felt trapped. I jabbed with the pole. He didn't stop. He didn't stop! He was lucky the pole was made of lightweight wood because I broke it and turned on him in a flurry of defensive moves that came from some nameless place in my past. Arms pulled me off him. I was turning to walk off the tension and form my apologies when I realized one of the people who held my arms was Rusty.

"How'd you get here?" I asked.

"It's amazing what a badge will do," he answered.

I shrugged loose. I felt sorry for attacking Andrew, flustered from the mess of emotions that drove me to it and betrayed that Rusty had come here knowing I didn't want him to. Now he was going to do precisely what I didn't want him to do.

Ramon stepped in, "Cassidy, we have choreography so nobody gets hurt. If you insist on really fighting your opponents you're not going to make it."

"I didn't mean to. Besides, these are experienced stuntmen. You'd think they could take on an inexperienced housewife."

"That's not the point. You have to follow the script because that is what the camera is going to follow. When you depart from the script you lose the camera. We're gearing up for a big scene. You have to be ready in three days."

I went outside and paced frantically trying to walk off the tension. I rounded a corner and collided with... Spike. He stepped aside, not recognizing me.

"Sorry," he said.

"It's okay. I wasn't exactly watching where I was going."

"Cassidy?"

"Yeah."

"That was you in there?"

"Yeah."

"And I was supposed to protect you? Looks like you do pretty good on your own."

"I don't belong here. Just hand over the prankster and send me home.

Sherri suggested I do this, but it isn't working. It throws me into flashbacks and these guys shouldn't have to cope with that."

"Why are you still here?"

"Because it's gotten personal. I've been nearly run over. I've had my Jeep tampered with, nearly causing a major traffic accident, I've been chased down by a speeding car. This isn't funny anymore and this person needs to be stopped."

"And you're stopping them, how?"

"I was hoping to talk to the extras and work my way into a position where I could catch them in the act. So far I have been running, leaping over fences, climbing walls, and trying to learn fight scenes without attacking anybody."

"I'll have to be more careful how I keep an eye on you. I didn't know you lived in attack mode."

"I don't. I really don't. I've just been through so much. I've got to find a way to stay out of trouble. The violence of the scenes brings on flashbacks and… and I'm afraid I've reacted badly to them a few times."

"It's called post war syndrome."

"But I didn't do this after Afghanistan. Life in Joshua Hills has been more traumatic than the war."

"Sounds like it's time for a move."

"It doesn't matter. Trouble follows me. Rusty will tell you. I'm a trouble magnet."

"Who's Rusty?"

A hand appeared over my shoulder.

"I'm Rusty," I heard behind me. "And you are?"

"Spike."

Rusty recognized that name. He looked Spike in the eye, "Thanks. Thanks for being there."

"Just doin' my job."

"Thanks for doing your job then. You saved my family."

His family. Family to Rusty was something very different than it was to me. Family was personal. Family was precious, not that I didn't care about my family. I did. To me my family was the people I was allotted to in life. I happened to have a loveable, agreeable family and I kept loose ties to them. To Rusty family was everything.

Spike was embarrassed. Rusty didn't care. He'd been in Spike's shoes before. He knew a big lunkhead like Spike would survive a little embarrassment.

"Who was it this time?" Rusty asked me.

"The men in the yellow van," I answered simply.

"Babe, this is tearing you up."

"I got through it the first time. They don't haunt me. They were just hired goons. It's the ones I hurt that tear me up."

Spike was taking notes.

"I need to get back in there. I'll never catch this person until I get out of this practice room."

"I'm sorry, Andrew. Can we try it one more time? I'll try to stay in the present."

We squared off and tried again. Rusty watched from the corner shaking his head. I had to keep a tight rein on my mind and it was very wearing, even more so than the physical activity. Spike joined Rusty off and on. Finally Ramon called a halt for lunch.

Ramon caught up to me before Rusty could.

"First you attack your partner. Then this detective follows you out. Are you in some kind of trouble?"

"Not the kind you're thinking of. He's my husband. What I don't understand is why he isn't at work. It's not like crime takes a vacation every time he worries about me."

"Why is he worried about you?"

"Memories. Threats. The fact that if something can go wrong it usually does. All the flashbacks that the fighting brings on? He's been my backup through all that. He knows what I see when Andrew suddenly turns into a threat. He knows how I feel. It hurts him to see me live it again. That's why I wanted him to stay out of this."

Rusty caught up so I led him to the dining hall, grabbed a chicken burrito and started a patrol of the area. I was still determined to find the woman who drove the Cadillac. I walked to Sherri's trailer and knocked on the side. No one was home. I tried the door and it was unlocked. No wonder Sherri had so many tricks played on her. I tried her cell number knowing she wouldn't answer it if she was working. She didn't. That meant she was on location.

"If anybody suspicious comes down this walkway let me know," I said and entered the trailer. The place was thrashed. The items on her vanity were swept off. Kitchen drawers were opened and emptied. The bed was stripped. The dresser was emptied, just like the kitchen had been. I flipped open my phone and called Arnie.

"Arnold Rodeo speaking," he said.

"Arnie, this is Cassidy. Sherri's off on location and her trailer's been thrashed. You know better what to do in these cases so I thought you should know."

He spent a good solid minute cussing, told me thanks and hung up.

I opened the door and stepped out.

"Maybe you should take a look," I told Rusty. "You've seen thrashed rooms before. See if you can tell what they were doing here. Hopefully Joe will be here soon. More likely it'll be Davin. If it's Davin he won't be much help but he ought to be entertaining."

We waited for Joe and while the two men checked out the trailer I put my eyes to the ground and, burrito in hand, examined the area for tracks. I knew if the trailer had been thrashed that morning I would have heard about it from Sherri. Since I hadn't heard anything, I could assume it had been done after Sherri left. I was excited. This was what I'd been waiting for. A clear case within a defined time frame. With Rusty there he'd have ideas. He and Joe would turn this into a real case. The place would be fingerprinted, evidence collected. If I could just come up with a suspect we'd be in business.

Right outside the door the tracks were confusing. As usual, many people had walked down the little corridor that morning. Davin rounded the corner.

"Davin, stop!" I called out. "Can you get me some orange cones?"

Instead of jumping to action he leaned against the trailer and grinned at me.

"Cassidy? Is that you?"

"Yeah, but stay off the tracks. I need to puzzle this out and I need people to stay off the tracks. Can you block off the walkway?"

"I can. It'll take a while to go get the stuff."

"Caution tape? Anything?"

"What are you doing in that get up?"

A woman walked by obscuring the tracks even more.

"Just get the cones. I'm rapidly losing information here."

This was tough tracking. There had to be tracks by the door. Whoever had thrashed the trailer had gone in first so there had to be matching tracks in both directions. I sorted through a dozen sets of partial tracks. Grouping, categorizing. Trying to figure out the timing of each layer.

These tracks belonged to the Hair people. Those were left behind by the Makeup people. Sherri's tracks were easily identified. Next I found Davin's tracks. Coming and going. Hmmm. There was another set, buried deep, just partial prints. I focused on Davin's tracks since they were the most readable of the possibilities, then I put the tracks aside because I could talk to Davin. This other set though, it was mysterious; it was a puzzle. How much time did I have left for lunch?

I couldn't profile, there wasn't enough of the tracks left to do that, although I was fairly certain it was the same woman I had seen at Sherri's shooting. As I made progress down the corridor tracking the woman, I soon realized the cones would be useless. I'd be moving them too quickly so I called Davin and canceled the order. He caught up with me again, watching my tracking with interest.

"One other set of tracks went to Sherri's door and back out this morning," I told him. "They were yours."

"Just making the rounds."

"Why didn't you check the other doors then?"

"Some doors don't need checking. Some of them I know are occupied. Some are offices. Some are open all the time."

"Was Sherri's door locked when you checked it?"

"No."

"What time was that?"

"I don't know."

"Did you go in?"

"No."

"Did you see anything unusual when you checked the door? What made you check it?"

"I just knew Sherri was away. I checked it to see if I needed to make more frequent stops there. I thought you were gone so no one was watching the trailer. So I added it to my stops. What made you come back?"

"I didn't leave."

"What made you do whatever it is you're doing?"

"Sherri thought I should mingle with the extras but when we talked to Nickolai about it he gave me this role. I don't know what I'm doing anymore. I'm in these fight scenes. I should be there practicing now, but I need to follow this through before the tracks are gone completely."

"Leave it to you to start out tracking, become a body guard and accidentally land an acting job. Do you know how hard it is to get a part like that? They're usually given to stunt men who have been in the business for years."

"I kind of figured that out. Now let me track."

I'd been tracking all along, Davin walking patiently out of the way of the tracks, but I really needed to focus and get back to practice. I was in enough trouble that I didn't want to add lateness to my list of offenses. But this could lead to something. This could be the end of my worries.

After I left the shelter of the trailers the tracking became tougher. I wasn't confined to one direction and had to move from track to track. I had slowly made my way halfway across the big open square when a kid ran up.

"Are you Cassidy Michaels?"

"Yes, get off the tracks."

He jumped aside, not knowing where the tracks were.

"Ramon wants you back in the practice room."

"Okay, I'll be there as soon as I can."

"But they're ready to start."

"Tell him something came up and I'm helping Security sort it out."

He hung his head, hands in pockets.

"Okay, but he's not going to like it."

Tracking partial tracks took studying and comparison. This was where a real tracker was tested. Anybody could see footprints in the dirt. It took a real tracker to decipher exactly which tracks to follow. The tracks on top were the most recent, but they did not belong to the person I was following. They lingered somewhere in the middle on top of old tracks and under new ones. The tracks led to a group and got lost in the jumble. I stopped tracking and looked at the group as a whole. They had milled around, shifting just as any group will as others joined in and they waited for something to happen. Apparently they were waiting for transport because they all boarded a van and the van had left. I couldn't follow them from this point but Rusty could. I jogged back to Sherri's trailer and updated the guys.

"I followed the tracks to the square. She joined a group of people waiting there and then boarded a van. Check around and see which van took off from the square this morning, where it was going, and who was on it. I have to get to practice."

"Good work kid," Joe said.

Rusty was in a somber mood but I didn't have time to talk. I gave him a hug and headed for the practice room. I wasn't in much of a mood to face Ramon or learn choreography.

"Did you get things squared away with Security?" Ramon asked.

"As much as I could under the circumstances. Joe and Rusty should be able to take it from there."

"What are you really doing here?" he asked.

"Sometimes even I don't know," I said. "I'll tell you all about it later. We have work to do."

Over and over and over we practiced the routine. I thought I could do it in my sleep. I thought I probably would. The actions became automatic and just when we thought everything was perfect Ramon reminded us that this was a life and death fight. He wanted to see the fight in our eyes, in our action. He wanted to see the force of the battle… so the flashbacks began again. Sometimes I closed my eyes knowing what would happen if I watched that face come at me, the strike coming. When Ramon dismissed us I hung back, knowing I owed him an explanation.

"I ended up with this job accidentally," I explained. "Sherri hired me to find the person who was playing practical jokes on her."

"Why would she hire you?"

"She thought my tracking skills would help find the prankster."

"Tracking skills."

"Yeah, that's what I was doing at lunch. I went to check on Sherri's trailer and someone had totally thrashed it. I found two sets of tracks that went both to and from her trailer. One set was Davin's. He had a logical explanation and didn't match my profile of the prankster so I followed the other set of tracks to the square where the person boarded a van. Sorry it took so long to figure all that out. The tracks were buried under hours worth of other busy tracks so it took some figuring."

"You're a tracker, hired as a body guard. How did you land a stuntman's job?"

"Sherri wanted me to get access to the extras because it's kind of obvious by now that the prankster is an extra. But when she took me to Nickolai and he found out I had a little military and police background he gave me this part instead. They filmed me running through the woods, climbing fences. It's been really weird and I haven't been able to do much for Sherri. So when I finally had a chance to track this person I had to take it."

"So you don't work for SundownPictures at all?"

"Only for two weeks, but these pranks have turned serious. Sherri's thrashed trailer is a minor nuisance. Whoever this prankster is, she has turned on me for some reason. She tried to run me down. She rigged my gas pedal to stick when I drove home. Another time she tried to chase down Sherri and I in a car and we only lost her by taking off cross country. I want this woman stopped and I seem to be the only one who can dedicate the time to do it."

"Tuesday is the big fight scene. Will you be ready for it?"

"I'll be ready."

"You have to be. It's a one-time shot. We can't go back and redo it. The whole set will be burned down in the shooting."

"I'll be ready. Is there shooting to do afterwards?"

"Yeah, but you should be through unless Nick wants to go back and fit you into more scenes. You'll be on call for the whole two weeks."

"Oh great. I was hoping after we catch this woman and do the big fight scene I'd be finished. My husband was against this job from the very beginning. Things I get involved in have a habit of turning dangerous and under the circumstances he has been... shall I say over protective?"

"Under what circumstances?"

I stood up but I guess the layers of costuming hid it.

"You mean you didn't notice?"

"Notice what?"

"I'm five months pregnant."

"What are you doing here? You know why they have stuntmen, don't you? Because they do things normal people can't. It's not a safe line of work.

You have to be a little crazy to do this work."

"Maybe Nickolai could see I'm a little nuts. I've got an easy part. I don't have to jump off any buildings. I don't have to do back flips."

"You just have to fight in a room full of fire. It isn't going to be pleasant. You're going to have to really focus. Everyone is going to look worse than whatever you are seeing in that head of yours. It's going to be hot and intense and you can't afford to slip. You switch to real fighting in the big scene and someone is going to get hurt."

"I'll work on that." He stood so I took my leave, "I better find Rusty. I'll see you tomorrow."

"Tomorrow's Sunday. You have tomorrow off."

"I do?"

"Yeah."

That worried me and cheered me at the same time. I'd totally lost track of time. No wonder Rusty was here. It was his weekend off. But I wondered what would happen to Sherri. Did she have the day off, too?

Rusty wasn't nearly as cheerful as I was. They were sorting through Sherri's possessions. A stack of papers was accumulating next to him.

"Here's another one," Sherri said handing it over to Joe, who passed it to Rusty. They'd been sorting as they went and Sherri's possessions were stacked according to where they came from. Some of them she was packing into a suitcase, which boded well for my Sunday.

"I think we have it under control if you want to go," she told Rusty.

He stood and surveyed the scene. Six large stacks of clothes. A dozen pairs of shoes. Unused pots, pans, utensils. Only the vanity had been restored to order. That made sense considering it was Sherri's trailer.

"You know what to do," Rusty said to Joe.

Joe nodded, "Will do, probably tomorrow."

"Good, I'll check in on Monday."

Rusty picked up the stack of papers. They were threats; mostly threats but there were other things in the stack too. Hate mail. Details about what the person wished to do. To me they looked more like idle ranting but everybody present had a much different outlook.

It was another brown couch evening. Rusty was worried. I didn't know enough to be truly worried. I could tell; something in those letters had touched him deeply. I was hoping Sunday could be a fun day. I sure was ready for a fun day. I wanted to put all the bad memories back where they belonged and replace them with fun.

Rusty just needed time. I could tell when he relaxed a little because his grip loosened and I could move a little. I could tell when the next stage came because he started talking.

"I wish I could stop you."

"I know. My part in this is actually very small. Two short choreographed scenes. We've been over them a thousand times. Everybody just gets into position we all do our part, and get out of the way and the whole scene won't last an hour. My part lasts about a minute."

"I can't go to work that day."

"That's silly. Of course you can. This is just a job. It's not Junior's first school play."

"I can't. I can't just go off to work when there's so much at stake. Joe's going to bring in more security. I'm going to ask Schroeder for a couple of officers. He'll give them to me, when he sees the threats. We'll be ready, as ready as we can be behind the camera."

I felt him tightening up again. Time to change the subject.

"We have tomorrow off. How do we want to spend our minutes?"

He flinched, pulling me close again.

"Don't say it like that," he said quietly. "I can't think of it like that today. I can't think we only have minutes. I need to think bigger than that."

"Would you take me hiking?"

"Babe, it's winter."

"We can still hike. I need to feel earth beneath my feet. I need to follow a game trail. Just for a little while. We could go rock climbing. We could invite Kelly."

"You're not climbing rocks. A fall would be too risky."

I was glad he hadn't seen me climb out of the alley.

"Even if we just walk in the hills behind the house, I'd like to get out. I'm feeling boxed in."

Chapter 22

We live in the desert. We don't get much rain here. Clouds hit the mountains behind our house and what little rain or snow falls hits the mountains. Some of it strays over our house and a very tiny bit of it hits the desert floor to the north. This was a dry winter. We were way behind on our rainfall for the year and everybody was talking about water rationing and wildfires. Strict was relieved. The cold temperatures in the mountains kept tourism down and the lack of snow kept the skiers from losing their way. The only snow up in the mountains was in deep, shadowy canyons or at the ski resort.

On Sunday I looked at the thermometer. Fifty two. A good hiking temperature. Once we got moving we wouldn't even need jackets. Rusty wouldn't let me carry the pack. It made me feel naked. I always had a pack on when I hiked. Usually it was thirty-five pounds. I would have been more comfortable in the pack even if it only contained a lunch, water and two jackets.

"It's only a day trip. There's no snow. Let's see if there's anything left of the hideout."

"Are you sure you want to know? You haven't been there in a long time. A tarp doesn't last forever. The hideout could have reverted to forest by now."

"I know. I kind of think there's as much of it left as I need there to be. If it's gone, then maybe that's a sign that I don't need it anymore. Even if the hideout doesn't exist anymore it's a pleasant picnic spot and an interesting canyon. I have climbed those rocks a hundred times. We can see the deer in the clearing."

The hideout was a camp I'd built. It was a simple affair. Just a huge tarp hung over two fallen trees. The floor was cleared and the tarp kept out water. I placed branches from the forest on top to cover it. Saplings grew up, around, and over it, so it looked like a wild patch of forest, but it was really a little tent/cave. A person standing in the camp couldn't see it. To get in I had to look around under the forest litter for a little flap of tarp. I lifted it and crawled under and inside was a snug little shelter. I kept a stove and sleeping bag there. An ammo box kept backpacker food dry and a couple of books waited for rainy days when I was trapped inside. I even had a fluorescent lantern that lit up the whole inside. I'd spent many a lonely night there.

I'd needed that hideout for a long time. I fled to it when I needed to get away and into the woods. Then I'd fled to it when my first husband passed away and left me alone at twenty-four. Many grief filled days had been spent hiking off sadness I thought I'd drown in. Many hours were spent in the canyon trying to figure out my future. I didn't know how to make a future out of what I had to work with. All I'd known was how to live in the woods. So that's what I did, off and on, until I met Rusty. The girl he met back then was bitter, woods wise, independent but full of sorrow and hardness.

I didn't know what Rusty could see in me. At first I ran from it. It frightened me. He didn't push. He didn't even really nudge. But he called on me and he nurtured me and one day I couldn't imagine life without him. He changed me from a borderline hermit into a woman. I had a purpose again. I had friends. I had a job to do. And I had him. I found less reason to hide and more reason to stay with Rusty and now a whole summer had gone by and I hadn't been to the hideout at all. Still, it sat up there, waiting for me. Maybe. Maybe Rusty was right. Maybe I didn't want to see if it was gone. If it was gone, then maybe the me that made it was gone, too. Maybe I should just let myself think it was there.

It was late morning when we took off from Creekside campground. Shadow took to the trail eagerly. He sniffed for squirrels and wandered from one side of the trail to the other, investigating everything.

I started out chilly but I knew I'd warm up quickly. There was no point in digging out my jacket. The creek was a trickle and I wondered if there would be any water at all up the canyon. I'd never seen it completely dry up there. I counted on a little water being in the creek for my cooking and it had never let me down. Most of the water came from snowmelt but there could have been a spring up there somewhere. I noticed that the trees were dry and the grasses were parched.

The cold had discouraged tourists from venturing out on a hike. Most of the tracks that I saw on the trail were very old, but one set looked familiar. And recent.

Rusty made me go first, partly because he was bigger, had a longer stride and he thought he might leave me behind if he went first. That was unlikely. The other part of it was habit. I was the tracker. The tracker goes first. So I walked ahead of him reading the tracks as I went. When the tracks left the trail I stopped, peering into the woods.

"What are you looking for?" Rusty asked.

"Kelly, he came through here maybe two days ago. I just thought he might be out here camping somewhere."

"In winter?"

"Rhonda's back east. She doesn't like to rough it. He might take advantage of the time and go camping for a while. I'd probably go camping if you went away for a week."

I continued down the trail and picked up Kelly's tracks again. He must have just walked down to the creek and back.

"Okay, I'm curious. How do you recognize one person's two day old tracks? To me the trail just looks like dirt."

"You know I've tracked Kelly. For many miles. You don't track a person without learning something about them. Kelly is left-handed. He tends to walk on the left side of the trail. It's got the right stride, the right pace, the right wear spots, the right attitude and personality."

"Hold it. Tracks don't have personality."

"Of course they do, once you learn the subtleties. When I track someone for a while I can tell how they are feeling."

He smiled. "So how's Kelly doing?"

"Good. He's enjoying the hike. He's looking forward to roughing it a little. He's been noticing birds in the trees. He's made mental notes about the condition of the trail, seen little things he might come back and fix later."

"You can't know all that."

"Okay, then ask him about it later."

Instead of getting warmer the day got colder. I was okay as long as I was hiking. When we stopped to rest I found myself standing with arms folded, eager to start walking again. I don't know why we stopped to rest. I didn't need it and Rusty didn't need it. It just seemed like the thing to do at the time. As I hiked I watched for sunny spots in the trail and slowed down in them, soaking up the warmth.

It was a good day. A day to feel free again. We followed Kelly's footprints when he turned up the canyon. At one time I would have been worried at the thought of footprints in my canyon but I was pleased that Kelly enjoyed it as much as I did. Every time we came to a climb Rusty made me go first and he stood beneath me. It made me feel strangely fragile. There were ways up the canyon that didn't require rock climbing but I liked the feel of the rock on my hands. Plus, this was the route Kelly had taken. I'd unconsciously followed his tracks.

I was pleased to see a small trickle of water in the creek. If there was water here maybe the deer would stay close to it. Water was scarce in these mountains. We stopped at the meadow but there were no deer. The grass was cropped low. The deer were running low on food. I looked around at the less desirable plants and they too had been grazed upon. I knew deer ate woodier plants in the winter. I hoped they were coping with the dry winter. As I hiked I noticed brush that the deer could have eaten so I felt better about their situation. I wished I could invite them to my house where we kept the grass watered. It wasn't exactly green but it was food. I left the deer meadow a little disappointed and, as I hopped back across the creek to start up the canyon again, a big rain drop hit me square on the head and rolled down the back of my shirt.

"Looks like we better make a run for it," Rusty said. "I just hope the roof is still intact."

"If it's not we can shelter in the rocks. Too bad Trent's Cave is gone."

We hiked quickly up the canyon but it was still half a mile to shelter. We were soaked to the bone by the time we arrived. Rusty kicked around where the flap usually was that led inside the hideout. He stood outside holding the flap as I crawled in. We were in such a hurry that I didn't even notice it was light inside and when I bumped something unfamiliar I looked up into the surprised face of Kelly sitting there trying to peel off his soaking wet clothes.

"Oh gosh, Kelly, I'm sorry!"

His pants were down around his knees and sticking because they were wet. He couldn't get them up and he couldn't get them down. I quickly sat with my back to him to save him further embarrassment while Rusty stood outside in the pelting rain, waiting for a chance to come in. Shadow whined beside him.

The problem was the hide out was snug when I camped there alone. It was downright cozy if Rusty was there. Three people were going to feel like a can of sardines.

There was huffing and puffing and silent curses as he fought his clothes. I finally decided he just needed space so I crawled back out.

"What are you doing?" Rusty exclaimed.

"Let me know when the coast is clear!" I called into the hideout.

The rain pounded as Rusty and I stood outside shivering and grinning at each other. When we got the all clear, I sent Rusty in first. Shadow pushed his way in and promptly gave himself a good shake. There was thrashing around and both men simultaneously yelled, "Arg! Shadow! No!" Then Rusty, "damn wet dog!"

Even standing out in the rain I smiled at the picture in my head of what it must be like in there. Did I want to go in? The first thing to hit as I entered was the overpowering smell of wet dog and damp clothing. Sitting scrunched into the back of the hideout were Kelly and his big black lab, Amos. Rusty sat in his damp clothes. Shadow stood square in the middle of the hideout taking up the most space. Everybody looked wet and crowded and a little uncomfortable. I pushed Shadow aside and found a spot to sit down. Yup, sardines.

It was amazingly quiet in the hideout. The branches that covered the outside muffled the sound of the rain. I looked around wondering if the tarp was still water tight. It hadn't been but a new tarp was in its place. I looked around further and I could tell. Someone had been taking care of the place.

"Sorry to crash your camping trip," I said to Kelly.

"We had one day off and Cass had to get out of town," Rusty continued.

"It's okay. I crashed your dinner party," he answered.

"No you didn't. You were welcome."

"Then you didn't crash my camping trip either," then he was embarrassed again and began explaining, "I don't come up here often."

"It's okay. The hideout needs someone to come up here."

"It seems lonely. I check on it. Stay a night or two. Fix a few things."

"Why?"

He bowed his head, still embarrassed.

"Because I can't let it die. It reminds me of you two and I can't let it go. If I need to get out, it's here. The least I can do is keep it up for you. It saves me packing in a tent. I can see why you built it here. If you want me to stay away, I will."

"No, Kelly, the hideout is yours as much as it is mine."

We sat in cold, damp discomfort as thunder rolled over the mountain. Thunder was rare in Joshua Hills. It didn't sound like a good sign.

Kelly flashed a grin. "You're lucky I wasn't armed when you first came in. What did you do to your hair? I couldn't figure out what you were!"

"Oh golly, I forgot about that. It's dyed for the movie."

"Cassidy started a job as a tracker and ended up a stuntman," Rusty said.

"Yeah, you should see me in the rest of the getup. Black leather jacket. Zinc studs. You can't even tell I'm female, or pregnant. If they end up using any of the clips I bet you won't even recognize me."

"We came up here to get away from all that," Rusty reminded me.

"I wonder if it's raining at the set."

"I doubt it. The rain hits the mountains and stops."

"That's good. We need it nice and dry on Tuesday."

"Babe, please drop it."

Kelly knew something was up but he knew not to ask. He looked to Rusty.

"I'll check in later in the day," Kelly said.

"After dark," I said. "They won't start filming until dusk because the fire has to show up in contrast."

"Cassidy…" Rusty said.

"Sorry, Rusty seems to think Tuesday is doomsday, or something. It's just a shooting. One big fight scene."

I could feel Rusty tensing beside me.

"Would it help if I knew what all the threatening letters said?" I asked,

"Joe took them. I only got to glance at the top one and all it said was, 'I Hate You' I assume that one was to Sherri since it was found in her trailer."

Rusty pulled me to him. He stuck his feet out. I sat in front of him leaning against his chest. He jumped when his wet shirt hit his skin. There was more room in the hideout this way but he really just needed me close. Kelly recognized the signs of stress. He knew Tuesday held more than anybody could predict.

"You're freezing," Rusty said rubbing my arms.

"I'm okay. It'll warm up in here with all these bodies."

The dogs lay around licking their paws, adding the smell of dog breath to the already stuffy interior.

"If I thought it would get you to quit I'd let you read them but I know you wouldn't. All I can do is hope you'll keep your eyes open, stay alert, and not let the flashbacks get the upper hand. You need to know that everybody is in their place every second. One change in the plan could mean disaster for you or Sherri. Joe is screening everybody who makes up that scene. We'll have backup right there. Security and police officers both. But we can't see what you see. We have to stay behind the camera unless all hell breaks loose and that's not the kind of trouble you'll be in. It'll be something quiet and sudden. Joe tried to get Nickolai to cancel the shooting but it's all set up for a go."

Joe took this seriously. That told me more than Rusty's worry. Rusty worried about everything. Not so, Joe.

Rusty opened up the daypack and handed me a sandwich.

"I'm not hungry. It's too cold to be hungry," I said.

"You barely ate breakfast, then you hiked four miles. You need it," Rusty said.

He's going to be unreasonable because he cares so much. I had to remember Kelly's words.

"Let's cut them in half so everybody can have some. I only want half anyway."

"I brought backpacker food," Kelly offered.

"We can't cook it in this close of quarters. I've only lit the stove in here a couple of times and had some scary flare ups so I quit. I've spent days in this place eating nothing but jerky, trail mix and cookies, reading books, and sketching."

"I've seen them," Kelly admitted. "Have you seen her sketches?"

"No, when we're up here we don't spend much time in here."

"It's just a way to pass the time," I explained. "I can only read so long. I never was good at art. Don't show him."

Sigh, too late, Kelly handed the book over to Rusty. I didn't even know what drawings were in there anymore. I hadn't seen the book for a year. The pages were yellowed and brittle from temperature changes. Rusty held the book tenderly. It was touching that he placed that much care on something I considered random doodlings. He turned the pages as delicately as his big fingers could manage.

"You had these just sitting up here in the woods when we could have had them up in the house?"

"I don't want those things up in our house. They're just...observations. Just little things I drew."

"No they're not. They reveal a lot about you. Most people would draw the scene with the rocks, trees and creek. You draw... a mouse, blades of grass bending in the wind, a tiny game trail that nobody on earth ever knew was there. They're beautiful. How could you let them weather like this?"

"It's just a sketchbook, something to pass the time on days like this."

"Can I keep it?" Rusty asked.

"Sure."

"Can I scan it?"

"Rusty, I don't care. I didn't sign any of those, did I? As long as they are just random drawings I don't care what you do with them."

"Why don't you admit to the talents you have?" he asked.

"I do, that's why I'm a tracker."

Rusty was good at helping me see there was more to me than a trouble magnet who could see invisible marks on the ground and find people. Drawing? A talent of mine? I laughed inwardly. Pencil scratchings. They were just pencil scratchings. They were just pencil scratchings that Rusty cherished. For some reason I was glad. He put the sketchbook in the pack and pulled out the fruit. The rain pattered outside.

"Are you warming up?" Rusty asked.

"Yeah, I'm fine."

After the long walk and getting some food in my system I was tired. At work I was busy all day. I didn't have time to get tired. This tiredness was so heavy and Rusty was so comfortable. Having him close was relaxing. I felt him lay me down and pull the sleeping bag around me, then he stretch out, easing out the cramps that I knew came from being in this place for any extended length of time. And the rain pattered on. The guys talked softly.

I woke to snoring, Rusty lying behind me, one arm around me, his hand resting where he could feel the baby. Kelly slept scrunched against the far wall. We were getting more like sardines all the time. Amos and Shadow...where was Shadow? He knew how to get out of the hideout but I didn't think he would in the rain.

The thunder rolled over the mountains. I could barely hear the rain.

I slid out from under Rusty's arm and crawled to the entryway. Amos followed. I lifted the flap and looked out. I expected to see a wet and bedraggled dog waiting but he was nowhere to be seen. Usually if Shadow needed to go out he nosed his way out and then barked to get back in. It was only raining lightly so I ventured out. I was amazed how green the woods had turned during the storm. I loved the forest after a rain. It felt fresh and clean. The temperature had dropped noticeably. I walked around watching the woods for a black and white Shadow. I walked to the creek in case he had gotten thirsty. The creek had swollen with new rain and again tumbled roughly down the canyon, over the trail below and on to Creekside Campground. I whistled, hoping Shadow would hear me. Usually I was his sheep and, being a Shetland sheepdog, he knew where I was at all times. I knew he couldn't be far away. Amos followed me around sniffing for new smells. I looked around on the ground for tracks. Only Shadow's, Amos's and mine were visible. I could track Shadow but I didn't think that was necessary. What I could see of Shadow's tracks looked like typical sheltie activity: a quick check of the camp and a bathroom stop, the scratching of the ground afterwards. I was following the tracks despite deciding not to, just out of curiosity when there was an earthshaking *CRASH!* and I was thrown over backwards. For a moment I was shaken, unable to move. What scared me the most was that I couldn't see. Rocks pelted the area and the rain began pounding again.

"Cassidy!" Rusty called. It sounded sharp… and startled.

I started to get up but I was still disoriented and my vision had only returned a little bit. I found my feet and felt my way toward his voice.

"Rusty, I can't see," I said feeling my way. Suddenly I felt arms around me, guiding me forward.

"How close was it? Did it hit you? Where did it hit?"

"What hit? I don't know what happened. I just know I got knocked flat and I can't see. And Shadow's missing. I was looking for Shadow."

"Lightning. It was lightning. Are you okay?"

"I think so. Everything is jumbled to me. Why can't I see?"

"Come inside. Rest your eyes. Maybe it was just the brightness. Where did it hit?"

"I don't know. Rusty, I don't know. I couldn't see it. Everything happened too fast."

He made me lie down but I was antsy. I laid back and closed my eyes. The guys dimmed the lantern and we waited, listening to the rain again. Lightning. Rusty said it was lightning. What would lightning do to a baby? I thought that was Rusty's big question, too. I lay still waiting for the baby to move. We couldn't call for help. We had no radio or cell phone reception in the canyon even in good weather. During a storm it was zero. We all felt terribly helpless.

"Rocks," I said, "I remember rocks falling. It must have struck the canyon wall or a tree near it."

Rusty was looking over my hands and feet for burns. What we were really waiting for was the baby to move. Please move little one. Just a flutter. I couldn't even think about my eyes. I was just waiting. I knew the baby frequently stayed still for hours and it wasn't unusual for him to not move. As the seconds stretched to minutes I couldn't help feeling frantic.

"Rusty?"

"I know, babe. Lay quiet. Just lay quiet."

"Is the creek water cold?"

"What?" Kelly asked.

"When I drink ice water it wakes him up. He will frequently move if I drink ice water."

"I'll go," Kelly said.

Thunder boomed overhead and rumbled over the mountains, shaking the camp.

I opened my eyes again. The white nothingness was looking more like somethingness.

"It's coming back," I told Rusty.

I didn't need to see him to know how he was feeling. If we'd been home he'd have had me to the doctor by now. He'd be pacing and nervous. As it was he couldn't do any of that. All he could do was sit and hope.

Kelly came in with a bottle of water. I felt the bottle, hoping it was cold enough. I thought it might be. I sat up, knowing it helped to be upright, and took a drink. We waited. I took another. It usually took several drinks before the now familiar fluttering would start. With the tension in the air it felt like it took forever. Please move, baby. For mommy? For daddy? I took another drink. I thought I felt something, a small movement and then more followed. Relief flooded me. I could breathe again.

"Okay. We're okay," I said, tears in my eyes.

"Where is it?" Rusty asked.

"Right here," I said pointing to the spot.

Kelly was embarrassed to be in on such a private scene but there wasn't anything that could be done. It took half an hour or more for my vision to slowly return.

"We need to head for home," I announced when I could finally see what objects were again. I couldn't make out details but I knew what things were.

"Cass...no. I can't force you to hike four miles after what you've been through."

"It's the only way home and you're not forcing me. I'm just doing it. We only had a day. We did the day hike. We got out and I got my dose of nature. It's time to go home."

"It's still raining."

"Not much."

"You're not climbing down that canyon."

"Rusty we both have to be at work in the morning. I'm supposed to be there at seven. We can't even leave in the morning and go straight there. If we got up at first light we'd still be late."

"I'll hike out and send a lift back."

"No, I'll be fine."

"Kelly? What was your plan?" Rusty asked.

"I've been here since Friday. I have to be at work in the morning, too."

The guys took stock of our supplies. Nobody had a tent. The best we could do was carry food, water, stove, and jackets. We put the basics in Kelly's big pack and stuffed in the sleeping bag, just in case. To my relief both dogs came running when the group crawled out of the hideout. We looked at the sky, hoped for the best and headed down the canyon.

"If we follow the dogs down we won't have to climb," I told the guys.

I had to walk very carefully. I couldn't see well enough to just walk so I felt with my feet as I walked. When it came to the steep downhill stretches I had to pick my way down very slowly. My feet slid out from under me a few times, scaring Rusty again.

The rain began coming down in earnest again but we kept hiking. Rusty called a halt when I was shivering uncontrollably. I would have kept hiking, thinking hiking was warmer than soaking wet stillness but Rusty wouldn't let me. There was no shelter and the temperature continued to drop. In school talks I warned kids about going on hikes prepared for anything and now here I was freezing my butt off on a long, wet trail.

"Cassidy, your lips are blue. We need to get you dry and warm."

"I'm-m-m okay-y-y," I shivered.

"You're not convincing me. What would you do in a survival situation?"

"With no t-time constraints? F-f-find shelter. Any shelter. Leaves, a log. I'd find a place with limited shelter and dig down in. If I were by myself and just had to get out, I'd pile on the insulation and jog it."

"You're in no shape to jog it."

"Says who?"

"Me."

"We're on the trail now. That means there's less than two miles to go. We can make it t-two miles. I don't have to worry about slips and falls on the trail. Let's just go for it. Once we get to the truck we can crank up the heat."

"What can we do to warm you up?"

"Without shelter? There's no way to get dry. Let's just hike to the truck. We know it's close. We know the way. All we have to do is keep on keeping on. That's the rule. K-keep on keeping on."

I headed down the trail shivering until an old cadence we sang in the Marines got into my blood:

Hey! Hey! All the way,
We love to run every day.
If I were President and had my way,
There wouldn't be a fat man in the Marines today.
Everyone would be fit to fight,
Whether you test them day or night.

The guys followed so I started singing it. They had never heard me sing, never seen me in such a state. I was just keeping on, like I learned so long ago. When that cadence quit working. I switched:

One mile
No sweat
Two mile
Better yet
Three miles
Gotta run
Four miles
To the sun

"Okay, we get the point." Rusty said.
Still in cadence:
"You missed the one that
sounds like me.
After seeing my sketches
you'll have to agree:

A little mouse
with little feet
was perched upon
my toilet seat.
I pushed him in.
I flushed him down.
I watched him spin
around and 'round."

"You're kidding. You learned *that* in the Marines?" Rusty asked.

"You learn all kinds of stuff in the Marines."

"Marines training or not, you wouldn't flush a mouse," Rusty said.

"Oh yeah? You didn't see the latrine in Afghanistan, although I don't recall seeing a mouse in the outhouse. And they didn't flush."

I'd achieved my goal. The guys were moving. The truck was not far. We'd make it. Today.

Every part of my body was frozen as we hiked into Creekside Campground. I crawled into the truck and huddled there, shivering, feeling a lot like the mouse that got flushed down the toilet. Rusty started the truck and got the heat flowing. We all drove to Kelly's house where he started a fire in the fireplace. He loaned me some of Rhonda's clothes to change into but they were too big, even over my big belly.

Kelly's house was small. It was an A-frame with a kitchen, living room, bathroom and bedroom downstairs and one bedroom upstairs. The downstairs bedroom was full of hobby stuff: camping gear, rock-climbing gear, a remote controlled glider, a sewing machine, a plastic see-through box with hundreds of pieces of fabric stacked inside neatly and labeled: fat quarters. A stitching project half finished. The house was old, needed painting, and had a lived-in feel. The dishes had stacked up in Rhonda's absence but Kelly didn't care. His whole house reminded me of the old brown couch. It had seen better days but it was settled in and comfortable being that way. Amos flopped down in front of the fire, the perfect picture of a black lab at home.

Rusty and I sat on the couch in the living room thawing out.

"Thanks for taking me hiking," I said to Rusty.

"You're thanking me? For that?"

"Yeah, I got my dose of nature in. I'm ready to stay home for a while now. It's not your fault the weather turned on us."

Chapter 23

Monday was a long day of drills. We went through the sequences over and over until we didn't even have to think to do them right. Then we moved to the set and did it again in our real positions within the scene. I kept track of my position in relation to Sherri so I'd know what to watch for during shooting. I examined the faces of all involved but the mysterious woman was nowhere to be seen. Every time I was given a break I walked over to Sherri's trailer, checked the door, checked the ground around it. Everything seemed unusually quiet considering we were gearing up to the climax of the movie. I hoped it was because everybody knew their job.

When things calmed down, and the trailer was checked out, I sat. I sure would be glad when this job was finished. I was not cut out for this. The people had grown on me. Even though I still considered Sherri a spoiled rotten California girl, I liked her and I was vigilant, wanting to prevent whatever trouble was headed our way. I had an advantage. I was used to trouble. Sherri was not and I wanted to protect her from it. After a while the quietness began eating at me.

"Something's brewing. I don't like it," Spike said from nowhere. I'd forgotten about him and I reminded myself to be more observant. At least Spike was a good guy.

"What is it?"

"I don't know but others feel it, too. I hope Nickolai feels it."

"Who knows about the threats?"

"Not as many as you'd think. But the feeling is still there, hanging in the air. You watch people. They're uneasy but they don't know why."

"Things that hang in the air can wallop you one," I said remembering the lightning strike the day before. I hoped this tension didn't have the same frightening results.

Spike and I walked the set checking for anything unusual but there were so many odd looking things around that I couldn't begin to guess what was normal and what was abnormal. There were props and fire starting devices and men crawling all over the set preparing for the next day. Electric screwdrivers were busy putting pieces in place. The set was large and it was hard to believe the whole thing would be ashes at the end of the day tomorrow. Even the demise of the set was saddening. It was a marvelous creation, a complicated construction job with many artistic architectural accents. It looked like a patio surrounded by a mansion. It looked like a place

I'd like to sit and sip iced tea. The fountain worked and the archways surrounding the patio provided windows of action. A wrought iron balcony overlooked it all. It was landscaped and tended and had taken on a short lived life of its own as the movie unfolded in and around it. That such a place could be created, earned its place in the imagination and then was burned down so quickly left me sad.

The flashbacks I had suffered had eased up as the practice had become a more casual rehearsal in our nice, normal street clothes. We had focused on the actions and less on the intent of the shots so there were far fewer angry glares and threatening movements.

One of the women from Hair walked by, glancing uneasily around her. She felt it.

Monday evening Rusty was a frightening sight to behold. Tight as a rattlesnake ready to strike. Dangerous Detective Man. If he looked as intimidating at work as he did when I saw him, he had a lousy day. Everybody would have steered away from him. He arrived home before me and he couldn't stand the thought of being cooped up in the house while I cooked dinner so we bundled up and drove into town. His driving was tight, precise and I felt like we were in a race even though we were only going the speed limit. The tension was contagious.

We found a booth inside Trujillo's and settled in.

"Hey, Rusty! Cassidy! I haven't seen you in decades!" Benny greeted us loudly. We used to come to Trujillo's frequently but it was a longer trip now that we lived out of town.

"We've been busy," I said.

"That's no excuse. Busyness is a reason not to cook. You should be here *more often* if you are busy." He had a point. "So tell me, what name you choose for this baby? Is it by any chance Benny? Benjamin? Benji?"

I laughed, "We haven't chosen a name yet."

"So how long you got?"

"Three and a half months."

"Aiyee, it's getting close. You better name that kid before he ends up nameless."

"He'll have a name, don't worry."

"How you been feeling?"

"I'm fine. I've been working and hiking in the woods. I'm doing great."

"That's good. What can I get you? No alcohol for you."

"Iced tea."

Rusty ordered a beer and then we both ordered a combo plate.

"How are you really feeling?" Rusty asked after Benny left.

"I'm okay. Things are tense at the set but nobody knows why. Even people who have nothing to do with the scene walk around with a wary glance and nervous energy. It's weird. How can one person's unspoken intentions spread like that?"

"What about you? Are you nervous?"

"Yes and no. Whatever is lurking doesn't worry me. I know what I'm supposed to do, so that doesn't worry me. I am mostly nervous for Sherri's sake and I don't look forward to all the cameras. I hate the cameras. I'll just have to tune them out, and watch for odd things that don't belong. It's going to be a tough scene just because there is so much to keep track of: the actions, the person I am working with, Sherri, people that don't belong, fire, cameras. If I am lucky I'll be too busy for flashbacks but I have a feeling the intensity of the scene is going to make that tough too. Tomorrow's the last of it though. I'm only on call after tomorrow. They may not need me at all."

Benny suddenly appeared at the table again.

"Ha! The hair! I knew it was something! I knew you looked different in some way but it took a while for it to hit."

He walked away again not waiting for an explanation.

"Benny's not very observant," I said.

"Most guys aren't. One thing I can count on. If something is out of place tomorrow you'll see it. You've got a good eye. I just pray it happens when you can deal with it."

"You're blowing this all out of proportion. What can they do with cameras recording every move? They do anything at all and it's going to condemn them. Who would be that dumb?"

"Someone who's warped and desperate and has nothing to lose."

Tuesday morning I had plenty of distractions. Bailee had a hundred and one questions. She almost didn't care about the riding lesson.

"What happened to you?" she asked when she saw my hair.

"Sherri got me into a stuntman's job. I didn't know they were going to do this to me when I sat down in the chair."

"So you are going to be in the movie? That is so cool! Are you going to have pictures made up? Will you autograph one for me?"

"My part in this movie might add up to thirty seconds. I'm not doing any acting after this so I'm not having pictures printed up. I have no desire to ever do this again and I almost don't know how I ended up doing it this time. I'll write my name on anything you like. You find a movie promo card or something. I'll sign it for you but I think it's silly."

"Who do you work with? Are you a good guy or a bad guy? Are you in a scene with Brock the Rock?"

"Bailee, one question at a time. I'm a bad guy and I work with a couple of different stunt men. I doubt if I'm in a scene with Brock although the camera might happen to catch us both in the same picture. I don't work with him directly."

On and on she talked and questioned me. It was good to hear her chatter. It meant a lot to me that she had progressed so far. I answered as many of her questions as I could and didn't burden her with the tensions of the day and after her lesson she went home all tanked up on excited energy and I went home and ate lunch.

Rusty was already out at the set making security arrangements. He probably wore a trench in the ground with his nervous pacing and the whole company was wishing I had never come on board.

Even though shooting wouldn't start until dusk I had to get there in the early afternoon. I'd have to spend an hour in Hair and another hour in Makeup. The people in Costumes had everything ready but I'd have to stand up to intense inspection and I was told I'd probably get sent back to Makeup again for touch ups. We'd practice the scene several times in full costume before the sun set. Since it was winter, the sun set early. It would be a busy afternoon.

The whole compound was a bustle of activity. I watched the ground as I headed for Ramon's office. I looked in the practice room. There were several pairs of people running though their routines. Donnal and Andrew were anxious to get started. They weren't in costume yet so I ran through my two sequences with them a few times. Ramon caught up with me and sent us to our respective stations. I grudgingly went through all preparations for the scene, jumped again when I saw myself in the mirror. I went to Costumes and got outfitted in the same bulky leather outfit I wore before. At least the outfit was warm. The temperature was in the forties and dark clouds loomed giving the set an ominous feel. The hustle and bustle of activity intensified as the light faded and last minute preparations were made. I caught a glimpse of Rusty talking to a group of people. They pointed out a direction and he strode away.

I took a look at the set. I couldn't tell who was who except for the officers. Ben Tomlin was as bad as Davin. He was basking in all the Hollywood trappings, ogling the girls, watching the cameramen, wishing he could get hold of one of the cameras for just a few minutes. This assignment had a very high GPS rating. There were cameras and light meters and TV screens and weapons and weapon look-alikes. I walked up to him.

"Hey there," he greeted me and I realized he didn't know who I was.

"Hi," I said.

His eyes narrowed and then got big. "Cassidy? Is that you?"

"So, what do you think?"

"Hey guys! Look! It's Cassidy!" he said, dragging me over to the rest of the group of officers. They all stood around me trying to find the me they all knew. They came up empty.

"Say something," Big John said.

"Where's Rusty?"

"No, I mean something from the movie," Big John said.

"I don't have a speaking part, which is a very good thing considering I am not very nice and I suspect I might even be male. I'm not sure. I can't tell by looking in the mirror."

"I don't know what they planned, but you're still female," Jacobsen said. "Not the sexiest costume they could have given you."

"Under the circumstances I don't think sexy is the right look for me," I said.

"Oh yeah? That's not what Rusty says," Ben teased.

"Sounds like Rusty talks too much."

"You seem awfully calm considering."

"Considering what?"

"What you're walking into."

"I don't know what I'm walking into except a big, fake fight scene where I manage to get caught on film for about thirty seconds."

"Thirty seconds of fame in a costume that makes you look like an outer space alien is not worth the risk you are taking."

"I'm not doing it for me. I'm watching out for Sherri. I never plan on getting within ten miles of another movie set again."

The guys all stood around exchanging glances that ranged from quiet amusement to flat out worry.

Things were really gearing up. Officers patrolled the area. Two fire trucks pulled in behind the cameras. I thought they would have been handy in any case considering the chances of wildfire were high in this part of the country. Security had been increased and Joe was kept busy giving out instructions and checking IDs. His expression was serious.

I walked to Sherri's trailer and she wasn't there. Bill stood guard on the door. He nodded to me, just enough recognition to let me know they were on the ball. I was used to that form of communication. The officers often didn't need words to communicate and they frequently just gave a questioning glance followed by an answering glance.

Sherri was probably in Hair or Makeup. She'd probably be in there until the last practice. I went to the door of Hair but Security quickly stepped in and stopped me. I figured the same thing would happen no matter where I looked for her. Wow, these threats were being taken seriously, I thought.

Ramon saw me walking around and pulled me aside.

"What are you doing just walking around out here?"

"I'm looking for something to do. I can't find Sherri. I can't find Rusty. You don't have practice going on."

"Don't walk around alone."

"How can I possibly be alone? Look at this place. It's crawling with people. There's more security and police officers than there are actors."

"Let's just hope they do their job."

He took me to the practice room, got on the phone and said a few words, then turned to me.

"Come at me," he instructed.

I started into my routine but he departed from it.

"What are you doing?"

"You're going to have to be ready for anything out there. Start with what you were taught. When things change I want you to cope with them. Remember you can't hurt me."

We started again and he came at me. It was tricky trying to stay in the routine and ward off his blows at the same time.

"It's not Donnal and Andrew that are after me," I said.

"This is still good practice. If you see something coming at you from any direction, be ready."

Ramon was fast. Each time he came at me my first reaction was defensive, just stay out of reach, then counter with any move I thought would take him off guard. I didn't want to fight him. A door opened and Ramon swung at me. I ducked and turned to see Rusty walking briskly across the room. As he gathered me up in a tense hug I felt a weight slip into my pocket. I pulled it out. It was my 9mm and badge.

"No," I said flatly. "I won't use it."

"You've got six senior officers who will stand up for you if you need to."

"I won't, though. I can't. If I did you might as well just lock me up in a nice padded cell. I can't use my gun that way."

"Keep it. Just in case you change your mind."

"Rusty, nobody's going to try anything. It looks like the place has been invaded. Security, cops, firemen, EMTs…they'd have to be nuts to try anything."

"Maybe they are. Maybe they want their fifteen minutes of fame any way they can get it."

Rusty had read the letters. I weighed his natural tendency to worry with what might be in those letters, then I kept the gun so he'd think I was more protected. I turned to Ramon again.

"Don't try to fight this woman," Rusty said. "How much does she know about you? Can she pinpoint your vulnerabilities?"

I stopped. "I don't know. She could know but she'd have had to be watching at key times."

"She was watching when the Cadillac almost ran you over. She might know."

People began filtering into the practice room. Time for final preparations. Rusty stepped in close and looked me in the eye.

"I wish I could see you for just a second the way I know you to be."

"Me, too," I answered.

He couldn't even kiss me, I was so covered with makeup.

"Remember it's not just you," he said solemnly.

"I will."

"Okay! Everyone in your places!" Ramon called out.

I took a look at Rusty and he hesitated a moment before backing out of the room. I could feel the pull of his hopeful wishing, that I'd just walk away, wash off the makeup and be done with it. But I had a job to do.

When I took a look at Donnal I knew this was going to be a tough assignment. Even in the practice room he was an intimidating foe. I fought down the alarm his appearance triggered in me.

Dodge, jerk, twist, duck, kick, twist and trapped. I stilled myself knowing it was just practice. The grip wouldn't tighten.

Then with Andrew: duck, charge, duck, twist, turn, block, block, kick, turn, block, jab, JAB, jab harder, push up with the pole, run forward two steps, turn. Andrew wasn't as intimidating as Donnal. Something was bothering him. This was too easy.

"Come on," I told him. "You're holding back."

"Again!" shouted Ramon.

Andrew put more force behind it but something stopped him.

"I can't help it. I found out what's going on. I'm supposed to be fighting you when I want to defend you."

"Forget what you know. If something happens just pretend it's planned and go with it."

"You shouldn't have hid your pregnancy."

"I didn't. And I'm not as helpless as you think." Block, block, kick. "Remember, when I started at this I had to learn to hold my punches."

"I know. I took one of those punches."

"Come on, put some effort into this."

Andrew did his flip over me but he was so distracted he almost didn't make it.

Ramon marched over.

He looked Andrew in the eye as he barked out, "We have time for one more try. Let me see this all work together! Ready and Go!"

We began and Ramon continued, "Remember, this is all or nothing. You've trained hard for this. We're going to do it and we're going to do it RIGHT."

I put my weight into the moves and jabbed more forcefully than I had before, trying to get Andrew to see, I was ready, no matter what happened. With the unexpected force he pushed, an angry scowl making him appear sinister. It was no longer a matter of going numbly through memorized moves, we'd moved to a different level for better or worse. He lunged, I pushed, he made the flip and we were ready to go.

We walked the short distance from the practice room to the set. It was like a parade. Background people stood watching us go by. Nerves were still on edge. They'd be on edge until this was over. I wished I could stop and read the tension in the tracks.

"Places everybody. Places."

I climbed up onto the fabricated mansion. Ramon, knowing I was inexperienced, followed me up and pointed out my camera. Before it had just been a direction to keep in mind. Now it was a direction and an angle. I couldn't see the camera. The lights were too bright, but I knew where to concentrate. As the others found their places I searched the area for Rusty but I couldn't see anything behind the lights. I had to turn away and preserve my sight. I could feel his helplessness over the expanse between us. I could feel the officers and the security men watching the scene go together, trying to catch anything that didn't belong. I took note of my position in relation to Sherri. I counted the steps in case I needed to close in that direction.

I looked around and was surprised how many other actors looked exactly like me. Could Rusty tell us apart? I felt oddly detached thinking I was missing that link to him. I knew he was here to prevent disaster. But more than that, he was here to protect his baby, his wife. What was I doing here?

Camera checks, position checks, the whole area was walked by pyrotechnicians making sure the fire would start in the right place, the right time and affect the right areas of the set for the right length of time.

It was like being in a nightmare. Like fighting things I knew I couldn't beat. Frightening faces appearing before me. Quick ineffectual reactions pounded into me by dozens of practices. It was eerily quiet for a battle scene. In the finished version there would be clanging and violence and music but right now it was quiet and unsettling. I expected noise with violence. It was all very disorienting to me. Blinding lights one direction, dark violence the other. We ran through the first half of the scene three times. We didn't need the fire for this part of the scene so we repeated it until Nickolai was convinced we had enough action recorded. Donnal was a natural at this. I was glad we had three chances to get this right because I was fighting flashbacks. It took all my control not to strike him, to remember the moves at the same time. When I saw Dirk coming at me and I knew that chokehold was coming I knew my eyes reflected a genuine fear. I had to force myself not to elbow him in the side and pull away from his grip. When we stopped for a break I could feel the collective relief of those watching, especially Rusty.

I kept an eye on Sherri. So far so good. Maybe all the tightened security had paid off.

Hair and Makeup people stepped in and did last minute checks. They fixed my smudged makeup. Ironically, they smudged it more.

The lights were adjusted. Places were taken again and the new action sequence was practiced. This time I faced Andrew. I could see the tension of the moment in his face as we fought. He knew. If anything was going to happen in a big way it was going to happen during the fire scene. He knew it would target Sherri. Or me. He knew either way, if something happened I'd be on top of it and it was something he couldn't allow to happen. I realized, if something did happen it would trigger a chain reaction and *I* couldn't allow that to happen.

Chapter 24

"Places!" called out Nickolai. He paced in front of the stage giving us a pep talk and a speech about the hard work and dedication everybody had shown in the six months they had been working together. This little lull in the activity was bad news for me. I didn't have time to stand there listening to a long-winded director. I stood on that red line with the number seventeen taped next to it and listened and waited and felt the blood slowly leaving my brain. I had to walk. I had to sit. I had to do something. On and on he talked and I felt weaker and weaker until I just had to sit. I lowered myself to the floor and sat cross-legged waiting for my head to clear.

Andrew didn't like what he saw. "Are you okay?" he whispered.

"Yeah, I'll be fine as soon as I'm allowed to move around."

I was just trying to get my blood flowing when I realized Nick was instructing us on the fire, reminding us this had to go through with a single take. I missed half the instructions. When Nickolai had finished he sat down with a flourish. "Places?" I stood back up hoping I was as ready as I needed to be. "Places? And action!" The clapper was slapped shut with a resounding bang.

Andrew looked at me with an "are you ready?" and I nodded. He magically changed into The Enemy and the sequence was begun. A swing at me. Duck. Charge in. His kick. My duck. A twist, turn. Why was everything going in slow motion? Was I just thinking clearer? Block, block and I was back in another fight for my life. I remembered being trapped in a dressing room, Trent pinning me to the wall. Kicking out at him. Kick, turn, block. Everything turned into a jumble of past and present. I wanted to run. I could feel Rusty out there somewhere and then there was the pop and flare of the fires. They caught quickly and spread into a fierce inferno. Andrew was still in sync praying I'd get through my part of it. He saw the flashbacks hit and saw me come back to reality when the fires started. Jab, JAB. A soft *thunk* beside me. Wait! That was wrong! What was it? Jab harder, push up with the pole. I felt Andrew's weight on the pole as he went through the flip. Okay Cass, run forward two steps, turn. When I turned there was a dark, costumed figure running toward Sherri. She was fast and light on her feet. I was supposed to look around and run, then follow the exit plan to get out of the fire. The look in my eyes matched the occasion perfectly because I really *was* looking for the enemy.

Sherri was busily involved in her own scene so I chased down the character that didn't belong. I was running on instinct, but a part of my mind was telling me I might be reacting to something that did belong. When I caught the person I knew; this was the woman who tried to run me over with the car. This was the extra that Sherri had pointed out. I grabbed her by the shoulder and spun her around.

I felt movement behind the camera. A massive shift forward. A hundred people wondering if they should do something or finish the scene. Ten cops watching little old me in a struggle I wasn't prepared for. Rusty watching his wife, his child. I didn't know what to do. I couldn't turn the woman loose. She'd go for Sherri. I couldn't drag her off the set. It would ruin the scene. So I pretended it was part of the scene, only I didn't hold my punches. All I had to do was keep her busy until the scene ended and then the guys could take over. I mostly fought defensively. I knew if I took one dangerous hit Rusty would be on the set in a flash. So I drove the woman away from Sherri back toward the mansion.

She was livid. This was not part of her plan. When her anger flared she went after me punching and scratching and I grabbed her wrists pushing, pushing for the background, out of the scene. She writhed around screaming every profanity in her wide vocabulary. She brought up a foot to give me a kick and I had to let go of a hand to catch the foot. I pushed up on her foot sending her falling backwards. I fell on top of her, took my gun out of my pocket and pointed it in her face.

"Don't move!" I yelled at her. "Don't move until I say. You hear the cut and you stay put. You move a muscle…"

She let out a blood curdling scream. Her back arched lifting the both of us. Her screams were not anger, though, they were pain. Only searing pain brought a scream like that. Only terrible pain gave a small woman the strength to lift another person even when her life was on the line, but that's what she did. She leaped to her feet dumping me on the ground and frantically pawing at her head. Then she took off running with her hair in flames! I ran after her pulling off my leather coat. I threw the coat over her head and rolled with her until the flames were smothered.

Curses filled the night as this wild woman tore into me, anger and pain driving her. She pushed me through the window of the mansion and we fell into the crawl space below the set. There was a frantic scrambling for control.

"Stop!" I yelled. "This plan of yours was a losing proposition from the start. You can't get out of this. Either you face the fire or the police. You can't win!"

"Damn you! You bitch! You ruined everything! I hate you!"

I could hear the pop and hiss of fire catching more wood overhead.

I heard a loud, "Cut!" and knew the actors would all be leaving the set.

They got all the action they could out of the scene and it would be allowed to burn down now.

"Make your choice!" I ordered her. "I personally would choose the police. It's less painful. You already know what the fire feels like. I don't think you want that again. Come on. We need to get out of here."

"Cassidy!" I heard Rusty shout over the crackling flames.

"Damn it! Move!" I yelled making a grab for my foe but she was running on some fury that I didn't understand. Every time I made a move to get her out of there she backed away punching and scratching and kicking at me. She just was not going to be caught and I didn't know how much I was willing to risk to bring her in.

"Cassidy! Babe, please! You can't do this!"

We could see the flames licking through the floor above us. This place could come down any time but she fled deeper into the woodwork until I was stooped over trying to follow her.

"Damn it! What do I have to do? Shoot you? That would be ironic if I had to shoot you to save you. Have you ever been shot before? I have. It's no fun. It hurts."

Ironically what saved us was the very chokehold that had frightened me earlier. She lunged at me grabbing me by the neck so I grabbed hold of her wrists and started dragging her out. She fought and squirmed but I held fast. She cursed and struggled but the position was so awkward for her, there wasn't much she could do. All I had to do was get to fresh air and backup before I keeled over, so I trudged towards the night air ahead. I heard voices ahead and picked up my pace but I needed air. I could almost see the officers through the haze. Just a little farther! But I couldn't make it. My senses dulled, my hands fell slack and I fell forward. The last thing I remembered was the woman struggling loose. She ran right into a wall of officers. I woke to water dripping on me from the fire charred beams overhead. The firemen had been called in to put out the fire on the set. I pushed myself up, fighting a wave of dizziness and staggered out the back of the set.

The reactions of the officers were mixed. Some of them snickered. Some of them were all business. Friends were concerned. But mostly it was amusement. I couldn't think of anything funny about the situation.

"Michaels! Over here!" someone shouted.

It took him a minute to get there and at first he was just stunned. When the relief and shock had worn off, he took off his jacket and wrapped it around me. It was then that I realized I had only been wearing underwear under the leather jacket. I hadn't even thought about that. When I was in Costumes I just changed into the garments they handed me. It wasn't the most comfortable get up but it was what they wanted me to wear so I put it on.

Then I went about my business thinking of it as an ugly leather jacket. It was only natural to throw it over a person who was on fire. So there I stood, in front of my friends and coworkers, nearly topless. Just a bra, leather pants bulging over my big belly. I could just imagine what I looked like: black and red hair, bad-guy makeup running down my neck and then... nothing. Bundled up in Rusty's coat, he led me to the EMTs.

"Rusty, there's nothing wrong with me that an hour in the shower won't fix."

"Hush, do this for me."

The EMTs had to call in someone from makeup. They couldn't tell where the makeup started and ended so Wanda came in with a huge bottle of makeup remover. Just taking off the stage makeup took a half hour. I had a makeup lady working on my face and arms while the EMTs were taking my pulse and blood pressure. They shined their little light in my eyes. As I gradually turned more normal looking they began their usual questions.

"When's your due date?"

"The end of June."

"Any pain?"

"Just the typical bumps and bruises I always get from a takedown."

"You do this often?"

"No, usually it's the other way around. Same result though."

"Tell me what happened," the one named Dave said. Dave was a kindly young black man. I was surprised I hadn't met this pair yet.

"How much did you see from behind the cameras?"

"We could see off an on until you fell through the window. You lucked out it wasn't a real window."

"Basically, we fell under the set and I chased and fought her deeper in. She tried to choke me and I grabbed her wrists and started walking. Only problem with that little plan was I ran out of air before I got out. So I lost her."

"The cops got her."

"That's good. When I got more air I found my way out."

"That doesn't sound like it took half an hour."

"She was stubborn."

They poked and prodded and felt for broken bones. I'd been through it all many times before. All I had to do was have patience.

"Well, we can't find anything seriously wrong with you," Dave finally said. "I don't know how you managed that."

When the EMTs turned me loose I came face to face with a group of concerned friends.

"You didn't call," Spike said.

"I was kind of busy," I said. "Besides you couldn't ruin the take."

"I would have, if you'd called."

"Cassidy, I was so scared!" Sherri said.

"I hope I didn't ruin the shot," I answered. "Now you know better than to hire me for a body guard."

"We need to extend your contract," Nickolai said.

"No, I'm through being a stuntman."

"I meant to cover the unexpected fight scene the cameras caught."

"I was just trying to keep her away from Sherri."

"There's still some useful footage in there."

"You mean you're going to give that woman air time after all the trouble she raised?"

"All in the name of entertainment."

Ben Tomlin, John Jankowski and Kent Jacobsen stood there with a "Well, we survived another Cassidy adventure" look to them.

Davin said, "Well, I took this job thinking it would be entertaining. I had no idea what an understatement that was. It was better than a trip to the movies!"

Chapter 25

When we got home there were six messages from Kelly Green. We looked at the clock. Twelve thirty a.m.

"If you don't call him he'll call again at one," Rusty said.

The phone rang four times before Kelly picked it up.

"Yo," he said sleepily.

"We survived," I said.

"Good. When do I get the whole story?"

"Tomorrow. Late."

"It's a deal."

We went to bed but it took us a long time to get to sleep. While we should have been dead tired we were wired from all the excitement. We needed quiet time. Time to feel the baby. Time to bask in a few minutes of peace.

At eight o'clock in the morning the phone rang. I groaned. I hadn't gotten to sleep until nearly two a.m.

"Hello?" I said.

"Cassidy! Have you bought a baby swing yet?" my mother asked.

"A baby swing? Why would I need a baby swing?"

"Why, to swing a baby, of course!" she said.

"I don't see why a baby needs a swing," I said, still groggy.

"Then you don't have one yet?"

"No."

"Good! Don't buy one. Are you okay?"

"Yeah, I'm just tired."

"Already? Usually you get up with the sun!"

"Not today. I was kind of busy last night. I survived a fight and a fire and I was trying to sleep in."

"Wow, you *have* been busy. You need to ease up now. It's not right for a woman in your condition to be fighting."

"Believe me, I don't plan any more fights. Good night, mom."

"Good night, no wait! Have you found out if it's a girl or a boy?"

"No, Mom, I won't know until the baby's born."

"Rats. Go back to bed. You can't get into trouble there."

Oh yeah? That's how I got pregnant. I fed Shadow and let him out for a minute to do his business, then I brought him back in and went to bed.

"That wasn't Schroeder, was it?" Rusty asked.

"No, it was Mom, we don't need to buy a baby swing and I'm supposed to quit getting in fights."

"I'll second that," he said.

At eight thirty the doorbell rang. I pulled on a robe and answered the door, Shadow barking beside me. It was FedEx. I signed for the big envelope and brought it into the house.

"Guess I'm just not supposed to sleep in today," I told Shadow.

It was addressed to me so I opened it. It was from Sherri. She remembered! Inside the envelope was an eight by ten photo signed to Bailee and one just signed with her name. Then there was a cast photo from the movie. She and Brock and Nickolai had all signed it. And there was a check for fifty thousand dollars. You'd think most people would be glad to get a check for fifty thousand dollars. I felt guilty. All I could say for Sherri was that she was still alive. I sure hadn't saved her from any pranks. I had probably caused her more trouble than she would have had without me. But, I reminded myself, she would have had countless sleepless nights.

"Who was that?"

"FedEx."

"What did they want?"

"They want me to go back to bed. And they want you to rub my back. And then they want you to take a shower with me and let me give you a nice soapy massage, maybe use the sprayer gently in all the right places."

"They do?"

"Mmm hmm."

"I should be at work."

"You'll be at work soon enough. I bet you'll be at work before we get to the shower. In fact I think you should just start with the front."

If there was one thing Rusty could do it was take a hint.

A grocery shopping trip made me go into town and I was looking forward to it because I was planning to stop by the cop shop to see Lawanda.

The little bell on the door jingled merrily as I entered and Lawanda greeted me, "Cassidy! I haven't seen you in weeks!"

"That's because I don't need cop stuff very often. I brought you something, just like I promised."

I handed her the big FedEx envelope. She read the outside but it only had the address of Arnie's agency on it. She reached in and slid out the photos.

"Hot damn, Cassidy! What were you doing the past few weeks?"

"Let's see, I trapped an electronic cat, chased a tarantula and a snake, I almost got run over by car, outran an angry woman in a Honda cross country on a dirt bike, tracked a prankster, accidentally landed a job as a stuntman. I was in a couple of movie scenes, saved the star of the show from an angry coworker. And nearly got burnt to a crisp."

"So, same ol' same ol'."

"Yeah."

"So, how'd you get the autographed pictures?"

"Spike gave me one and Sherri sent me the other."

"Sherri? Sherri Champlain herself?"

"Yeah."

"Who's Spike?"

"Brock's bodyguard. He's a nice guy. I wish I could have gotten his picture. I got a cast picture but the two most interesting people I met weren't in it. I'm saving that picture for the baby's scrapbook. So I can show him what he did before he was born. Then he can tell his school friends that he was this close to Sherri Champlain."

"You said 'he'! Does that mean it's a boy?"

"No, I still don't know and I still want it to be a surprise."

"Rats, I was hoping to find out if I won the bet."

"The bet?"

"Yeah, there's a pool going on around the station."

"That's illegal."

"It's just for fun. Everybody knows it's just for fun."

"So, how did you bet?"

"I ain't telling. That might tip the scale."

"It's not like I can change it to what you bet!"

"Oh, all right, most of the station thinks it's gonna be a boy. Cause they're betting he's going to be another cop in the family, like Rusty is. So I say it's a girl just so's I can argue with all the guys that come in."

"You're in good company. My mom's betting on a girl, too."

"I say there's no reason a girl baby can't grow up into a cop, too."

The baby was growing. Rusty could feel the taps stronger now. I could feel a growing bond to the little person inside me. We did everything together. He affected my every move and, I was sure, he was affected by mine, too. I started feeling guilty when I drank cold water. After all, how would I like it if my nice warm bed suddenly turned chilly? I'd move, too. I'd reach for the covers or snuggle up to Rusty. I still couldn't stand the smell of cooking eggs. Occasionally a smell would send me running for fresh air. Food that I used to enjoy somehow lost its appeal to me and foods that I thought I'd never like looked interesting to me. I quit buying ice cream because I ate too much of it. Every time I got hungry between meals I'd get a bowl of ice cream. Not buying ice cream didn't help much in the diet department, though. When we didn't have ice cream I started thinking cookie dough was the perfect thing. Pretty soon, the police station had a steady stream of chocolate chip cookies coming in. I wondered if the officers had to loosen their belts a notch like I did on a weekly basis. Rusty got teased but nobody was complaining.

Chapter 26

The search calls always picked up in early spring. It was the worst time of year for tracking. Warm days lured people out. Cold nights and unpredictable weather took them by surprise. If there was ever a time when heavy rains were going to obliterate a trail it was early spring.

It didn't take long, once the weather warmed up a little, for someone to get lost. Strict was reluctant to call me but I was more than ready to get out of the house.

"How are you feeling?" he asked.

"Fine. What's up?"

"I've got a rough one for you. I tried calling Chase. He wants you to take it. He didn't say he wouldn't. He thinks you need the chance to do it."

"Why did you call Chase first?"

"This is rough territory. It's going to be a challenge physically."

"And the tracking?"

"It's going to be rough, too."

"How old is the trail?"

"Three days. Like I said, it's going to be rough. The good news is we know where he started and where he intended to go. Why he wanted to hoof it and go cross-country we don't know. He obviously didn't know what he was getting himself into."

"Outdoor experience?"

"Enough to be dangerous."

"Water?"

"Yeah, he took water, food, a jacket. He expected to make the trip in a day. There's no way to do what he was planning to do in a day but he should have made it by now. I mean, he should have made it *somewhere* by now."

"Three days?"

"Yep."

"That means I need my big pack."

"Problem?"

"I don't think so. I'll figure it out. Give me an extra half hour. I need to empty my pack and prioritize."

"Don't prioritize too much."

"Who am I going with?"

"Victor."

Oh man, I had to bring everything if I was going with Victor.

"Why Victor? I mean, I like Victor. He's a good partner."

"He's better suited to this job and he's a dad. Nothing you can come up with will surprise him."

"Oh yeah?"

"Don't push it."

"Okay, I'll be there as soon as possible."

Next I had to call Rusty. He was not going to be happy. He wouldn't even let me carry my groceries in from the car and now I was setting out on a four day backpacking trip over rough ground.

"Hey there, how are you?" he asked when he answered the phone.

"I'm fine. I have a job to do."

"A search, right? Not a job. Last time you had a job didn't work out very well."

"Okay, I have a search. I'm betting it's at least three days long, although I hope not. I don't know how long this guy can hang on. He's been missing three days and he had a goal in mind so unless he gave it up he's getting farther away all the time."

"Where are you starting from?"

"I don't know yet. I'm supposed to meet Victor at the compound and Strict will show us on a map what we're up against."

What I saw on the map seemed impossible. Well, not impossible, just impossible the way our ten sixty-five thought to do it. He was camping and he decided he would hike home. Only problem with that little problem was he had twenty miles of the most dry, rugged mountains in the southwest to cross. Walking home as the raven flies would require several mountain climbing expeditions and walking home via the odd pathways of valleys and canyons would more than double the distance and probably disorient even a seasoned hiker. The canyons all look very much alike and directions get confused when all you can see are hillsides and dry washes. Follow a canyon heading west and it would turn without notice and head north or south without a person even recognizing that it happened. On the bright side there were roads crisscrossing the mountains. Our ten sixty-five should have stumbled onto a road and waited for help. Unfortunately, macho men on a mission could be terribly stubborn. So far the mountains remained silent. No motorist had dropped him off in town. There had been no phone call from a house deep in the woods. Three days running on empty was just plain stupid but I'd reserve that judgment until I talked to the man myself.

"Look, he had to cross these two roads if he was still on track," I pointed out on the map. "If he did what looks like the logical thing to do he should have gotten fed up with mountain climbing and followed this canyon. The canyon leads nowhere but it would have pointed him toward this highway." I tapped the map.

"That hasn't happened, though. We've got to go," Victor said.

"Couldn't we drive up these roads and see if he made it that far? It could cut our search by a day."

"We could. But you're the only one who might know it was his tracks and there are miles of roads where he could have come out. You're not walking all those trackless roads just in case he crossed one of them," Lou said.

"Okay, so let's get to it. What's the guy's name?"

"You won't believe me," Lou said.

"Try me."

"Homer Gent."

"You're kidding!"

"I told you."

"Sounds like a vanity plate on a baseball player's car," Victor said.

"Description? Tracks?"

"The family is in Pasadena. They called local authorities to report Homer missing and they contacted us since this started on our side of the mountain. If this progresses into their district we can call on them to help but it might be easier to just keep going."

"You think he made it that far?"

"No telling."

"Okay, let's back up again. Description?"

"Five ten. Two hundred twenty pounds. Gray hair."

"Age?"

"Sixty nine. Overweight but not a couch potato. He's used to being in the outdoors. He walks regularly. I doubt three days in the mountains killed him, might even have helped a little. That is, if he's unhurt. Last seen he was wearing jeans and a flannel shirt."

"Race? Color?"

"White, green."

"Shoe size?"

"Ten."

"I don't suppose you have any idea about the wear spots on his shoes. A guy in his shape usually has more distinctive wear spots than a normal person. Health issues, age and habits have left permanent patterns in old shoes of someone like him."

"No, but we have an idea of how determined the guy is. If he's still mobile he's still looking for a way home and he isn't going to ask for directions."

"Great. And I suppose he probably doesn't want to be rescued by a woman."

"Probably not, though after three days maybe he's mellowed a little."

"Maybe he'll feel better about it if we can trade war stories."

"You have war stories?" Victor asked.

"Sure, a few, although we have plenty of storytelling just covering the past three months. I sure hope you want chocolate chip cookies. I've been baking almost every day."

"Why do you bake every day? Why don't you just do a double batch once a week?"

"Because I don't get hungry for cookies. I get hungry for cookie *dough*."

"You're not going to go crazy on me, are you?" Victor asked.

"Me? No! Why?"

"Three days without cookie dough isn't going to bother you?"

"No, I don't think so."

"Good because when Natalia craved something she wouldn't let me rest until I'd found whatever it was."

"I haven't had cravings yet. Although, if you brought those gooey cinnamon rolls it wouldn't surprise me at all if your pack got invaded by critters in the night."

"You wouldn't."

"If I did, I'd make up for it with chocolate chip cookies."

"I didn't bring cinnamon rolls."

"Rats."

With the family gone back to Pasadena and the camp left empty I had a hard time finding Homer's trail. The campground was covered in tracks. Three days was a long time for a track to deteriorate. Size ten was not much of a clue to go by. The description helped a little more. Still there could have been a dozen men in the campground about the same size as Homer. After two hours of searching the area for tracks that were definitely Homer's I found Victor taking a nap on the picnic table bench waiting for a go ahead from me.

"Lou, I need more to go on. There are too many tracks to try and pick out one person. It'll take all day to narrow it down. Do you have the family's phone number?"

"What do you need to know?"

"I need a site number, any clues about direction. Even if they say last time I saw him he was headed for that big rock up that crooked canyon or...hell, I don't know. I just need a place to start. Right now I'm looking for vague three day old tracks somewhere in hell's half acre. No, it's worse than that. If it were only half an acre I could do it easier."

"Okay."

I left him to his interrogation. He came back ten minutes later.

"You're not going to like this."

"It's okay, anything more than what I've got will help."

"Homer's an old fashioned Gent. He swears by his old Army compass. He turned west, pointed at the horizon and said, 'See you all at home,' then he marched west."

"Where was he when he said these things?"

"Standing at the picnic table. Campsite number forty-two."

Campsite number forty-two was right next to base camp. We sort of knew that. Three campsites had been taped off and forty-two was one of them. Even with the tape in place there were tracks all over the campsite. Knowing Homer was standing at the picnic table and headed due west helped incredibly. It didn't take much zig zagging in a westerly direction to find Homer's tracks.

"Victor!" I shouted. "We got a trail. Let's go!"

Then, as I waited for Victor to put his pack on and join me, I looked due west and stopped. Oh, hell. Due west was a mountain climbers' nightmare. Mountain after mountain of dry, rugged land. The mountains were not your typical rock climbing rocks. They were brittle rock that flaked off when you put pressure on it. No water, no relief. Just twenty plus miles of sheer punishment. I prayed Homer wasn't set on going due west. It was insane.

Okay, Cass, one track at a time. Don't look at the big picture. Just follow the tracks. This was going to be slow. Three day old tracks took some studying.

When we'd officially gotten underway, which meant we were out of Lou's earshot and I had my eyes to the ground, the usual trail conversation flowed very naturally. In a way I was glad to be going with Victor because Landon already knew about my stuntman adventures. To Victor all this was new.

"Now I've got this check for fifty grand sitting in my bills basket and I feel guilty cashing it in."

"Why? You earned it."

"I don't feel like I did a good job."

"You were a body guard right?"

"Sort of, kind of, not exactly, yeah."

"And the body survived, right?"

"Yeah."

"So you earned it."

"I don't know. I feel like, well, say Lou called me out on a search and when we got to the highway I flagged down a truck and got a ride into town and attended a ping pong tournament and then came back and on my way back to my tracking job I happen to spot my ten sixty-five on the road looking for help. I wouldn't feel like I did a good tracking job."

"A ping pong tournament?"

"That was just an example."

"I still say you earned it. Spend it."

"I wasn't going to spend it anyway. I was going to put it in a bank account for the baby."

"So do it. The kid earned his share, too."

Homer couldn't go exactly due west. Rocks, trees and generally rough terrain prevented him from staying on track, but I had to give him credit, he stayed as close to due west as a guy possibly could. He sure knew how to wield a compass. As I followed him uphill and down I wished he'd drop the compass and step on it. Oh man. He did some strange things, things he never would have done without the compass. At first his trail passed through reasonably pleasant forest, but in these mountains the forest gives way to desert at the drop of a ridge. One side of the ridge would be shady, with trees and brush and wildflowers. That's because where there is green there is water. On the other side of the hill it could be as dry and barren as the middle of the desert. And so I tracked Homer out of the forest to a rocky ridge and when he reached the ridge he found a way to go west. It was a terrible risk. Victor and I opted for ropes. The rock on the mountainside was sharp and rolled under our feet. How Homer made this decent without injury we didn't know. It was easy to track him down it. There was only one direction he could go once he started down. His tracks bit deep and small avalanches marked his way. Occasionally he slipped and made a grab for the mesquite or dry roots that poked out of the loose soil. Stopping two hundred pounds of falling man with a skimpy mesquite branch left plenty of secondary sign. I wondered how Homer's hands were feeling after stripping several branches of their leaves. I thought a couple of these near misses would teach Homer to follow the canyon at the bottom, but no such luck. He went right up the west side. It wasn't quite as steep as the east side but it was just as rocky and difficult. In fact it was worse because it was uphill. Now we were in a bit of a fix. I needed to track but Victor had the experience climbing with ropes. But when we looked at the incline before us we didn't know what we'd attach a rope to. It wasn't solid rock. It was crumbled, loose rock scattered over loose sand. It was not a place a sane person would choose to go. There was a perfectly good canyon to follow. Why was Homer torturing himself with these impossible climbs? At sixty-nine? So he was used to the outdoors. So he walked a lot. He needed a dose of common sense. You don't hike home by pointing yourself in the right direction and sticking to it. There was stick-to-itiveness and there was life-sticks-it-to-youness. I thought Homer had met his match in these mountains. The ascent looked like an all-day endeavor.

"What do you think?" I asked.

"I want to say, if he can do it we can do it, but I'm not sure it's the right thing to do."

"If we leave his trail we'll lose him. Going around this mountain is a day's work and there's no telling if we can find his trail on the other side. And we can't assume he went west. He should have given up that plan long ago."

"So you want to follow his trail up this mountain?"

"No. But it's the only way to stay on it."

"How long has Homer been traveling due west?"

"A couple of miles."

"What are we going to hit on the other side?"

We got out the map.

"Looks like there's a flat area up top. We can camp there and continue this wild goose chase tomorrow."

"Think we can reach the top today? We don't want to get stuck half way."

We both looked at the incline. It was going to be murder. If we made it to the top we'd be all done in.

"There's nothing to tie into."

"I know."

"Rusty is not to hear about this. It was a rough track. That's what he'll hear. Okay?"

"If we find a place to tie in, I say we stop and tie in. That way if we fall we only fall the distance we've climbed from the piton."

I nodded agreement and we began climbing. We tried to stay together but Victor gradually pulled ahead. I had to keep an eye out for sign. In a way it helped to be tracking and climbing because I couldn't push myself and overdo it.

Homer had a slow deliberate way of climbing. He made use of plants and trees. He chose his footholds carefully. If not by sight, at least by feel. He tested the ground before trusting it to hold his weight. At times it took him a couple of tries to find a solid enough spot to proceed. So tracking up this mountain was easy even if the climbing was not.

I heard hammering above. Victor had found a place to tie in.

"Heads up," he said and I found the rope he lowered to me. I clipped in and kept climbing.

By the time we reached the top we could not have gone farther. Light or no light, we had to stop. We didn't even have the energy to set up camp. We shed our packs and sat down on the ground regrouping. I had gone through too much water. Normally a desert rat, I got thirsty much quicker now. I knew resources were a radio call away but I still determined to make do on my own. I told myself to keep a sharp eye on my water situation.

"Are you sure you're up to another day of this?" Victor asked. We'd been sitting in the same spot for half an hour, still too spent to move.

"As long as we take it slow and careful. We can't risk a fall."

"What's the likelihood of finding Homer?"

"Oh, we'll find him. When we do you'll have to stop me from wringing his scrawny little neck. But we'll find him. I can deal with people who just make mistakes, who take a fall or get turned around. I can deal with people who just took on more than they could handle. What I can't take is people who set off on something everybody in their right mind would count as a foolhardy endeavor and then just plow ahead trying to prove it's not."

"Do you mind if I quote you on that?"

I thought about that for a moment.

"No, you better not."

"Why? It makes perfect sense to me," he said, smiling.

"You know why. Because I often do things that Rusty thinks is a foolhardy undertaking, like this body guard job."

"And then when things turn bad, you plow ahead trying to prove it's not."

"Rusty has too many bad experiences. He thinks everything is going to turn on me."

"Maybe it's time to close your eyes to foolhardy endeavors."

"Oh, come on. If a spoiled movie star offered you fifty grand to babysit her for three weeks you'd do it, too. That's over half a year's wages in three weeks. That's a swimming pool for the kids. That's the vacation you've had planned ever since you and Natalia dreamed one up ten years ago. That's a new car, a remodeling job. You can't say you wouldn't take it."

"I'm not a trouble magnet. You take a job like that and it turns into mayhem, then you take the money, buy that new car and end up in a car chase with some psycho killer. You take that vacation you dreamed of and your plane crashes in some remote place and you have to walk out."

"So what would you do with fifty thousand dollars?"

"Get out of debt, put some away. Invest a little. I don't have any big dreams. I like life the way it comes to me. A little here and a little there. At least until you come along. Then there's no telling what will happen."

When the light began fading we had to set up camp and cook. It was a hardscrabble camp. The top of the ridge was just wide enough for a tent so there was no wandering off to the side. We lined up our tents along the ridge and left a cooking place in between. After we cleaned up dinner we checked in with Strict then we both went to bed beat and spent a long night recuperating.

When the sun woke me up I didn't want to move. My legs ached and I knew all I could look forward to was more up and down, slow tracking. If Homer had done the usual thing and just wandered wherever the land led I would have been having a great time. This mountain climbing was hard work.

Victor fired up his stove for breakfast. I eyed his freeze-dried eggs hoping they didn't affect me like normal eggs did. I distanced myself from him.

"What's wrong with you this morning?" he asked.

"Your eggs. Sometimes the smell of eggs cooking sends me to the bushes. I don't know about backpacker eggs, though. Frying eggs do it every time."

"I don't have to eat eggs." He put the eggs away and pulled out a cheese Danish.

I started drooling.

"You said you didn't have a cinnamon roll."

"I don't."

"You have a cheese Danish."

"A cheese Danish is not a cinnamon roll."

"I know, it's worse! It's almost cheesecake."

"Is there anything I *can* eat for breakfast?"

"If you're smart you'll eat all the cheese Danishes. But you can eat whatever you want. Just keep in mind that if you don't eat the cheese Danishes they are in mortal jeopardy."

"What are you eating for breakfast?"

"Oatmeal," I said with newfound distain.

"Aw come on, you can do better than that."

"You know I always eat oatmeal and hot chocolate for breakfast on the trail."

"I'll make you a deal. I can't stand to watch you eat oatmeal when you want a cheese Danish. I'll eat my eggs at a distance and I'll trade you a cheese Danish for three cookies."

"You can have all the cookies. I only make them so I can eat cookie dough."

He ate his eggs. I gave him the cookies and he gave me two precious cheese Danishes. I ate one for breakfast and saved the other for later.

There's a certain way to eat cheese Danishes. Ever since I was a little kid I ate the outer edge with the icing first and saved the cheesy middle with just enough pastry to keep it interesting for last. Okay, so I know I'm weird. I eat muffins upside down, too.

With breakfast finished and tents taken down, we were ready to hit the trail. With a sigh of resignation I found the tracks and we set off down another steep incline. We were halfway down the slope when things went from bad to worse. Homer's trail down the mountain looked like a giant snowball took out a trail downhill. I was guessing he sat down and scooted down on his bottom.

With easy sign to read, I'd gotten ahead of Victor. I heard rocks sliding and did a heads up to make sure it wasn't coming my direction. When difficult parts of the trail come up we usually give each other space to work and time to figure things out. But when I saw Victor teetering on the brink of tumbling down the mountain I made a lunge for him. He saw the motion out of the corner of his eye and yelled, "Cassidy, no!"

When he turned toward me it set him off balance and he tumbled ass over teakettle down the mountain. All I could do was stand there and watch.

Chapter 27

Okay Cass, don't hurry. You have to think clearly and you can't fall, too. Whatever you do, don't make this worse. First rule, do no harm. I don't know where that came from but it made sense. I made my way slowly and carefully to where Victor lay. The force of the fall had ripped the pack off one shoulder. He was all tangled up in a small pine tree.

"Victor?"

No answer. My heart skipped a few beats.

"Victor, you can't do this to me. You're the EMT. You know what to do. At least tell me what to do."

No answer.

Good news was he'd landed on his side. I could get his pack off without moving him much. His pack contained more first aid gear than I knew what to do with.

Bad news was he couldn't tell me what to do with it. More bad news. The radio was shattered. There were little bits of yellow plastic scattered down the hillside. I unclipped the remains of it knowing the case didn't actually do anything except hold the contents together. The little electronics board was broken and I couldn't make any noise come out of it. If I could talk to Strict he'd have Victor out of here within a few hours. But I couldn't talk to Strict.

Okay, first things first. No radio. Limited abilities. Unconscious EMT. Plenty of first aid supplies. Panic stricken tracker. I undid the fastex buckle on his pack and I gently eased the remaining shoulder strap over his arm so I could open his pack.

I checked his pulse. It felt fast to me but my pulse would be fast, too, if I'd just fallen down a mountain. I thought it would settle down soon. Okay, what did they always do next? Blood pressure. I looked around in Victor's pack and came up with the blood pressure cuff. Yay! It was digital. I wasn't sure how to read the other kind. Of course I wasn't sure what the numbers meant. I knew the doctor was always pleased when mine came out around 120/85. But I didn't know what dangerous numbers looked like. When I tried it on Victor it said 140/98. What did that mean? I'd have to ask him when he came to. Next I thought they would check my eyes. Since Victor was out like a light I thought the eye test was a good thing to try. I knew it had something to do with head injuries.

Shine, shine. Look, look. I felt like a little kid playing doctor. I didn't know what I was doing. I just hoped if something was drastically wrong I could tell. But what would I do if I did discover something wrong? I couldn't leave him here on this steep hill. I couldn't move him to the bottom of the hill without risking both our lives. I couldn't talk to Strict. I couldn't get help. The list of things I couldn't do was growing by the second while the list of things I could do was dwindling.

It felt strange touching a man who wasn't Rusty. I worked my way down each arm, not knowing exactly what a broken bone felt like. When I'd checked everything I could check in the position he was in and thought about the fall he took I narrowed it down to a possible broken arm, some cracked ribs and a knock on the head. I cleaned and disinfected the large bump on his head and scrapes on his elbows. I found a cold pack and held it to the bump on his head while I thought about what else I could do. I totally forgot about Homer Gent.

I remembered the inflatable splints the guys carried. I ran my hands down Victor's arm again and he flinched. That was a good sign to me. Maybe he was coming around. It also meant he felt pain right where I'd have pinpointed the break. I looked through the little plastic packages until I found one that looked right. I opened up the packet and unfolded the splint. As gently as I could I slipped the splint over his arm, positioned it as good as I could and blew it up until it fit snuggly. A few minutes later I pinched the valve and eased up the pressure because it looked like his hand wasn't getting enough blood. I replaced the cold pack and sat.

I couldn't leave Victor like this. One move might cause him to slide downhill. If I did have to hike out which way would I go? Going back the way we came would take most of a day and it was even riskier alone and in a hurry. I didn't consider that an option. I pulled out the GPS and the map and pin pointed my location. Damn. Homer had put us in the most desolate place possible. If I followed the canyon below it led to a giant maze of canyons. If I went up canyon it dead ended into a risky climb that led nowhere. If I climbed up and followed the ridge, it eventually ended in a mountain top and I'd have to go back down again. Okay, plan B. Where was the nearest road? I located the road on a map and figured out, on paper, the best route to take to get there. So far plan B was not an option either. I wouldn't leave Victor in this precarious position. Plan C involved waiting for Strict's morning check in. But I knew it would take several tries before he would grow concerned. Just because we didn't answer didn't mean we were in trouble. It just meant radio reception was poor, but he expected it to be poor in these deep canyons. No matter how I looked at it we were stuck for most of the day.

I began preparing for a long wait and possibly a very cold night. I scooped out a ledge in the mountainside. It wasn't level and I had to move a ton of dirt but I thought the tent would stay put. I spread out a tent, for visibility and for shelter if we were still here when the light failed. As I worked I talked to Victor, going over the options out loud, just in case he could hear me. I knew it was iffy. When I was coming out of an unconscious state it helped to know someone I knew had things in control. Even if they didn't, the voice gave me something to focus on. I rambled on and on and wandered back to the situation at hand, "I'd go for help, but you know what a search is like when you have a group and some hero has to go off for help and then you have two searches instead of just one. Plus, I didn't know if you'd stay put when you came to. So I couldn't leave. One wrong shift and you could end up at the bottom…"

"What are you doing?" he mumbled.

"Victor! Don't move. At least until you're all here. Just wait."

"What are you doing?"

I knelt beside him. "Setting up for a wait."

"It's still morning."

"Yeah, that's a good thing, too."

"Give me a hand. What's with the splint?"

"Your arm's the only thing I knew, even remotely, what to do something for."

He looked around at the pack contents scattered, the tent spread out in a cleared area.

"How long was I out?"

"Too long. Your pulse and blood pressure didn't scare me. I'm worried about broken ribs. When you move take it slow. How do you splint broken ribs?"

"You did all this?"

"I had to do something."

"Okay, let's take stock of the situation."

He began untangling himself from the pine tree. There was a lot of grumbling and attempts to not cuss. Victor, in spite of the language he heard in his work, kept his language clean. I blamed his kids. He stopped and felt his leg. It probably hurt like hell whether it was broken or not because it had been bent backwards.

"What is Strict doing?" he asked.

"You crushed the radio, so he's probably making his third attempt at a morning check in, wondering what's up."

"He doesn't know?"

"I had no way to contact him."

"Did you try a signal?"

"The only thing we have to signal with is a gun. I didn't think the sound would carry that far."

"There may be a ranger closer."

"How much ammo do we have?"

"Not much."

"We need to save a couple of shots just in case."

I got out my 9mm.

"No, use mine. It's louder."

I took his sidearm from him and pointed it at the sky in the general direction of base camp. I fired off three evenly spaced shots, paused.

"Again."

I repeated the three. If Victor wanted to signal help it meant he wasn't hiking out.

"Tell me what we're up against," I said.

He was still trying to make his way over to the tent. Every movement was painful. The flattened area was only a few feet away but it took him a long time to untangle himself and make his way over. Lowering himself to the tent brought another gasp of pain.

"I think you're right about the ribs. I'm not sure about my left leg yet either. I'm not going anywhere soon. Hand me the stethoscope."

He listened to his lungs and seemed satisfied with the results. He poked around at his ribs and didn't like the results of that.

"If we can set you up here and you will be okay, I can hike out. I plotted out a route to the nearest road. It's about five miles. It isn't all up and down, but it is cross country."

"Let's give the signal a chance to work."

"That could take all day and it might not work at all. You can't count on the right person hearing those six shots and coming to the right conclusion about them. We need to get you out of here."

"I don't want you off in the mountains alone. You already said we don't want to turn this into two searches."

"We won't. I'll trace my route on your map. If someone shows up here you will know where I am. I'll be fine until I get to a road. Then the trick is to find a ranger truck or a search and rescue car making the rounds."

"How long will that take?"

"In this country? The rest of the day."

"Then at least wait until morning. I don't want you to get caught out there at night with limited supplies."

It was decided. We'd give rescuers until morning to find us and, if they didn't, I'd follow plan B and hike out. Surely Strict would know something was up if we didn't answer our radio all day. We spent the rest of the day on the little ledge. Victor lay as still as he could and I cooked lunch and dinner. When storm clouds moved in we figured we better set the tent up. It was a trick erecting the tent on the ledge because first Victor had to move off of it, then when it was up he needed to crawl into it. There was no room on the ledge for two tents. In fact, the one tent took the whole space and hung over the edge so we ended up sharing, which was against the rules, but we were kind of stuck. Outside the tent door there was just enough space to sit next to the camp stove without getting burnt. I worried about it being so close to the tent.

In the morning I woke with the first light, ready to eat a quick breakfast and strike out for the road but when I opened the tent flap I was greeted by a shower of snow that fell off the tent flap and into the tent. Outside was a pristine blanket of clean, crisp snow. I wasn't hiking anywhere.

"Victor? Are you going to be okay for another day?" I asked.

He didn't answer for a full minute and at first I wondered if he was unconscious again but eventually he opened an eye and looked out the door of the tent. I went to the door of the tent and brushed the snow away so I'd have sure footing for cooking. Then I crawled out and started shaking the snow off the tent.

"What are you doing?" Victor asked.

"Making us visible again. Are you warm enough?"

"I'll be okay as long as I stay in my sleeping bag and we close the door."

I zipped the door closed and then went to my pack and began putting on any layers that would help protect me from the cold. I'd have to be outside to signal searchers. I took the clothes from Victor's pack and put them in the tent where they would warm up a little, just in case he needed them, then I cooked breakfast. I had to hold my breath and step away from the pan to cook the eggs but at least backpacker eggs cook quickly and easily. I put the water bottles in the tent to keep them from freezing. Frozen water wasn't much use for cooking or drinking. One of the water bottles had frozen so I immersed it in the warm water on the stove before drying it off and putting it in the tent. I kept Victor fed, and made sure he had enough water. There wasn't much more I could do.

We listened. Constantly listened. We were very familiar with the sound of a helicopter. We'd heard it a hundred times up close. Sometimes we showed up to begin a search with the *choppa, choppa, choppa* blowing around us. This time we were hoping it brought friends. All we could hear was silence. Not even the animals were out and they certainly wouldn't be found on this God forsaken ledge in the middle of nowhere. I don't know how many times we reminded ourselves: "They know where to look. We're less than a quarter mile away from our last GPS reading. They have to know where we are. All they have to do is decide we need help and they'll be here."

"I'm surprised Michaels didn't commandeer a helicopter himself after no word for a day."

"We don't know what's going on out there. They may have had another call come up, too."

"Strict has a lot of faith in your survival skills."

"Oh yeah, I can fry freeze dried eggs with a clothespin on my nose. Big deal. First of all, survival skills work a lot better if you have something to work with. When it comes right down to it we have nothing outside of our own supplies to work with. I could light a fire, if we had wood. I could trap food to eat if we had wood and a game trail. There's lots of things I could do but most of it involves not being stuck in an eight square foot area."

"I bet if we needed to you'd figure out something."

"Hopefully it won't get down to that. We still have two days worth of food."

"How are *you* doing?" he asked me.

"I'm fine. A little stir crazy, wishing we could get out of here, but I'm fine."

"How's...you know."

"He's fine, he moves around about like normal. I'll be glad to get some real fruits, vegetables and ice cream again. Maybe cookie dough, too."

"It doesn't bother you to be stuck out here?"

"No, this feels like home, in a way."

I could see the question: this? Like home?

"You have to understand where I come from," I explained. "Before I met Rusty this was more normal to me than living in a house. I spent a lot of time wandering the mountains, looking for tracks. I'd still be doing that if I hadn't gotten car jacked. That's how I met Rusty. Then he found out I was a tracker and focused my skills on search and rescue."

"You've changed a lot since that first search."

"I know. I had to. I wouldn't have survived all this trouble without changing."

"So many times we thought you wouldn't. Natalia asks over and over again why I would work with you. She says you're going to go too far and..."

I waited but he looked away. I didn't understand. This was something his wife had said. These weren't even his own feelings. Victor didn't have to maintain a macho image with me. I saw the dad behind the rescue worker. I saw the humor in his eyes. I knew he'd give up a cheese Danish. I didn't even need to trade him the cookies for it. He was just like that. I didn't ask "and what?" But he finally said, "And break every heart on the force."

"You can't look at it that way," I said, a big lump in my throat. "I'm just one person, one tiny piece of a huge organization. The whole force feels any mishap that happens to any one person. It's not me. It's being part of the family."

"That's true, but when push comes to shove you see what a person is made of. They know what you're made of. And if it's a family, which I guess you can liken it to, then you're the little sister and you've got fifty-six big brothers just on the police force, half the fire department and three quarters of Landon's coworkers all in your family, who know the stuff you're made of. Even when they joke about you being a trouble magnet they hope that when push comes to shove they come out on top like you do. They live so close to that edge. They just hope they can claim that attitude that keeps them going when they need to. That they can bounce back like you do."

"That's silly. I'm a lousy cop. I can't even be trusted in uniform. I'm like a little kid playing cops and robbers. I go on an apprehension and I end up being the hostage."

"Even then, you keep a clear head. I've heard the stories."

I poked my head out of the tent. It was snowing again, lightly. I went back inside and batted at the tent fabric to knock the snow off.

"I don't know about that. You didn't hear most of what I said to you while you were unconscious. I wasn't thinking very clearly then!"

"Sorry, I thought you were going to try and stop me and I thought we'd both end up at the bottom of the canyon. What I see here shows a pretty clear head. How'd you know about the splints? How'd you know how to take my blood pressure?"

"I knew about the splints because I had to splint Landon's leg once. And I knew all the usual steps you take. I've had plenty of practice being the patient during triage. I didn't know what the numbers meant but I knew the routine. Pulse, blood pressure, eyes, broken bones. Nothing seemed scary. I thought I'd at least recognize scary numbers."

"You did fine. You followed everything you knew to do and you stayed level headed. Just the fact that you stuck around showed you had your head on straight."

I saw Victor's ears perk up. It took a second and then I heard it, too. The distant *chopachopachopa* of a helicopter. I climbed out of the tent but I couldn't see the helicopter because of the snow. Then suddenly it topped the mountain and came down the canyon. I waved but I was on the pilot's side of the helicopter and he was having navigational troubles of his own. He had to concentrate on flying. It passed us without slowing down. I knew how noisy a helicopter was, knew it would do no good to yell, so I whipped out my 9mm and fired three shots up into the air, away from the chopper. It slowed slightly. I saw it lift and circle around. This time the spotter was on our side of the canyon. I jumped up and down waving my arms around. A point of recognition, then a wave. I waved back.

"We're in good shape now," I called to Victor. "It wasn't search and rescue but they know where we are now. Hopefully they'll come back with EMTs."

Another turn and a ranger, dangling on the end of a cable, was dropped off on the ledge. Kelly unclipped, then clasped me in a nervous hug.

"Trouble, what did you do this time?" Kelly asked.

"It wasn't me, it was Victor this time."

He poked his head into the tent.

"Victor?"

"Hey, what's up?"

"Not you, obviously," Kelly said crawling into the tent. The tone turned business like and there was a quick radio exchange. Patient serious but stable. We'd need a basket. I paced outside the tent in the few feet there was to pace in. I just wanted Victor where he could get treatment. Now that the situation was back under control my thoughts turned to Homer Gent. Where was he? Did he get caught in the snowstorm, too? How prepared had he been? His tracks were buried under snow now. There was no way to track him. But where was he? Half of me said he was sitting in a bar in Pasadena bragging about his trek through the mountains. And half of me knew he could be a Popsicle out in the woods somewhere. Part of me saw frostbitten toes and frantic wading through the brush and snow trying to get home again. And part of me still pictured the stoic Gent bullying his way up hill and down oblivious to the weather.

Kelly crawled out of the tent, "Good job, kiddo."

"Kelly, I still have a ten sixty-five out there. There's no tracking him now. What's the next step?"

"The next step is you go home and show Rusty you're not dying out here in the woods. You know how he gets. He checked in with Strict every night. First night everything seemed fine. You two checked in just like usual. When Rusty checked in the second night, nobody knew anything. Next morning the same thing. He's scared."

"But I'm fine. It was the radio that was dead, not us. I'd be out there tracking Homer but I couldn't leave Victor."

"Go home, this has turned into an air search."

"Then let me go. He's my ten sixty-five, too!"

"It's not up to me. That's Strict's department."

"Where's Rusty?"

"Probably at base camp. He tried to stay out of the way. He tried sticking to work, listening to the radio. He was going nuts."

About an hour later a second helicopter made its way up the canyon and stopped above us. Two EMTs rappelled down and while they were bundling up Victor, Kelly and I rode cables up. We waited for Victor and the remaining guys down below and then took off for town. They stopped briefly at base camp to drop off Kelly and I got off, too.

"I'll come visit as soon as I find out what happened to Homer Gent," I told Victor.

As I ducked and jogged out from under the chopper's blades I saw Rusty waiting. I must have made quite a sight: big belly, four layers of clothes, backpack haphazardly tossed together, sun burned face, red and black hair. He grabbed me in a hug to the hoots and whistles of the guys standing around.

"My girl, I've got my girl back. Kelly wasn't thinking. He just said patient serious. He didn't say who. I wanted to wrestle Strict for the radio. I asked, but they had more important things to talk about and I just got left hanging."

"Victor took a tumble. He's going to be laid up for a while."

"Why didn't you answer your radio?"

I took off my pack and dug around until I came up with the remains of the radio.

"Victor smashed it in the fall."

He took the pieces from me.

"It's not supposed to be possible to break them that bad!"

"What can I say? Victor's got talent."

Rusty took the radio to Strict, "What did I tell you?" Rusty asked Strict.

Strict ignored the barb, "Good job, Kid," he said.

"I still have a ten sixty-five to find."

"No chance, the tracks are gone. We're spending one day on an air search before we throw in the towel."

"Then let me go. I know better what to look for. I told Victor I'd see this through."

"You've done enough. Go home and regroup."

"I can't regroup until I see this through. Just let me ride along. An extra set of eyes can't hurt."

"It's been nearly a week. You really think there's somebody out there to find?"

"If he died he died on his feet. I have to go see."

"If he died you'll be in a world of hurt."

"I'll find out either way. I did right to stay with Victor. No matter what happened to Homer Gent. I couldn't leave Victor. Not only was it dangerous for Victor if I left, it was just foolhardy to continue up and down those canyons alone. I had no choice. But I do now, and I'm asking to be taken along on the next pass."

Strict stood up to me, arms folded, half drill sergeant, half grandfather. He didn't call me Kiddo for nothing. Half the guys did, even guys younger than me. But Strict truly cared. This was like a teenager asking for the keys to dad's sports car. He knew I'd be responsible. He knew I could help the efforts. But he wasn't sure he wanted me out there.

"If the pilot can find the spot where I was picked up. I can lead them the way I think Homer went. Homer went due west as much as he possibly could. He was nuts, but that's what he did. Even if he strayed from that plan I will know it when I see it. I can find him even from the air. If the snow clears up, maybe I can find his trail again."

"Cassidy, you just spent two days stranded on the side of a mountain and now you want to go back. How are your supplies holding out?"

"I can combine my food with Victor's and I'll be fine for another two days on the trail. But I won't be on the trail. It's just a fly over. I shouldn't even need supplies unless we find a trail. We're more likely to find Homer than we are to find a trail, but I want to go."

"Go get checked out by the EMTs. If they say you're up to it you can go on the next pass."

"Yes Sir!" I said and went off to where the rescue squads were parked.

"Cassidy, babe, what are you doing?"

"Finishing what I started."

"Why?"

"Because I know where to look. Does anybody else?"

"You could just tell them then. Just tell them where to look."

"You can come, too."

"Go back to where you found me and Victor," I told the pilot, "Then go slowly due west."

"Due west? He'd have to be insane to go due west."

"Yeah, that's what I thought, too, but I followed him all day due west. Believe me, I questioned his sanity, too."

As long as the terrain was simply up and down we continued due west but finally the route became too rocky and steep even for Homer Gent.

"Okay, go back and let's look at this canyon. He'd walk across the floor of it and hit those rocks. I doubt he could climb those rocks. Where's the easiest climb that's closest to due west? What about that crevasse, right there? That's what I would do if I was bound and determined to go due west."

"Why's he going due west?"

"Walking home to Pasadena."

"Damn, idiotic, hard headed son of a bitch," said the pilot. When the snow gave out on the west side of the mountains I almost asked to be let off but I knew our chances were better up here. To be accidentally dropped off on Homer's trail would just be asking for too much of a coincidence. When we got to the west side of the mountains the canyons began going east west and midway down a canyon we found a lone man, stumbling along.

"Look! He matches the description."

"It can't be him. Not after a week. He shouldn't be standing."

"There's a flat spot. Land there."

"Cassidy… oh hell."

Homer was oblivious to the helicopter that landed within hailing range. He stared at the ground, marching, stumbling, marching again. As I drew near I could hear him mumbling:

"Mama Mama can't you see
Mama Mama can't you see," he sang both sides of the cadence.
"What this road is doing to me
What this road is doing to me."

"Mama mama don't you care
Mama mama don't you care
I've got sweaty underwear.
I've got sweaty underwear."

"Homer," I called.

"Joined the army to get in shape
Joined the army to get in shape
But all I do is hurry and wait
But all I do is hurry and wait

They took away my life of fun
They took away my life of fun
Now I don't even shoot my gun
Now I don't even shoot my gun"

I'd learned it, "Now *all* I do is shoot my gun." Maybe I learned the Sniper School version.

"I used to date a beauty queen
I used to date a beauty queen
Now I hump my M-16
Now I hump my M-16"

I smiled. This could be fun. "Gentlemen! Ladies present!" I called out after him. He stopped. He turned around and blushed, though I thought it impossible to blush brighter than his exhausted, sunburned face already was. He turned back around, almost falling over, and kept walking.

"They took away my gin and rum
Now I'm up before the sun"

I followed Homer.
"What branch?"
"Army."
"Marines."
"Naw, you?"
"Yeah, you done good Homer. It's time to stop."
"Caint. Aint there yet."
"You've been marching for a week. It's time to stop."
"I made up a new one. Wanna hear it?"
"Sure."
He sang off key, "They took all my water away, now I think I'm gonna die."
"You're not going to die."
"Can't quit till the mission's accomplished."
"You've got new orders. Look, they sent a helicopter. You've got new orders."
He turned to look at the helicopter, saw the uniforms following him and pitched over backwards.
"He's all yours," I told the EMTs.

Homer was taken to the local hospital where he was treated for dehydration, exposure and general orneriness. I bet he discharged himself and walked home from the hospital. I don't know. I went home to my nice warm bed and my eager husband, glad to know my mission was complete. My next mission was a kinder and gentler one.
"The baby grew while you were gone," Rusty said.
"Of course he did."
"I missed you. And I missed those little taps, too."
"I felt them. I felt you missing us, too. I knew you'd worry when the radio died but there wasn't much I could do. We tried firing three shots into the air. I don't know if it did any good. Second time I know it did. I fired again when the helicopter flew down our canyon."
"What would you have done if they hadn't found you?"

"The plan was for me hike out but the snow put a stop to that. There was no way to get off that ledge with snow on the ground. So I suppose we'd sit tight until the snow melted and then I'd hike to the nearest road."

"What would you have done if the snow hadn't melted?"

"Rusty, it doesn't pay to play the what-if game. We knew a whole day with no radio contact would start Strict on a new search, we weren't stuck there forever, and we weren't without options."

"I think Strict is going to be a little leery of sending you out again."

"I don't know why. Nothing that went wrong affected me much. None of it was my fault. I think I did the right thing in the situation. So he should have no qualms about calling me again."

"I can always hope he will, anyway."

Chapter 28

It felt weird walking into a hospital. So many times I had been wheeled in. I'd followed ten sixty-fives in when they got flown in. I rarely just walked into a hospital. I knew the layout from emergency around to the front lobby, where we usually met to exchange paperwork or find rides home. After that I always got lost.

I joined a group of people waiting for an elevator and followed as they all entered. Nearly every floor was lit up so I waited for the fourth floor and got off there. I stepped into a small lobby. A woman in colorful scrubs sat at a counter.

"Can I help you?" she asked.

"I'm here to visit Victor Gomez," I told her.

"That guy needs to go home and get some peace and quiet," she said. "I wish I had so many friends."

"Victor's a great guy," I admitted.

"Room 412," she said, handing me a card with the room number on it.

I signed in and entered through the double doors into lostville. I don't know what it is about hospitals. I always get lost in them. All the corridors look alike. There are no visible landmarks, just dozens of doors and an occasional counter. I walked and walked and walked reading room numbers and not looking into open doorways. I thought it was intrusive to look into people's doorways, especially when the people inside didn't feel well and were stuck in skimpy hospital gowns.

424...422...420...418...16...14...the end of the corridor. Sigh, I'd done it again. I'd gotten lost on one floor of a hospital. Drop me in the middle of nowhere and I could find my way home, but put me in a hospital and I got lost at the drop of a hat. I didn't even know where the elevator was anymore.

Okay, it had to be one of the open doors. I'd read the numbers without being intrusive. I walked the corridor again. I came to an open door. Number 440.

"Come in," a woman said weakly from the bed closest to the door.

"Excuse me?" I said.

"Please come in, I haven't seen anybody in months," she said.

I entered the room. There lay an old woman and when I say old I am being kind. She was ancient. She was barely there. Her thin form was almost unrecognizable beneath the thin blankets. An IV stand stood by her bed and a bag hung on the side. The color in the bag did not look good.

"My name is Lily," she said. Her hair hadn't been brushed in weeks. Her eyes were kindly. Her face lined with years of experiences I would never know.

"My name is Cassidy," I said.

"Don't pay no attention to her," the woman in the next bed said. "She don't know nothin'."

Whoever that other woman was had pretty much sealed it. I would sit and visit with Lily if it killed me. To say someone didn't know anything grated on me. Lily had a lifetime of experiences, family, history, advice and it might take some patience but I knew there were some gems in there somewhere. If there was one thing I had it was time.

"You're expecting," Lily observed. "How exciting. I remember when I was expecting. It was a bad time to be pregnant. Nobody had nothin'. We cleaned out a dresser drawer and that was our crib for the first four months. Then we got a cheap old playpen that probably would be recalled now 'cause the slats were so far apart. Coulda strangled the kid, they say, but it's what we had and we didn't know no better back then. He was a big tyke. Couldn't carry him round long afore my husband had to take over. He was a big strapping guy, my husband was. You'd never guess it looking at me now. Oh, he was a doll, though. You take time while you're young. Savor each moment cause they don't last forever. My baby is sixty-one now. My husband is gone. When that little one drives you nuts jus' remember it only lasts a little while. You won't remember the hours of fussing but you'll remember the joys. When they come, savor them like they was rich chocolate. Don't hurry them along. Let them last. When you take the kid to a park don' rush around. Let him meet Mickey Mouse on his own terms. Let him poke his nose in flowers. If'n he has his heart set on seeing the tigers at the zoo, you find the tigers at the zoo. Seein' his eyes light up at the tigers is better'n seeing everything else in the place. I ain't gonna be around much longer. All things gotta come to an end. But it's nice to talk to someone every once in a while."

"I wish you could meet my husband," I told her just to keep the subject going.

"Is he big and strong? You need a big, strong guy. You're just a little thing, like me."

"Yeah, and he's a doll, too. Would you like to see his picture?"

"Oh! You'd share your pictures with me? Oh! I haven't shared pictures with a girlfriend in oh so long. We used to go to the Woolworth's for coffee and share pictures. If we was feeling really good we'd get a root beer float. Or maybe an Orange Crush if the weather was muggy. But we'd share pictures. I just love pictures. So many memories."

I stood by her bedside and showed her the pictures in my wallet. My mom always kept me well supplied with pictures. I stood by and listened to her exclaim about each one.

"Oh my! You weren't kidding! He is a doll! He's more'n a doll, he's a hunk!"

I flipped to the next picture, "This is my nephew, Patrick."

"Oh! Would you look at the little tyke! All dressed up like a cowboy! Ain't he the cutest thing! How'd they get that rope to stay all stiff like? It must'a been starched or glued or something."

"Patrick is a little cowboy. The rope isn't starched. He's turning the rope himself. Here's his brother, Wyatt. Wyatt's the quieter, more creative brother."

"Oh my, he is a doll, too. You can see it in their eyes. This one has a mischievous streak to him and this one has a kind heart and a quiet way."

"Yeah, the mischievous one takes after me."

She talked about how different I and my sister looked and how my mom looked like the TV mom of old and how my dad looked like he meant business.

"Aint no two ways about it. You don't back talk that man. Now your husban' he got a heart. He'll take a little back talk, but that man? No way Jose!"

"My dad has a heart, too. It just takes a little patience to find it."

"You're such a dear to stop and visit with me. But I know you have more important things to do so I'll let you go."

"Actually, I was here to visit a friend. He fell down the mountain while we were on a search and rescue call and I need to see how he's doing."

"What are you doing out on a mountain in your condition?" Lily asked.

"I was looking for a man who was lost but I ended up tending to my partner instead. He'll be okay, but he's waiting to hear how the search ended."

"Sounds like you don't need that big strapping husband of yours. Out in the mountains on search and rescue. Sounds like you can take care of yourself!"

"I need Rusty. Even if I'm out on a mountain taking care of myself. I need to know he's home waiting for me."

"That's the woman in you and it's jus' going to get worse when that little one gets here. You jus' wait and see. Now you run along and tell your friend Lily says 'hi'."

"Okay, I will."

By the time I located Victor he was alone again.

"You'll be glad to know we actually found Homer Gent," I told him. "I don't think he got caught in the snow storm. He was still on his feet, though just barely. He'll be okay."

"Where was he?"

"Still heading due west. He had to take a detour or two but he was as due west as he could get."

"Why do I get the feeling that's not what's really on your mind?" he asked.

"I met someone while I was looking for your room. You know how I always get lost in hospitals. I stopped to read a room number and next thing I know I'm talking to this little old lady."

"What wisdom did you manage to pry out of her?"

"What?"

"You always seem to learn something from old folks. You're like an advice magnet when you get near old people. That's how you learned so much from Old Frank."

"You're right, I learned a lot from this lady. But it's stuff you know already because you're a dad."

"Tell me anyway."

So I replayed the conversation to him and he smiled and nodded in all the right places.

"You're coming back, aren't you?"

I hadn't thought of that. Come to think of it, maybe I would. I had plenty of pictures. Maybe she would like to see the pictures from my wedding and honeymoon.

"Yeah, maybe I will."

"You will, because if you can make someone's day better you usually try and do it. You just need opportunities presented to you."

I didn't think of myself like that. I mostly tended to think of myself as antisocial. But it took so little to brighten some people's day. All Lily wanted was to feel like a part of something. So, yeah, I'd probably be back. Just like I came back for Bailee.

"Would you mind doing something for me that might make you a little uncomfortable?" I asked Rusty.

"Uh oh, I don't like the sound of that."

"If you lose patience you can always just go down the hall and talk to Victor. It'll just take a few minutes on your part but it would mean so much to Lily."

"Lily?"

"Just a few minutes?"

I was putting baby things in a bag. Anything to let Lily think her opinion mattered. I stuck a scrapbook under my arm and headed for the door.

"Will you come?"

"What's in it for me?" he asked, still apprehensive.

"Nothing. Maybe. Maybe you'll get what I get out of it. If you do you'll be glad you went. Some things I do, I don't do for me."

Cookies? Check. Baby stuff? Check. Pictures? Check.

I peeked into Lily's room and she brightened instantly.

"You came back!" she cried.

"And I brought somebody with me. This is Rusty. Rusty, this is Lily." I set the bag on the side of her bed. "I've been shopping," I fibbed. "But I don't know what I'm doing. I've never had a baby before. Do you think these will fit?" I started pulling things out of the bag, letting her be a mom, a grandma, whatever she chose in her mind. Her eyes twinkled as she fingered the tiny sleepers.

"You don't know if it's a boy or a girl?" she asked.

"I want to be surprised. My doctor asked if I wanted to know. The ultrasound technician asked me if I wanted to know. My mom begs me to find out. Rusty's work has a pool going on whether it's a boy or girl. We're keeping everybody guessing."

"Turn sideways," she told me.

I turned sideways giving Rusty a wink.

"If I had to guess I'd say it was a little girl because you're carrying so high. Course it could be because it's your first."

On and on she went, parceling out old wives tales and little bits of wisdom and memories. She looked through the scrapbook exclaiming once again about each picture.

"Cassidy, what was all that about?" Rusty asked as we continued down the hall.

"Just letting someone know that life didn't really leave her behind. That wasn't so bad was it? She said you were a hunk. A real live hunk visited her today. She'll brag about that to the nurses for days."

"You didn't give her any cookies."

"I don't know if she's allowed to have them. But Victor can."

We made a cookie delivery and I let the guys talk guy talk. That was another reason I brought Rusty. Victor and I had covered every topic and he really just needed to talk guy talk. We could rehash the search ad infinitum but it didn't do any good. Natalia and I talked girl talk.

A couple of days later I went to see Victor and stopped by Lily's room on the way. We exchanged pleasantries. She gave me her usual dose of reminiscing, advice and predictions about the sex, size, and personality of the baby.

"You're just a little thing. You better hope that baby is little too. She takes after your husband and you might have a very long labor! What do you crave?" she asked.

"I wouldn't say I crave anything. The only unusual thing I get hungry for is cookie dough."

"Hmm, if you crave sweet stuff it means you're having a girl. If you crave salty stuff it means you're having a boy."

I took a lot of her sayings with a grain of salt.

"Something's on the tip of my brain," she admitted, "I can't place it. When your husband visited it got to perking in my brain. Then, when I saw your wedding book it got worser. I know I know you from somewhere, but where could it be? I seen your husband somewhere. And I seen something in your wedding book before. What could it be? It's gonna bug me to my deathbed if I don't think of it."

"Would it help to know I'm usually blonde? I'm stuck with this hair because of a movie job I landed. As soon as it grows out I'm getting it cut."

"Why don't you just bleach it back out?"

"What color does black and red turn when it's bleached out? I could just make it worse."

"You got a point. You're usually blonde?"

"Yeah."

She took a good look at my face and then closed her eyes, presumably trying to put blonde hair on the little kid face. Her expression lighted up.

"I gotchtes it! I remember! Sometimes I have a heck of a time remembering but I remember you now. You was on the TV some time ago! I remember. You was stuck in a mine and it was all over the news and then they found out you was engaged to that detective and they showed the invitation to your wedding! An' the whole world fretted that you wouldn't be found. An' your poor husband was at his wits end. He couldn't even talk to the cameras. An' I cried my eyes out when you came outa that mine. I couldn't believe you made it an' the kid too."

"Trevor."

"Yeah, Trevor. An' I cried at your wedding when it was on the news. To think you came so close to that wedding never happening and you were so beautiful. You really need to go back to being blonde. You was so beautiful in that sparkly gown. You was stunning!"

"Thank you, Lily."

"An' now you're expecting your own little one. An' it's a girl. I can tell, because you crave cookie dough and you're carrying high. That's a sure sign. What are you going to name her?"

"I don't know. The choices are rather limited."

"Oh no! There's thousands of names. Ten of thousands if you jumble the letters around."

"Well, my dad has a tradition of naming kids after old west legends and heroes. That's why we have Cassidy, Jesse, Patrick and Wyatt. So I have been looking for a name of an old west hero that would fit. There's too many Bills back in history. I think I can come up with something a little more original than Bill Michaels."

"You know who my old west hero always was? I always thought he was a good guy. Some folks think he was a bad guy. But he always led the most fantastical life. I used to read about him and day dream that I was living his adventures out in the old west. You know, I remember the west when it was hardly even there. I remember Tucson before paved roads. I remember when cars first appeared on them dusty rutted old roads. They was rutted from wagons, not cars. But I always wished I could be Kit Carson. I always wondered what I would do if I were captured by Indians. And even though he hunted Indians he had a heart for them. He often stood up for them if they was wronged. It was like he lived on a fence tween white folks and red folks."

"Kit Carson? I hadn't thought of that one. It's certainly more original than Bill."

"There, you see? Now you got a name."

"Well, not really, but it's something to consider."

Hmm, Kit Michaels for a girl. Carson Michaels for a boy. I tried picturing what Kit Michaels would look like and I came up with a lithe young girl at home in the woods. And when I thought about Carson Michaels I thought of a no nonsense young man, maybe a cop like his dad. I walked down the hall, my thoughts filled with possibilities, ready to ask Victor what he thought of the names. He'd let me rattle on about it and I'd come to my own conclusions and he'd nod agreement. I knew all that as I rounded the corner into his room. I wasn't even thinking about him not being there and when I looked into the bed I saw a younger black man, bandaged and obviously in pain but his eyes narrowed when he saw me.

"Sorry!" I said. "My friend was obviously moved to another room."

"Obviously, but I don't think so. I think you're here on purpose."

"Well, in a way I am. I was coming to visit a friend…"

"Tha's what you say. I don't believe you for a second."

He raised his cell phone, speed dialed and said simply, "Get her."

I backed out of the room and walked briskly toward the elevators. When I was out of earshot of the room I did my own speed dialing. I didn't wait for a hello.

"Rusty? I think I made a blunder."

"What? Are you okay?"

"Yeah, for now. Just get over here."

"Where are you? What's wrong?"

"Just get here! Bring a couple of uniforms. I'm scared to get in the elevator. I don't want to get cornered. I need to find the nurse's station. I need witnesses. Where's the stupid nurse's station!"

"You're at the hospital?"

"Yeah, I went to see Lily and Victor and when I went in Victor's room he was gone and some kid recognized me and I don't know who he is but he sure knew me. And he called someone. He told them to come 'get me'."

"Who was it?"

"I don't know. It wasn't Manny Mo. It was a tall black kid, short hair, looked like he'd been stabbed. He was bad off enough he couldn't come after me himself. He thought I was there for a reason. He didn't believe I was there to visit someone else. I don't know how far away his buddies are. The ladies room! They won't check the ladies room, will they?"

"If they're thinking ahead they might. Find the nurse's station and have them call security."

"I can't find a nurse's station. Everything looks the same. It feels like I'm walking in circles. Where is everybody? Oh shit."

"Cassidy!"

"Sorry. It's them."

I could hear car noises through my phone. I knew Rusty was on his way. I heard the siren come on as his sense of urgency grew.

"Stay on the phone as long as you can. Make a scene. Do whatever you need to attract attention."

"Well, well, if it isn't the little snitch," said Manny Mo. "You picked a handy place to get caught. Lots of people know how to revive you here."

Chapter 29

There were three of them. Manny Mo pulled a knife out of his pocket and flipped it open. I wondered if one of them was D Dawg and the other was his stick man. Of course the man in Victor's room might be D Dawg. I wondered what name he used to check in that the police hadn't noticed. Funny the things my mind comes up with when I am backed into a corner. It just started sorting facts, putting puzzle pieces together. Somehow I needed to stop this altercation before it turned violent, not just for my safety, but for the patients, nurses, and security officers. I hated making a scene. It was so unlike me. I backed away from the three young men advancing on me.

"If anybody can hear me!" I called out. "Call Security! Stay in your room and call Security. If you can lock your room, do it!"

Stupid, stupid me. As soon as I made a scene people started walking out and standing in their doorways, wondering what was going on.

"Get in! Get in and call for help!" I said, still backing away.

The three didn't like the extra attention. Suddenly they stopped and Manny Mo stood taller, grinning smugly. He tossed the knife over my shoulder and the man behind me deftly caught it in one hand and pointed it at my back. I took a look at my situation. I didn't see any more weapons. If the only one with a weapon was the man behind me I thought I could take him on.

"Somebody! Call security!"

There was a ding in the background and a young woman came around the corner, took in the scene before her and quietly turned around and ran back to the elevators. So much for security. I had about five seconds. I turned and gave the man behind me a swift kick to the side that bent him over in pain. The three rushed in and I barreled through them, shoving them aside. Hands groped for me and I pulled loose, running for my life. The elevator dinged and the doors opened. The woman ran right into Rusty! I was a step behind her. Rusty pushed the woman behind him and drew his side arm, two officers pushed their way out and followed Rusty down the corridor. The woman hid in the corner of the elevator whimpering. I hit the button to close the doors, saying a silent prayer.

"It's okay," I told the woman. "They were just after me. I don't think they'll hurt anybody up there except maybe the officers."

The baby was moving like crazy.

"Are you okay?" the woman asked me. She looked like maybe she worked in one of the offices down stairs. Her hair was up in a ponytail. She was dressed in a crisp blouse and pressed slacks. She was carrying a clipboard and pulled her glasses out to read the paper on the clipboard.

"Yeah, I'm fine. I just hate running."

"I think it was the wise thing to do."

"You didn't have to leave your husband up there to deal with it."

The elevator doors opened and two more officers tried to rush in.

"Number four," I told them.

"How many are up there now?"

"Rusty and two officers against four high school kids, but one is injured."

"Thanks, Cassidy."

"Who was that?"

"I don't know, but they know me. I'm the cookie queen. I'm Rusty's wife. I'm their little trouble maker."

"You're a trouble maker and police know you by name and it doesn't bother you?"

"Well, I wish I wasn't such a trouble maker. But I don't do it on purpose. It's always situations like this," I said as I walked with the woman back toward the offices. We almost walked into the lobby to go down the other corridor when I saw another group of high school kids in the lobby. I grabbed the woman by the shoulders and pulled her back.

"You can't be seen with me," I told her.

She led me down a little-used hallway. We hurried to the end and she pushed me out and followed. I just thought she knew the hospital better than me and wanted to be out of sight. When I came to a stop outside the door I realized I was outside, facing two more kids. The woman took off her glasses, tossed the clipboard aside and asked the taller, rougher kid, "So? Am I in?"

The taller boy grinned, "I'll think about it."

"You sure as hell will! Six brothers in there and *they* didn't get her!"

She advanced on the boy but he stood up to her.

"Someone put a leash on this bitch," he said.

The girl made a move to strike him and the other kid stepped in grabbing her by the shoulders. She struggled kicking out at him and he laughed at her.

I thought this would be a good time to make a run for it. I sprinted down the backside of the hospital as fast as a pregnant woman can sprint. I rounded the corner with them gaining ground. It's pretty sad when a woman six months pregnant can outrun a group of high school kids. I ran toward the squad cars in front of the building. I yanked on a door. Locked! Damn it guys! Why do you have to be so darned careful! Who's going to steal a police car? I tried another door and another. Finally one door was unlocked and I flung myself inside and locked the doors. The kids pounded on the car. They could break in but they'd have to make a big scene to do it.

"Hey!" Someone yelled, running across the parking lot.

More kids appeared. They began pounding on the squad car. One kid had a rock. A couple of guys climbed up onto the hood and jumped up and down on it.

The man running across the parking lot had a cell phone in hand. Within minutes more black and whites came screaming into the parking lot. Cops in full riot gear advanced on the group. The kids cursed the police, some of them standing up to them, some fleeing on foot. The ones who stayed behind were wrestled into other squad cars. I sat in the passenger's seat of car number fifty-one; the windshield and one window were smashed. I was lucky it was shatterproof glass. When most of the chaos had been put down one officer noticed me sitting in the car. Kent Jacobsen. Why did it have to be Kent Jacobsen?

He didn't know which of several actions to take. His first inclination was to yank me out by the scruff of my neck and demand an explanation. Then his second inclination kicked in and he knew I had a perfectly logical explanation. I always did. He pointed at me and glared. "Don't move a muscle!" he said. When the parking lot was cleared he marched over and tried the door. It was locked. He pointed to the lock.

"Find out what conditions are like inside first. I almost got cornered on the fourth floor. There was a group waiting in the lobby and a couple by the back door. I think you got the back door group."

He gave me an "oh come on" look but he radioed the officers inside, then he came back and indicated the lock again. I unlocked the driver's door and he got in and sat down.

"You? You're the cause of all this?" he asked. Smoke wasn't quite coming out his ears, but he certainly wasn't pleased with me.

"I just came to visit Victor Gomez."

"What happened to Victor? Don't tell me, he went on a search with you…"

"Well, yes. But it wasn't my fault he fell down the mountain."

"It's never your fault. I suppose this wasn't your fault either."

"It is, if there was something wrong with visiting Victor. I couldn't help it if a member of D Dawg's gang was in Victor's room! I couldn't help it if I was on their want list. I didn't even know I was! I go visit a friend in the hospital and all hell breaks loose."

"Could you possibly make all hell break loose in a more remote location without a whole building's worth of victims to protect?"

"Next time I'll give it a try."

"Are you okay? Did they hurt you?"

"They stuck a knife to my back but the kid that did it was upstairs. I gave him a good solid kick in a place that hurt and busted through the others and ran into the elevator. The other kids just chased me around the building. Why do you guys lock your cars? I had to try three cars before I could get in one. I'd think if you were wrestling criminals into your car you wouldn't want to take the time to unlock the doors!"

"I like your logic, up to a point. I'll leave you to reason that one out yourself. I know a couple of guys who are going to wish they'd locked their doors."

"Oh…" I said looking around. "Who?"

There was a knock on the window and Rusty stood there with that same look that the guys all had when they saw me as the root of their troubles. Basically it looked like, "Oh, no, not her again!" Only Rusty already knew it was me. He pointed to the lock and I unlocked it. He opened the door and I stepped out.

"You got any more surprises for us?" he said looking over the car.

"I don't think so. You got the four upstairs? The three by the backdoor chased me around front. The cleanup crew got most of the rest. Oh! I did get a suggestion for a name for the baby! I need to do some research and see if it fits."

"Hello?" Victor said when I called.

"Victor? Could you do me a favor?"

"I doubt it but I can try. I'm kind of stuck here."

"This won't take much effort on your part."

"Okay."

"Watch the news tonight and see why you might want to let me know you were discharged from the hospital."

"I should call you?"

"Ordinarily it probably wouldn't matter but in my case it was a mess."

"A mess. When you say something was a mess it means…"

"Just watch the news."

I watched the news that evening hesitantly. I didn't want to see it, but I thought I ought to know how deep my rivalry with D Dawg really went. It was embarrassing.

A female reporter in a tight red dress began the news story, "Believe it or not there was a riot at Joshua Hills General Hospital, triggered by a woman who tried to visit a friend, and accidentally prompted local gang members to hunt her down. Can you believe that, John?"

"Pretty hard to believe, Marsha."

"This young woman was found hiding in a police car because she was chased from the hospital's fourth floor unit. Here you see, the gang using violent means to get at the poor woman trapped in the car!"

Wow, I didn't even notice they'd tried to lift the car! I'd felt the rocking and the pounding, saw the glass break.

"When we questioned the local police commander he refused to comment until a proper investigation was conducted."

Standard procedure. They should have expected that.

The phone rang.

"Cassidy? What happened?" Victor asked.

"The trouble magnet was really strong today," I said and then sat down for a very long and weary explanation. "I thought the whole gang thing would have blown over long ago, but I guess the longer D Dawg had to run from the police the more ticked off he got."

Rusty switched off the TV and patted the big brown couch.

"You know you're going to get grilled tomorrow."

"I know."

"So you better sort it all out in your head before you go in."

"Did you get D Dawg?"

"No, D Dawg won't be found in any hospital."

"Who was it?"

"We did luck out there. He was one of the higher ups in the organization. The gang is pretty messed up right now. We had eight arrests."

"You were right about gang members being smart. The woman you pushed into the elevator with me acted like she was helping me out and she helped me right into a trap."

"What?"

"Her job was to lure me away. She was trying to earn her place in the gang and when she demanded her place there was a confrontation and I managed to run away while they were discussing it. That's when I found a squad car to hide in. I couldn't go back into the building. I couldn't make it to a building farther away. It was the safest place I could find."

"If I'd known what I know now, things would have been done very differently. My only goal was to find you. When I saw you leave with that woman I thought I'd isolated the problem."

"Me too. I thought I was helping her and then all of a sudden the tables turned. The sad part is I can't go back. Lily will be all alone again."

"Babe, you can't be everything to everybody."

"I know, but she was so pleased to have a visitor. And there's so many people like her. It breaks my heart. She didn't even care that she didn't know any of the people in my pictures. She just liked that someone was sharing with her."

"And you say you're hard. Can you explain it to me from beginning to end? I'll help you with what you should say to Schroeder."

"Usually, when I talk to Schroeder he can't deny that my logic makes sense. He just isn't sure how I come across it."

"I can identify with that. Still, let's go through it all the way one time."

So I told the whole story to Rusty and then the next day I did it again with Schroeder. I had to identify the gang members who confronted me. They were not concerned with the ones who attacked the police car. Those people had been caught on film. So I pointed out the three who had confronted me in the hospital, the girl who had acted like a hospital employee and the two boys who cornered me in back of the hospital.

"Do us all a favor, lay low for a while," Schroeder finally said. Seemed like he always said that after one of my disasters. "You have two very tense months between now and delivery. We can't afford any risks. If I were you I'd consider having that baby at a different hospital."

"But Rusty has to be there. Nothing will keep him away."

"I know. You should have seen his Dad when he was born. Rusty's just like him. If D Dawg is still on the loose, you'd be crazy to put yourself in that hospital."

"But my doctor works at that hospital."

"We're working on D Dawg. You work on staying safe."

Chapter 30

The baby was growing fast now. Instead of little taps and flutters we could watch as a little elbow or maybe a heel would travel across my abdomen. Things were getting crowded in there. Sometimes the baby would get the hiccups. That's the best way I could think of to describe it. I could imagine the baby all curled up in there, having the hiccups. Didn't do much good to hold his breath. He didn't have breath yet. Couldn't drink a glass of water backwards. It was all watery. And the hiccups would go on for hours, keeping me awake at night. Rusty felt the movements, fascinated. It was right about this time that pregnancy really set in. I felt clumsy. I couldn't sleep. I got tired easily. The movements were becoming uncomfortable. I got hungry an hour after eating. And then, finally, the cravings hit. It was never the same thing twice but they seemed to hit at the most inconvenient times. We learned where all the twenty-four hour stores and fast food places were. We kept a stash of candy bars in a drawer. Fifteen miles seemed a bit far to drive for a Three Musketeers bar at two in the morning. There was always a cheesecake in the fridge. There was no telling what flavor of ice cream would be in our freezer. But even with all these precautions I'd get up in the night and search the kitchen. Always cautious, Rusty would get up too, because he knew I'd go to the store by myself if he didn't wake up.

"What is it, babe? Just tell me and I'll go."

"I don't want to go to town again. How can I be hungry for the one thing we don't have?"

"Ask your mom. I bet she's got a rule number for this. Is there a list of Murphy's laws for pregnancy? What kind do you want this time?"

"Chunky Monkey."

"Did you check the website? Last time you sent me for Ben and Jerry's the flavor had been discontinued."

"They can't send Chunky Monkey to the flavor graveyard. It's on the top ten list."

"We have three different flavors of ice cream."

"I know, and it's silly to want a different one. Don't go. I'll go to the store in the morning."

"Then I'd rather go now. When you go by yourself there's no telling who you will run into."

And so he'd go just to settle it in his mind that I wouldn't be out by myself. Usually, since I couldn't sleep anyway, I'd go, too.

Doctor's visits changed from once a month to every two weeks.

"You're doing great!" Doctor Ron would tell me, "What are you eating? Are you taking your prenatal vitamins? Are you still exercising? Make sure you drink plenty of water. Have you had any calls lately?"

"I doubt if Strict will call me now. He'd do nothing but worry. It would take a life and death situation to get me on the trail now. Only problem is that Schroeder wants me to have the baby at a different hospital. I've been black listed by a gang in town and he's worried I'd be a sitting duck at Joshua General."

"And what do you think?"

"Did you see the news report a few weeks ago?"

"I don't have time for TV. I'm doing my rounds right about then."

"It wasn't a pretty sight. And it was a very close call. I'm sure the hospital is still talking about it."

"You don't mean..."

"Yes, exactly."

"Where do you want to have the baby?"

"Joshua General, but I'm not sure if I should. Do you work with other hospitals, too?"

"Yes, but only as needed, which usually means special medical conditions that can only be treated in L.A."

"So my choices are Joshua General or your hospital of choice in L.A.?"

"Here, let me give you the paperwork."

Rusty didn't give me a chance to even talk about the hospital situation. I came home and he was packing.

"What are you doing?"

He turned, knowing he was going to have a fight on his hands. He held out his arms. His eyes looked so sad.

"Rusty? What's wrong?"

"I'm sorry, babe, you're going to the ranch."

"No!"

"You know I don't want this either. You can't see the developments. The tension in town is getting worse than I've ever seen it. The gang detail reports new developments every day. D Dawg has a price on your head and it isn't in dollars. I won't risk it. I can't. I can't go through this again. I need to know you're safe. When I think of what they could do... it paralyzes me. I can't think enough to do my job and my job is to put an end to this."

"I can't go now! It's getting so close. I want you to be there."

"I know, believe me, I know. I want to be there, too. And I will. I'll be there."

"You won't. You'll be here."

"Babe, you pick up the phone and I'll be there."

The tears were so close to the surface.

"I want... my minutes," I said and he scooped me up and took me to the old brown couch and he sat with me while I cried, and cried, "I don't want to go, you can't leave me there."

He buried his face in my hair and held tight.

"The baby's going to miss you," I cried.

"I'll call, you can tell me all about it."

"It won't be the same."

"No, but we'll be safe, all three of us."

"But I won't know that. The place is turning into a war zone. I've seen a war zone before."

"Hush, I'll be here. Try to think of something positive. Just think how excited your mother will be. Just think of Patrick's questions. Think of Martha trying to figure out what to fix for dinner when you change your mind on the hour. You can watch Elan and Patrick track. You can visit with the hands. Just think of what kind of a bet Zack has going when you get there. You can listen to all Jesse's horror stories about week-long labors."

"But I just want you."

He was quiet for a moment. I felt a deep shuddering breath and then he said quietly, "Thank you."

"For what?"

"For wanting me. Sometimes I think you married me just because I was selfish and couldn't live without you. You're so strong. You never need anybody."

"No, I need *you*. I just need you."

We sat there and the minutes stretched.

"When are we leaving?" I asked.

"In the morning. It's got to be a quick drive, too. Too much is changing here. I have to stay on top of it."

"In the morning?"

"Yeah."

"Then we better make the most of it," I said. "I need something to hold onto. Please?"

"Oh, babe, you don't even have to ask. We will, just be with me. Have patience. And take it slow."

Savor it, I could hear Lily say. And slowly things turned from holding to kissing. And I savored those kisses and I put my all into them and when the world turned it turned slowly. I needed him, oh how I needed him, all of him. His strength, his eagerness, his sexiness, his touches, his caring. How he could want me in the shape I was in I couldn't imagine, but I drank it in and when we lay exhausted, the half packed suitcase knocked off the bed he was quiet, feeling for the baby.

"How could he sleep through all that?" he asked.

"He'll wake up soon. He's awake a lot more now. It's a relief when he stops. Seems like if it's not movement, it's hiccups or contractions. Something is always going on."

"I wish I could feel it."

"He's getting stronger every day. Doctor Ron thinks he'll be a good-sized baby. He's guessing a little over eight pounds."

"Has he made any guesses about the sex?"

"Yeah, but I can't trust him. He knows we want to be surprised so he keeps waffling. He says it's a boy because of one thing and a girl because something else. I'm supposed to see him once a week the last month. How am I going to do that?"

"I'll talk to him. He'll refer you to someone up north."

"Oh Rusty, I don't want to do this."

"Shh, don't start. We'll get through this."

Chapter 31

"Oooooh would you look at you! You're so cute. Look at your little tummy!" My mom squealed. "What happened to your hair?"

"Little tummy? Mom, I'm huge! And my hair was the victim of a job I had for a few weeks."

"A job? What kind of a job requires red and black hair?"

"It's a long and very funny story best saved for dinner."

"Speaking of dinner. We've got roast venison tonight," Martha said.

"It sounds wonderful," I said, hoping I could eat it. It was likely to be grouped in the eggs and fish category but I was sure there would be plenty of side dishes, too.

Wyatt's eyes got big, "That's my baby cousin?" he asked.

"Your baby cousin is growing in there," Jesse explained. "Pretty soon he'll be old enough to be born."

"How'd he get in there?" Wyatt asked.

"He was, um, conceived in there," Jesse said, a little embarrassed.

"Well, how's he getting out?"

"Wyatt we'll talk about this later," Jesse said, not wanting to have the bird and bees discussion with the whole ranch watching.

"It's just like the mares," Patrick said.

"I never seen a baby horse be born," Wyatt said.

"Well, you should. It's interesting," Patrick said. "They're all wet and wobbly and they look so cute when they take their first steps. I love seeing the colts be born. Will our cousin be all wet and wobbly, too?"

"How come baby people take so long to learn how to walk?" Wyatt asked.

And we thought Patrick would be the one with all the questions.

"Cause people only have two feet to balance on. Horses have four so it's easier for them," Patrick explained. Sounded good to me.

"See? It starts already. You'll be fine here," Rusty said. "I wish I could stay and listen to it all. Martha? Do you have space in your freezer?"

"I think so. How much space?" Martha answered.

"A cooler full."

"A cooler? What have you got?"

"Sixteen flavors of Ben and Jerry's, two each of every candy bar you can think of, a cheesecake, beef jerky, sweet gherkins, cheese and crackers, cookie dough and a can of asparagus."

"Well, what's all this for?"

"Umm, midnight munchies?" I said sheepishly.

"You don't look like you eat all this stuff!" my mom said.

"I don't eat much, I just get hungry for a little bit of one particular flavor and there's no telling what it's going to be next. It's not like I can run down to the store here."

Rusty carried the cooler to the kitchen and then I heard them go to the chest freezer out back. He took my suitcase to my room, gave hugs and handshakes all around and I couldn't stand it anymore. He was leaving. He saw the tears coming so he led me down to the Explorer.

"I'll call every day. I'll be back when this has blown over."

"Gangs don't just go away. Arresting D Dawg isn't going to suddenly make everything bright and rosy."

"When I call I'll want a full report, okay?"

"Okay, be careful out there."

"I will. No jumping, no racing. You take it easy."

"Okay."

"And don't ride Apache. Touch a doe for me."

"I love you."

"I love you too, babe. Take care," he said wrapping me in a protective hug, we shared a quick kiss and then he was gone, waving as he pulled away. I watched the Explorer travel down the long driveway to the "big road" and turned to face my family. What I really wanted to do was run up to my room and cry but I refrained.

"Them bad guys better watch out! Uncle Rusty means business!" Patrick announced.

"You can't fault a guy for doing what he knows is right," my dad said. "Welcome home, Cassidy."

"Thanks, Dad," I said and gave him a hug.

"Hey Cass, we're going to hold you to it. You've got to tell us the story of your new hairdo," Randy said.

"I was hoping Jesse would know how to get rid of it."

"I do!" said Zack. "*Buzzzzzzzzzzz* it off!"

"No way. In L.A. I fit right in. They just expect to also see body piercings and chains attached to my clothes."

"Where's Shadow?" Patrick asked.

"I don't know, but I'll pay you five bucks to track him down."

"Five bucks? Why?"

"Just to make it worth your time. He's around here. He knows that when he's here he's a ranch dog. I'm not worried about him. But it would be good practice for you to track him."

"Cool! Five bucks!" Patrick said running off to where he knew the truck had been parked. He stared at the ground and began slowly tracking Shadow to the back of the barn where I knew he ran to greet the ranch dogs.

"That's no fair!" Wyatt said. "What can I do for five bucks? I can't track."

"You want to earn some money too?"

"Yeah!"

"It doesn't matter what the job is?"

"Umm, why?"

"You have to be careful what you volunteer for. I might send you to go help Randy muck out stalls."

"Ewe."

"But I think what I would like is for you to draw a picture of your family so I can hang it in the baby's room at home. Can you do that?"

"Yeah!"

"That would be the best thing you could do for me."

"I'll do it as soon as I go home to my art stuff. I got lots of art stuff. Crayons and water paints and tempera and charcoal and finger paints. What do you want me to use?"

"Whatever you think would work best."

I could see the wheels turning as he followed his mom into the house.

After I had unpacked and rejoined the family down stairs my mom wanted to show me something. I followed her up the stairs and to the room across the hall from mine.

"This is the play room," she said opening the door wide. Inside was a twin bed, a crib, a changing table, and shelves of toys for kids from about age ten down.

"Mom! You've gone grandkid crazy! The kids don't need all this!"

"Yes they do!" Wyatt said, "I think it's cool!"

"I think it needs books," Patrick added.

"We can add books!" Mom said brightly. "We'll have to put the big kid books up high and the baby books down low. Do you think you can keep your big kid books out of reach of the baby?"

"Course I can. I'm big. I can reach this high," Pat said.

"You'd be surprised how high a baby can reach," Mom said. "By Christmas the baby will be ready for toys. Let's go shopping!"

"Mom, there's nothing you could possibly add to this room!"

"But you need all kinds of stuff. We're bound to find something."

"We're all set. We even have things I see no use for. What am I going to need a baby swing for?"

"Oh Cass," Jesse said. "You'll love it. A baby will swing for hours. If you need to cook dinner, just stick them in the swing and cook away. Anything that buys time, you want."

Mom gave me a "so there!" look.

"Clothes! You must need clothes."

"I'm not buying anything new. I've only got a month to go."

"Party pooper."

"If we could find a way to make me blonde again, I'd be interested."

"Hmm," said Jesse. "We could bleach it all out and dye it. That's dangerous though."

"But if I wait until it grows out it'll be red, black and blonde striped."

"Like the snake!" Patrick said. "Red and yellow kill a fellow. Red and black won't attack."

"That's funny, because my hair was dyed like this so I'd look like a bad guy."

"You? A bad guy? That's funny! You a bad guy!" Patrick laughed.

"Just wait till you see the movie," I said.

"A movie!"

Oh hell.

"I'll tell you the story at dinner."

"Aw, Aunt Cassidy, that's no fair! You get us all curious and then we hafta wait!"

"Not for long."

"I say Patrick's right. This room needs books," Mom said. "Let's go to the book store. We can't buy the whole store but we have to start somewhere. Boys, you can each start your library with three books. You choose three books and we'll start a children's library."

"Yay!" Patrick said.

There was a little single room bookstore in town. The boys ran in, banging the door and jingling the little bell. Wyatt ran straight to the kids' section. Patrick began perusing the shelves of grown ups' books.

"These are all big, long, boring chapter books," Patrick said.

"You're in the romance section. What are you looking for?"

"Field guides."

"Look in the Nature section."

"I'm not tall enough to read the signs on top of the shelves."

Ten minutes later Patrick had an outdoor survival book, a field guide to North American wildlife and a book about backyard birds.

"Patrick. I said this was a children's library we were starting," Mom said.

"I *am* a children. If I'm a child and I like these books then they're children's books. Besides, if Cassidy's baby takes after her she'll be reading these books when she's seven, too."

"Oh, Lord help us," Mom said.

Wyatt was sitting cross-legged on the floor reading the very first book he'd seen that was interesting. I was glad to see it was, indeed, a kid's book, and that he wasn't having any trouble with it.

"Wyatt, we're choosing books to read at home. We're not at the library."

Wyatt stuck the book under one arm and looked for another. When he had two books he went to the front desk where he found he was too short to be seen.

"Scuse me, Ma'am," Wyatt said. "Scuse me."

"How may I, oh! There you are," the woman said looking way down at Wyatt.

"Could you show me where the art books are?"

"Art books? What kind? Surely not the classical works of art."

"I want a book that tells how to draw people."

"Oh, you do?"

"Yes Ma'am."

"My, what a little gentleman! Follow me."

I was glancing through a baby name book and over the bookshelves I heard, "Oh man, How to Draw People, How to Draw Animals, How to Draw Dogs, How to Draw Cars, How to Draw Cartoons. Aunt Cassidy! Do you want a serious picture or a funny picture?"

"It doesn't matter, it's for the baby's room."

"Then it should be happy. Rats, I can't decide."

I made my way around to the art section.

"Wyatt, I won't let you spend twelve dollars on drawing books to earn five dollars. I'll buy the books and you do the picture."

"But, which ones?"

"I'll get you the cartoon book and the people book because I know you'll find them both useful. Now Grandma will get you one more reading book."

Once again he sat at the bookshelf, pulled a book down and began reading oblivious to what he was supposed to be doing.

I bought the drawing books, the baby name book and *Heroes and Legends of the Old West*.

Mom went over and took the three books that Wyatt had.

"But Grandma! I read that one already!" he said.

"Find three to buy," she told him. "Buy ones you'll read more than once."

Wyatt appeared with another book.

"What about you?" Mom said to me.

"Mom, the baby won't need books for a year."

"Nonsense, babies love books. You read to that baby before they can talk and they'll talk sooner. You read to them before they can read and they'll read sooner."

"We're ready to go. I don't want to read a hundred kid books to find three to buy."

"I know a good one!" Patrick said.

"Me too!" said Wyatt.

They ran off again.

"I like this one."

"But I like this one."

"But this is Aunt Cassidy's baby. Aunt Cassidy's baby isn't going to like dolls and sissy stuff."

"How do you know? Somebody's gotta be a sissy in this family. I bet she's going to be a cute little girl and I bet the boys are gonna try and kiss her in kindergarten."

"Boys don't kiss girls in kindergarten. Girls kiss boys in kindergarten. Boys get cooties from girls in kindergarten."

"Just mean boys. Some boys like girls in kindergarten. I play with girls. I play with Madeline."

"Woohoo! Wyatt's got a girlfriend!"

"I do not! I just play with her."

I waded into the argument before it could get out of hand.

"I think it's great that you'll play with girls," I told Wyatt. "And I don't know what kind of a kid this baby is going to be. What have you found so far?"

"I like these books!" said Patrick. "I even have this one memorized. It's funny."

"And I like these books," said Wyatt.

"You've got twenty books here! We only need three. If a book's good enough to memorize it's good enough for me," I said choosing that one.

Patrick handed me one more from his stack and Wyatt after much thought drew one book from his stack.

"Good!" My mom said, looking triumphant.

Mom brought in a bookcase and placed it in the playroom. The eleven books looked lonely sitting there in mostly bare shelves. I knew it wouldn't be long before it was half full of all kinds of kid's books.

Dinnertime was boisterous, filled with lots of chatter about the upcoming race. Frank's Choice was finally deemed ready to go and seemed fit as a fiddle. The guys joked about his knees and Old Frank's name came up more than once. Wyatt tried time after time to get a word in edgewise but they were all excited. Finally Wyatt resorted to what usually worked in school. He sat there quietly with his hand raised. Finally my dad acknowledged him.

"Yes, Wyatt?" Dad boomed over the table.

"I can hear about Frank's Choice every day. I've been dying of curiosity cause Aunt Cassidy has a story to tell us and I just gotta hear it."

"Trouble, you still gettin' in trouble?" Steve asked.

"I try not to," I replied. "It just doesn't always work."

"I want to hear about the hair and the movie!" Wyatt said.

All eyes turned to me.

"Well, did I tell you about the time I tracked a movie star because she'd gone hiking and broke her leg and they thought she was missing?"

"I don't think so," Zack said, but I didn't trust Zack. He was pretty scatterbrained.

"Okay, the story just got longer."

I started from the very beginning telling about tracking Sherri Champlain through the woods and about the paparazzi and the helicopters and the news reporters. And then skipped to Sherri hiring me as a body guard just as dinner ended and Martha started clearing away the dishes.

"But, I haven't heard anything about the red hair or the movie!" Wyatt said, alarmed that he might never hear the end of the story.

"I'll finish, don't worry, but if Martha wants to hear it too I should help her clear away the dishes so she can come listen to the rest."

"Don't you dare," Martha said. "I'm sure I'll catch enough of it to scare me without hearing every word. Besides, we've got dessert."

"Okay, so this movie star hired you as a body guard because she was tired of some practical joker. What a baby!" Wyatt said.

"That's what I thought, but fifty thousand dollars was a lot of money. Uncle Rusty didn't want me to take the job. He said it would turn on me. He said there had to be a catch. He was suspicious because of the amount. But I ended up taking the job and I met lots of interesting people."

I continued my tale until I'd safely emerged from the smoking ruins of the set.

"I can't believe you did all that while you were pregnant! What were you thinking?" Mom exclaimed.

"Mom, a fence is a fence. They didn't ask me to do anything I hadn't done in the Marines or Police Academy. And I'll probably get a good sized check in the mail from the movie company, too. Not bad for three weeks of work."

"And does that have anything to do with why Rusty wants you out of town for a week or two?"

"No, that's a different set of trouble, but there's not much to tell. And it's not finished yet so I should probably hold off until I find out what happened. Did he really say a week or two?"

"Yes. He said everything was supposed to 'go down' Friday and if everything went well for the police he could come get you the next Wednesday."

"Did he say what was supposed to 'go down'?"

"No."

"What does it mean to 'go down'?" Wyatt asked.

"It can mean a lot of things. Rusty tends to take on some of the language from the kind of case he's working on. It could be that the gang has some big plan for Friday or it could mean that the police have a big raid. I try to stay out of police business but I think I should pay closer attention. He should have told me more."

"He just didn't want to worry you," Mom said.

"Well, it didn't work."

"Aunt Cassidy, don't be sad," Patrick said.

I was sitting on the floor of the playroom, half playing with baby toys and thinking, half leafing through the baby name book.

"Why'd you get the old west book?" he asked.

"Because it's a Gordon baby name book. Look up Kit Carson."

"Why Kit Carson?"

"I met a lady in the hospital and she was nice and wise and her favorite old west character was Kit Carson."

He looked up Kit Carson in the index and turned to the right page. He began reading and didn't stop for a long time.

"What's an Indian agent?" Pat asked.

"I think it's a hunter or someone hired to make sure the Indians in a certain area were kept under control. Why?"

"Kit Carson sounded like a nice guy until it talks about what he did to the Indians."

"You have to remember, the old west was a different place back then."

"I know, but Elan's my friend. I don't like someone who killed Elan's family."

"I'm named after a bank robber. Do you think that's any better?"

"Are you thinking of naming the baby after Kit Carson?"

"Yeah. I haven't talked to Rusty about it but Kit would work for a girl and Carson would work for a boy."

Patrick looked pensive for a moment.

"I think we should ask Elan. I think it's important for some reason. You don't want him to think of the baby badly because of her name. It might be like Mom naming me Barton Fartston."

"You heard about Barton?"

"Mom doesn't like him either."

"Well, if you think we should talk to Elan, go get him."

Patrick left the book behind and ran off to find Elan. I picked up the book and started reading. Patrick was right. For a while Kit Carson sounded a lot like me, but I, too worried about what Elan would think. Patrick was gone for another half hour, perhaps because Elan had a job to do. Patrick knew not to interrupt Elan's work. Finally the young Indian man stood in the doorway.

"Patrick says you wish to speak with me." He was always so precise.

"Sit down, Elan, you know my father's tradition of naming his children."

"Yes."

"I was thinking of the name Kit Carson but we read that Kit Carson was not a friend of the Indian people."

"Yes, in a way that is true."

He wasn't helping much.

"Would it be insulting to you if I named the baby after Kit Carson?"

"Insulting to me? No!"

"Would it be insulting to Indian people in general?"

"For a white woman to name her baby after a white man's hero?"

"If I named him after Kit Carson it would not be because he was a white man's hero. It would be because he was capable. He survived in the wilderness. Others trusted his abilities. He knew hunting and trapping and tracking, things necessary to live in the wilderness at that time. But, Elan, he was involved in the Long Walk. He killed your people."

"And mine also killed yours. It is past. Cassidy, Kit Carson was a formidable man. Any man who could take on my people and accomplish what he did is to be admired. My people were not peaceful in his time. The whole country was in arms. No white man was safe. Kit Carson knew many Indians. His friends spoke of him well and his enemies spoke of him with admiration. Either way you look at it a person who has his heritage in their name has big shoes to fill."

"Well, I'm not counting on that. I don't think Kit Carson's abilities are as appreciated today as they once were."

"Honesty and strength of character are never a bad thing. From what I hear of this baby's parents strength of character should be no problem."

"I don't know who you've been talking to..."

"Steve, James, Jesse, Patrick, Chase. Your father has an interesting way to put it, but in the end he says the same thing."

"My father thinks I'm an irresponsible kid."

"Your father says, 'One thing with Cassidy being a trouble magnet. She's learned to hold her own. You can throw anything at that kid and she takes it on.' My people were Kit Carson's trouble. They threw many things at him and he took it on. So I think the name very appropriate."

"Has Steve told you all the old stories of when I was kid?"

He didn't have to answer. His lopsided grin said it all.

"Do you still think the name appropriate?"

"Perhaps you should consider Daniel Boone."

"Daniel Boone?"

"How does the old song go? Killed him a bear when he was only three?"

"That's from an old TV show."

"Look him up."

"I didn't kill the coyote. How's the tracking going?"

"You owe Patrick five dollars."

I smiled. I knew he could do it but I expected him to come running back to claim his reward.

"Why didn't you collect your five dollars? You could have bought something at the bookstore."

"I don't track for money. I track to learn stuff."

"You can always use five dollars. I know you. You're always saving for something. What are you saving for?"

He looked embarrassed. "Moccasins."

"It shouldn't take long to do that. Are your moccasins wearing out? You know your mom will buy you new ones."

"Not for me, for the baby. I didn't want the baby to grow up in cowboy boots. I wanted her to learn to walk like a tracker from the very beginning. If I used your money to buy the moccasins it would be like you buying them and I wanted to."

"Well, here," I said, handing him a five-dollar bill. "Put it in a different fund. I'm sure you have plenty of time to buy those moccasins. Babies don't walk until they are close to a year old. Thank you for thinking of the baby."

"I've been waiting a long time for a baby cousin. I've had a lot of time to think of things a baby cousin needs to know. I'm going to be a good big cousin. I'm going to teach her everything I know. And I'm going to keep her in line."

"Keep her in line?"

"Somebody's got to teach her to explore without killing herself."

"I'm sure you'll do a great job, Pat."

"I'll warn her not to jump off the barn roof unless she knows there's not a pitchfork in the hay. And I'll show her where the hole is that the rattlesnake goes into, so she won't get bit. And I'll show her the game trail by the fence in Snoopy's paddock where you can lay in the grass and the rabbits will walk right by. And I'll tell her how soft rabbits are and show her how to touch one."

"You're still sure this is going to be a girl."

"And she's going to be just like you."

Jesse stuck her head into the room and called Patrick home for the night. Elan left too and I was alone with my thoughts again.

Rusty called. He had gotten back to town and checked in at the station. The house was too quiet, he said. He'd picked up dinner in town but he didn't feel like eating it.

"How was your day?" he asked.

"I guess it was as good as it could be. Mom made a playroom for the grandkids. We went to the bookstore."

"Just a bookstore?"

"Believe me she wanted to do more, but I couldn't see the point in buying new clothes if I was only going to wear them for one more month. I bought a baby name book and a Gordon family baby name book."

"Did you find any good names?"

"I'll keep looking. I'll make a list and you can see which ones you like."

The more I talked to him the further the miles stretched and the sadder I became.

"Cass, what's eating at you?"

"What's happening Friday?"

The line went still.

"Don't worry about it."

"I have to. You should have told me. I'd rather have a specific worry than this vague cloud of doom that hangs over me."

"Friday is a deadline of sorts. D Dawg gave his people until Friday to bring you in but he wanted to make a big deal of it. He wanted to show other members what happens to a snitch. At first I just wanted to get you out of the picture. Now the goal is to keep Manny Mo alive."

"You said the price wasn't in dollars. If it's not in dollars what is it?"

"Something these kids value more than money. Prestige and drugs. That's another thing that makes this meeting so important. If we can catch D Dawg in this we'll have the evidence to put him away for a very long time. We can confiscate anything they brought as a payoff. Nearly every kid that shows up will have something on them."

"On Friday."

"Don't dwell on it. If all goes well you can come home soon. I want you here where I can see you. Try and be happy. Get out and do the things you love. Ride Shasta. Go tracking with Patrick. Play pool with Steve. Did you touch a doe for me?"

"No, we haven't gotten out to the deer flats."

"Get out of the house. You'll feel better if you are doing active things."

"I'll try."

I did try. I rode Shasta around the corral, wondering what the baby thought of the odd movements. Mentally talking to the baby, telling him, "This is a walk. This is a trot. This is a canter. The fast one is a gallop." But my heart wasn't in riding. And it wasn't in tracking. I just longed for home.

"Martha, can you give me a job to do? I need something to do but my room is clean, the playroom is way too clean. A playroom should look played in."

"Go down to Jesse's house. She always has her hands full. She'll put you to work."

So I walked down to Jesse's house. I rang the bell and she answered it.

"Martha won't put me to work. She said you always have chores to do."

"You've got to be kidding. You want work to do? I've got six loads of laundry, dishes to wash, a floor to mop, a suitcase to pack."

After I'd washed the dishes I helped Jesse fold clothes.

"Just wait until the baby comes. You'll be up to your ears in laundry."

"How can one little baby cause so much extra laundry?"

"Ha! You just wait and see!"

"Can I bake cookies?"

"Are you sure you're not in nesting mode?"

"Nesting mode?"

"Right before women go into labor sometimes they suddenly feel like cleaning everything, making sure everything is ready for the baby, kind of like a mother bird building a nest."

"I don't think so. I still have four weeks to go."

"Are you sure?"

"I better be."

"Here," she said placing cookie ingredients on the counter. "Set the oven five degrees hotter than the recipe says. My oven is off a little."

"Are you going grocery shopping any time soon?"

"Maybe, why?"

"I'm out of Brownie Batter."

"I have a mix here in the pantry."

"No, it's an ice cream flavor. I guess I should just settle for a different kind. I have ten others to choose from. But nothing is like Brownie Batter ice cream."

"Now you're making me hungry for ice cream."

"I've got lots at the big house. You want to go on an ice cream binge?"

"You're a mean cruel sister. Yeah!"

The cookies were forgotten. We bent over the freezer behind the ranch house.

"Cassidy! I'm going to go buy stock in Ben and Jerry's! Golly, how much ice cream can one girl eat?"

"What kind do you want? Chunky Monkey, Cherry Garcia, Phish Food, New York Super Fudge Chunk…"

"How about Peanut Butter Cup?"

"Sure, sounds good to me. We can split it. Do you want Reese's on top? Fudge?"

"Cassidy, how do you eat like this and stay so skinny?"

"Maybe the baby likes ice cream, too."

"We have to finish before the boys get home from school. If they see us eating this they'll clean out your whole supply."

Half a container of Peanut Butter Cup, two Reese's and a little fudge sauce later I was washing all the dishes in the ranch house kitchen. Then I dusted the living room.

"Cassidy, I swear you've got nesting syndrome. Quit working!" Jesse scolded. "Martha dusted this morning."

"Can we bake those cookies?"

"No, it's too close to dinner time and the boys will eat them all as soon as they walk in the door."

"Then I'll go help Steve."

"No! You are not mucking out stables or grooming horses. Just sit."

"I can't just sit. I have to do something."

"Okay, let's run through the baby things and make sure you have everything you need. Crib?"

"Check."

Bassinette? Changing table? Diapers? Clothes?…a stroller?

"A stroller? I don't have a stroller."

"A backpack?"

"Of course I have a backpack. I live in a backpack."

"One for a baby?"

"No."

"Mom! Hey Mom! I found something we need to go shopping for!"

Before I could even blink we were in the big ranch truck on the way to town.

"What about the boys? You said they'd be home from school soon!"

"They know to check in with James. Patrick will do homework and then report in for chores. If Elan's handy he'll get away with tracking first. If he finds Steve or James first he'll be put to work. Wyatt is dead set on drawing a perfect likeness of everybody in the family. Trouble is, he's a perfectionist lacking in abilities. So he tries over and over."

"Poor kid. I didn't know I set him onto an impossible task. I expected smiling stick figures standing in front of a stick house."

"Not with Wyatt. He's actually got a very good eye for a five year old. He just needs practice."

"Maybe I can help later."

At the store we stood in front of a whole row of strollers. Umbrella strollers that folded up and fit under the seat in a car. Strollers that looked like small cars. Strollers that doubled as a car seat and high chair.

"Push them around. Look this one is too little. You have to stoop over to push it. It'll irritate you to stoop over all the time. This is a nice basic one. Here's a jogging stroller."

"A jogging stroller?"

"Yeah, see the big wheels? That's so you can push it at a jog and not worry about getting hung up on rocks."

"That's what I need! Then I can jog around the block when I get cabin fever. My block is almost two miles long."

My mom appeared with a stack of baby clothes.

"Mom, I've got all kinds of baby clothes. Size newborn through six months," I scolded her.

"I know, but the baby is not coming home from the hospital in yellow and green. They're coming home in a little dress or a little play outfit. It's not that big a deal to buy one of each. Look at the little jeans. Aren't they cute? And here's hiking boots!"

"Hiking boots for a newborn? No way."

"Don't let Mom buy the jeans," Jesse warned me, "Don't buy anything without snaps in the crotch!"

"Oh look! Here's little overalls with a police car on the front! You have to have this! Rusty's going to bring the baby to work and he can wear this!"

"What about backpacks?" I asked, trying to distract my mom from cleaning out the baby clothes section of the store.

The backpacks did look very handy. This was a baby product I could identify with. Now we could get out in the hills together!

Before we checked out Jesse inspected all the outfits.

"Not this one, no snaps. Not this one, the elastic in the sleeves is too tight. Not this one, the eyes on the little doggie appliqué can come off and get swallowed. Not this one, baby fingers can get tangled in the little ribbons…"

When she was through we were still left with two little girl outfits and three little boy outfits. Mom was determined. I had to have the overalls with the police car on them, no matter what.

"If it's a little girl, I'll sew lace around the edges so they'll be pretty."

She bought little black and white saddle back shoes saying they looked like police cars.

"Mom, Rusty's a detective. He doesn't drive a squad car."

As the days passed the Ben and Jerry's supply got lower and lower and the candy bar stash was in a sorry state. I still craved cookie dough. One night I couldn't stand it anymore and got up in the middle of the night and baked cookies. Martha wandered in at three a.m.

"Cassidy, what are you doing?" she asked as she squinted into the light.

"Baking cookies."

"I'll make you cookies. Any time you want!"

"I don't want to eat cookies. I want to bake them."

"I think Jesse's right. You have some odd form of nesting syndrome. You're not going to make it to the end of June. You've been dusting and washing dishes and straightening rooms that are perfect. It's one of the classic signs."

Martha went back to bed. I finished the cookie baking a little before five and washed the dishes, so Martha wouldn't wake up to a mess. Then I went to bed and slept until ten. When I got up there were two cookies left.

"I'm sorry, Cassidy, the boys didn't know and they were half gone before I found out."

"The boys ate all those?"

"Yes. I think Zack had ten!"

"Oh!" I said, relieved, "I thought you meant Patrick and Wyatt! I couldn't eat all those cookies. I'm glad the guys liked them. I just wanted to eat cookie dough while I baked."

Chapter 32

Friday I was in a sorry state. I woke up nervous and I called Rusty as soon as I thought he'd be up and around.

"Babe? You okay?"

"Yes, I just had to hear your voice."

"But we just talked last night."

"It doesn't matter. I need to hear it again. What are you doing?"

"Getting ready for work."

"Wear your tweed coat. I love the tweed one."

There was a long pause and I realized he wasn't getting ready for the office. He would be in riot gear today.

"Wear it when you come get me then."

"I will."

"Be careful."

"I'll call you when it's all over."

"No matter what time it is."

"No matter the time."

"I'll stalk that deer today. I need to do something alone and I need to concentrate on something else today. So I'll stalk the deer."

"That's my girl. I wish I could watch you."

"You can. I'll wait for you."

"You know that's not what I meant."

Sigh, "I know."

"You take care."

"You too."

"I love you," we said simultaneously.

I hung up and cried. When my tears were spent I packed a lunch and headed out. I stopped at the barn.

"Steve? I'm walking to the deer flats. If I'm not home when Patrick gets home from school can you send him out there after me?"

"Ride Shasta."

"I need to walk. If I lead Shasta he'll nudge me in the back all the way."

"I'm telling you. Take a horse along. If something goes wrong you need a way back. You're either taking a horse or a hand, so take a horse. I need all the hands I can get. Elan and Randy are gone to the race."

"Frank's choice is running today?"

"Yeah."

"Can I get a bet in?"

"You never bet on the races, least of all a horse's first race."

"I've rode Frank's Choice. I know the horse he is. I know the odds are not going to be in his favor, so that works in my favor. He beats the odds and my money pays off, right?"

"Right."

"So I want to bet ten thousand on Frank's Choice."

"Ten thousand! Where did you get ten thousand dollars?"

"Three weeks as a body guard. It's only a fifth of it."

"And you want to bet all that?"

"Yeah."

"Rusty will kill you if he loses."

"No he won't. I wasn't even going to cash the check. It felt like ill-gotten gains."

"Ten thousand on Frank's Choice. To win?"

"To show at first. If I come out ahead use the initial ten to try for a place. Consider the ten thousand play money and the profits untouchable. I'll stay with it until the odds start shifting. How long do you think it'll take for Frank's Choice to prove himself?"

"It's hard to say. The racing world is a fickle place."

"What time's the race?"

"If you want to catch it be home by three. Your dad will be watching on the big screen upstairs."

"Okay, I'll take Shasta."

I went to the tack room to get my saddle but Steve beat me to it.

"You have no business lugging saddles around. And let me groom him when you get back."

"Steve, I'm pregnant. I'm not an invalid."

"Let me do it for you. There's not much I can do for you anymore."

I gave him a hug before saddling up. Steve had been watching over me ever since I could remember. He was the ready, steady hand I could always count on. Somehow, I felt he needed to retain that position no matter how old we both got.

My need to get out had been dulled a little. I climbed up into the saddle and went out the back gate of the ranch. I rode like I did as a kid. I let Shasta lope and felt the free, easy feeling of the wind in my hair, the gentle rhythm of the gait. When we were a couple of miles from the ranch I pointed him toward the deer flats. I tied him to a tree about a quarter mile from where the deer grazed. I could see a couple of does even from this distance. I kept a couple of trees between the deer and me as I walked the short distance to the clearing. Shasta snorted as he noticed he was being left behind. He hadn't been stalking in a long time. He was used to being with his rider.

The deer grazed lazily. The weather was really warming up and the deer didn't want to be out in the sun. Several of them were bedded down in the shade. In a way it made my job harder. The grazing deer would be distracted but the deer resting in the shade would be on lookout for the whole herd. That meant if I was going to sneak up on one it would have to be the closest one. I kept a sharp eye for the first deer. I found her bedded down in a little spot of shade about a hundred yards away. I stood quietly, planning my route, then set out in a low crouch. I soon found out a low crouch wasn't as easy when you're eight months pregnant. My thighs bumped up against my belly when I crouched down. It was distracting, to me and Junior. He started bumping back. When I froze, the baby didn't but I don't think the deer were observant enough to see my shirt move as a tiny elbow or heel went across from one side to the other. I wondered what he was doing in there. I pictured him doing back flips, winding the umbilical cord around himself. I wondered how there was room in there to do anything. The deer perked up and I froze again. She stared at me for half an hour and I stayed frozen for half an hour. I was still twenty feet away when the doe rose to her feet. I knelt down in the grass and waited for her to decide if I was friend or foe. I knew touching a doe today was impossible but I sat enjoying the view. I hadn't been out with the deer in a long time. It was peaceful watching the deer milling around, gradually heading for the brush away from me. After a while they decided I wasn't a threat and settled down again. I move forward a foot at a time on hands and knees and sat whenever they noticed me move. I wasn't really stalking now. It was more of a game between them and me. They knew I was there. They were bigger and faster. One leap and they'd be gone. I'd let them go. So we were all happy together. When I got hungry I stood and headed back to where Shasta was tied. I got out a sandwich and ate as I rode back to the ranch.

"Any luck?" Steve asked as he took the reins from me back in the barn.

"You could say so. I didn't come close but I had a good time and I got to watch the herd for a long time."

He took the saddle off and I grabbed a brush.

"Go on, I'll do it," he said.

"It's relaxing to me. Let me do this side and you can work on that side."

I still admired Shasta's dapple-gray coat. I'd chosen him from amongst all the bays and chestnuts and sorrel horses because of his temperament and because of his flashy, yet friendly look.

"Rusty didn't call, did he?"

"You'd have to ask Martha that."

"He'd probably call my cell phone, but if he couldn't get through he might call here."

"You sound like you're expecting a call."

"I doubt he'd call this early, but there's always a chance."

"What's the big news?"

"That he survived the day."

"At least he's got luck and skill on *his* side."

"Plus as many officers as they could spare for this. I think Schroeder will help as much as he can. This case has a lot of ripple effects if they can catch some key people. If they catch the right people, I can go home again."

When Shasta was all brushed out from his ride Steve and I headed for the house. Inside the mood was festive. As a kid I was never really interested in the races. To me horses were friends, not a business venture. And even now, with ten thousand dollars on the line, the bet seemed more a validation of friendship than a business risk. I had faith in Old Frank, in Steve, Randy and Elan. They knew their job and if this horse was good to go I thought he'd win. I knew it was important to get my bets in on these early races, because as Frank's Choice proved his worth as a racehorse the odds would change very quickly. Frank had wanted to hit the racing world by surprise with this horse and I meant to take advantage of it.

The talk upstairs was jovial. Everybody was ready for this race. It helped that they showed shots of the warm up. People gawked at Frank's Choice. I had to admit he didn't look like much of a winner, but that's what we were counting on. He was shorter than most of the other horses but on closer inspection I thought he still had the reach. It was his spirit that won out in my mind. He just flat out loved to run. When I rode him I could feel the ease of his run, the power. A quarter horse race was a jog in the park for him. He'd be disappointed to have to stop.

Dad sat in his big, leather chair and everybody else stood around talking and watching the horses.

"See there? That's the one favored to win. He's won five in a row."

All the hands knew the horses. Dad was showing me.

"He's a good horse," I replied. "I'd pick him over Frank's Choice if I were just out at the races for a day."

"Hopefully you'd pick almost all of them over Frank's Choice. I'm almost embarrassed to enter him. He's a sorry looking SOB but he sure runs like the dickens."

"I assume you've run him in groups so he'd be used to running with other horses."

"Only problem is no horse here can keep up with him. We aren't a big outfit. We don't have a dozen racehorses. We got our one or two favored horses and the rest are workers."

"Just keep your fingers crossed that he keeps his cool in real competition," Steve said.

Randy rode Buck next to Frank's Choice and a man helped close him into the gate. Was that Elan? I didn't know how these things worked. This was Elan's first race, too, so I didn't know how involved he would be.

The horses tensed, waiting for the gate to open. I couldn't see the tension but I'd felt the tension of a horse that wanted to run. Even if they were already in motion there was a tension there. To put that tension behind a gate invited an explosion of action.

The gate opened and the horses sprung out! Frank's Choice got off to a rocky start. He bolted crooked and was bumped by another horse. The jockey pointed him down the track and Frank's Choice took off like he was chased by a swarm of bees. He bolted into the group and had to sort things out. Funny thing, though, the other horses were more bothered by it than Frank was. Once the initial scare was over he ran well. The announcers and the crowd went wild as he pulled ahead one horse at a time.

A quarter horse race doesn't leave much room for error. There is no time to make up for mistakes but Frank's Choice didn't believe in mistakes. He believed in running. And he wanted to be the leader of the pack, just like at home. He saw the lead position was getting away from him. It wasn't a matter of competition. He knew his place. It was out front, so out front was where he headed and he almost made it before the finish line. He came in second and when the other horses slowed down, he took his place at the front triumphantly, but late.

Steve was disappointed but unsurprised. It was a first race after all. Frank's Choice was young and inexperienced. There would be more races with better results. Once the thrill of the race got into his blood there'd be no stopping him.

"You're lucky you played it safe," Steve said. "You didn't make megabucks but you didn't lose either. You sure you want to continue?"

"Sure, for four or five races anyway. He had a rough start today. With a clean start he'd have won."

The rest of the afternoon dragged by. I paced the house imagining all the ways things could go wrong for Rusty. We'd practiced over and over these kinds of raids in academy but academy was very different from real life. In real life there was no going back and fixing the mistakes, no gathering back in the classroom to pick apart the fatalities. In real life it was permanent.

Dinner was quiet. Nobody needed to rehash the race. Nobody felt like celebrating even though we hadn't exactly lost. When Randy called we made it sound like a win. He was happy with the race. We'd started out worse and come out better before. Randy was good at seeing the bigger picture.

I paced the house. I tried straightening the playroom, tried imagining a little Rusty playing with the toys. I sorted laundry and ran a load, hoping I'd need to pack and head for home on Wednesday like Mom said.

"Cassidy? What are you doing starting laundry at eight o'clock at night?"

"I won't be able to sleep, anyway. I'm waiting for Rusty to call. I told him time wasn't an issue."

"You need the rest."

"Mom, I can't rest until I know and I can't settle down. I'll do the laundry, maybe sweep the porch. Do you need the windows washed? I can do the insides."

"The windows are fine. You need to rest."

"Maybe I should wash my sheets, too."

"Rest. You'll have enough to do soon. You'll need all the energy you can get once labor starts."

"I can't rest for three and a half weeks. I'll go nuts."

"Tomorrow we'll go shopping."

"There's nothing more to buy, Mom. You've bought everything baby related you can get your hands on."

"I still wish we knew if it were a boy or a girl."

"I'm sorry, Mom. We'll know soon."

The washer stopped and I switched the laundry to the dryer.

Where was Rusty?

Nine o'clock rolled around. Nine thirty and the dryer finished. I stopped it before it buzzed and disturbed people. I folded clothes and fretted. Ten o'clock. I walked down to the barn and walked among the horses. Apache was looking good. Shasta greeted me and nudged my shoulder. I went to the little refrigerator in the office and got out carrots for each horse. Mack and Chet's stalls seemed lonely but I knew Randy had Buck and another horse down at the racetrack. Satan was now used to me coming and going. He no longer charged the stall door when I came in. I tried giving him a carrot. He laid his ears back and I took the carrot away.

"You be nice or you aren't getting anything," I scolded him. His ears stayed back so I continued on. His ears perked up as I turned away and he looked hopeful when I came back. "Be gentle," I warned him. "Gentle...gentle...ahah!" I closed my hand. "Be gentle!" He took the carrot gently and I tried to pet him but his ears went quickly back again. Good for nothing horse. All I could say about him was he was beautiful. Jet black, perfect form, the perfect quarter horse, except for his bad-tempered nature. He wasn't bred. Nobody wanted to chance his temper being passed on. But he was good advertising. Put him in a paddock out by the road and people stopped to take his picture.

Eleven o'clock. Where was Rusty? What was he doing? Why wasn't he calling? Another container of Ben and Jerry's later and I was still waiting. It's amazing the terrible things the mind can think up if given enough time to worry about them. I tried to remind myself that even I knew how to keep from being shot. Body armor was now standard gear so he'd be wearing his vest.

I caught myself dozing and got up to pace again. I checked my cell phone to make sure it still had plenty of charge and that I hadn't missed a call. I walked down to Jesse's house. I didn't want to disturb them but I had to do something so I walked the quarter mile in the dark and climbed up into the tree house I'd built for the boys. It was comforting to feel the smooth wood of the floor. The paint had been worn away by busy boys playing rough and tumble imaginary games in the tree house. I was glad to see it was used often. I sat with my back to a corner enjoying the cool night air, fretting quietly by myself. When the baby started bumping against my ribs I lay on my back so we wouldn't be so scrunched. I stared up into the sky. The night sky was a blanket of jewels in the darkness of the ranch. I tried to imagine my way back home. I tried to picture myself in my very own bed in my very own room with Rusty lying quietly beside me. I felt for him and was met by rough plywood. The baby quieted again and slowly the night faded.

I was startled awake by the cell phone and nearly jumped out of my skin.

"Hello?" I said automatically, even though I knew it was Rusty.

"Cass? Did I wake you?"

"It's okay. Mom would be panic stricken if I stayed here until morning."

"Where are you?"

"In the tree house."

"Babe…"

"I was just doing things to stay awake. I didn't want to miss your call. I've been waiting forever for your call."

"I'm sorry. I called as soon as I could."

He sounded weary. I knew the conversation would be short, but I knew the one thing I needed to know. He was okay.

"Are you okay?" I asked.

"Yeah. I'm okay. You?"

"Now I am. Now that I know. How did it go?"

"I won't know for sure for a day or two. We accomplished a lot. I'll know more tomorrow, after I talk to some people. It's been a very long day."

"When can I come home?"

"I'll know more tomorrow."

"You mean tomorrow Tuesday or tomorrow today?"

"I'll let you know as soon as I can."

"I'm ready to hitch hike home if I need to. I need to be home. I ache whenever I'm left alone to think. I want you so bad."

"Climb down and walk home. We both need to go to bed. I won't hang up until I know you're back at the big house. What did you do today?"

"I tried to stalk deer…"

"Did you touch one?"

"No, the conditions were wrong and it's not easy to do when I can't bend over without crowding the baby. But I got to see them and watch them for a little while. I bet ten thousand on Frank's Choice's first race."

"You what?"

"It was a risk, but it's not like I didn't have the money. I played it safe and gained a little. He came in second. I told Steve to bet the ten thousand and not risk the profit. Just for four or five races. From what I saw today he's capable of winning. He's got the speed and the drive. The odds are against him so the profits are large. Did you know that if I guessed the top three horses in the order they win I could make a year's wages?"

"I thought you didn't like to gamble."

"I don't, and I'm not exactly gambling."

"What do you call betting on the horse races if not gambling?"

"I call it showing faith in the abilities of my family and friends. Four or five races and that's all. For Old Frank. I know he knew what he was doing. I just know it."

"And you said the body guard paycheck was ill gotten gains."

I'd climbed down from the tree house and I made my way down the dirt road to the big house. The little false labor contractions started up again and subsided.

"Maybe that money just has a future in ill-gotten gains. What other shady operations can I invest in?"

"Cass…"

"I'm just kidding."

"At least you seem to be feeling better."

"I just needed to hear your voice. Now I need to see you. I need a hug."

"Me too, Babe. Soon."

"You want to know something weird?"

"What?"

"The baby's shifted or something. Everything feels different. About four days ago. I think everything is fine. I feel good. The baby moves like crazy. But isn't that weird?"

"I don't know. I'll ask Doctor Ron."

"I have an appointment next Friday if I'm in town." I climbed the steps and entered the front door of the ranch house. I locked it behind me. "Okay, I'm back. I'm in the ranch house. Thank you for calling. I waited and waited and I was getting scared."

"I know. I knew you would. I almost had Schroeder call you earlier but I knew hearing Schroeder's voice would have scared you more. I'll call after dinner. I need some sleep and tomorrow's going to be tense and busy. I'd talk all night but I'd be wasted tomorrow and I need to have my head on straight. You take care."

"I'll be okay now. I'll talk to you soon."

"You're back for sure?"

"Yeah, I'll be waiting."

"Okay, sleep good."

"You too."

I yawned as I turned off my phone and went up to my room. I undressed for bed. The baby started hiccupping. Sigh. Was this a sign of what sleep as a new mom would be like? I slipped into bed and tried to relax as my abdomen twitched and jerked. Rusty, if you could feel your baby now, you'd be amazed. He is getting so big.

I awoke to bright blue skies and a hunger that wouldn't quit. I showered quickly and went down to the kitchen. Breakfast was long gone. I searched the kitchen and then searched for Martha. It wasn't nice to use up ingredients she had plans for.

"Is it okay if I make a few pancakes?" I asked.

"Of course! But I'll do it."

"It's okay, I need something to do. If I don't cook breakfast I'll do laundry. I'm feeling stir crazy. Besides, I feel like a particular kind of pancake and I don't know how they'll turn out."

"What kind are you making?"

"Banana pecan caramel."

"Pancakes?"

"Yeah."

"If it works I want the recipe."

"Okay, I'll try and keep track of what I do."

I was a little worried about getting the proportions right if I started from scratch so I made pancakes from a mix and added mashed bananas and chopped pecans to the batter. Then, while they were cooking I drizzled them with caramel sauce, flipped them over and cooked the other side. I made four, but I doubted I could eat four. I put them all on a plate and drizzled on more caramel sauce and then thought blueberry syrup sounded good, too. I ate all four pancakes and two scoops of Ben and Jerry's. I waddled about the kitchen cleaning up and then waddled upstairs to sort out the last of the laundry.

"Cassidy, you know Martha will wash whatever you drop into the laundry chute," my mom said.

"I know Mom, but I talked to Rusty last night and I might be able to go home soon. I want my clothes to be clean. Plus, I need something to do. If I don't do laundry I'll clean my bathroom again and it doesn't need it."

"I'm calling Rusty," she said. "There are some things he needs to know. That baby's on its way and he needs to be here!"

"What do you mean, it's on its way? I have three weeks to go!"

"One: the baby's dropped."

"Dropped?"

"Oh god, you didn't know? It's been obvious for nearly a week!"

"Mom, I don't know anything. You didn't tell me it mattered. What does it mean that the baby has dropped?"

"Why… it means it is in position to be born! It happens within a week or two of birth! Your doctor didn't tell you?"

"I haven't been able to get to the doctor for the past two visits."

"Oh my! Oh dear. I'm calling Rusty!"

"Mom, you're overreacting!"

"Overreacting? One: the baby's dropped. Two: you've had nesting syndrome for several days. Three: hmmm, three. Your water hasn't broke has it?"

"I don't think so."

"You'd know it if it did. But two out of three is pushing it. You need Rusty either here or you need to be home. He'll be devastated if this baby is born and he isn't there."

I ran two loads of laundry, cleaned my bathroom, and spent an hour packing all the baby stuff my mom had bought. My mom in turn began packing as well.

"Mom! What are you doing?"

"It's been decided. I'm taking you home tomorrow."

"Tomorrow?"

I was elated! I was going home! I'd see Rusty again! My life would be back to normal! I'd be in my own home, amongst my own things. I could relax. I could be me again.

"Why are *you* taking me home?" I asked.

"Well, it was agreed that I'd be there to help you after the baby was born, right?"

"Yes, but…"

"And Rusty needed a few more days to finalize some things at work."

"Yes, but…"

"Cassidy, I think that baby is coming sooner than you think. I think he'll be born in the next week."

"But I'm not ready! I need to go home. I need to get things settled. I need time on the big brown couch!"

"The big brown couch?"

"It's how Rusty and I spend our together time. The just-you-and-me-time."

"Honey, you'll get your big brown couch time. But, you're displaying all the symptoms of an imminent birth. I'm surprised you didn't know."

"Mom, I've never had a baby before!"

Chapter 33

Within a week! I didn't exactly panic but I went into overdrive. I washed all the laundry. I made all the rounds to be sure I'd had a proper visit with everybody. I brushed Shasta even though he didn't need it and I told him all about what I thought might happen in the next week or so. I packed. I made sure we were ready to transport Shadow. And then I paced the house, finished off the Ben and Jerry's and finally ate the can of asparagus. What was it about asparagus? Usually I didn't care for it. And I fretted. I wasn't ready to be a mom. I must have been nuts to let this happen. What was I going to do with a baby? A helpless little baby. I went to the playroom and looked at the nursery part of it. All the little containers of baby products. Baby wipes, disposable diapers, baby powder, tearless shampoo. What was mom thinking buying all these things so far ahead of time? They'd be useless by the time I came back. Grandmotherly nesting syndrome, I thought.

"Aunt Cassidy, do you *have* to go home tomorrow?" Patrick asked behind me.

"I'm afraid so, Pat. Grandma thinks the baby is going to be born soon and I need to get back to where my doctor is."

"How come you have to have a doctor there?"

"Well, you don't have to. But if something goes wrong it is safer to have that happen with a doctor handy."

"What goes wrong when babies are born?"

"It's nothing you need to worry about. My doctor says everything looks good. He's happy with the way the baby has been growing."

"What about you?"

"Me? I'm fine. Nothing's going to go wrong."

He wasn't convinced. He was used to things turning on me. Maybe I shouldn't tell him so many stories.

"As soon as the baby is born Grandma will email pictures back and you'll be able to see, everything is fine."

Wyatt came in, sad.

"Aunt Cassidy, I tried to make your picture but I couldn't."

"What happened, Wyatt? You're such a good artist! I know you can do it. I think you are just trying too hard. Can you show me what you've done so far?"

"No, it's embarrassing."

"I'm sure it's wonderful. Show me. Or go get some art stuff and we can do it together. I'll help you."

There was a sketchbook in the playroom. Mom knew her grandkids, that's for sure. Wyatt found drawing tools.

"Okay, draw an oval for a face," I instructed.

"People don't have oval faces."

"An oval is good to start from."

He insisted on narrowing the oval at the bottom for the chin.

"Now add eyes," I said.

His people were not going to have dot eyes. They were almond shaped, had irises and pupils, eyelashes and lids. He ran into problems making the eyes match. He got ready to crumple up the paper but I stopped him.

"No! You're doing great. Start on the other eye slow. If things are not going well just erase back to the part you know is right. Take it slow, erase gently, draw lightly. When you know it's right you can always go back and darken your lines."

Even though I wasn't much of an artist myself, I coached him from one feature to another, stressing things that I knew distinguished each person: his mom's long wavy hair, his dad's piercing eyes and freckles. He put moccasins on Patrick and put a rope in his hand and he drew himself a quiet little boy in cowboy clothes with little to distinguish himself from any other kid. I wanted to tell him to put a paintbrush in his hand or something, but he had drawn himself the way he wanted me to see him.

"Wyatt, see? You can draw. You did a terrific job! I'm going to frame this and hang it in the baby's room. He'll be able to see you guys every day."

"Can I draw a picture of the baby?"

"We don't know what he looks like. We don't even know if it's a boy or a girl."

"When Grandma sends pictures I'll draw one of the pictures."

"That would be great. Can you run and get my pack from my room? I owe you five dollars."

He ran across the hall and back in the time it would take me to stand up. I gave him his five dollars and he stuffed it in his pocket where it would probably get washed when his mom did laundry. Wyatt was creative but he wasn't very conscientious.

My laundry was done. My room was clean. The bathroom was scrubbed. The clothes in the closet were organized. My riding boots were shined. I sure wish there was more to do around the ranch but Martha did everything before I could get to it.

I went downstairs wondering if there were tortilla chips and cheese dip in the kitchen. Chili on top would be good, too. Martha was in the kitchen preparing dinner so I didn't push the chips and dip. Instead I cut up vegetables for her and snitched a few as I went. The meat in the oven smelled wonderful. The more time I spent in the kitchen the hungrier I got. Martha stirred a sauce on the stove that started my mouth to watering. I sure hoped my appetite settled down after the baby was born.

Dinner was lively that night. Randy and Elan brought stories from the races and everybody was talking about the baby, mom insisting there was going to be a new family member by this time next week.

Rusty called after dinner.

"Hey!" I said cheerfully. I was feeling closer to home already.

"It's good to hear you be happy."

"I'll be happier when I get that hug."

"How are you?"

"Besides huge? I'm fine. The baby's so big. You can see his kicks easily. I'll be sitting still and suddenly a little bump will go running across my shirt. The first time Wyatt saw it he jumped. It was funny. 'It looks like there's a mouse under your shirt,' he said."

Rusty laughed but I could tell he was still tired.

"I want to see it."

"You will. Tomorrow. How's work going?"

"You wouldn't be coming home unless it was going well. These kids fight every move we make, even in custody. They don't give an inch. They know every inch they give can add to their time. They are caught in such a web of violence and drugs. An inch of information could snowball on them. They aren't stupid. But it sure makes for a weary week."

"Maybe we can turn this week around a little."

"If I can see you, it'll turn around a lot."

I went to bed early even though I was just as stir crazy as could be. I wanted to get plenty of rest and wake up early. I wanted to pack the truck and eat a good breakfast. The baby did back flips as soon as I laid down. It felt like he was excited to go home, too. I wondered if he even knew Rusty existed. Could he hear Rusty's deep thundery voice as he gently felt for the taps and kicks? Could he feel the love soak through? Come on, baby, sleep time. Ouch! He hit that one sensitive spot. I ran names through my head trying to put myself to sleep. Kit, after Kit Carson; Daniel or Danielle after Daniel Boone; Shane after the character in the book; Dalton after the Dalton gang; Garret after Pat Garret; Riley after *Riley's Luck*; Kenzie, Darby, Darcy, Carson...

I woke to a dark room. I checked the clock. Five a.m. Normal wake up time. I'd drive mom and Martha nuts if I pushed to go too early. Still, I couldn't just lie there. I got up and showered and shaved my legs. I blow dried my hair, curled it and put on makeup. I chose one of my favorite maternity tops so I'd feel good. I visited Shasta and talked to all the hands as they went about their morning chores. I saw Patrick out getting a quick scan of the ground before he had to go to school. Something caught his eye and I smiled, recognizing the shift in his focus. He squatted down beside the track, followed the direction it pointed and off he went. I hoped he didn't miss the bus.

The peacefulness of the place settled around me. I sat in the porch swing and watched the horses. I wondered if I needed a rocking chair. Better not bring it up until Mom had gone back home again or she'd have to go furniture shopping. As I rocked the false contractions started again. That reminded me that I was hungry. I went to the kitchen and found Martha busy putting breakfast on the table.

"Sit down, Cassidy. Get off your feet or your ankles will swell up."

I sat down.

"My! You look nice today," my mother said as she sat in her usual spot. "Are you almost ready?"

"I am ready. I just need to load up."

"As much as you've been working I'm surprised the truck wasn't loaded up already. How do you feel?"

"Fine. I keep having those weird contractions and the baby has been quiet this morning. Maybe it's because he was up half the night."

"In honor of Cassidy we are having banana pecan caramel pancakes," Martha announced. "With a side of scrambled eggs, sausage, biscuits and gravy."

Martha rang the triangle to call the hands to breakfast. Mom and I dug in and pretty soon Dad came down the stairs. Slowly the hands wandered in from their early morning chores. I thought it was strange that Big Wayne Gordon looked lonesome. My parents never showed much outward affection towards each other but I wondered if he missed Mom already.

After breakfast Dad actually carried her suitcases out to the truck. Normally he would send Randy to do all the fetching and loading, but he walked with Mom down the stairs and loaded the suitcases himself. I brought my suitcase down and Randy quickly took it from me. My dad gave me a rare hug.

"You take care. We'll be expecting a call."

I suspected the pictures would get here before the call. Mom and her camera were inseparable. We looked around and Shadow was nowhere to be seen.

"Patrick?" Dad said. "Go fetch that ornery hound."

"Yes, sir, I just hope I ain't late for school. That'd be a shame to miss the bus on account of following orders. I might have to take the whole day off of school!"

"Smart ass, boy," my dad mumbled.

Pretty soon Patrick appeared dragging Shadow by the collar.

"I said heel! I know I'm not the boss but I say heel, anyway!"

"Shadow! Come!" I called and Shadow almost dragged Patrick across the yard. He ran up and sat at my feet. His ears went back when Randy grabbed him and stuffed him in his crate in the back of the truck. After hugs all around Mom and I climbed into the truck.

"Can I drive?" I asked. "I'd rather drive than think."

"Okay. I never liked driving these big old trucks anyway," Mom said. I climbed in and readjusted everything there was to adjust. I rolled down the window and waved as I eased the truck down the lane and out to the big road. The school bus was just pulling up at the stop and we stopped the truck. Mom rolled down her window and yelled, "He's on his way!" Then she got on her cell phone and called Jesse.

Driving the truck was uncomfortable. I had to get close enough to reach the pedals and far enough away to not bump the steering wheel with my belly. That made the steering wheel an uncomfortable distance for my arms. After a while the discomfort grew until I was squirming in my seat. Half an hour down the road the silly contractions started up and driving was no longer fun. Four and a half hours to go. Mom was chattering away about how exciting it would be when the baby was born, how I had to see Rusty's eyes when he held the baby. She went through an impossibly long list of things she would go shopping for if it was a boy or if it was a girl. I listened patiently and fidgeted and squirmed and ached. These contractions were stronger than I'd remembered them in the past. They had been a little painful in the past, like cramps, but these were even more so. Maybe Mom was right. Maybe the baby would be born this week. The thought filled me with uncertainty. I needed to psyche myself up for this. I thought I better start.

The road got longer and longer and the contractions were not easing up. I realized with a start that I was no longer concentrating on my driving. I was fending off cramps. I pulled off onto the shoulder.

"Mom? Can you drive now? I'm feeling rotten. The seat position is impossible and these contractions are hurting me."

"Contractions?"

"My doctor had a name for them. Braxton-Hicks? I've had them for a month now but today it's worse. I don't want to feel bad when I see Rusty. I was so excited to see him again but now all I can do is hurt."

"Are you sure they're just Braxton-Hicks?"

"Of course, I've still got three weeks to go. Maybe it'll go away. If it eases up I'll drive again."

I opened the door and hopped down and a sharp cramp took me by surprise.

"Cassidy? Are you sure you're okay? We can go home again. Rusty would understand."

"No, I want to be home. I want to see Rusty."

I climbed into the passenger's seat and Mom started up the truck and merged onto the highway. I tried to phase out the cramps. I tried curling up in the corner of the passenger's side but curling up made the cramps worse. When stretching back out didn't help I went for a new level of determination. I'd just have to tough it out. Four more hours.

Mom kept glancing at me. I knew what she was thinking but I wouldn't let her voice it because she'd head for the nearest town.

"I'm fine, Mom. Keep driving," I must have told her ten times.

The cramps got worse and worse. I tried telling myself that this was not labor but as the miles went on even I had to admit, if it wasn't labor, I needed help and if it was, well, I still needed help.

"Mom, this really hurts," I almost cried. "I'm calling Rusty."

Boy, did I have bad timing or what? Just as I said that my water broke and a great big contraction hit me like a ton of bricks. I gasped, tensing, tensing until it passed.

Chapter 34

"Cassidy!"

"Keep driving! Rusty will get us an escort. Just keep driving!"

I speed dialed Rusty's cell.

"Hey beautiful," he said brightly. "You left early. How far away are you?"

"Rusty, you need to come. Any way you can. We're on the 5!"

"Cass! What's wrong?"

"I thought it was those contractions I always get! I didn't know it was real!"

"And you're on I-5? How far away?"

"I don't know. Maybe three hours. Labor should last more than three hours. But this hurts. Can you come?"

"Tell your mom to put the emergency lights on. CHP will find you. I'm on my way! If you pull off call me!"

"There's no place to pull off on the 5, you know that."

"Watch for the CHP. If you see an ambulance, pull over. We'll make a transfer. I have to hang up to make a call or two. Keep your phone handy."

"I will. Oh! Oh here comes another one…"

"Cassidy? …Cass answer me…"

I know it must have felt like forever to him but finally it eased up and I talked again.

"I can't talk when they hit. It just hurts too much."

"Okay, I've got to go but I'll be back. I'm on my way. I'm in town so I can get on the road quick. You can do this. I know you can. Be strong. I'll be right back."

I tried to think of how he would find us. One truck, on a busy freeway, out in the middle of nowhere.

"Mom, put your emergency lights on so the police can find us. If they pull in front of us with their lights on just follow as close as is safe. If they come up behind and use their siren, pull over."

"I should have known you'd do something like this! Leave it to you to have your baby on the freeway in an old ranch truck! I hope you were kidding about naming that baby Otto! It better be a girl. You wouldn't dare name a girl Otto!"

"Mom! Just drive. Think of something positive! You wanted to be in the delivery room! Maybe you will. Maybe this is the delivery room! Oh, Mom, here we go again!…"

The phone rang. Mom looked at me, saw there was no way I was answering, and picked it up.

"It's okay, Rusty, she'll be here in a second."

When the contraction ended, and Mom handed me the phone, I was still breathing hard.

Rusty was in an ambulance. I could tell by the kind of siren in the background.

"Cassidy?"

"It's okay. I'm here," I said.

"How far apart are the contractions?"

"I don't know. I can't keep track of time."

"Okay, let's time them. When the next one starts tell me, and then tell me when it's over. We need to do that two or three times. Can you do that?"

"Yeah. I didn't want it to happen this way! I wanted some peaceful time. I wanted you to feel the baby move."

"I'll feel him move. Don't worry. Relax between contractions. Save your energy. Relax. Relax. Are you okay?"

"Yeah, it's hard to relax. Everything feels tense even when it stops."

"You're doing good. Do you know where you are?"

"No, there's farm land all around. You know how the farm land goes on for miles."

"Okay, just try to pass on useful information."

"Oh! There's a sign for McKittrick Highway!"

"Gotcha."

I could hear him radioing our position to the CHP. The tightening started again. Tighter, tighter!

"Okay! Start timing! Oh! Ouch..."

I could hear him saying encouraging things through the phone but I couldn't hold the phone up to my ear. My breathing came in short bursts. I forgot the phone and grabbed the headrest of the truck. Tighter, tighter! It seemed as soon as I thought I couldn't stand it anymore it started easing.

"Okay, it's passing. Oh, man."

He said something and I wearily searched for the phone on the seat.

"Cassidy? Are you there?"

"Sorry, I had to put the phone down."

"It's okay, you're doing great. Just stay calm, ride it out."

"You sound like you've done this a dozen times!" I told him. "You sound like Landon with a patient."

"Thanks. Actually I have done this once, except I was in the car."

"You delivered a baby? In a car?"

"Only once, and I was scared to death! Now relax, time to relax. Let me talk to your mom a second."

I handed the phone over to mom. I heard a series of okays and there was a glance over at me.

"She's doing fine. I don't know how she does it. I didn't mean to raise her so tough. When the going gets tough, Cassidy gets tougher. She'll be fine. I know what it's like and she's doing great. Just find us! Okay, I'll watch for it."

She handed the phone back to me. After a few minutes a CHP car passed us going about eighty. He pulled in ahead of us.

"Here's the CHP," I told Rusty.

"Is everything okay? Can you hang on another half hour?" he asked.

"I don't have much choice, do I?"

"If you need help I'll tell him to pull over. If you're good to go we'll keep going."

"Mom, follow the police car," I said.

Mom shifted in her seat and changed into racecar driver mode. At least, now we had the road to ourselves. Most of the cars pulled over to make way for us. I could feel another contraction coming on.

"Okay, here we go again! Rusty!"

"I'm here, babe…" I lost the rest of what he said as the contraction took over all my thinking. I gripped the seat, waited, waited, were they getting longer or was it just my imagination? I waited and waited… Finally it let up.

"Okay, just a sec. I need to find the phone… Rusty?" I panted. "I'm back."

"We're looking at eleven minutes apart. You're doing good. If it stays at eleven minutes for just a little while that's just two or three more contractions before I see the truck. You can do that. Just hang on. We're coming. You there? Are you okay?"

"I'm tired, Rusty, I'm so tired."

"It's okay. Maybe if you're tired it'll help you relax between contractions."

"I'm sorry," I said. "I'm sorry to put you through all this. We were going to have a nice peaceful time at home and then a nice predictable labor. We were going to have a suitcase ready for a trip to the hospital. We were going to have the station waiting on the phone call."

"The station is still waiting on that phone call. We're doing fine. Just keep a good attitude and we'll sail right through this."

"It's too early!"

There was some talk and then Rusty said, "Landon says three weeks isn't too early. The baby should be fine. If the doctor has been pleased with the way the baby has developed then three weeks early isn't dangerous. Plus, we don't know your exact due date. It might only be two weeks early."

"Doctor Ron is not going to be happy with me."

"He's been through this before. Everything is going to be fine. An overnight stay and we'll be home again, just us."

The conversation tapered off as we both fell into our roles. I knew he was there. All I had to do was tough it out until the ambulance found us. Why'd he have to ask Landon? I didn't want Landon to deliver my baby. This was too personal for a search partner to do. I was embarrassed. Of course he'd been the one to see me through the miscarriage. There was no telling what he'd had to do to me to save me from that.

The next contraction hit hard.

"Okay! Time!" I gasped. Just wait it out, Cass. Wait, wait. Every second felt worse. I was beginning to have my doubts I could do this, but I wasn't going to be a wimp. I'd get through this. If millions of other women got through this I would too. Yeah, and millions of women got epidurals and painkillers, too! I was giving myself a good talking to but I didn't voice any of it aloud.

Two more very rough contractions and I was resting. Rusty was talking into the radio, or to Landon, or the driver when I noticed the truck was acting different.

"He's pulling over to the left," Mom said. "Why would he pull over to the left?"

"Rusty's coming from the other direction and he needs to cross the median. The officer can talk to the ambulance driver over the radio. He'll guide Rusty to us."

She followed the police car to the shoulder of the road and came to a gentle stop. The officer sprung out and jogged over to my door.

"Cassidy Michaels?" he asked.

I wondered what would happen if I said, "Who? I don't know any Cassidy Michaels!" But I didn't.

"Yeah."

"We're going to transfer you over to an ambulance. Just sit tight."

If he knew what labor felt like he wouldn't tell me to sit tight.

"Boy! I am sure am glad Rusty knows how to use his resources!" Mom said, "Just think, emergency personnel at your beck and call."

"Mom, they'd do this for anybody."

"I never saw an ambulance driver go pick up the husband before going out on a labor call!"

"Okay, Landon's different. Landon would do anything for me."

I saw the ambulance come bumping over the median. Yes! Rusty was coming! I knew everything would be okay now. No matter what happened, Rusty would be there. I tried to step out of the truck but the officer blocked my way.

"Let them come to you," he said, cop faced.

"Oh, come on. I know you're just looking out for public safety and all but…"

His look stopped me. He wasn't used to back talk. I flipped a mental page in the procedure book and knew they'd get out the gurney and wheel it over to the truck. Oh, hell.

"Look," I told the officer. "These guys are just glad this didn't happen five miles up a mountain on a search and rescue call. Walking ten feet to an ambulance…"

His look stopped me again.

"You must be new around here," I muttered and then a new contraction hit and I was glad I wasn't standing. Rusty appeared at the door. I was white knuckled on the headrest, waiting, waiting for the tightness to ease. His brow furrowed and he tried to reach out when he saw my pain.

"Okay, babe, you're doing good," he ran his hands down my arms. "This is a good thing. Now we'll have plenty of time to make the switch without worrying about the next one."

"It's passing…okay…I need my hug. I've waited so long for this hug. I've been dying waiting for this hug," I cried stepping out of the truck. "A two week long hug," I cried burying my face in his coat. The old tweed coat. He remembered. I asked him to wear it and he remembered. It smelled so good.

"Cass…we need to go…"

"I know. I know we do. I'm soaking up strength."

Rusty was a little embarrassed. He'd seldom seen me like this and the other guys never had. Even Landon seemed embarrassed but I didn't care. If I didn't get my hug I was going to fall apart. I was stressed and scared and lonely and tired and having Rusty there was all I needed. I soon found out I also needed to get in that ambulance. Landon lowered the gurney so I could sit on it easily and Rusty helped me lie down. I could feel the tightness starting and about the time I was pushed into place in the ambulance the next contraction was in full force.

Landon drove. I was surprised, but it may have been standard procedure for the partner to remain detached in a situation like that. I read the EMT's nametag. It said Vance.

"We're down to ten minutes," Rusty said. He got out his cell phone, pushed a few buttons. "Mrs. Gordon? You have your headset on? Okay… I'm just going to stick the phone in my pocket but you can listen."

Things were happening fast. I was draped and prepped. They hooked me up to a monitor that gave them a pulse and blood pressure reading every few minutes. The ambulance rocked as they made their way onto the freeway again. I heard the siren on the police car and then I felt the ambulance speed up as it merged onto the freeway. I heard the siren come on and we were on our way.

"You settled in?" Rusty asked me.

"I'm looking for something to hold onto. I need something."

"Okay, just grab my hand."

"I don't want to hurt you."

"You won't hurt me. I want to feel it, too. Just grab my hand and hold on."

"Six centimeters," Vance said.

There was a collective note taking. The number meant something to everybody except me. Rusty shot Vance a look that asked if we'd make it to the hospital and Vance shrugged that there was no way to predict.

Vance was a lot like Landon. I wondered if there was some EMT gene out there. But while Landon was fair and blonde. Vance was dark. Dark eyes, dark hair, dark complexion. He was a little taller and a little heavier.

The next contraction came suddenly. I gasped and reached for Rusty. I held on for dear life. Oh! Oh! Tighter and tighter.

"Cassidy, breathe, it's okay, you can breathe," Vance said but all I could think of was the pain and the tightness and then the blessed easing. "Regular breaths, come on, you're doing good. Okay, almost over. There you go. One more down."

And it *was* easing. How did he know? I released Rusty's hand but he took mine back. I laid back catching my breath.

"Concentrate on breathing during the contractions," Vance said. "If you think about breathing it'll take a chunk of your attention away from the pain. If you feel like pushing, and you don't have the okay yet, breathe quickly and shallowly. You can't push while you are breathing like that. There's no point in pushing until the baby can come so wait for the okay. Use your breathing to your advantage. Show me how you breathe if you feel like pushing. *Hehehehehehe*," he demonstrated.

I copied him, feeling silly.

The tightness built. I gripped Rusty's hand.

"Breathe, Cassidy, breathe. There you go, keep it up," Vance said.

And Rusty, "There you go, babe, you're doing so good. You're so strong."

I eased up on his arm but he assured me it was okay. Tighter, tighter, oh golly…the miles flew and the contractions multiplied. One on top another. I was getting exhausted. I hardly had the energy to fight the contractions. Sweat dripped off my brow. The siren wailed and it started getting under my skin. A contraction ended and I let Rusty's hand go.

"Rus…can they stop the siren. Please cut the siren."

"We're just getting to the city. We're going to need it."

"I don't want the baby's first sound to be sirens. Please. Even if we don't make it to the hospital. I'll feel better with it off. Oh no, here we go again! Oh please..."

Later I heard the numbers go up. Seven, seven and a half.

"I see poppy fields! Almost to town," Landon announced.

Eight.

A different feeling came over me. It was overwhelming! My body reacted to it instantly.

"Rusty! Help!" I grabbed his arm.

"What is it?"

"Arg! I don't know!"

"Cassidy! Wait! Wait!" Vance exclaimed. "Breathe quick. Shallow. Look at me! Cassidy! Look at me. Breathe like I showed you: *hehehehehehe.*"

"*Hehehehehe,*" I breathed and it helped a little but the feeling grew and grew!

"Breathe! Keep it up! Good girl! You're doing good. Eight and half! Dad get over here!"

Rusty wrestled loose.

"Arg! I have to! *Hehehehe*, I have to, oh make it stop!" I pushed. I had to. I pushed some more.

"Okay Cassidy, you're doing super. Come on girl, you can push now. Let me see you push!"

I bore down with all my might. Anything to make that feeling go away. Anything!

"You're doing great. Again! Push again! You can do it. One more time! Here you go dad, right here. Here we go. Okay Cassidy, last one! Last big one. You can do it. As soon as the feeling hits go with it! Hard!"

OH! Push! Push! I felt a slithery giving feeling and the guys were all business. Oh! Push again!

"Give me another one, come on, almost done."

Rusty caught the baby. He was the first one to hold her. And he cut the umbilical cord himself, hands shaking even though he knew how it was done. One more push and I felt something different. Then suddenly there was a cry. A cry!

"Oh babe, she's beautiful," Rusty said. He wrapped her in a blanket and carried her to where I could see. "She's just beautiful." Tears fell down his face and he sat back holding his daughter close. He laid her on me and I brought my hands up. The blanket was warm and damp and moved. My daughter. I had a daughter. I was a mom, now.

"Uh oh, we lost the truck," Vance said, glancing out the window.

"It's okay," I said. "She just pulled off the road to have a good cry. She'll catch up."

Rusty pulled the phone out of his pocket and listened a second. He smiled and nodded.

"Mom!" I said. "You have a new baby granddaughter!"

"I knoooow!" she wailed back happily.

"Landon, can we stop and let my mom have a peek?"

Landon pulled over and Mom pulled in behind. Vance opened the ambulance door and she took a first picture: Vance, Rusty, me and the baby looking out the ambulance door. Rusty handed the little squirmy bundle to Mom who stood there and cried, looking at her new grandbaby.

Chapter 35

For once I was glad to have a few days in the hospital. The ambulance pulled up to cheers from the hospital staff and a crowd of officers. They slapped Rusty on the back and shook his hand as I was wheeled into emergency. Doctor Ron was waiting. The baby weighed in at six pounds seven ounces. Doctor Ron counted her fingers and toes and pronounced her healthy. She was bathed and I finally got to see what she looked like. Fine, dark baby fuzz covered her head. Bright intelligent baby eyes looked back at me. She was little and pink and newborn but oddly enough she had my nose and the big blue eyes that Rusty had as a child. Oh man, what was I going to do with a kid having Rusty's eyes? I was a goner. I was told the hair color and eye color could change but blue eyes were predominate on both sides of the family.

The nurses showed me how to hold, feed and bathe a new baby. They instructed me on everything, and I sure needed it. Mom must have taken a hundred pictures. And Rusty couldn't get enough of his new daughter. When he came into the room he gave me a kiss and hug and then searched for her and if she was in the nursery he finagled a way to get her out.

"Babe," he said quietly holding the baby in the rocking chair in the corner of the room. He rose and brought the baby to me. "We need to name this kid. What have you been thinking? I know we were talking about Kit Carson."

I shook my head. "No, I want to save the name Carson for a boy."

"Okay, do you have any other suggestions?"

"I have a list in the baby book in my suitcase."

"We need to name her before we go home. They'll be here in the morning with the paperwork."

"You sound like you have a suggestion."

"I do. I don't want you to agree to it unless you really like it."

I waited for him to continue.

"I'd like to name her Kaitlyn Elizabeth. I know, you think it sounds too sissy. But you can shorten it to Kate or Kit and we won't be using up the name Carson for a boy."

"Let's use it for now and get a feel for it. We'll see if it sticks."

I liked the idea of letting her choose just how much of a sissy name she wanted to live with. Over the next few hours she went from Kaitlyn to Little Katie. But in the morning when the nurse arrived with the paperwork we agreed and she officially became Kaitlyn Elizabeth Michaels and Mom cried all over again even though we had totally forgotten that her given name was Elizabeth.

Mom came to the hospital with an armload of baby size dresses and little pink sleeper suits. She had added lace to the little overalls with police cars on them. She dressed Katie up in the dresses and took pictures and emailed them home.

Mom was still determined to have a baby shower but I couldn't imagine a houseful of cops playing games so we had a Welcome Home Katie Party. Kate's second day home Mom decorated the whole place in pink baby shower decorations and invited everybody to stop by and meet the new addition. She had a ball playing hostess and showing off her new grandkid, while I just sat back and visited with friends. Anybody who would hold Katie also got their picture taken and added to a wall. The evening was especially busy as people got off from work.

A big, shiny, black limousine pulled up to the house in the middle of the evening, at the busiest time. I wouldn't even have noticed, but Lawanda was in the living room visiting with her cop friends and she suddenly ran to the front window.

"Oh my god! I can't believe it! I can't believe it! Cassidy! It's her! I can't believe it's her!"

I took a look. It wasn't just "her". It was "her" and Brock Larone and Spike. Mom didn't know who they were, which is just as well, she made each of them pose for a picture to add to the wall, just like they were the checker at the cop shop, like Lawanda. I'll always cherish the picture of Spike, all dark, tough looking, three hundred and fifty pounds of hard muscle holding Little Katie, almost in one hand with an expression clearly showing he didn't know what he was doing. I was proud of my police friends. They welcomed Sherri just like any other friend, "Hi, I'm Kent, I work with Rusty and I rescue Cassidy about three times a year. Sometimes we track together. How do you know her?"

"Oh, I'm Sherri. I worked with Cassidy several months ago."

There would be stories told around the station for the next few months as word of Sherri's arrival at the party made the rounds.

"So, Cassidy, are you ready to go back to work?" Sherri asked.

"No!" said Rusty. "She's not going anywhere."

"Oh, come on, not even for Hawaii?"

"I don't care if it's in the wilds of Canada, which *would* be tempting for Cassidy, she's not going anywhere. You've got a room full of cops. If you're bound and determined to hire a body guard I'm sure you could find a volunteer."

"Oh my," Sherri said. She zeroed in on Landon. "What do you say, Landon? Ready for a change of scenery? Six months? Hawaii?"

I never did keep track of whether or not Sherri found a bodyguard. I was saved by the baby. I took her to the changing table and did my motherly duty, wondering if I'd ever get used to it.

"Mom, how did Sherri, Brock and Spike know about the party?" I asked.

"Why, they were listed in your cell phone! I just borrowed your phone and called everybody while you were in the hospital!"

I spent much of the evening sitting, watching my baby get passed from one person to another. My mom was in her element bragging about her grandkids, making sure the table was full of food, and adding pictures to the wall of honor.

Strict took a seat beside me. "So, you ready for another call?"

"Not quite. Why?"

"Just asking."

"I need the world's best babysitter to get lost on a weekend that Rusty has off. Then she will be so grateful for being rescued that she'll volunteer for free babysitting if I ever need to go out on another call."

"I'll watch for that call," he said with a wink.

"Deal."

www.ingramcontent.com/pod-product-compliance
Lightning Source LLC
Chambersburg PA
CBHW050406260626
47156CB00003B/890